HAUNTING INVESTIGATION

a Chesterton Holte Mystery

Saint-Germain, Olivia and Madelaine Series
Hotel Transylvania
The Palace
Blood Games
Path of the Eclipse
Tempting Fate
A Flame in Byzantium
Crusader's Torch
A Candle for d'Artagnan
Out of the House of Life
Darker Jewels
Better in the Dark
Mansions of Darkness
Blood Roses
Communion Blood
Come Twilight
In the Face of Death
A Feast in Exile
Night Blooming
Midnight Harvest
Dark of the Sun
States of Grace
Roman Dusk
Borne in Blood
A Dangerous Climate
Burning Shadows
An Embarrassment of Riches
Commedia della Morte
Night Pilgrims
Sustenance

Fantasy
Ariosto
A Baroque Fable
The Vildecaz Talents
To the High Redoubt

HAUNTING INVESTIGATION

a Chesterton Holte Mystery

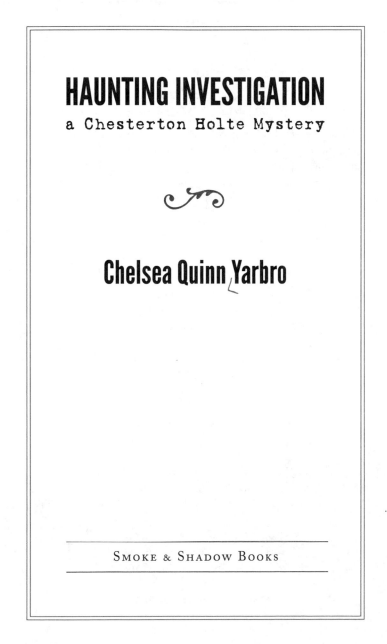

Chelsea Quinn Yarbro

SMOKE & SHADOW BOOKS

Smoke & Shadow Books
Cleveland Writers Press Inc.
31501 Roberta Dr.
Bay Village, OH 44140
www.clevelandwriterspress.com

Printed in the United States of America

First Edition: December 2015
10 9 8 7 6 5 4 3 2 1
Smoke & Shadow Books is an imprint and trademark
of Cleveland Writers Press Inc.

The publisher is not responsible for websites
(or their content) that are not owned by the publisher.
Library of Congress Cataloging-in-Publication Data on file with publisher.

Hardcover ISBN-13: 978-1-943052-01-1
Softcover ISBN-13: 978-1-943052-00-4
eBook ISBN-13: 978-1-943052-04-2

Cover Design by Patricia Saxton
Cover Photo by Dave Ward
Edited by Patrick J. LoBrutto

Mystery

For the memory of my Aunt Norma's friend
M. J., whose reminiscences of her work
reporting the news in Milwaukee, St. Louis,
Tulsa, Detroit, and Chicago from 1921-1956
provided a jumping-off point for this book.

PROLOGUE

IT REALLY WAS A BEAUTIFUL DAY, THOUGHT CHESTERTON HOLTE, AS HE LOOKED up into the endless blue of the spring sky. The little Belgian inn was worthy of a postcard, the trees were leafing out, and the Great War seemed much farther away than eighteen miles; even the four German soldiers facing him looked to be more likely to burst into song than to shoot him, their rifles like props for one of Franz Lehar's operettas rather than deadly weapons. Holte glanced at the crumpled form of the American journalist left beside the midden, and felt a stab of regret — it was unfortunate that he had become a casualty in a conflict that America was not part of, but war was like that — and was sorry that journalist had been mistaken by the soldiers for the spy they had been sent to get rid of. But weighing this one death against the nine hundred soldiers his dispatch would protect, he could not fault his decision to allow the Germans' their error: the soldiers had been looking for someone speaking English, and could not tell the slight difference between an American and a Canadian accent. "Poor fellow," Holte said as a kind of benediction for the dead man, and turned to face his executioners. He had been able to deliver his coded pages to the young man on the red bicycle, and they were now on their way to the coast; his mission was over, at the cost of only two men.

A blow struck his chest, vast and wet and too enormous to be pain. Holte felt his legs give way, and then his face struck the earth, where he saw a small insect crawling up a stalk of grass. And then he no longer saw anything as he drifted away from his body, his world, into dim mists and nothingness.

ONE

❧

"DAMN!" POPPY THORNTON SWORE AS THE KEYS ON HER SMITH TYPEWRITER jammed again. After she pulled the two strikers back, she wiped her fingers on the damp sponge she kept in a small glass dish next to her reading lamp, cleaning off the ink from the typewriter ribbon that transferred to the letters on the strikers and from them to her fingers. Suppressing a yawn, she resumed working on the story she would have to deliver to Cornelius Lowenthal at the Philadelphia Clarion by eight in the morning.

A gentle cough came from the area by the curtained windows.

"Duchess?" Poppy called out softly, wondering how her aunt's aging spaniel had got into the library without her noticing. At least the cat was in the kitchen, as he usually was at night; Maestro had an unnerving habit of wanting to sit on her pages as she stacked them up beside her typewriter. "Duchess, come here, girl." She whistled soft encouragement, but there was no response.

The clock on the library wall chimed one, and Poppy almost swore again. Her exasperation was growing with every word she put on the page. It was galling to have to report on the Fine Books Society when what she wanted to cover was crime, or at the very least, the police blotter. But that was not allowed for women from good families who had concerned relatives with political and business connections throughout the city. She reminded herself, an assignment was an assignment, as trivial as it might seem to her — and her colleagues, for that matter — and she had yet to prove herself to Lowenthal: the one crime story she had reported — a matter of high school students defacing old buildings with colored chalk — was hardly enough to ensure her preferential assignments, no matter how well she had done her job, and how clearly she had described the vandalism of the eight young men responsible. She pounded the stiff keys, taking out her irritation on them, and hitting the carriage return with more force than necessary.

The sound came again, but there was no sign of the taffy-colored dog. The hood-shaded library lamp on her desk flickered.

Poppy stopped typing and swung the shade of her work lamp up to better illuminate the long, narrow room, the walls lined with bookcases filled to overflowing. "Duchess. Come here." She was brusque now, no longer cajoling. "Duchess!"

"I'm afraid I'm not Duchess," said a male voice about ten feet from Poppy's left shoulder, in the window embrasure that looked out on the small stretch of garden which ran along the side of the house.

Poppy was too startled to be scared. She blinked twice and slid open the drawer on her right which contained three pairs of scissors. Locking her grip around the largest of them, she called out, "Who's there?"

"You don't have to shout." By the tone, he intended to reassure her. "I can hear you."

This served only to make Poppy more apprehensive. "Who are you?" she demanded in her best professional woman voice.

"Chesterton Holte," said the voice; his accent was somewhat British, educated but not snooty, and he pronounced his rs. "Gentleman haunt, at your service." The manner was cordial enough, no sign of menace beyond being a bodiless and unfamiliar presence in a dark house at night.

"Very funny," said Poppy with more moxie than she actually possessed; a strange voice in this room at so late an hour was deeply unnerving. Her hands were starting to shake, so she clasped them together tightly so that neither she nor her illusion — for surely that was what it had to be — could see them. "Chesterton Holte. Chesterton Holte, gentleman haunt. Ye gods! Where did you come up with that?"

"It's my name," the voice insisted. "Chesterton Holte. I'd write it down for you, but I'm afraid that I can't."

"You're armed?" Poppy's alarm escalated. Grasping the scissors as tightly as possible, she rose from her chair and glared at the section of curtain from which the voice came.

"It isn't possible. And even if I had a gun, it would be as ghostly as I am, and could do less damage than a gnat," he answered, a bit sadly. "Sometimes I can make electric lights flicker, or a 'phone line crackle, but that's about all."

"Oh, so you're saying that was you," said Poppy. "Why would you bother with the lights in here?" She wanted to keep him talking, to find out what he wanted. If he were talking, she told herself, he might not attack, and she might be able to pry some useful information out of him. "How did you get in here?"

"You have nothing to fear from me," the voice went on. "I couldn't do anything to you even if I wanted to. Noncorporeal, you know — ghosts are."

"Noncorporeal. As in, no body?" She glanced at the narrow opening in the curtains, trying to figure out how he had managed to get there. She had been working at the typewriter for more than two hours, so it struck her as odd that he should have waited so long to reveal himself — assuming he was real. "Ghost?"

"That's what happens to ghosts," he said. "We lose our bodies."

"I'm sure." Her sarcasm gave her a boost in confidence.

"I wish there were some way to prove it to you," he said, sounding genuinely rueful. "But I can't think how."

She summoned up her courage and said, "Show yourself," at the same time hoping that nothing would happen.

There was a kind of shadow that moved out of the curtains, roughly the size and shape of a grown man; he seemed fairly tall and slim, but there was little more to see of him. "This is the best I can do just now," he said apologetically.

"And why would that be?" Poppy asked as she watched in fascination as the shape drifted nearer her desk.

"Because you don't believe in ghosts. Your dubiety is robbing me of my full definition." He seemed to be cocking his head, watching her.

"How very inconvenient for you," said Poppy. "But you can't blame me: this is 1924. No one believes in ghosts any more."

"I'm aware of that," he said. "And right now, you're trying to decide how we come to be having this conversation."

She admitted to herself that he was right, but would not say so aloud. "I must have fallen asleep over my work and I'm in one of those very realistic dreams. But any moment now, a purple-spotted camel will drift through the room, and I'll know I'm asleep." She still held the scissors, but she sat down again.

"It isn't a dream. Sorry to disappoint you, but I am haunting you."

Poppy tried to swallow, but her throat was suddenly dry. "And why are you doing that — granting for the moment that what you say is true?" She waited for his answer.

"It seems I owe a kind of debt to you and your family." He coughed again. "I'm afraid I was the man who got your father killed in Belgium. The Huns thought your father was my contact, and, to buy a little time, I let them think it. That's why he was shot. They shot me, as well, a bit later, if that's any consolation."

Poppy's eyes filled with tears; she found it difficult to think of her father even now, when he had been dead for almost eight years. "That's a wretched thing to say."

"I know," said the filmy shape. "I'm sorry it happened at all."

"My father was identified as press; he was covering the British troops. America wasn't even in the Great War yet. He should never have been harmed," said Poppy, a sinking feeling in her chest, as if someone had struck her.

"No, he shouldn't have been," the form agreed. "It was my risk, not his. He shouldn't have got caught up in my activities."

"And why have you taken so long in getting here?" Poppy challenged him. "My father died in 1916. I presume you did, too, from what you said."

"Yes, About two hours after he did." The form shifted, as if wincing.

She shook her head. "This dream is turning nasty," she told the air. "I should consult Doctor Freud, perhaps."

"And what does a young woman like you know of Doctor Freud?" the shape asked.

"Don't be daft. I'm a reporter; I'm almost twenty-five, and a college graduate. I've read far more scandalous things than Freud, I promise you."

She tried to pinch herself so she would wake up, but it didn't work. "This is ridiculous."

"You're following in your father's footsteps, reporting," said the figure. He was a little clearer now, a tallish man in his mid-to late-thirties with light-brown hair falling over his brow and hazel-green eyes. His face was long and pale, with strong cheek bones and a straight, aristocratic nose; his mouth was harder to see, which puzzled her. Why would that part of his features be unclear? She could not see his lips move when he spoke, which perplexed her. His clothes were less defined, but seemed to be a high-necked sweater under a tweed jacket, and dark tan slacks. She could not make out his shoes, or even his feet.

"It's a good job and I want to do it," she said, a bit defensively. "It's what I trained to do, in college."

"And it honors your father," said Chesterton Holte.

"My father got me interested in the work," Poppy allowed.

"But did he encourage you to go into it? That's the question, isn't it? Journalism isn't women's work, is it?"

"Almost nothing interesting is," she told him, completely serious now. She watched the filmy shape drift nearer her place at the desk, and tightened her hold on the scissors.

"Why P. M. Thornton? To disguise your sex? Since you know Freud, you won't mind my direct language," said Holte.

After a minuscule hesitation, Poppy explained. "P. stands for Poppea, and M. stands for Millicent. I'm named for my grandmothers; the family calls me Poppy because my brother couldn't — or wouldn't — say Poppea when I was young, and came up with Poppy instead — you know how brothers are. Ye gods, wouldn't you use initials with names like that?"

"They are a little cumbersome," said Holte, coming around the Mayes Brothers sofa. "And initials are becoming fashionable again, even for women."

"It isn't for fashion," Poppy insisted, not wanting to admit what a disadvantage a female name could be in the newspaper world.

Holte made a sound that might have been half a chuckle. "You know your own mind on this. And you intend your initials to be taken seriously."

"At the least," said Poppy. "Starting with my male colleagues." She was about to ask Holte why he had picked on her of all her family to haunt, when a flurry of black fur entered the room, body and tail abristle, hissing in fury, headed directly for the tenuous shape of Chesterton Holte: Maestro, the big, long-haired, soot-colored cat, had arrived.

TWO

❧

"Ye gods! Maestro!" Poppy exclaimed, as the furious animal hurtled himself at Holte, springing towards him, claws extended for a lethal swipe at the intruder. When he encountered nothing but a glancing impact on the modesty panel of the desk, he looked about in baffled wrath, and whipped around, attempting to resume his attack, tail lashing, and growling musically.

"Noncorporeal. I told you," said Holte, looking down at the cat while he tried to rake him with his claws.

"He can see you," said Poppy in surprise.

"Yes, he can. Most animals can, and some babies, too. A very drunken sailor saw me once, but I don't count that. I send parrots into screaming fits." He moved back in an effort to mollify the cat, and half-vanished into the draperies. "He can see me, but he can't smell me, or touch me, and that bothers him."

Poppy could not think of any rejoinder to that, so she patted her knee, hoping to lure the cat to her lap. "I'm sorry he's being so inhospitable."

"He'll calm down in a bit," said Holte as he side-stepped Maestro out of courtesy to the animal. "Cats usually do."

"If Maestro can see you, I guess I'm not dreaming. So I guess I've gone a bit crazy." She lowered her head, confused at this abrupt change.

"No, not crazy," said Holte in what might have been a soothing tone, but Poppy didn't find it so. "You're just haunted. And to answer your earlier question: it was you or your brother I would have to haunt, and you seemed the likelier subject. More open to it." The filmy figure gestured, offering what might have been an apology.

"I didn't say anything to you about that," she said, startled at his perspicacity. "I didn't mention it."

"You were thinking it," he responded.

"And that makes it better? Now you claim to be a mind-reader?" Poppy was incredulous.

"Not a mind-reader. The question was obvious. I was expecting it. And I've observed your brother." He let Maestro make another try at clawing him — to no avail.

"And why is that?" Poppy asked, a surreal calm coming over her. "I mean, why did you come to me?"

"You may not believe in ghosts, but you've got a lot of curiosity and an open mind, very unlike your brother, if you don't mind my saying it. That should count for something. You aren't dogmatic in your thinking, nor do you deny the evidence of your own eyes. I think your brother isn't as flexible as you are."

Poppy smiled ruefully. "I'd say not. Tobias is pretty rigid."

"And after a little invisible surveillance — since it appears that I have to haunt one of you, I decided to begin with you. I thought I'd have a better chance of success." Holte moved to the wing-back chair in front of the brick-and-tile fireplace, did something that looked like calisthenics and in the next instant seemed to be sitting down, but in the blank air a little above the chair's seat.

Maestro gave a yowl of frustration and began to stalk Holte.

"When I wake up in the morning, I'm not going to believe any of this," said Poppy with strong conviction.

"No, probably not, not for now," Chesterton Holte agreed. "But that doesn't mean it isn't happening."

Poppy looked at the unfinished paragraph on the page in the machine. "I have to get this done," she said, doing her best to concentrate on what she had written.

"For your work tomorrow. You have to be at the paper by eight, as I recall." He waited for her next question, and when none came, he said, "I've been observing you for over a week."

"A week, is it?" She began to type again, making herself concentrate on the Fine Books Society. As she worked, she pretended she couldn't see the filmy outline of Chesterton Holte hanging in the air, or hear Maestro muttering curses in what her aunt called High Cat. "I'm not going to get much sleep tonight," she remarked as she got to the end of the page and inserted another into the machine.

"That's unfortunate. But you didn't get back from the Fine Books Society meeting until nine forty-five. And that sandwich Missus Flowers made for you wasn't much of a meal, for all it had roast beef and cheddar cheese on it. You need rest and nourishment, and you're not getting much of either. Of course, Missus Flowers is just the housekeeper, not the cook, so you could hardly expect more than a snack, especially so late in the evening," said Holte as if sympathizing with Poppy. "Missus Boudon doesn't stay after eight most nights, does she? unless there're guests in the house."

"You seem to know a lot about this household," said Poppy, keeping up her determined typing.

"I know you and your widowed aunt are the regular occupants, but that her surviving sons — your cousins — come for weekends and holidays: one is married and has children, the other is still single and likely to remain so; that there is Missus Bertha Flowers, who lives in, having a suite of rooms in what used to be your summer-house behind the kitchen garden; and Hawkins, the butler and chauffeur, who lives over the old coach-house which is now the garage. Missus Boudon, the cook, lives about two miles away with her feckless husband; she arrives every morning but Sunday at six. There are two grounds-keepers, father and son, the Jefferies, who live half a mile away; they tend to the garden twice a week. And there's Eliza, Eliza van Hooten, who comes in three days a week as general help for Missus Flowers. There are seventeen rooms in this house, it is more than five thousand square feet, and there's room for three autos in the garage, which used to be your stable." He recited this as if presenting a report.

"You have been snooping, haven't you?" Poppy asked as she typed the heading on the page, trying not to think about what he might have seen in his reconnoitering.

"Well, that's what spies do," he said apologetically.

She was more shocked than she let on, and somewhat offended, as well. Who was Chesterton Holte, to investigate her? Being a spy was no excuse.

"You believe you're in enemy territory?" The last two words were given in an angry whisper as she recalled that the rest of the household — her aunt, their housekeeper, and their butler — was asleep.

"Well, in life I was a spy; it's hard to lose the habit," he said in a mixture of pride and disconcertion. "I need to know what I'm getting into."

"Not just a dispatch courier, then," said Poppy, stopping to adjust the strikers again.

"No. But so few couriers were just couriers, on both sides," said Holte. "As everyone knew."

"I suppose you expect this will persuade me that you're genuine; I'm not so credulous as that," she said as she ended her article with an emphatic punch to the period key. "Delusions often do that — try to convince the delusional person that they are credible — or so I understand. Your demeanor doesn't seem delusional, which proves my point. This is my first experience with a delusion, so I have nothing to compare to it."

"I was hoping it might increase my credibility, to use your word," he admitted, and nodded to Maestro. "He's convinced."

"He's a cat," said Poppy.

"All the more reason to believe me — I cannot easily deceive a cat. No one can. Animals don't respond to misrepresentation as human beings do. A false smile might sway a person, but no animal is impressed. Babies still haven't learned what they're supposed to notice and what they're supposed to ignore. If I weren't here, Maestro wouldn't think I was."

"I don't know about that. I've seen him do a full arched-back-and-puffed-out-fur at a blank space of air," she said.

"That's not the same thing," Holte protested. "At least, not often the same thing."

"If you say so," Poppy told him, taking a moment to check the spelling of Auralinda Thistlewaite's name.

Holte sighed once and glanced at the clock. "Are you planning to rise at seven, as you usually do, or a bit earlier?"

"Six-thirty. I'm surprised you didn't know that, too." She was making a neat stack of the pages she had prepared, paper-clipped her notebook pages to them for reference, and got to her feet.

"I am aware that you are inclined to get up at seven," Holte said with a touch of formality. "But I haven't made a habit of lingering in your bedroom. I am aware when you wake. Not because I watch you, but I can tell when you're not asleep."

"I can't afford to rise at seven when I have to deliver an article by eight, at the paper. The trip to the paper takes half an hour on the streetcar, and I need at least forty-five minutes to get ready and have a little breakfast. I don't often wake up quickly; I do better staying up late. But I guess you know that already. I could have Hawkins drive me, but I think it sets a bad example." It also made her seem less like her colleagues; she reached to turn off the desk lamp, remarking as she did, "I don't know why I'm justifying my habits to you. You've figured our many of them for yourself."

"Because you don't think I'm real," he suggested. "You're right: there is no cause for you to do so."

She turned off the light, and was at once aware of the faintly luminous presence of Chesterton Holte; he seemed more real now that the library was dark. "Are you going to remain in here?"

"I don't know," he answered. "I may take a turn around the house, or I may slip away for a short while."

"Slip away to where?" Poppy couldn't help asking.

"To the dimension of ghosts, of course, where all of us go from time to time," he said as if it were obvious.

"How often do you do that? Are you going to leave now?" she asked sweetly. "Don't linger on my account."

"I've tried to call in here once a week or so, just to get the sense of the place, and you. Originally I'd planned to keep out of the way, but in this instance, though, I probably won't." He sounded almost apologetic. "I want to see how you manage tomorrow, get accustomed to your schedule. So I'll have to stick around."

"Oh, no," said Poppy firmly. "Get that out of your mind at once. This is all very well for a late-night delusion, when I can account for it as an aberration, or an especially vivid dream, but come tomorrow morning, you'll be nothing but a figment of my imagination, and I won't want any reminder of you loitering about. So you might as well go to your ghostly dimension and forget about this family."

"I wish I could do that, but I can't," said Holte contritely. "Necessity compels me to remain with you until I've — " He stopped suddenly.

"Until what?" Poppy prompted him.

Holte answered slowly, as if translating from a language he had heard but had never before spoken. "Until the premature loss of your father has been cosmologically recompensed; I can't leave until the balance is restored, hence my haunting."

"Oh," said Poppy rather blankly. "Table-rapping and spirit boxes too, I suppose?"

"Of course not. Those are dramatic illusions, not — "

" — a haunting?" she finished for him as she slipped her story and notes into a manila envelope she had removed from the center drawer of the desk, and started down the library toward the door. "You introduced yourself as a gentleman, so I presume you won't follow me."

"Not tonight," Holte said, amused. "At another time, when we're better acquainted."

"That's outrageous," she said, ruining her outrage with a yawn. She put her hand on the brass door-knob and turned it, attracting the attention of the cat.

"No. You have nothing to fear from me. Noncorporeal, remember?" He was already dissolving into shadows.

"Noncorporeal," she repeated as Maestro sauntered over to her. "Of course."

THREE

ORDINARILY, THE CLARION CLANG OF HER ALARM CLOCK BROUGHT POPPY awake at six-forty. This morning it was the telephone in the upstairs hallway, its cord extending down into the entry hall; it rang at two minutes to six. She came half-awake, reached out to turn the alarm off, but recalled dimly that she had put it on her vanity, not her bed-stand, so that she would have to get up in order to silence it. Blinking against the faint pre-dawn morning light that came through her heavy linen curtains, Poppy managed to get out of bed and totter across the floor to her vanity. "All right, all right," she murmured. "I'm up." Then she realized that it was the telephone, and she stumbled into the corridor and felt her way to the telephone.

"Dritchner residence," she said, yawning at the end.

"Miss Thornton? This is Carlotta Upshaw? Matthew Pike's secretary?" She paused. "Are you awake, Miss Thornton?"

"Yes?" Poppy said, catching the upward lilt from her. "What can I do for you?" She shoved the fingers of her free hand through her messy hair, wondering why the night city editor of the Philadelphia Clarion was having his secretary call her; he had little to do with the kinds of stories she usually did, and she had only a cursory acquaintance with Missus Upshaw, who usually arrived at the paper fifteen minutes before Poppy went home. Aside from greetings and small-talk they had never conversed.

"Mister Pike has left, but he asked me to 'phone you and ask you to come in half an hour early today. It's about an assignment?"

"What assignment?" She had a second when she thought she was still asleep — after all, last night she seemed to have a conversation with a ghost — and now this. She almost hung up and went back to bed, but she couldn't quite do that.

"I don't know. Mister Lowenthal will be expecting you." For once, this statement didn't sound like a question. "He's come in early, and wants you to do the same."

"Half an hour early. I'll be there." Then, mindful of courtesy, she added, "Thank you for calling."

The usually crisply demure Missus Upshaw gave a single crack of laughter before she hung up.

As soon as the connection was broken, Poppy stood for about thirty seconds before a sharp buzz reminder her to replace the receiver; why, she wondered, hadn't she asked what assignment was so important that it merited a special 'phone call? To receive such a summons was something new in her experience. At least, she thought, she had left a note for Missus Boudon about her early breakfast before she had retired. She frowned, more at herself than the telephone, and made her way back to her bedroom, wanting to go back to sleep, but going to her vanity table. She sat down on the padded stool and stared into the tall oval mirror. "Ye gods," she exclaimed as she caught sight of her pale image in the gloom. She had almost added she looked like a ghost, but after her experience — if that's what it was, and not some lingering dream — of the night before, she couldn't bring herself to utter the word aloud. Picking up her silver-backed brush, she began to put her fine, fashionably short-cropped brown hair in order. A second glance at the mirror reminded her that while she was an attractive young woman, she was no beauty: her face lacked the softness to be pretty, though her skin was flawless. Her chin was firm and had a hint of a cleft, her mouth was too full to be a true cupid's-bow, and her eyes — a somber grey-green — were much too keen to be pretty. Added to that, she was coltishly angular, a bit too tall and lean for current fashion. She didn't have to wrap her bosom to achieve the proper flat-chested look, for Mother Nature had been skimpy in that part of her body. "Still," she told her reflection as she did most mornings, "I'm not going to frighten horses and small children."

When she had bathed and dressed, she emerged from her room in a neat but not too fashionable business-suit of dull-green wool crepe with long, shawl-cut lapels over a blouse of ecru cotton with a narrow edging of lace at collar and cuffs. A single-strand necklace of red Baltic amber hung around her neck, and a discreet gold pin ornamented her lapel. She carried a slim brief-case and a small purse of embossed leather into which she put a pair of matching gloves. Her high-heeled shoes also matched her bag and the seams of her silk stockings were properly straight. What little make-up she wore was in discreet shades.

After leaving a short note on the occasional table outside her aunt's bedroom door explaining her early summons, Poppy went to the library to collect her work from the previous night, glancing at the curtains as if half-expecting to discover the hallucination from last night still lingering in their folds. "Ghosts," she scoffed at herself. Chiding herself for foolishness, she left the library and found Maestro waiting at the top of the stairs, as if he expected an explanation from her. "Come on, cat; let's have breakfast," she said, resting her hand on the bannister as she went down to the main floor.

Missus Boudon was in the kitchen, just beginning her work for the day. She was smiling brightly in spite of the bruise on her jaw. Short, round, with her sleek dark-blonde hair done up in a French bun, she was good-looking and relentlessly cheerful. "Good morning, Miss Poppy; thank you for the note about your early day. Eliza brought it down to me after informing Missus Dritchner. Missus Flowers will be up in half an hour. Your aunt will be down shortly, to join you," she said brightly, as Poppy came into the kitchen. "I've put your eggs to coddle and I'll have your toast ready in a moment."

"You might as well feed Maestro while you're at it," said Poppy, reaching for the cup of coffee the cook held out to her. "He had an active night last night."

"One sugar, a dab of cream," said Missus Boudon.

"You know the way I like it," Poppy approved, and went into the breakfast room to wait for her meal, leaving Missus Boudon to put her food in order while she attended to Maestro, who had begun to express himself vociferously. She contemplated the flower prints hung on the wall, trying not to imagine what the Clarion wanted of her.

"Oh, there you are," said Josephine Dritchner as she came into the breakfast room to take her place at the head of the table, Duchess trailing after her with forlorn determination. "You're ready to leave, I see." Unlike her niece, Josephine was in a pale-blue silk wrapper over her nightgown, and her badger-gray hair was in a single braid down her back. Elaborate slippers kept her feet warm. "I think it's unconscionable for you to have to be there so early. You're not a drudge, or shouldn't be."

"Good morning, Aunt Jo," said Poppy, getting up to give her aunt a kiss on the cheek. "You didn't have to rise early for me."

"Yes. Well, we'll see about that," Josephine said, a bit obscurely.

"I'm sure we will, Aunt Jo," said Poppy, used to her aunt's early-morning pronouncements. She sat down again and had a bit more coffee.

"You were up late last night, weren't you?" Josephine pursued. "Past midnight, no doubt."

"Yes. I didn't go to bed until about one-thirty," said Poppy, aware of what was coming.

"I don't know what to think," Josephine declared. "When I was young, ladies didn't keep such hours except after balls. You need your beauty sleep."

"A lost cause, I'm afraid," said Poppy, turning as Missus Boudon came in with her coddled eggs and toast. "Thank you," she said.

"I'll bring more coffee directly. And you, Missus Dritchner. What may I get for you this morning?"

Josephine pretended to think. "Well, it's Wednesday, so oatmeal to start, with brown sugar and milk," she said, as if this were a novel treat instead of what she had had almost every morning for sixty-four of her sixty-nine years. "Then two rashers of bacon and a basted egg. And a pot of strong, black tea: the English tea this morning, if you please."

"Very good, ma'am," said Missus Boudon, who whistled for Duchess as she went back into the kitchen.

"That woman is a treasure," said Josephine.

"She is," Poppy agreed, unscrewing the top of the egg-coddler and picking up her spoon.

The two women sat silently while Poppy ate her breakfast and Josephine opened the Constitution, the Philadelphia Clarion's morning companion paper. It was a smaller, less modern publication than the evening newspaper of the Addison Newspaper Corporation; the Constitution put emphasis on business and political affairs, with six columns of type and no trace of banner-headlines.

"Oh, dear," said Josephine as she skimmed page two. "I see that Judge Hammersmith has handed down another unpopular opinion. Not at all like Judge Flanders. Alfred used to go hunting with Judge Flanders." Her late husband — now twelve years dead — had had a brother-in-law on the bench, and Josephine had retained her interest in such things for his sake. "Judge Flanders is more inclined to pay attention to public opinion than Judge Hammersmith has ever been."

"Because Judge Hammersmith doesn't answer to the public, he answers to the law and the Constitution," said Poppy around a mouthful of buttered toast.

"So he claims," Josephine said, clearly not accepting this explanation.

"And no doubt he's had good reason to go against public sentiment," Poppy couldn't keep from adding.

"That's his contention," Josephine sniffed in open doubt, looking up as Missus Boudon brought her a bowl of oatmeal, a jug of milk and a small bowl of brown sugar, on a lacquered tray.

"Tea will be ready shortly."

"Thank you, Missus Boudon."

Missus Boudon offered another smile. "More coffee, Miss Poppy? Something more substantial."

"Yes, coffee, please, and a glass of tomato juice if we have any to spare."

"We do," said Missus Boudon with a hint of disapproval.

Before the cook could leave the breakfast room, Josephine stopped her. "Oh, that sounds lovely. Will you bring me a glass, as well?"

"Certainly," said Missus Boudon, as she went through the swinging door back into the kitchen.

"While you were up last night, did you notice anything unusual?" Josephine said rather abruptly, as if the question had only now snapped into her mind.

"Unusual how?" Poppy asked carefully.

"Oh, I don't know. Odd. Peculiar. Uncanny." She poured milk on her oatmeal. "Out of the ordinary."

"Why do you ask?" Poppy felt a twinge of uncertainty now, and tried to decide how much to tell her aunt.

"Duchess was restless for an hour or so. Not in her usual way, meaning she wants a treat, or to be let out. No, this was more distressed, uneasy, fretful. I feared someone might have broken into the house. But it was nothing I could discover. What my grandmother called seeing spooks. No doubt that accounts for it." She laughed to make it clear how ridiculous she thought this to be.

"Oh," said Poppy, to show she was listening.

"I heard Maestro crying at one point, and I thought perhaps — " She broke off as if she had said something rude. "It was probably some wild animal out at the dustbins, or perhaps a stray dog. Don't you think?"

"It sounds plausible; there're plenty of stray dogs around, and more than a few wild animals, although you wouldn't expect them to come this far into town," said Poppy, glad to agree on a topic more acceptable than she thought Chesterton Holte would be. "Or maybe it was a wandering raccoon. You know what nuisances they can be."

"I gather you didn't notice anything?" Josephine pursued.

"Nothing like that," Poppy answered, uncomfortably aware of her evasion. "But I'm pretty preoccupied when I work."

"I know, dear. It's your father in you. He was like that from the time he was born: once something caught his interest, the rest of the world vanished. He spent half of my wedding reception watching tadpoles in the fishpond. Not even the promise of cake could tempt him away from the tadpoles." She managed an uneasy smile, as she often did when talking about her youngest brother. "Esther encouraged him, of course," she added, her disapproval of her older Suffragette sister turning her features to harsh lines.

"I remember how he worked; his concentration was prodigious," said Poppy. "He could wrestle with details for hours." She had been starting her junior year of high school when her father had left to cover the war in Europe, and she still recalled their last meeting with poignance.

Fortunately Missus Boudon chose that moment to return with a tray holding tea for Josephine and more coffee for Poppy, and two glasses of tomato juice, allowing the two women to interrupt what could rapidly become painful memories. "Tomato juice, as requested. When do you want your bacon, ma'am?"

"Ten minutes, I should think. I want to enjoy the oatmeal." She smiled as she watched Missus Boudon leave the room.

Poppy added a little more sugar to her coffee and looked at her aunt. "I won't be back until about eight-thirty tonight; if you don't mind, have supper without me," she said.

"Do you have an engagement?" Josephine asked hopefully.

"I'm meeting Mildred Fairchild at Wendover's for an early dinner."

"Mildred Fairchild — how nice," Josephine approved faintly. "Please convey my regards to her and her mother."

"I will," said Poppy. She took a long sip of coffee and tried not to think about her freakish incident of the night before. Perhaps she'd tell Milly about it when she saw her. Then again, she thought, best not.

"I'll let Missus Flowers know that you'll be late. And Missus Boudon." Josephine sighed in a display of ill-usage. "You don't have to work, you know. Your father left you well provided for. I still think you should consider traveling."

"I want to work, Aunt Jo." It was a discussion that they had had often enough to have become a ritual. "I'd be crazed with boredom if I didn't do something more than entertain and keep house, or spend my time on trains and ships. I like being a reporter; if I had to give it up, you might as well bring on the straight-jacket."

"Entertaining and keeping house are excellent employments for any woman's time," said Josephine firmly. "And travel with the apposite companion is an appropriate occupation for a lady if she no longer has a household to keep: if you feel you must work, when you returned from Europe or Asia, you could write a book."

"They may be the best, but I'm not suited for any of those things, and well you know it. I can't plan a menu, I don't care about inventories. I want to be useful, not decorative. Not at all characteristics most men are looking for. " Poppy finished her coffee and wiped her mouth with her napkin, which she slipped back through its ring for use tomorrow morning, reached to the empty chair beside her to retrieve her briefcase and purse, then smoothed her skirt.

"How can you be certain, when you never give any of them a chance?" Josephine turned distressed eyes on Poppy as she rose from the table and came to kiss her aunt on the forehead. "Yes, it's all very well for you to try to sweeten a bitter pill, but if you're left an old maid, don't put the blame on me. You'd think with Esther for an example, you'd understand — It's not as if I haven't tried to — "

" — make a proper lady of me, yes, Aunt Jo, you certainly have. And I adore you for it. But I haven't the talents. You know I don't." She moved past the table and to the hall door. "I'll call you later."

"How do you know you haven't the talents, when you've made no effort to acquire them?"

This was the stalemate position they always reached; Poppy abandoned the topic. "I hope you have many good things planned today."

"The Jeffries and I are going to see to the new planting in the back garden, if the weather holds. And I'm expecting Eustace tomorrow evening, so I have to put his room in order for him." There was a remote look in her eyes: whenever she mentioned either of her surviving sons — the oldest and the youngest — she also remembered Cosmo, who had been killed in the Great War at age thirty-four, and Reginald, who at twenty-eight had died of the 'Flu.

At the mention of her cousin, Poppy smiled. "Ye gods, I forgot he was coming. How long does he plan to stay this time?" She came back to the table.

"I don't know, precisely. I so rarely do with Eustace. He's supposed to attend some sort of grand function at the Moncriefs on Friday, but I have no idea what his other plans may be. I'm assuming he will stay for the whole of the weekend, but he hasn't let me know." Fondness and vexation mixed in Josephine as she spoke of her perplexing youngest son, now thirty-two. "He's been doing very well in New York, you know. International Business Associates is thriving."

"Yes. You've mentioned that once or twice," said Poppy, with a wonderfully straight face.

"He's a very devoted son," said Josephine with strong determination, as if she expected Poppy to argue with her.

"Yes, he is. And with such a mother as you, he should be." She reached down for her cup and sipped the last of the coffee. "Sorry, Aunt Jo. I really have to leave, or I'll miss the streetcar and be late into the office."

"You could have Hawkins drive you in, or take a cab."

"Aunt Jo, I need to know things about the streetcars and the buses, and the way most people travel about the city. Reporters don't like to see one of their number riding about in high-style; it creates a bad impression."

"But a lady shouldn't have to — "

Poppy held up her hand. "I've got to go. Lowenthal puts great importance in promptness, and I've been ordered to arrive early, and I need to be on my way." This was as much regret as she was willing to express. "I don't want to get on his bad side if I can help it. He would like to have an excuse to keep me on the society desk forever." She picked up her brief-case. "Drink my tomato juice for me, if you please." She offered her aunt an apologetic smile.

"Oh, all right," said her aunt.

"Remember: I'll call you after lunch." It was her usual promise, and most of the time she kept it. "Have a pleasant morning."

"We'll have a dinner party while Eustace's here; Missus Flowers and I will work out the details today, after I talk to Eustace," Josephine called after Poppy. "You'll be expected to attend."

"That's fine. Tell me when and I'll make sure I'm here," Poppy called back. She had paused at the coat closet to take out her raincoat, and, after a moment's consideration, her umbrella, before she hurried out to the streetcar passenger kiosk, to begin her journey into the heart of Philadelphia and her work at the Philadelphia Clarion.

FOUR

CORNELIUS LOWENTHAL, SEATED BEHIND HIS CLUTTERED DESK, APPEARED massive, his large, square head with a choir-boy face, his barrel chest, and thick arms dominating his body. This was emphasized when he rose, for it revealed his short, skinny legs in well-cut trousers. His thinning, ruddy hair was already looking storm-tossed from his mauling it with his fingers; usually it took until after the morning meeting at ten o'clock for this to happen. "There you are, Thornton," he said, stabbing his index finger in her direction a she came through the door to his office. He glanced at the clock on the wall: it read seven fifty-three. "Just made it, didn't you?"

"Yes, sir," Poppy said, handing him her story on the Fine Books Society. "The auction information is in the third paragraph, as you stipulated. It and the next two can be used separately, if you like."

Lowenthal took the four sheets of paper and glanced through them. "I'm going to cut half of this, you know." He sat back down, his wooden office chair tipping with the force of his movement.

"Yes. I expect you will. But you said you wanted more information than you knew what to do with, and this gives you plenty," Poppy reminded him, used to his intimidating exterior and aware that he was much more bark than bite. "So there you have it. Every scrap of information I could glean in three hours over tea."

"That's what I asked for," he agreed, flipping through the pages again. "You sure about the names?"

"I checked the spellings twice. If you like, I can telephone their chairwoman and ask her to confirm them," said Poppy, her mouth a little tight.

"Nope. That won't be necessary. I'll have Miss Stotter do it if there are any questions." He sighed. "What's your current assignment?"

"You haven't given me one; you have the most recent in front of you," Poppy reminded him. "Mister Pike's secretary said you had one for me. She called me this morning."

Lowenthal nodded and sighed again. "I do have an assignment or you — Pike and I agreed. Gafney is covering the Dales Warehouse arson investigation, Harris is on the Porto trial, and Westerman is out sick, worse luck. And anyway, he's been assigned to the Chapin Street murders. Which leaves you."

The mention of the second-rung crime reporter grabbed Poppy's attention. "Is there a story you want me to cover? More than a bicycle theft? A real crime story?"

"I don't want you to cover it — far from it — it's not the way we like to do it, but sometimes press of circumstances — In this case it could be an advantage — and right now, you're my only available reporter with any crime experience who isn't already assigned," he said. "The trouble is, it involves acquaintances of yours."

"A crime involving my acquaintances?" she echoed, trying to think who this might be, and what it was about the crime that had so rattled her editor. She decided to try the direct approach. "What kind of crime?"

He stared at the framed photographs on the wall as if to remove himself from their discussion. "It's a hell of a thing — a hell of a thing." He shook his head, one hand tugging at his hair, creating more havoc. "You know the Moncriefs, don't you?"

Poppy looked startled. Where had that come from? "If you mean Madison and Louise Moncrief, they're friends of my cousin Eustace. I know them to say hello. Why do you ask?"

"I need you to get over to their house, and quickly. I take it you know where it is," Lowenthal said, his rather prominent blue eyes evading hers.

"Yes, I know where it is," said Poppy bluntly. "What's this all about?"

"Well," said Lowenthal slowly, "it seems that Madison Moncrief has hanged himself, according to the first reports. At least he was found dead this morning by the housekeeper; they say he was in the dining room. Used the chandelier, according to the police. It's not exactly a crime, but it takes a crime reporter to cover it, just in case. Think you can handle it, he being someone you know, that is."

"The chandelier?" Poppy asked, appalled; the chandelier was a treasure of Viennese crystal and brass, originally fitted for gaslight, now electrified, and the pride of Madison and Louise's house. "Ye gods."

"The report didn't say, it just gave the basics. Madison Moncrief found hanged in the dining room. Missus Moncrief was asleep in bed — on some kind of medication."

"She's recovering from a — she lost a pregnancy a little over a week ago; she's only been home from the hospital for a few days, and from what I've heard, she's been very upset: small wonder, considering," said Poppy awkwardly, the whole implication of this catching up with her. "They were going to give some kind of party on Friday. I remember thinking she was awfully brave or awfully foolhardy to plan such an event so soon after her tragic loss. I can't imagine that her physician would approve such a strenuous — " She made herself stop babbling. "My cousin Eustace is arriving from New York to attend it."

"It isn't going to happen now," said Lowenthal with certainty. "Not with Madison Moncrief dead."

Poppy took a long, deep breath and steadied herself. "Do they know how — ? Could there have been foul play?" That seemed so much more plausible than Madison Moncrief committing suicide; foul play made his death much more acceptable. "Was there any sign of a break-in or other violence? Was there a note?"

"That's what I want you to find out," said Lowenthal. "I want a preliminary story by two. Get as much out of the police as they're willing to give, and boil it down to the essentials, so we have it for the metropolitan edition. We're not going to make the first edition on this one, but the second, yes, if you hurry. You can put together something more complete tomorrow; for now you need to get just basics from the cops, no speculation, unless it's something shocking. For that, we can chase the paper if we have to, but I really don't want to, not if it's a suicide, which Wyman says it probably is, but coroners like suicides — over and done with quickly. If it turns out that's what it is, I'll save you three inches on page one, below the fold. If it's murder, you'll get four inches above the fold; our readers like murders, especially society murders." He looked at the clock. "Seven minutes past eight. You better get going. You can draw taxi fare from petty cash on your way out. Hop to it."

"You want me to take taxis?" she asked in astonishment.

"Time matters on this one, Thornton. Chop-chop, as they say in China." He made shooing motions with his hands.

Realizing she would learn nothing more here, Poppy said, "Yes, sir. And thanks." The word sounded peculiar to her, under the circumstances.

"Don't thank me yet, Thornton. Wait until you find out what happened. I hope you have a strong stomach — you'll need it for this one." With that for dismissal, Lowenthal leaned back, slid open the partition between his office and that of his secretary, and all but bellowed her name. "Miss Stotter! Get in here!"

Hurrying through the main room of the editorial division, Poppy heard the ubiquitous clatter of typewriters, punctuated by occasional rings from the half-dozen telephones that provided service to the twenty-two desks, seventeen of which were occupied by harried reporters. Stopping at the frosted-glass door of the Accounting Department, Poppy was issued a generous four dollars for cab-fare while she consulted her red-leather address book for her destination. Clutching her money in her hand, she went down to the street and flagged a passing cab: it was a two-year-old Dodge Brothers sedan, and the driver was so recently arrived from Scotland that his burr sounded almost like a foreign language.

"One twenty-eight Hamilton Place," said Poppy, settling into the rear seat.

"Aye, ma'am," said the driver — at least, that's what Poppy decided he had said. She made allowances for his accent.

They swung around into traffic, barely missing a large wagon pulled by two hefty draft horses the color of good custard — American Creams. From there, the driver barreled past three delivery vans — two motorized, one horse-drawn — and reached the main intersection without mishap, and only three times having recourse to use his horn. For the next fifteen minutes, the taxi cut and dodged his way out from the center of the city to the venerable neighborhood marked by streets named for signers of the Constitution and members of the first three Presidential administrations. Hamilton Place was a tree-lined cul-de-sac, usually quietly dignified, now bristling with vehicles. The cabbie braked energetically, pulling up behind a cluster of police cars, and put the cab in neutral. "Is this where you want to go, ma'am?" the cabbie inquired, pointing to the surrounded house, taking unusual care to make himself understood. He was uneasy about the place. "It's a dollar thirty."

"Yes, thank you," said Poppy, handing him a generous dollar fifty. Accepting his appreciative salute with a nod, she got out of the car, carrying her bag and her brief-case with her, along with her umbrella. She was glad that now that she hadn't worn a hat, for it would be one more thing to get wet if it rained. She walked quickly but not so rapidly that she would seem rushed; it would not do to seem flustered.

The taxi reversed, double-clutched, then turned around, and headed back toward busier streets.

As she hastened up the driveway to the handsome house, Poppy prepared herself to deal with the investigating police. She knew most of them considered reporters a necessary evil, and women reporters as a calamity on a par with major felonies; she needed to be ready to counter any resistance she might encounter.

Two uniformed officers stood in the open doorway; the younger of the two glanced at Poppy. "Sorry, ma'am. The Moncriefs aren't receiving visitors today."

Poppy had pulled out her press credentials and held them up. "P. M. Thornton of the Philadelphia Clarion. I understand Mister Moncrief has been found dead."

The older officer frowned at her. "A reporter, are you?" His tone made it clear that he didn't believe her.

"That's what this says," she pointed out politely but firmly. "If you'll be good enough to let me in, and tell me who's in charge of the investigation?"

"Ask for Inspector Loring," said the older officer, grudgingly moving enough to allow her to pass.

"Inspector Loring," Poppy repeated, and stepped through into the entry-hall of the Moncrief house.

The building was not quite fifty years old, a fine example of carpenter Gothic, with a front and back parlor to the left of the entry hall, and a small sitting room in front of the dining room on the right. Just at present the sitting room was filled with policemen and a pair of morgue workers, all speaking in lowered voices. Beyond them, the double pocket-doors stood half-open, revealing a corner of the long, highly polished mahogany dining table, the green-marble mantle of the fireplace, a bit of the brass-and-crystal chandelier canted on one side, and another group of men standing in a semi-circle, most of them looking down, as if embarrassed to stare up. There was something laid out on the carpet, the face covered. Shocked in spite of all her preparation for this sight, Poppy recognized Gregory Swindon of the Pennsylvania Ledger and Wilfred Bishop of the Philadelphia Informer, standing at the fringe of the police, and she steeled herself for what was to come.

"Inspector Loring?" she said, approaching the group of men with as firm a step as she could muster. "P. M. Thornton, Philadelphia Clarion. What can you tell me about Madison Moncrief?" She held out her hand, curious to see who among the police would take it.

FIVE

❦

A MAN IN HIS LATE TWENTIES OR EARLY THIRTIES WITH EXHAUSTED, ANCIENT eyes, looked around. He was wearing a dark-grey suit, white shirt, a red-and-black regimental tie, and tan overcoat. Unlike the other policemen, he was not in uniform; his suit — from what little Poppy could see of it — was rumpled and inexpertly tailored, his shirt-collar was wilted, and he needed a shave. In return, he took stock of Poppy, eyes narrowing. "The Clarion is it? What in the name of Beelz — Black Jack Pershing made Lowenthal send a woman on a story like this?" he asked of no one in particular.

Swindon and Bishop exchanged glances that made Poppy want to crown them both with cast-iron skillets.

"You'll have to ask him why he chose me; I have no idea." This was not quite the truth, but it served its purpose. "What matters is that I'm here," she said, finally dropping her hand. Little as she wanted to admit it, she was feeling a bit queasy.

"So I see," Inspector Loring said, as if taking on a new and unwelcome burden. "I hope you aren't the squeamish type, Miss Thornton," he went on, deliberately stepping aside to reveal the upper half of Madison Moncrief's body lying like a discarded marionette on the floor, a heavy rope around his neck, his tongue bruise-purple and protruding. From his nose up, his face was concealed by a linen handkerchief.

Much as she wanted to steady herself, Poppy knew that if she touched anything she would be banned from the scene of the crime and Bishop and Swindon would find a way to spread the story among their colleagues, so she closed her eyes a moment until she was sure she could maintain her composure, then said, "Ye gods, poor Louise. This, on top of everything else — she must be beside herself. "

Loring stared hard at her for several seconds. "You sound as if you know these people. Do you?"

"Slightly," said Poppy. "They're fairly good friends of my cousin Eustace." Belatedly she realized that Lowenthal might have had some reason beyond her being female to hesitate sending her on this assignment — not that she wasn't determined to handle herself well, but she could see it might be trickier to do than she had first thought.

"Oh, great," said Swindon.

Loring considered her a few seconds more. "Perhaps you can help us. Since you know the Moncriefs."

"I told you; I don't know them very well. I've been to this house perhaps four or five times in the last three years, always with my cousin," said Poppy, becoming cautious. "They are more acquaintances than friends."

"That's more than the rest of us put together — none of us know them at all," Loring said. "At least, tell me what you notice."

"If it will help." Poppy made herself look down at Madison again. "How horrid. He must have suffered terribly."

"Strangling is a hard way to go," Loring said, then pointed up at the chandelier. "He wrecked that, in killing himself. It wasn't designed to hold so much weight off-center, and, as you can tell from the rope, he used the outer rim with the gas-jets. A strange choice; if he had chosen the center of the chandelier, he would have hung there all night. He might still be there."

"You mean hanging from it?" Poppy asked, and felt questions rising within her.

"You have a vivid imagination, Thornton," Bishop muttered.

"No, I don't," she replied calmly. "It just strikes me that since it was possible to hang from the strongest part of the chandelier, it's strange that he didn't. If I were about to hang myself, I'd do it from the sturdiest, not the weakest, support."

"He'd probably have had to move the table," said one of the policemen.

"That's no big problem, not if you're going to do away with yourself," said Loring. "He had to get up high enough to do it, but a chair would have worked as well — maybe better."

"Also, it doesn't seem like Madison, to ruin something as fine as the chandelier." Poppy shook her head emphatically.

"He was going to kill himself," Loring said.

"Even then, Madison Moncrief is . . . wasn't the kind of man to make a mess, and certainly not with the chandelier. The chandelier is valuable, you see, and even if it weren't . . . This is much too . . . untidy for him. Ye gods, the man's an accountant at one of the most conservative firms in the state." She hesitated, then plunged on. "I didn't know him well, but I do know he was very meticulous, and I can't believe he'd deliberately ruin a fine chandelier. There was no reason for him to cause so much damage. He could have hanged himself from the balustrade along the gallery in the entry hall. That's much sturdier." She wondered if she were saying too much, if she had failed to maintain the proper perspective on the case. She decided to be a bit more circumspect.

"Maybe he didn't realize the chandelier wouldn't support him," Loring suggested.

"It was the most obvious way to do it," said another of the policemen, not allowing Poppy the chance to respond. "People don't think about other people, not at a time like this."

"But that's what I'm trying to tell you: Madison Moncrief would think about such things, and he wouldn't leave this kind of destruction behind. Not with his wife asleep upstairs. Not with the housekeeper coming first thing in the morning," said Poppy, knowing she was being narrowly watched. "He was discreet, very discreet."

"Yeah. And he'd still have been up there when the housekeeper arrived, or his wife came looking for him, assuming he had decided to hang from the center of the fixture, and not the rim. If he'd hanged himself in the basement or slit his wrists in the bath or took poison in the library and just drifted away, it would be neater: but his wife would be shocked, no matter what." Loring saw the other reporters making notes and he raised a quizzical eyebrow at Poppy. "No notes?"

"Not so far," she said, and forced herself to go on. "How soon after he suffocated do you think he fell?"

"Hard to say," Loring said, and was supported by nods from the other policemen. "The blood has pooled to the low points of where he's lying, so he probably fell pretty soon after. You can see where his shoes and legs hit the edge of the table, and his arm. It's broken, by the way, and one ankle snapped, but that most likely happened after he died." He pointed to the scuffs, chips, and scratches on the glossy mahogany.

Poppy nodded. "It could be much worse, I'd imagine."

"Oh?" Loring prompted her.

"Well, yes: think about it," Poppy said, and glanced up at the lop-sided chandelier. "The whole fixture could have come down, which would mean there would be gas in the house — a great deal of gas if it continued to leak for half the night. The gas could have exploded, having had several hours to build up, and that would really be unlike Madison, taking a chance of harming others, especially since his wife . . . " She met Loring's surprised gaze with a deliberately candid one of her own. "That's assuming this isn't a suicide, after all."

"Un-huh," said Loring. "And do you have any reason to think it isn't a suicide?"

"Only that the method seems foreign to the man I knew," said Poppy, finally taking out her notebook and opening it, and making a few scribbles in it.

"Slightly," Loring added for her.

"Yes, slightly."

He stepped back from the body. "We got all the measurements?" he asked the men standing with him.

"Distance from the walls, from the fireplace, from the table, from all three doors. Height of the chandelier. Dimensions of the room. Made a sketch of the positions of the furniture and distances from the body," said the nearest man in uniform as he patted the well-worn notebook in his hand. "Approximate length and condition of the rope. We'll get that exactly when we can start moving things about. The morgue workers will take a photograph before they move the body when they get in here."

"The morgue workers are here, waiting in the sitting room," said another of the policemen. "And the hearse. They want the body so they can — "

Loring nodded. "I'll see to it in a couple minutes. I want to make sure we have everything covered before we let them have him. Dillon, I'll want you to go with the body and sign off on the transfer, and collect his clothes."

Dillon, a fairly young man in a well-pressed police uniform had just come in from the kitchen. "Aw, Inspector."

"Just do it, Dillon," Loring told him wearily.

Bishop spoke up, "Is there anything more, Inspector?"

"I don't think so. Not right now. Check with the precinct this afternoon." Loring was paying them very little attention; he frowned at the body. "Poor sod."

"Come on, Inspector, give," Swindon protested. "We have to file by one."

"Call the precinct. If we have anything more to release, we'll make sure you have it. If we haven't, then file what you have so far," said Loring, and turned to Poppy. "Lowenthal can't object to that, can he?" He regarded the other two reporters. "Nor will van Meder or Constantine."

Swindon snorted. "You think so, do you? When did you ever work for van Meder?" He nudged Bishop. "Come on. Let's get out of here."

Poppy stepped back, ready to leave. "Thank you, Inspector Loring," she said as a matter of good form. "I'll call you at three."

"Not you," Loring told her. "I want you to stick around for a while. I've got some questions for you. About Louise Moncrief." He pointed toward the sitting room. "Don't worry. I'll give you a ride back to the Clarion myself if I have to."

"Oh!" Poppy was nonplused at this unexpected turn of events; she wondered what Lowenthal would expect her to do now.

"I need to find out some things from you, before I ques — interview the widow," Loring explained as he led the way into the sitting room, pointing back into the dining room where the men with the stretcher were waiting impatiently.

"Does she know — "

Loring nodded. "She's upstairs. Her maid has called her sister, who will be here as soon as she can. I wanted to give her some time to . . . collect her thoughts. I understand that she isn't . . . quite well."

"We're done here, Inspector," one of the policemen called out.

"Okay. Stick around until the hearse goes. Make sure the house is secured before you leave." He signaled the morgue workers. "He's all yours. Make sure you check his pockets and account for any money, jewelry, or other possessions he may have on him, and see to it that Constable Dillon has a copy of your inventory when you hand over his effects. I'll find out who's visited the house in the last three days, why they were here, how long they stayed, and anything about the visitors that was unusual." He pointed to a wicker couch. "Miss Thornton. If you would?"

Slowly and carefully, Poppy sat down.

SIX

❧

"YOU WERE QUESTIONED BY THE POLICE?" MILDRED FAIRCHILD SUPPRESSED A shriek as they closed the curtains on their booth at Wendover's Continental Restaurant. "About Madison Moncrief? Who's dead?" She was very elegant in a mauve cashmere coat with a beaver collar over a drop-waisted dress of printed fabric designed by Klimt. Her very modish hat was set on her sculpted auburn waves at a rakish angle and she smelled of lilac and violets.

"Yes, Milly," said Poppy, feeling a bit foolish discussing it with her old friend; only the thought that the story was in the evening papers rid her of the conviction that she shouldn't discuss an assignment while she was working on it.

"So tell me: what did they ask you?" She folded her arms on the table and looked straight into Poppy's eyes. "Were they gruff and ill-mannered?"

"More brusque and suspicious," said Poppy with a slight smile. "Inspector Loring was as polite as he could be, given the circumstances."

"But wasn't it exciting," Mildred kept on. "I mean, if the police should question me, I think I'd just faint!"

"It's nothing like that," Poppy said, becoming flustered, now that she was away from the scene. "Inspector Loring is trying to determine how Madison Moncrief died, and, since I have had a little social contact with the Moncriefs — "

"Isn't that bullying?" Mildred asked. "The police are always bullying, aren't they?"

"They don't bully reporters, particularly ones on the scene who might be able to help them," said Poppy drily.

"On the scene." Mildred shook her head. "You mean you actually saw the body?" she shrieked.

"I saw it, at least most of the upper half," Poppy said soberly. "It was pretty awful." Sufficiently upsetting, she thought, to make her forget about her lunchtime 'phone call to Aunt Josephine.

"Good Lord!" Mildred turned a paler shade under her foundation and powder. "What on earth were they thinking, to show you the body?"

"I'm a reporter. I was sent to cover the story. The other reporters there saw the body, so why shouldn't I, as well?" Poppy said, as if she had to defend herself.

"But still — " Mildred interrupted herself. "I think it's just too ghastly."

"You may be right; it was pretty unpleasant, and perhaps worse because I knew him, however slightly," said Poppy, glancing away from Mildred. "But, Milly, I hope you won't think me ghoulish to say that this story could be the making of me as a reporter." That thought had kept her calm during Loring's questioning. "If I can work this story all the way through, make it everything Lowenthal wants, then I'll be in a position to do the kinds of stories I want to do: stories with substance on real issues. No more Fine Books Society meetings for me!"

"But corpses — Poppy, that's so lurid. I mean . . . dead bodies. Good gracious, I don't understand why you don't simply find the sort of man who can appreciate you and — "

"Now you're sounding like Aunt Jo. Twenty-four is not the end of the world, you know." Poppy shook her head, and sternly corrected herself: twenty-five in a little over a month. "I'm not about to waste my life, and my education, simply waiting for some man to come along and bestow himself and all his goods upon me. For one thing, there's a shortage of good men, or haven't you noticed? Between the Great War and the 'Flu, there aren't enough left to go around for everyone. Some of us have to make other plans, and I have the temperament for it. If I'm going to be an old maid, I'd just as soon I do something worthwhile with myself."

"But staying single! Deliberately? Aren't you worried?"

Little as she wanted to admit it, Poppy was a bit worried, but was not about to acknowledge that to Mildred. "I have a good job, and if that fails, I have an inheritance. I'm more fortunate than a lot of women. I don't have to settle for a man just to keep a roof over my head."

"And, as you say, you do have ten thousand a year from your father's trust," Mildred said with a little frown. "That's quite an independence."

"Yes, it is. I'm grateful to my father for providing it, though I'd rather have him still alive than have the money."

"Well, of course you would," Mildred agreed. "You value your father's memory." She gave an impatient little sigh. "Perhaps a little too much? What man can live up to him?"

Poppy bristled. "I am not trying to find a substitute father, Milly, and well you know it. But I'm not about to — "

" — Settle for the first man who asks you. Yes, Poppy, I know. You've said the same thing for ages. But still."

"He would have to be the right man, one who wouldn't try to hedge me in, or turn me into an asset, or would resent my work. The thing is, Milly," Poppy confided, "is that I like being a reporter, and I'm not so sure I'd like being married, especially if it were to the wrong man. That would be dreadful."

"Why don't you let me look around for you? I'm a pretty successful matchmaker, if I say so myself. If I had some idea of what you want in a man, I could start looking for someone who wouldn't want to limit you, or any of the rest of it. You said yourself that I did well for Timothy and Bess Rymer, and Howard and Katherine Hall, and Dorian and Roberta Mitchell, and — "

"Thanks, Milly, but I don't think so."

"But why not?" Mildred exclaimed.

"The trouble is, I'm not like you: I don't know what I want, only what I don't want," she explained, surprising herself. "You knew what you wanted, and you got him."

"My Humphrey is a prince, an absolute prince," Mildred declared staunchly. "I am a very lucky woman."

"And he's right for you in every way. You two are clearly made for each other, and I'm very happy for you. He'll be the god of your idolatry and he'll dote upon you until you're both doddering ancients. But, Milly, he'd drive me nuts, if I had to live with him, and I'd do the same to him," said Poppy, making no apology for her slang.

"You're being too hard on yourself, or too hard to please," said Mildred, then glanced speculatively at Poppy. "What about Todd Powers? He seemed very interested in you. You could probably still get him back, if you wanted to."

"Ye gods, why on earth would I want to saddle myself with someone like Todd Powers? He's got money and position, as well as influence, but he's just the kind of man who makes me savage, and I don't mean that in a flattering sense. He's arrogant, superior, and self-centered in the extreme. He likes to be gallant and protective because it makes him feel superior to poor, helpless women, and he says so. Oh, not in so many words, but in his condescending manner. When he crosses the street with a woman, he takes hold of her elbow, which doesn't help at all, and forces the woman to lean on him." Realizing that she had raised her voice too much, Poppy took and deep breath and went on more levelly. "He does say that behind every great man there's a great woman, which is often true, sadly. When he says behind, he means that's where a woman belongs — subordinate and devoted. Well, I don't want to spend my life furthering someone else's ambitions, thank you very much. I have ambitions of my own."

"But Poppy, you're going to be twenty-five. You're running out of opportunities," Mildred said with so much sympathy that Poppy had to stifle the urge to yell at her.

"Twenty-five isn't antediluvian, Milly," she said, though between Aunt Jo and Mildred, she was beginning to think it might be.

"You're so much like your Aunt Esther," said Mildred, thinking of Poppy's father's other sister, the one who had made a life for herself without a husband, traveling the world for the National Geographic Society and was presently somewhere in eastern Russia. "Always ready to take women's parts, no matter what the circumstances. Sometimes I wonder how your family managed to breed two such different women as Esther and Josephine — don't you?" She shook her head, and touched the corner of her mouth with a red-lacquered fingernail. "Esther hasn't realized that there's no need for Suffragettes any longer, or demonstrations, or protests. We have the vote, and the way is clear."

"Milly, Milly, the vote's just the beginning, a first step, not the end of the fight," said Poppy. "And Aunt Esther is right: there's a long way to go to true equality; the vote's a good start, and we need it, but there are so many other matters we need to address. We have a great deal more to do." She found herself breathing a little faster. "Don't you want the right to control your own property? To bequeath and inherit without some male being part of the process? Don't you want to be able to sign a contract without your husband co-signing? Don't you want to be paid the same salaries as men earn?"

"Why should I bother myself with tedium? Oh, Poppy, you can't tell me you want to have to handle all those details?" Mildred laughed.

"I'd certainly like the option," said Poppy.

"But don't you see?" Mildred persisted. "This way — with a husband — you can have the best of both worlds? You can vote and run for office and all the rest of it, but you don't have to be on your own. You're protected."

"Protected means immature, incompetent, incapable," said Poppy. "We protect children, not adults."

"Oh, stuff!" Mildred exclaimed. "How can you say such things?" She was becoming distressed, and it showed, as she reached for her embroidered linen handkerchief and began twisting it between her hands.

"I say it because it's true, and we both know it," Poppy told her, softening her words with a smile. "Things are a little better than the way they were twenty years ago, and there are far worse conditions in many other countries, but — "

"Oh, there's room for improvement, I grant you, but the real fighting is over, like the Great War." Mildred smiled back. "And I'm glad of it."

"Perhaps," Poppy allowed, though she was tempted to argue.

"You're always looking on the dark side of things, Poppy. I can't understand it, someone like you being caught up in all that darkness. You're not willing to make allowances, or to take the time to concentrate on the good in people. Don't you think you should try the light side, instead?" Mildred's tone was rancorous, her eyes were severe, but her lips continued to smile.

"When there's light enough, I will," said Poppy, then sat back.

"Poppea Millicent Thornton, you are the most impossible — " She stopped herself, touched the brim of her hat, and said in another tone, "Do you think we should ring for the waiter and order something?"

"It wouldn't hurt," said Poppy, mentally chiding herself for becoming so insistent; she would never change Mildred's mind, and she knew it.

Mildred was glad of the distraction ordering their meal would provide. "That would be a good idea, I think." She reached up and pushed the small bell at the edge of the door. "I'm going to have soup instead of an appetizer. What about you?"

"I like the lobster bisque here," said Poppy, aware that they had drawn back from a terrible, invisible brink.

"It's one of their better offerings," Mildred agreed. "I think I'll have some, too, and cod to follow." She slipped her handkerchief back into her coat-pocket. "Hasn't it been a dreary spring? Don't you long for sunny days?"

Glad to change to this innocuous topic, Poppy agreed that the spring was disappointing so far and that she would welcome a break in the weather. "But I hope we have a cooler summer than last year."

"Wasn't it appalling?" Mildred agreed at once, and turned to open the curtain for the waiter.

They ordered, and unfolded their napkins, each telling the other how hungry she was. From there, they went on to catch up on what their college friends were doing, how each other's families were, what their plans were for the summer, and the astonishing progress of Mildred's three-year-old twins, Portia and Miranda, both of whom promised to be real beauties, according to their proud mother. With the children to discuss, and Mildred's recent purchase of three arm- chairs from Mayes Brothers, they dined convivially enough and parted on good terms, each promising to telephone the other within the week.

Splurging on a taxi-ride home, Poppy found herself in the back seat of a year-old Cadillac, her briefcase lying on the seat beside her, her purse in her lap, her umbrella propped against her leg. As she rode through the damp streets, her thoughts began to drift back to the Moncrief house and the story she had filed four minutes before the metropolitan edition deadline; she hadn't waited around to see what Lowenthal thought of it, too worried that he might spike it after all. If more important news superceded the Moncrief story, Lowenthal wouldn't hesitate to take it out. She'd wait until she saw the paper before she congratulated herself. Dinner with Mildred had eased the lingering questions about Madison Moncrief's death, but now she harkened back to three minutes to five, when she handed the two sheets to Lowenthal, she had held her breath before obeying his wave of dismissal. She wanted to figure out the significance of every nuance of gesture, every inflection of tone, and what it meant to Lowenthal, keeping her on the Moncrief story. She patted her briefcase as if to console the carbon copy of her article inside.

"It was a good story, if a bit terse," said a voice beside her in the dark of the passenger compartment.

Poppy almost jumped. "Ye gods! Don't do that!"

"Read your mind?" Holte asked.

"Sorry, ma'am. The road's a bit uneven here," the cabby said.

"Yes. Yes, of course," said Poppy, looking about. She closed the glass partition between her and the driver, then stared into the space beside her. "What's going on here?" she whispered irately.

"I'm haunting you," said Chesterton Holte in a conversational voice. He had almost appeared on the seat beside her, but seemed to be a hovering shape, not a presence. "Remember?"

"Shhh," she admonished him.

"He can't hear me," he reassured her, lowering his voice to match hers. "Only you can. He can't see me, either."

"So if I talk to you, he's going to think I'm crazy," Poppy muttered.

"Ghosts aren't perceptible to most people," Holte reminded her.

"Just me, animals, some birds, and the occasional baby," said Poppy very softly. "And one drunken sailor."

"That's right," Holte concurred.

Poppy resisted the urge to shout at him, and instead, she said very softly, "Other than haunting me, what are you doing here? Do you only come out at night?"

"Hardly," said Holte, continuing after a slight pause. "I've been following you all day. Part of my haunting."

"All day," Poppy repeated, reviewing her day in her thoughts, her frown deepening.

"From when you went down to breakfast until now." He was like an exhaled breath on a frosty night: a white smudge in the darkness of the taxi's interior.

"Ye gods," Poppy said, aghast at what Holte must have witnessed. "All day." She lowered her voice again. "Why?"

"I told you last night: I owe your family something for what happened to your father." His tone became thoughtful. "At the time, I thought it was justified, a reality of the Great War — unfortunate but unavoidable. But after I died, I came to realize that it was another senseless loss in a sea of senseless losses, and that I had deprived your family of someone who should not have left you so abruptly." He made a coughing sound. "So now that I grasp the . . . ah . . . error of my ways, I feel compelled to make up for the misfortune of his absence in your life. And it strikes me that your current assignment provides me a good opportunity to make a start."

Poppy briefly asked herself if all of this could be an illusion, but she set that aside for the time being: she had some questions she wanted answered. "What do you mean?" she whispered; she would make up her mind about Holte's reality some other time.

"Your story on the Moncrief killing was interesting. You had all the basic facts, and you presented them clearly, to the extent that you know them."

"Thank you," she said at her most acerbic.

Impervious to her tone, he went on, "You missed one point, however."

"Oh?" Her tone offered him no encouragement.

"It's an important point," he said.

She couldn't resist asking him, "And what would that be?"

"The point," said Holte, "that Madison Moncrief was murdered."

SEVEN

"MURDERED?" SHE EXCLAIMED IN A HUSHED VOICE, GLANCING SWIFTLY AT THE rear-view mirror and the driver's face. "Ye g — what makes you think so?"

"Because he told me," said Holte as if this ought to be obvious.

"He told . . . Of course," she said sarcastically. "He's a ghost now, too, is he? You've become acquainted?"

"Ghosts can converse with one another, you know, at least they come as close to it as their condition makes possible, " he said, sounding huffy, then he took a more accommodating tone. "Not as we're conversing now, but there are ways we're able to exchange information and experience when we need to."

"And you're certain it's murder, not some incomplete memory or a cruel game? I imagine dying can be perturbing when it happens, and one might not pay close attention to what went on around one." She wouldn't have thought that Madison would do anything so beastly, but if he had become a ghost under violent circumstances — if there were actually such things as ghosts — might he try to seek revenge through a misleading report? She tried to banish the whole farrago from her thoughts. "Besides," she added, "is he sure?"

"That he was murdered?" Holte asked. "Yes, he is. That isn't the kind of thing you make mistakes about, once you remember how it happened."

"I guess you should know," said Poppy, struggling to keep her voice low.

"I . . . um . . . witnessed his experience, as he had it, and it seemed to be murder to me, since he vaguely recalls someone got him up onto the chandelier: he didn't do it himself," he said, then added, "He couldn't reveal who killed him."

"Couldn't or wouldn't?" Poppy challenged, and noticed she was speaking more loudly again, and mentally shushed herself.

"Couldn't, I think," said Holte. "When a ghost is revealing something to another ghost, it's nearly impossible to lie or obfuscate."

"I suppose I should have known that," said Poppy with a sarcastic glance at Holte, and noticed that the cabby was eyeing her in his rear-view mirror. She bent over her briefcase and went on in a whisper. "Can we do this later? I'm apt to end up in the asylum if I keep talking to you; the driver thinks I'm talking to myself and that worries him."

"Very well." As he fell silent he also vanished.

Left suddenly alone, Poppy felt very much, and very irrationally, abandoned. "Don't be ridiculous," she muttered. She told herself she was acting like a schoolgirl, that Holte wasn't anything real, that ghosts, helpful or not, did not exist, but she discovered that she missed him, and that it didn't matter whether he was imaginary or not. She sat back, amazed at herself, and doing her best to make herself feel at ease; for the rest of the journey, she did her best to make her mind a blank.

"That'll be a dollar fifty," said the cabby as he drew up in front of Aunt Josephine's house, looking relieved to be rid of her.

Poppy sighed, handed the cabby a dollar seventy-five and let herself out, taking care to make sure she left nothing behind. She was mildly surprised to find the porch-light out. She glanced along the street and saw all the houses were dark. "Damn," she said aloud, in case Holte should be listening. "The butler's in his apartment over the garage at this time of night, and there's no bell: the power's out again." As she slipped her key into the lock and went inside she waved a dismissal to the cabbie; the taxi pulled away from the curb.

Two candles were set on the highboy across from the telephone table in the entry hall, their light doing little to dispel the gloom. The glow of more candles in the rear parlor caught Poppy's attention and she went toward them.

Josephine was sitting near the fireplace, a crocheted throw over her knees, an open book on her lap, a cup of tea on the table beside her, and her reading-glasses perched precariously toward the end of her nose; there was a silver candelabra on the table as well, set so that it would drip no wax into the tea. She looked up over the rims. "Poppy, dear, is that you?"

"Yes, Aunt Jo." She came into the parlor and dropped into the chair opposite her aunt's. "It's been quite a day."

"How was your dinner with Mildred?" Josephine asked, closing her book and removing her glasses.

"Oh, you know Milly. She lives her life in italics." Poppy stretched out her legs and set her purse and briefcase on the floor next to her. "She says she's happy; she certainly looks it, and prosperous, too. Her clothes must have cost at least three hundred dollars, and her perfume was French and sixty dollars a bottle, or I know nothing about scent. From what she told me over dinner, her husband's doing well, her twins are extraordinary, and I'm delighted for her."

"You could have her way of life for your own, you know," Josephine prompted her. "I wish you'd reconsider."

Poppy shook her head ruefully. "It wouldn't work, Aunt Jo. Milly and I aren't very much alike even though we're friends. What suits her would quickly pall for me." Without warning she yawned, and didn't see the shocked look on her aunt's face. "It was a long day today, and it will be a long day tomorrow."

"Well, with the lights out, you might want just to go up to bed, then; catch up on your rest. Missus Flowers took a branch of candles to her quarters almost an hour ago," said Josephine. "Get some sleep for a change. I shudder to think the kind of day you must have had. You're walking as if your feet are sore, and that means you have been out and about again."

Poppy did her best to smile, wanting to change the subject. "How long has the power been off?"

"An hour and a half or a little more. I telephoned the radio station, to see if they knew anything, as you taught me to do, and they said they would look into it."

"Have they called back?"

Josephine shook her head. "Not yet."

"They probably will," said Poppy. "Ten minutes after the lights come back on. But they may know what happened, and will tell you about it." She pushed herself up from the chair, picked up her things, and went to the door. "I'll see you at breakfast, Aunt Jo."

"Remember Eustace will be here at dinnertime tomorrow," Josephine said; she picked up her glasses once again. "I do hope you'll be in."

"Is he still coming?" Poppy asked in some surprise.

"Why wouldn't he be coming?" She sounded genuinely bewildered. "He's been planning this trip for more than a month."

Caught up short, Poppy tried to smooth out her answer. "Well, he's coming for the Moncriefs party, and now that it's been canceled — "

"Canceled? Whatever for?" She gave Poppy a narrow stare. "Is there something you aren't telling me?"

It was just what Poppy had surmised: her aunt knew nothing about the events of the day. "Because," she said as she came back into the parlor to Josephine's side, "Madison Moncrief . . . died this morning."

"Madison Moncrief is dead? That's absurd." Josephine stared at Poppy, her expression changing from derisive to concerned. "You're serious, aren't you? I'm surprised it isn't in the evening paper."

Poppy kept silent, thinking that by morning, Josephine would have a volley of questions to ask over breakfast. She didn't want to point out the short notice on page one, a bit below the fold, knowing it would give her aunt real distress to see it.

"I haven't read either paper yet, not with the lights out, but such an event must surely be sufficiently deserving of notice. The Moncriefs aren't generally inclined to seek public attention, but they're not nobodies, are they, so a death in their family ought to be reported," said Josephine, and continued, "Madison's a young man. How could he die now?" she asked Poppy. "He's always been the picture of health. Do you know what happened?"

"Yes, Aunt Jo, I do." She reached out and took her aunt's hand. "The police think it might be suicide."

Josephine laughed angrily. "Suicide? That's the most nonsensical thing I've ever heard," she declared. "Madison Moncrief isn't that kind of man. Louise can't have told them that, can she? It's a mistake."

"It's a complicated story, Aunt Jo. If you like, I'll tell you tomorrow evening, when I learn more. Right now, all I know for sure is he's dead and it wasn't an accident. I've been assigned to cover the case." She patted Josephine's hand before releasing it. "The police don't know much yet. When I left the house, the police hadn't yet spoken with Louise." The twenty minutes she had answered questions for Inspector Loring were still fresh in her mind: had the marriage been sound? It certainly seemed to be so. Was everything solid in their finances? As far as Poppy knew, yes. Had there been any difficulties, any tension between them recently? There was the miscarriage, but nothing else that Poppy knew of, but she wasn't one of their circle of intimates, and most of her information was second-hand from her cousin. There had been no gossip about them that she was aware of, at least not recently. What about outside interests? Did the inspector mean hobbies or lovers? Both, if they applied. It had taken Poppy a little time to recall what she knew about either kinds of interests but she was able to tell Loring that Madison built ships in bottles and sailed a forty-foot sloop in the summer; Louise attended horse shows and races and raised orchids at their seaside house. As to lovers, there had been rumors a year ago, about Louise and a man from New York, but nothing came of them; Poppy had not paid much attention to the whispers.

"She'll set them to rights about Madison. Suicide! Preposterous! I knew his mother, and she would never have allowed such a thing." She gathered her throw around her as Poppy walked away. "Go get some sleep, my dear. Thank you for telling me; I'll send a sympathy note and appropriate flowers around in the morning, and I'll call Eustace as well, to find out if I should expect him."

"Tell him I'm sorry about Madison when you talk to him," Poppy said, making her retreat. "You don't have to mention I'm on the story."

"No. Certainly not. There are candles on the table at the top of the stairs. Take one along to your room," Josephine called after her, then added reluctantly, "There's a letter for you in the entry hall, from Esther. The postmark is Vladivostok. Why does she go to such remote places? No doubt you'll want to read it."

"Will do. Thanks, Aunt Jo." She picked up the letter before she went up the stairs to the landing and saw Maestro curled at the top of the flight, next to the table with the candles, in just the right place to be tripped over;

Poppy stopped and looked down. "You are a nuisance, Maestro," she told him affectionately, before she bent to move him out of the way as she resumed her climb up the remaining steps. "You don't want to get stepped on, do you?" The cat uncoiled himself and hissed at something behind her. "Seeing spooks?" she asked Maestro, adding to the vacant air, "I suppose you're here."

"That I am," said Chesterton Holte, as the shell-sconced light at the top of the stairs momentarily flickered, blinked twice, and faded.

"A nice trick," she said, trying to rid herself of the eerie sensation his antics caused her. "I'll remember to look for it."

"About the only one I have — that and static on the 'phone line," he said as Maestro fled down the hall ahead of them, spitting and growling to himself. "I'm sorry I can't carry something for you."

"So am I," she said, picking up a candle in a boat's lantern.

"You're thinking I'm an illusion again," he said, his outline blurring; he made an effort and his presence became a bit clearer. "What can I do to impress my reality — tenuous though it is — upon you?"

"You've certainly impressed the cat," she said as she turned toward her room. "I suppose I'll have to accept you for the time being."

"And that is no answer," he told her, remaining more or less at her side. "May I come along and explain about Madison Moncrief."

She gave it a moment's thought. "Why not? You'll probably do it whether I agree or not, so come along." She decided to read Aunt Esther's letter in the morning, when it was light, and she would have a better chance of making out Esther's unorthodox penmanship. She led the way down the corridor. "Not that you don't know where my room is."

"Second door on the right after the green bathroom; the first door's a linen closet," he confirmed. "Windows face east and north."

Turning the doorknob was awkward; she used the hand in which she carried her purse and briefcase. "I should have remembered: of course you know," she said, and stepped through her door, Maestro twining around her ankles in a figure eight. "Damned cat," she said affectionately, as he abruptly froze on the threshold.

"If you fall over him, I'm sorry, but I can't catch you," Holte said, sounding unusually contrite.

"Noncorporeal. You've told me," she said, setting down her purse and briefcase on the bench at the foot of her bed. "Repeatedly."

Maestro lingered at the door, pacing unhappily, then let out a plaintive yowl; Poppy went and let him out, then returned to the bed. Lit by the single flame of the candle, she found her bedroom unfamiliar and perhaps sinister. She bent to unbuckle her ankle-straps, then stepped out of her shoes, examining her swollen feet. "I could do with a little noncorporeal just now. Ye gods, my dogs are barking; Aunt Jo was right."

"Yes, there are advantages to not having a solid body — not many, but a few," he said, and almost sat on the chair in front of her vanity; Poppy shuddered and looked away. "Does this bother you?"

"It does. You hover there, about three inches above the seat and act as if you're actually on it." She set the candle on the nightstand and looked back at him. "Now you're sunk about four inches into the chair." With an impatient wave, she said, "Just do whatever you want. Sit cross legged in mid-air, if that makes you happy."

"I would like you to feel comfortable," he said. "I suspect you'd prefer it if I matched your corporeal notions of comfort more carefully than I've done."

"So I'll be more likely to believe in you?" she guessed. "For now, I'll give you the benefit of the doubt when you hang in the air."

In response he rose from the chair and spread out about four feet off the floor as if reclining in a hammock. "This will suffice me if it doesn't bother you."

"Go ahead," she said in a tone of capitulation. "And tell me what you found out from Madison Moncrief."

"Well, you'll have to understand that he's still pretty disoriented — everyone is when they leave the body, Moncrief more than most, because his departure was unexpected. But he has been able to recall a little of what happened; he'll remember more in time." He looked around as if he expected to be overheard, then went on, "He said he was drinking some cognac — the real thing, from France — as he usually did before retiring. He had a meeting scheduled for the morning, and was reviewing what he would have to present, and he thinks he fell asleep, which was most unlike him. He's fairly certain he spilled the cognac."

"Where did he spill it?" Poppy asked, planning to discover if the police had learned anything about such a spill.

"He believes it was on his trouser-leg, and the snifter fell on the carpet next to his chair. He said his thoughts were woolly."

"Woolly?" Poppy repeated.

"You know: thick, slow, muzzy." Holte sat up and folded his arms. "He also said there was a funny taste in his mouth." He watched her, seeing how she evaluated this information.

"Was he drugged, then?"

"It's likely," said Holte carefully.

"Who'd want to drug him?" Poppy asked while she flexed her toes, interested in hearing more in spite of her wish not to.

"He isn't sure about it," said Holte, with a kind of melancholy amusement. "But that's not surprising under the circumstances. He told me he had a slight memory of being hefted onto his feet, and the noose slipped around his neck, but he doesn't know who did it, or even if it happened."

"Drugged and hanged by someone else. Or could he have been drunk and despondent, and hanged himself." Poppy looked over at Holte.

"He said he'd only had half of what was in the snifter."

"But how many times had he poured into it? Was that his first drink, or his third? How long had he been drinking that evening? You say he claimed it was French, but could it have been something cooked up in a basement vat?" Poppy sighed as she set her shoes in front of the nightstand; she wanted to get undressed and into bed, but was unable to bring herself to do it while Holte was in the room. "If he were drunk, he might have — " She broke off. "But if he were that drunk, how could he get on the table? And where did the rope come from?"

Holte unfolded his arms. "Your cousin should be able to tell you whether or not Moncrief was inclined to drunkenness. Ask him, and decide for yourself." Still in his sitting posture, he drifted toward the door. He hesitated, then said, "He liked his work, but felt that one of the partners had it in for him, but that didn't make any sense to him, because Quentin Hadley had got him into the firm, and Grimes isn't involved with that side of the business."

"You mean he was set up?" Poppy asked sharply, as all her journalistic nerves began to tingle.

"I don't know, and Moncrief doesn't know, either — but he's confused. That's why I wasn't sure I should mention it." He regarded her narrowly. "It might be nothing, you know."

"It might," she agreed. "Are you leaving?"

He nodded. "You're tired, and you have a busy day tomorrow. I saw the memo Lowenthal gave you; you'll have another early morning."

"So I will," she said, and watched him slide through the door. As soon as she was sure she was alone, she rose and unbuttoned her jacket, then went to the closet for a hanger. Tomorrow, she decided, it would be the russet dress with the peplum jacket. Her blouse was sadly wilted and would have to go into the hamper, but the dress would not show the wear of the day as the blouse had. Satisfied, she removed her underclothes and drew on her nightgown. Before getting into bed, she remembered to blow out the candle and to put the alarm clock on her vanity table, set for ten minutes to six.

EIGHT

ARCHIBALD HUBERT WYMAN, M. D., PHD., CHIEF CORONER FOR THE CITY OF Philadelphia, stood on a low platform behind the podium facing the cramped room filled to capacity with journalists of every stripe, some from as far away as Boston and Washington. In the smoke-fogged chamber, he looked every one of his fifty-six years, his eyes sunken in shadowed and pouched sockets, his greying hair not quite neat, his suit a bit too large for him. A veteran of the Great War where he had headed up a graves registration unit in France, he was one of a small group of anatomists who had done extensive studies of 'Flu victims, which gave him a straightforward way with death. "Good morning, gentlemen, Miss Thornton, Missus Ackersley. If I may have your attention?"

The rumble of conversation straggled into silence as the seventeen men and two women turned in his direction, almost all with notebooks and pencils at the ready.

"First, let me tell you at once that the results of my examination of the body of Madison Moncrief are not complete, and I have not yet fixed on a cause of death. I am not satisfied that he killed himself, and it is possible that his hanging was staged to appear to be suicide but in actuality was something else — but exactly what else I have yet to determine. There are questions to be answered before I can give you my findings, whatever they may be." An energetic buzz of speculation passed through the assembled reporters; Wyman held up his hand for silence. "As you know, Mister Moncrief was found yesterday on the floor of his dining room; he had been hanging from a brass chandelier in his dining room; the chandelier was broken, it appears that his weight was too much for it. One of his household staff found him.

The chandelier will be removed for testing. Tests on Mister Moncrief's blood showed faint traces of alcohol and what may — and I mean may — be an opium derivative, but it is so far unidentified. Samples of his blood have been sent by courier to New York for further analysis."

"You mean he was poisoned?" one of the reporters asked on behalf of them all.

"I mean it is possible that there was an opiate-like substance in his blood. Nothing like arsenic or strychnine; it may have been a strong sleeping pill — I'm waiting for word about that from his doctor." Wyman cleared his throat. "It could have been given to him, or been self-administered. I'll know more about that when the test results are returned to me."

"It was an unfamiliar poison?" another voice inquired.

"That's what I said." He glowered at the reporters and continued, "The condition of the body was consistent with hanging, though how he came to hang is still uncertain. There was a welt on his neck and a rope-burn next to his left ear. His tongue was distended, and his eyes showed a network of burst capillaries usually associated with death by strangulation. Other than these injuries, and post-mortem broken bones that resulted when the chandelier broke and the body dropped to the floor, striking the dining table in the process, Mister Moncrief was generally in good health, with a scar on his shoulder, that I have been informed was the result of a sailing accident some seven or eight years ago. There was a stain on his right trouser-leg from the mid-thigh to the calf, composed of alcohol and what seems to be the same unidentified possible opiate found in his blood. His bladder had released as well, leaving urine trails down the insides of his trouser-legs. The police are continuing their investigations until such time as the cause of his death is determined. At present this is the extent of what I know to be the facts of his death." He put the accordion file back down, signaling his readiness to take questions.

The room was silent for perhaps two seconds, and then erupted in a babble of queries, the reporters competing in volume in order to be heard.

"Do you think it's murder?"

"Are there any suspects yet?"

"How soon will you know what killed him?"

"You said broken bones — which bones were broken?"

"What about the police investigation?"

Hearing that next-to-last question, Poppy smiled, for she had detailed the broken arm in her short piece that appeared in the metropolitan edition of the Clarion yesterday evening. With Wyman's remarks to bolster her, she could now expand on the damage done to the body when she submitted her next story — which, she reminded herself — was due at three this afternoon. She tried to press toward the front, but the men were unwilling to make way for her, so she went to the wall in the hope that she could get around the others.

Waiting near the door, the only other woman in the room, Phyllis Ackersley, doyen of the Tribune, smoked while she wrote in one of her custom-made notebooks; everyone in the room was aware of her presence: her silver hair and her fox coat had been seen at all crime-related public announcements since the start of the Great War, and she knew the rhythm of these events better than anyone in the room, including Doctor Wyman. She tapped the ash off her cigarette, closed her notebook and put it in her unfashionably large purse, then turned and left the room, unofficially signaling that the meeting was at an end. She was followed by Jefferson Scott of the Tri-County Spectator and Pierce Cummings of the New York Register. The exit was on.

A few of the remaining reporters gathered in front of the podium, persisting in asking questions, none of which got much in the way of answers; on the platform, Dr. Wyman gathered up his accordion file of papers and ignored the burble.

"Would you like me to follow the coroner after he leaves here?" Chesterton Holte spoke in Poppy's ear. "I could tell you what he says and does. If you like."

Poppy put her hand up, more startled than annoyed. "Don't do that."

"Do what?" A shimmer in the air next to her revealed where he was. "Not go with the coroner? Why not?"

"Just . . . just sneak up on me," she said in an intense whisper. "Especially not in a place like this."

"Oh. Then you do want me to follow the coroner?" He sounded

enthusiastic. "I could find out if he held any information back."

"Yes." She shook her head. "No."

"If you don't like what I find out, you don't have to use it, do you? Why not take advantage of me? I can get places you can't." He made a sound like the tisking of his tongue; Poppy wondered how he managed that — come to think of it, she thought, how does he make himself heard at all, being noncorporeal?

Roy Tarriser from the Pennsylvania Bulletin nearly backed into Poppy as he raised his hand in the hope of being recognized before the coroner left. "Have the police determined if Moncrief's death was a crime?"

"You'll have to ask them, thought it is a very real likelihood at this stage," the coroner shot back. "And I remind you that suicide is a crime in this state, as well as murder. I don't believe it was accidental, unless it was some kind of prank that went wrong. For the time being, the cause of death is undetermined." Another chorus of shouts burst forth and the men did their best to move closer to Dr. Wyman, as if nearness could make him say something more final; the coroner retreated a step, holding his file tightly. "I'll let you know when I have more information. I'm not going to indulge in speculation, so don't bother to ask. Thank you for coming." That said, he turned abruptly and left through the side door he had used to enter the room.

Poppy sighed, frustrated at having failed to make herself heard. "All right," she said quietly. "Go after him; after we talk, I'll make an appointment with him. I've got to talk to Inspector Loring before this gang gets to him. He's expecting me in fifteen minutes."

"You'll see me before the end of the day, when you're on your way home," Holte assured her, his voice fading.

It was a brisk three-block walk to Police Headquarters, which was located not far from the Philadelphia Superior Courts Building. The day was pleasant enough to make the walk a pleasure. Poppy reached the steps of Police Headquarters in less than ten minutes. A half-dozen men in uniform flanked the door, some of them looking more like building guards than men at their shift change.

Poppy approached one of the more friendly looking of the policemen, an older man with sergeant's stripes on his sleeve. "Pardon me, but can you tell me where I can find Inspector Loring? I have an appointment with him."

The sergeant looked her over, gave her a wink. "Second floor, take the right corridor, and it's the fourth door on your left." He sketched a salute to her, and watched her make her way into the building.

Stepping into the rotating door, Poppy was at once struck by the noise of the place: there were a number of people in the marble-clad lobby, most of them in front of the reception desk, seeking attention from the two harassed men behind it. Near the broad stairs were a number of benches where more people waited, many of them dejected or fretful, whom Poppy assumed were the victims of crimes, or perhaps arrested criminals. She went up the stairs and turned right when she reached the next floor, where tall windows in need of a good cleaning provided a dusty kind of light. In a sudden attack of unaccountable self-consciousness, Poppy smoothed the front of her jacket and walked more briskly down the corridor, making note of the policemen who were in the corridor, some of them clearly on missions, a few leaving the shift-change a little late.

At the fourth door on her left, she paused, then opened it into a room about the size of the music room at Aunt Jo's; five medium-sized blond-oak desks, each with a chair behind and a chair in front, were crammed into the space, jig-saw fashion, all of which had a telephone and a reading lamp with an outward-facing name-plate set out on them, with in-and-out baskets at the edge of the large blotters at the center of every desk; a dozen filing cabinets, three tall wastebaskets, and half a dozen straight-backed chairs ranged along the walls. An unused fan stood atop the tallest filing cabinet, its cord dangling. Two of the desks were occupied, one near the side-door, by a man in his fifties, the other, at the back of the room, by Inspector Loring. Today he was wearing a blue-and-brown tweed jacket over a newly ironed white shirt with a simple blue tie; his eyes were no longer eons old, but bright, and a surprising shade that was almost turquoise, Poppy noticed as he looked up while she threaded her way to his desk.

"Miss Thornton. Right on time." He smiled, deep creases framing his eyes and cheeks, and he half-rose, indicating the chair across from him. "Do sit down," he added as he did. "Thank you for coming."

"Thank you for seeing me, Inspector." She held out her hand, and after a slight hesitation, he took it. "I'm grateful for your invitation. I know you have a great deal to do, so I appreciate this opportunity to talk." Hearing herself, she winced, thinking she sounded worse than Mildred Fairchild. To cover this awkwardness, she glanced at his name-plate as she sat. "J. B. Loring. What does the J. B. stand for?" To her astonishment, she blushed.

"Jeddidiah Beaufort. I was named for my father's brothers; I never use it. My family calls me J. B. It's easier."

"Ah. Me, too." She felt herself grinning at him, as if they shared a secret. "Grandmothers though, not uncles or aunts."

His smile came and went again; if he noticed her reddened face, he made no sign of it. "My colleagues call me Loring, for the same reason."

"I . . . I didn't mean to . . . intrude."

"As you told me," he said, sounding amused. "Poppea Millicent. Must have been a problem in grade school."

"It could have been worse; I had a classmate named Constance Payne," she said. "You'll have to forgive my asking about your name. I'm just curious. All reporters are." She decided she had made a good recovery, and opened her purse to get her notebook and a pencil. "Are you willing to pass on some more information, as you said you would?"

Loring's office-mate rose from behind his desk. "I'm taking an early lunch. I'll be back in an hour or so."

"Okay." Loring said, and watched the older man trundle off. He turned back to Poppy. "Where were we?"

"We're about to trade information," Poppy told him, both relieved and unnerved to have the other policeman gone; his use of soldiers' slang didn't offend her.

"Right." He took a dozen sheets of typed paper and made them into a stack on which he rested his folded hands. "Case reports. You shouldn't see them."

"I understand," she said, feeling a sudden need to establish a more professional ambience to their discussion. "You, first."

"You told me yesterday that the Moncrief marriage had gone through a rough patch a year ago, but you couldn't remember any details. Have you

been able to recall anything more about it? When did it end, if it ended."
He grabbed a pencil and shoved it into a small pocket sharpener, twisting it
to restore the point.

"I've remembered some of what my cousin — "

"Eugene?"

"Eustace. Stacy. He told me, oh, perhaps eighteen months ago, that
because of Madison's promotion at Hadley and Grimes, he had been
working longer hours — and since he hadn't been working there long, he
wanted to do his best for them. He had a raft of clients to handle. Louise
had taken to going to social events with other men — most of them were
friends of theirs, and Eustace — Stacy — said that it had been Madison's
idea, so that Louise wouldn't have to sit home all the time. Even he squired
her to the symphony once, Stacy did."

"Had she been sitting home?" Loring asked with just enough doubt in his
question to make Poppy answer more sharply than she had intended.

"Yes. At least she was, compared to how things had been before Madison
became a junior partner at Hadley and Grimes. Her sister came to stay with
her a few times, but she has a family of her own, in Baltimore, and couldn't
spare many days for Louise." She paused. "Her sister is Neva, she's Missus
Theodore Plowright."

"And lives in Baltimore," Loring said, writing quickly.

"Yes. I don't have their address. Stacy probably does; we're expecting him
this evening." When he said nothing, she added, "Would you like me to get
it for you? I know Stacy would be glad to help you."

"I'll get it from Missus Moncrief, or the lady herself, when she comes to
Philly. I'll be going to see Missus Moncrief later today. The housekeeper —
a Missus Haas — said Missus Plowright was expected at seven." He stared
at Poppy for a few seconds, which for her seemed to be ages. "What was the
second thing?"

"Second thing?" she asked, then shook herself mentally.

"The second thing your cousin told you about the Moncrief's marriage?
You said there were two things," he prompted.

"Oh. Yes. Stacy remarked when Louise announced that she was pregnant,
that this should take care of the problem. He didn't elaborate on what

the problem was, but I suspected it had something to do with giving her some purpose to fill her time, and when I mentioned it, he didn't disagree. Missus Moncrief couldn't go to charity balls and horse shows forever, and both she and Madison were hoping a child would be more rewarding than another charity event." She felt a little uneasy, telling Loring so much, but she excused herself with the realization that what she had said could help this policeman to identify the murderer.

"Hum," said Loring, making more notes. "Okay. Your turn." He tapped the base of his desk lamp as it flickered. "It's the weather."

There was that soldiers' slang again. Poppy flipped her notebook open. "How is your investigation progressing? What line of inquiry are you planning to follow?"

"That's two questions," he said.

"I gave you two answers," she countered.

"Yes, I guess you did at that." He set his pencil down and stared across the room. "Since we still have no firm information from the coroner, we're proceeding carefully. I don't know if you realize how closed-mouth Wyman can be, and we don't want to create more difficulties for the Moncrief family. Once we have Wyman's official determination, we'll have a better idea of what we need to do. For the time being, we're trying to learn as much as we can about Madison Moncrief and what may have led up to his death, whatever the cause — even if it's suicide after all, there's a chance that there may be a crime connected to it. Which means I will want to speak to your cousin; he may know something one way or another."

"I'll tell him when I see him," said Poppy.

"I appreciate your help." He tapped his fingers again, not as a sign of impatience, but as if he had recalled something he wanted to mention. "One thing, though; don't tell him what I've told you here, if you please, tell him only what you've put in the paper. He's likely to be more candid if he hasn't had to wrestle with a lot of theories, or feels we're fishing."

"It may be too late for that. Stacy has a very quick mind and prides himself on his ability to deduce. He's fond of wrestling with theories; says it keeps him from getting intellectually flabby." She studied his face for a second or two, then added, "But I'll keep my conjecturing to a minimum."

"Very good of you, Miss Thornton. I'd be grateful for that. If you'd let me know what time it would be convenient for me to call upon him? I doubt he wants to come here, the ambience being what it is."

"Very neatly put," said Poppy, checking her shorthand to be sure she had it all. "Do you mind if I quote you?"

"You mean to your cousin or in your articles? and do you mean to use my words alone, or use my name?"

"Both," she responded promptly. "You are in charge of the investigation, aren't you? I should use your name in the paper, and my cousin will ask for it."

He frowned, then glanced at her. "I can't see any harm in it. Go ahead. But check what you're saying with me before you print it."

"I will. You'll hear from me before the end of the day; or call me if I don't reach you," she said, and waited. "And the second thing?" She couldn't help but smile at this reiteration of his question.

"The second thing would be the one about how we'll conduct our investigation: that will depend on whether Moncrief committed suicide or was murdered, doesn't it?"

"You mean if suicide is connected to a crime," Poppy added, knowing Loring expected it.

He didn't quite smile, but there was a softening around his mouth that erased the harshness from his features. "That's right."

"I suppose that's possible. Not probable, you understand, but possible." She tapped her open notebook with her pencil. "What do you plan to do if it turns out to be murder?" And what would she do, she wondered, if the coroner brought back a cause of death as suicide? That would end the story with hardly a ripple, and she would be back at the Society page and more Garden Club and Book Club and Bridge Tournament coverage. She comforted herself with the thought that Holte had said it was murder; to her surprise, she was becoming convinced of it; Holte seemed to be on to something beyond illusion.

Loring took a long, slow breath. "We will talk to everyone who knew him, everyone associated with his work, with his household — "

"That might be difficult. Louise won't tell you anything out of turn, and neither will their servants. Gossip remains inside the household walls."

" — or who might have a stake in his survival and find out as much as we can about how things stood between him and these people. We'll talk to his family members, if they're local, to fill in any gaps we might have. We'll go over his bank records and his travel records to see if there has been anything suspicious in his recent activities. If his firm will allow it, we'll review his list of clients. We'll check up on his business dealings and his personal habits, to see if anyone could be putting pressure on him, or if he could be pressing others who might resent it. We'll interview members of any clubs he belonged to, or any sporting organizations. If there's no trail to someone likely, then we'll look for someone not on the immediate list; we'll try to find that person or persons and determine if there's any reason for them to want him dead, or might know why he would want to kill himself." He leaned forward. "Then we'll hope someone confesses or we find a suicide note."

Poppy almost laughed. "That's how it's done, is it?"

"That's the way it works most of the time. The guilty party gets so rattled that he — or she — comes to us with their story. Or someone rats the killer out. That's a little more problematic, since not all informers actually know what they're talking about, or has a private agenda for providing the information. Think of all the shell-shocked dough boys in the Great War — it's not just the guns that drove them 'round the bend, as the Tommies say."

"My father said much the same thing in his letters to me," Poppy said.

Loring looked at the cover of the file top of the pile on the corner of his desk. "The trouble is that the evidence can tell us just so much, and the rest is shoe-leather, persistence, and luck." He smiled once more. "I don't expect you'll want to put that in your story — in fact, I hope you won't. But keep it in mind if we have to investigate this as a murder."

"I'll keep it to myself for the time being," she said, returning his smile. For several seconds all they did was smile at each other, then Poppy, remembering her purpose, asked, "Do you have any more questions for me?"

"Not yet. But I may." He sat back in his chair.

"Let me know if you do," she said, closing her notebook and tucking it and her pencil back into her purse. "I won't keep you any longer. Thanks for giving me this exclusive. Lowenthal will be glad."

"I didn't do it for Lowenthal," came Loring's answer in a self-effacing tone, as he rose. "I'll walk you down."

Perturbed, Poppy said, "Thank you, Inspector, but it isn't necessary." She could feel color mount in her face again, and she attempted to move well ahead of him.

Loring came around the desk. "I know it's not, but I want to." He motioned toward the door. "After you, Miss Thornton."

NINE

AS SHE COMPLETED HER STORY IN ONE OF THE SIDE-OFFICES OF THE CITY ROOM of the Clarion, Poppy found herself wondering for the third time that afternoon about her time with Inspector J. B. Loring. Her call to him twenty minutes earlier to review his quoted remarks had been taken in the manner of an unwelcome obligation, but he had been cordial when he wished her a pleasant evening. What was his reason for his candor about the case — if it was candor and not something more strategic? Did he want to keep on her good side, in case the Moncrief case needed help from the press? There was another possibility, she told herself, and tried to stop the heat in her face without success: had he been flirting with her? Or was his quirky charm a device he used to disarm those from whom he was seeking information? Was he curious about her, and her possible role in this case? The chance that he might be attracted to her seemed ludicrous to her, so she discounted it, deciding instead that Loring wanted to keep as much goodwill with the press as he could. Reading her short account of the coroner's conference, she spotted two typos and got out her inkwell and pen to correct them. Still mulling over Loring's apparent interest, she got up and walked her story into Cornelius Lowenthal's office.

Lowenthal regarded her skeptically as he took the typewritten sheets. "Are you milking this story?" he growled.

"I don't think so," Poppy answered. "There are some unanswered questions, and the coroner hasn't established a cause of death yet. It's our job to report the state of the investigation, and the state of it is undecided." She was pleased at how confident she sounded.

"Think he might hold a formal inquest?" Lowenthal asked, an expression of eager anticipation on his cherubic features.

"He didn't say so. As you see in paragraph three, samples have been sent to New York for analysis, and there should be results in a day or two. I suspect Wyman'll make up his mind about an inquest when he has the results." She folded her hands and waited while Lowenthal continued to read.

"Who is this unnamed source you mention?" Lowenthal inquired a bit too nicely. "Is this a cop, or what?"

"It's someone . . . close to Madison Moncrief." That wasn't quite a lie, she told herself. Chesterton Holte had provided the information, and so far, nothing she had learned had flatly contradicted what he had told her.

Lowenthal pounced on this. "What kind of close?"

"Confidante close. That's why he doesn't want his name used. I haven't found a second source yet, to confirm it; that's why I phrased it the way I did."

"Yes. Artfully done. Your father would be proud."

Poppy swallowed hard. "The cops don't know about him — the guy who told me about Moncrief — yet." It was a facile explanation, but it made enough sense to be acceptable. Not that she was planning to tell anyone, least of all the cops, about Holte.

"You know this unnamed source? Can you vouch for him?"

Poppy knew she had to choose her words very carefully. "I do know him — not terribly well, but — "

"But you move in the same circles, I suppose? You said your cousin was Moncrief's pal? Your cousin might have put you on to him." He nodded before she could say anything. "And this guy thinks it's murder?"

"For the reasons mentioned, yes, he does. I made sure that what he said is identified as opinion."

Lowenthal nodded approval. "Keeps us safe that way."

Poppy wanted to remain calm, but she could feel her shoulders tighten. "As you see, I'm not endorsing anything he's told me, only reporting his concerns."

Lowenthal continued to read as if he were alone in the room. Finally he put the two sheets down. "All right, this is how it'll go. I'm going to take out the unnamed source paragraph and hold it in reserve. If Wyman says murder, we'll use it in your next report, if not, it's spiked." He coughed, a sure sign that he was up to something. "I don't suppose you could attend the funeral? The coroner will have to release the body when he gets the tests back, and then the family will want to bury him."

"My cousin is likely to attend. I could probably go with him." As she said it, she wondered how much she should explain to Stacy.

"Do it. And keep on this until Wyman decides on the cause of death. I want to have another four inches on for Monday, minimum, and not just a reworking of what you've already said, and then something every day until the coroner's finding is in. If it's murder, you can stay with it. If it's suicide, the least said the better." He worked the fingers of his left hand through his hair. "You're doing a good job, Thornton. Keep at it and you'll be Harris' back-up in a year." Then he glowered at her. "It's three-forty-five. Get out of here. Take the rest of the day off. Go see your cousin. Just remember that I'm going to need you to be prepared to follow the story any time for at least a week."

"I thought you'd want me to stay later," she said.

"You've done a good job and you needn't linger."

Poppy was instantly suspicious, wondering to whom he would assign the story now. "I can still get over to Hadley and Grimes this afternoon and see what I can find out."

"Yes, you could. But you've been running full steam and you look tired. And with Moncrief dead, the office is probably in disarray, so it'll be hard to get anyone to talk to you today. I'll call over and try to set something up. I want you wide awake and full of vinegar tomorrow, and through the weekend: half days Saturday and Sunday, unless we learn it's murder. There's still a lot to do on this story, and I won't have you dragging through it." He slapped his hand on his desk blotter. "Go on, now. And get in tomorrow morning at six-thirty, and plan to be here until seven in the evening."

"All right," she said, feeling somewhat reassured. "Six-thirty tomorrow morning it is."

"Oh, by the way: get yourself some comfortable shoes. You're walking like an amputee." He shook his head as if amazed that she had not done so before now.

"I'll do that on the way home," she said, for once not wanting to question his motives. "Something simple, with a lower heel."

"That's the ticket. And make sure you bring an umbrella. My lumbago says rain's coming." He pointed her in the direction of the door. "Make sure you ask your cousin about the funeral, and if you can, find out where it will be, and when. Get going." He leaned back. "Miss Stotter! Bring your dictation pad! Chop-chop!" Then he glanced at Poppy. "I'll expect a thirteen-hour day from you tomorrow, so don't think you'll have Friday evening to yourself. Make the most of this evening instead."

"I'm on it," she promised him while she thought about what Lowenthal had in mind for her. She returned to her desk, where she picked up her carbon copies and put them into her briefcase, removed her purse from the locked bottom drawer, and put the cover on the typewriter. She took the elevator down to the main floor rather than use the stairs.

"He likes you, you know," Chesterton Holte observed as Poppy raised her hand to signal for a cab.

She glared at him. "Only so long as I get the story," she said, hoping no one on the street noticed she appeared to be talking to herself. She realized that she was becoming used to his spontaneous arrivals.

"He doesn't care about that at all," said Holte. "He's smitten."

"Don't kid yourself, the story is the only thing he cares about," said Poppy, waving her raised hand to show urgency.

"Hardly."

"Oh, come on, he's an editor. The paper comes first and last."

Holte chuckled. "Not Lowenthal; Inspector J. B. Loring."

Poppy was so startled, she almost stepped off the curb and into the cab that had pulled over to answer her summons. "You were there? You were listening? How could you? I thought you were following Wyman." It was an effort to keep her voice low as she opened the door of the cab and gave the driver her instructions. "Turnbull Shoes and Accessories. Do you need the address?"

"I know where it is," the cabbie said as he put the car in gear and headed off. "It'll cost you about four bits to get there."

"Fine," she told him, and lapsed into a thoughtful silence while Holte floated a few inches above the seat next to her.

"I did follow the coroner, who went to the saloon behind his office for a plate of corned-beef-and-eggs. I went back to his office later, after you left the Inspector's office."

Poppy shook her head, astonished at his audacity.

"He's extending himself because he likes you — not the way Loring does," Holte said in her ear after the cab had gone four blocks. "There were no other reporters in his office, were there? Just you."

"Ye gods, not here," she said quietly, then added for the benefit of the cabbie, "Sorry. I thought I saw someone I know."

"Not one of your favorites," said the cabbie with satisfaction as he swung around the corner, dodging a woman with three children in tow crossing the street.

"And Loring does like you," Holte insisted. "And you like him."

Had they been alone, Poppy would have told him just how ludicrous a notion this was, but she kept her mouth shut and tried to fix her mind on the traffic outside, and the passers-by on the sidewalks. She was on the verge of opening Aunt Esther's letter, which she had shoved into her briefcase before leaving the house, but was stopped by Holte's next remark.

"You do like him. Why were you blushing if you don't? There's nothing wrong with liking someone, is there? Not all policemen are louts, don't you know?" He asked this sensibly enough; her fulminating glance cast in his direction showed her disagreement.

"We're both assigned to the Moncrief case. That could have something to do with it," said Poppy in a half-voice.

"Oh, yes, he has an excellent excuse to talk with you: you're being helpful to him on Moncrief's murder, but just wait. When this is over, he'll find one excuse or another to seek you out. Just wait," he repeated. "You'll see."

"You're certain of that, are you?" she asked, whispering.

"As certain as I can be." He left it at that.

"An ambiguous answer," she muttered. "Which way do you want me to take that?"

"As a statement of the obvious," said Holte.

Poppy considered what to say next. "Pardon me if I don't get my hopes up."

"He'll want to see you. You may call me a dunce if he doesn't." He was semi-reclining in the air, undisturbed by the driver's negotiating skills. "I suspect his men will razz him about your visit. Police have strong sensitivities in such matters."

She bit back her challenge to his statement, and counted the remaining five blocks to Turbull's. Getting out of the cab at her destination, she tipped the driver ten cents and was thanked with a broad wink and grin.

Turnbull's was a large, well-laid-out shop, with displays of shoes on two walls — men's on one side, women's on the other, or as Poppy liked to think of it, meeting-house style — and assortments of gloves, hats, handbags, satchels, wallets, and briefcases set out on tables among the fitting chairs. The light was bright enough to show off the stock, but not so bright as to be jarring. The clerk who helped her made several attempts to convince her that fashionable shoes with two-and-a-half-inch heels would be preferable to the simple, inch-and-a-quarter-heeled black pumps that she settled upon. After presenting her with a pair of bronze Chanel evening shoes with plain gold buckles and pointed toes, Poppy gave in and bought both pairs, telling herself that she could always use shoes that went with her new evening dress, which was in blonde satin. Besides, she added inwardly, she hadn't bought shoes in over a year and was due new footgear, so the outrageous thirty-six dollars was well worth what she bought.

"Good choices, both of them," Chesterton Holte told her as she flagged down another cab and gave Josephine's address. "I like the Chanel pair very well."

"I'm glad you're pleased," she mouthed to him.

"I'd think you are, too," he said, as if unaware of the edge in her words.

She did her best not to look at him as the cab followed the streetcar tracks toward her aunt's house, waiting at one intersection as an overturned delivery truck was pulled out of the road by a pair of Cleveland Bays, leaving a scattering of bread so fresh that the air was redolent with its new-baked aroma. The rest of the ride proved uneventful until they turned the corner for the last time; Poppy sat up straighter, seeing a new, black Lincoln with white sidewall tires parked in front of the short walkway to her front door.

"Very elegant," Holte murmured. "Whose is it?"

"I've never seen it before," said Poppy.

The driver whistled through his teeth and said something in Portuguese.

Poppy shook her head. "I wonder if we have guests," she said quietly, and as she said it, decided it probably had something to do with Eustace's arrival. "Unless it's someone calling on the Norths, across the street."

"I'll pull in ahead of the Lincoln, Miss, if you don't mind," said the cabbie. "Handsome auto, that."

"Yes, that will be fine; and it is a . . . splendid car," said Poppy, gathering up her shopping bag, her purse, and her briefcase. "Thank you," she said to the driver.

"Not too flashy," Holte approved.

Poppy found herself sharing that opinion. "Costly to maintain, I'd guess. Large autos like that can be expensive to keep up." She handed the driver a dollar-eighty, and got out, studying the Lincoln and concluding that one of Stacy's friends might well have brought him from the train station, or that Stacy himself had bought the Lincoln to flaunt his success. She pushed the doorbell, and saw the overhead light flicker. "You're here — I know. I suppose you're coming in with me, whether the door's open or closed."

Before Holte could respond, Hawkins answered the summons of the doorbell, dressed in full butler's regalia to receive guests, "Good afternoon, Miss Poppy. We didn't think you'd be home until later."

"The boss gave me time off for good behavior," said Poppy with a faint smile. "I gather we've got company?"

Holte came into the entry-hall directly through the door as Hawkins was closing it; his arm went through Hawkins' shoulder.

The butler rubbed his shoulder, giving Poppy an apologetic look. "Yes we do. Mister Eustace is here with Mister Warren Derrington, from International Business Associates in New York. They're in the rear parlor with Missus Josephine. Would you like to join them?"

"If you're willing to take my case and my shopping bag up to my room, I'll go in now," she said, handing him the items in question while doing her best to place Warren Derrington. She had a faint memory of a reserved and maladroit friend of her cousin. "Do I look presentable, Hawkins?" She slipped out of her coat and handed it to Hawkins. "I'll want this in the coat closet."

"Your hair is a bit mussed in the back, but nothing that can't be fixed with a smoothing touch," the butler assured her as he nodded in the direction of the rear parlor. "Go in and make yourself known. I'll tell Missus Boudon you're here, and Missus Flowers, who is setting the dining table. I should add another leaf to the table."

"That's good of you, Hawkins," said Poppy, running her hand down the back of her head before starting toward the double pocket-doors. She knocked once, counted three, then pulled the doors apart, establishing her smile firmly on her face as she did.

Aunt Jo was sitting in the grandest chair in the room — a high-backed, wing-sided grandmother's chair, upholstered in heavy damask of dark-gold and ochre. She was in a lace-and-silk afternoon ensemble ten years out of fashion, her best pearls looped twice around her neck, with pearl cluster earrings to compliment the necklace. "Ah, you're home; I was hoping you'd be here before we sat down to dinner," she said as Poppy came up to kiss her cheek.

The two young men with her had risen and now Stacy, turned out in the height of fashion, with a dark-blue blazer over a crisp white shirt with a stiffly starched collar, a silk tie, and dove-grey slacks, came over to kiss Poppy on the cheek. "Hello, Cousin Poppy," he said with his most engaging smile.

"Hello, Stacy," said Poppy, taking his hands in hers.

Aunt Jo, who often disapproved of nicknames other than her own, like Stacy, and Hank — by which her oldest son, Galahad, was known — sighed her opinion.

"Is that gorgeous vehicle in front yours?" she asked him, returning the kiss.

"Alas, no; it's Warren's. You remember Warren Derrington, don't you, Poppy?" He indicated his companion.

"I believe we met two years ago, at the Moncriefs' Christmas Eve banquet," said Poppy, offering her hand to the good-looking fellow in the well-tailored dark-grey suit with the self-effacing manner and the cleft chin.

Derrington shook her hand diffidently, and held it for a bit too long, as if using it to help him decide what to say. "Kind of you to remember, Miss Thornton, among so many guests you must have met that night." He let her hand go. "I'm sorry that such an occasion as this should provide a second introduction."

He seemed distant to the point of Poppy's remembered maladroitness, but she thought it might be grief rather than self-doubt that was the cause. "Very true. My condolences to you both."

"Thank you. It's been a shock. I never thought that Madison would do anything so — Mother's been telling us that you have been one of the reporters on the case," said Stacy.

"Yes, from the first," said Poppy in a deliberately neutral voice. "I got the assignment early yesterday morning."

"She went to the house while the police were there," Aunt Jo said with a disapproving moue.

Derrington studied her face. "How unpleasant for you."

Poppy managed not to say something dismissive and instead told him, "Crime often is, Mister Derrington."

"Crime?" Stacy exclaimed; for once his smooth facade cracked a bit. "I thought they had decided it was suicide."

"But it might not be suicide?" Derrington asked.

Poppy realized everyone was looking to her for an answer. "The coroner has yet to determine a cause of death, and the police are considering making an investigation. Once there is a finding on the cause of death, they'll proceed appropriately," she said, hoping it wasn't too much information for the two men, that she hadn't exceeded the limits Inspector Loring had imposed on her.

Maestro sauntered into the parlor, his fluffy tail held aloft like a flag.

"I told you Madison Moncrief couldn't do away with himself," Aunt Jo announced with an expression of triumph.

"Nothing is certain yet, Aunt Jo," said Poppy, going to the smaller of the two couches that flanked the coffee table. She sat down, wishing she had decided to wear her new, low-heeled pumps home, so as to ease her feet. "We're all waiting for Doctor Wyman to get the results of the tests he's having made on Moncrief's clothes."

"So unsavory, to think that his clothes are being examined, to say nothing of his body," Aunt Jo grumbled. She glanced toward the rear door. "Oh, where is Missus Boudon with the drinks and canapés?"

"Probably making allowances for my arrival in the food she's preparing; I didn't know I'd be home for dinner," said Poppy. "And I apologize."

"Nothing to apologize for," said Stacy. "I'm glad you were able to come home early." There was just enough speculation in his tone to prompt Poppy to answer.

"Oh, it's a trade-off. Lowenthal expects me to do a thirteen-hour day tomorrow, and so he's letting me have a little extra time now."

"Isn't that a little high-handed?" Derrington asked.

"Not for a managing city editor, it's not," said Poppy. She was about to launch into a short description of the nature of her newspaper work when the double-doors opened again, and an angular fellow with tawny hair and chiseled features, in a conservative three-piece suit, burst in.

Maestro hissed and took refuge behind Josephine's chair.

TEN

❧

"WHAT BRINGS YOU HERE, TOBY?" STACY ASKED, AND WAS ANSWERED WITH A look that bordered on revulsion; Stacy smiled innocently.

"Do you have to ask? You, of all of us, should know, shouldn't you?" Tobias inquired stiffly of Eustace. "Good afternoon, Aunt Josephine, Poppea." He swung around to face the other man in the room. "And you're — ?" he asked.

"Warren Derrington." The two men shook hands warily. "A friend of Stacy's from New York. We met at Haverford, Stacy and I. Dritchner, Derrington, you know how it is." He tried to sound genial, but was unable to pull it off.

Tobias looked him over critically. "Tobias Thornton. I'm Missus Dritchner's nephew and Poppea's brother."

"Not to be rude, Toby, but what are you doing here?" Stacy asked.

"You really are a knuckle-head, Eustace," said Tobias. "This dreadful business with Madison Moncrief, of course. I thought even you would remember that I have some connection to the Moncriefs. His stepbrother, Russell, has come home to be with the family through this difficult time; his grandmother requested an escort for the lad, and I was assigned to accompany him, since I have relatives in the city and my stay to look after young Moncrief will not put a charge on Alexandrian Academy. I will have to be here for a week; the funeral hasn't been scheduled yet." He looked about importantly. "When I first arrived in the city three hours ago, I had planned to leave Russell with Louise, but when I saw Julian Eastley was at the house, I thought better of it and took the youngster along to his maternal grandfather and grandmother. They're very close with Russell, you know, and have been since his grandparents took him in after his father and mother — Louise's stepmother, you know — died of the 'Flu.'"

"Julian Eastley!" Derrington scowled at the name, ignoring the rest of Tobias' account. "What on earth would he be doing at the house?"

"I don't know. Neva's with Louise, so his presence is only awkward instead of scandalous; I am aware that there are mitigating circumstances, and that there is good reason for Louise to want a man's presence just now," said Tobias and drew up a leather-upholstered wing- chair. "Eastley is hardly the sort of person who'd make a sympathy call, I would have thought, and I doubt I am the only one with such an opinion."

"Probably not, but I wouldn't call his presence unexpected," Poppy observed; out of the tail of her eye she saw Maestro slink into the parlor and sidle along the baseboards, hackles up, staring at the air behind the smaller sofa. "He's a fixture in the Moncrief house, as I understand."

Stacy cocked his head. "Nothing to worry about, Toby. Eastley has been stringing after Louise since before the Great War, as all her friends know. Madison never minded him coming about; he understood about Eastley's idolization of Louise, that there was no harm in it. You could have settled Russell with Louise without a qualm, Toby. There's not a jot of impropriety in Eastley's presence."

"Stacy, for heaven's sake," Derrington chided. "The man's a hero."

"That's inconsiderate, Eustace," Tobias reprimanded him as if he were one of his students. "Eastley's far from the only man whose lungs were burned in the trenches."

"More than his lungs were damaged," said Stacy, putting his full attention on Tobias. "But he's not alone in that, either."

"All of you — please!" Josephine admonished them as Missus Boudon came in bearing a large tray with a platter of canapés and four bottles of genuine spirits from Europe — Scotch, brandy, cognac, and gin — an assortment of glasses, a glass pitcher of water, a bowl of ice- cubes, a pair of silver tongs, a bottle of tonic-water, and a stack of small plates.

The room went fairly silent for a second or two, and then Tobias said, "I trust I may command a room from you, Aunt Josephine?"

"Of course you may, Tobias. I'll tell Missus Flowers to make up the Blue

Room. And I'm sure she's already set a place for you at the dinner table." She beamed at him, delighted to have so much of her family around her even for so unhappy an occasion as Madison Moncrief's death. She moved forward in her resplendent chair. "Come; tell me what you would like to have? Ordinarily I'd begin with Poppy, but she lives here, so I imagine Mister Derrington should have first choice, he being the only full guest in the house who isn't family."

Derrington shrugged clumsily. "I . . . a gin-and-tonic would be very nice, Missus Dritchner."

Aunt Jo prepared it with three ice cubes and held it out to Derrington, who took the glass and returned to his chair.

"Tobias is older than you, Eustace," Aunt Jo pointed out, "So he shall have his choice next. What do you want, Tobias?"

"I shall have ice water," Tobias announced, stiff with disapproval. "Drinking alcohol is illegal, Aunt Josephine."

"Don't be tiresome," she replied, but put two ice cubes in his glass and filled it with water, then gave it to Tobias. "If you will be such a stickler." She smiled at Stacy. "Scotch, I suppose, no ice?"

"Yes, Mother, if you would?" Eustace confirmed, offering her one of his best seraphic smiles.

Poppy asked for cognac. "Go light on the amount, please. I want to be clear-headed first thing tomorrow."

Aunt Jo served herself brandy as well, but without water or ice. She raised her modest snifter. "To welcome guests," she declared, and had the other four echo her.

Missus Boudon picked up the platter of canapés and offered them around the room, saying nothing until Stacy asked her what time dinner would be ready. "You have two hours yet, Mister Eustace," she said. "Your mother asked me to serve at seven-thirty."

"A bit earlier than usual," said Tobias, not quite approving. "I would have thought eight would be a more appropriate hour."

Poppy held her tongue with difficulty, not wanting to wrangle with her brother so soon after his arrival. She sipped at her drink, thinking that Tobias was a stuffed shirt.

"Mister Eustace and Mister Derrington have been traveling," said Aunt Jo. "They'll want to retire early, to recruit their strength for tomorrow."

"Dinner will be ready at seven-thirty." Missus Boudon reiterated, then nodded to Aunt Jo, and set down the platter. "I'm going back to attend to dinner, Missus Dritchner."

"Yes, thank you, Missus Boudon." Aunt Jo sipped judiciously at her drink.

"Are we going to change?" Poppy asked as Missus Boudon left the room.

"Oh, I hope not," said Stacy. "I think we can consider dinner en famille, don't you? Besides, Warren would have to go home to fetch his dinner jacket, and what's the point of that? His home is in New York."

Derrington shrugged uneasily. "I don't want to be a — "

Tobias bristled. "You may do as you like. I will change." He regarded Stacy with hauteur. "You're becoming very lax in the niceties, Cousin."

"The nineteenth century's been over for more than two decades, Toby," said Stacy, unfazed by Tobias' umbrage.

"Do as you like, gentlemen," said Aunt Jo. "But remember, we sit down at seven-thirty."

Poppy set her snifter on the end-table leaving most of the cognac untouched; she rose, motioning to Stacy and Derrington to remain seated. "If you'll excuse me, I'm going to go freshen up. This is a special occasion, though it is a sad one."

Tobias shot her a look of cautious approval. "Of course we'll excuse you, Poppea."

Poppy resisted the urge to object to his officiousness, and said only, "I'll see you all at dinner." She turned toward Aunt Jo. "The cognac is excellent, as always. Your man in Canada does well by you. Thank you." She could feel the sizzle of disapproval from Tobias; as she left the parlor, she heard Maestro hiss.

"You can understand, can't you, why I preferred to haunt you?" Holte said in her ear as she went up the stairs.

"He can be a little . . . stiff," Poppy allowed quietly.

"How diplomatic of you," Holte marveled, then said more bluntly, "By the way, you might want to look into the death of James Poindexter, five months or so ago, while you're looking into the Moncrief case."

"Poindexter." Poppy stopped her upward climb. "I remember that. It was judged a suicide, wasn't it?" As she heard herself, she felt her curiosity spark. "Why should I look into it?" She kept her voice low, not wanting to be overheard conversing with the air. "Is there something irregular about his suicide?"

"Suicide? no such luck. There's a connection between him and Moncrief, and you can solve two crimes if you can unearth — no pun intended — the perpetrator of both. They both worked for the same firm, for a start."

"Were either of them so obliging as to tell you who that perpetrator is?" Poppy inquired.

"No." Holte sounded disappointed.

She turned down the gallery to her bedroom. "Are you going to keep digging up — no pun intended — previous suicides to keep me on the case? That's Lowenthal's decision, not mine, and not yours."

"I just told you — If you take the time to study the two cases you'll see that they are linked, and so are their deaths."

"You're certain of that? That they're linked?" She felt suddenly tired, and simultaneously, spurred to action, yet she could not summon up any enthusiasm for another complication in this case, not with dinner so near.

"I am. I've told you: it's difficult for ghosts to dissemble to one another."

"So Poindexter told you because he knows Madison Moncrief?"

"In a manner of speaking." He waited while she opened the door. "Moncrief took over Poindexter's post at Hadley and Grimes. That could be a good place to begin your investigation. Did you know Poindexter?"

She considered what Poindexter was like, saying, "I knew him as one knows people on sight, but not in terms of personality or character. As I remember him, he was studious and earnest, a bit stodgy, but nothing artificial about him. I was told he was something of a roisterer when he was a student — but I don't know anything specific about it. He was a widower, and it was supposed that he killed himself — "

"By hanging," Holte interjected. "Alone in his house."

"Hanging," she repeated.

"Hanging," he confirmed. "By himself."

"All right. Hanging due to grief and loneliness, or so the coroner determined. If there was a note, they never found it, but everyone said he had been melancholy for some time." As she said it, the explanation seemed thin and unconvincing.

"I see you take my point. It probably means extra work for you, but it could be a coup, if you can carry it off. The public would lap it up: nefarious doings at an old, respected accounting firm. Two men dead. Possible scandal. Lowenthal wouldn't dare send you back to the Society page after such a story." He became a clearer image as Poppy closed the door and went to open the draperies to let in the last of the afternoon sun; he stared directly at her. "So you do believe me. Moncrief and Poindexter would appreciate it."

"But would Lowenthal, if it doesn't pan out? His opinion is more important to me, don't you think?" Poppy asked, as she picked up the shopping bag set on her vanity stool. She pulled out the two boxes and sat on the bed, bending over to unbuckle the ankle-straps on the pair she was wearing. "Oh. That feels good." She kicked the offending shoes off her feet.

"Which pair will you wear tonight?" Holte asked.

"The Chanel, with the long puce skirt and my mulberry sweater with the gold embroidery platten. It shouldn't show up Stacy and Mister Derrington, or be woefully underdressed for Toby." Before she sat up, she made sure the seams of her silk stockings were straight. "Aunt Jo likes to observe the traditions when we have guests."

"Will your brother actually dress for dinner?"

"Yes. They do every evening at the Alexandrian Academy — black dinner jackets in the fall and winter, white in the spring and summer. His wife tells me he hardly ever dines at home — but you probably know that, don't you? You said you observed him before you came to me, and there was your remark on the stairs." She opened the Chanel box. "I think Toby would be mortified if he didn't have on the right clothes. I wouldn't be surprised if he wears a dinner jacket to an afternoon picnic."

"I wouldn't think that would be the right clothes for a picnic," said Holte. "Picnics aren't sufficiently formal for dinner jackets."

"You know what I mean." Poppy removed her skirt from its hanger in the closet, then opened her chest-of-drawers to take out her sweater. "Missus Flowers is so good. If it were left to me, every drawer would be in chaos."

"Would you like me to leave?"

The question startled her. She considered it, and said, "Yes, if you would. Please. It's silly, isn't it, but I'd prefer you didn't watch me."

"With pleasure. I'll return in twenty minutes, if that's sufficient?" Before she could answer, he vanished.

By the time he came back she was finishing up her hair, checking it in the mirror. When she saw the shadowy shimmer that marked his appearance, she was no longer startled. "You're three minutes late."

"Apologies. It isn't easy keeping track of time when there are no clocks, or other timekeepers about. Time doesn't mix well with noncorporeality, I'm afraid." He became more visible, his figure taking greater definition. "So, have you given any more consideration to the Poindexter matter?"

"Not yet," she replied.

He sank down a few inches so that his feet appeared to touch the floor. "It's worth exploring, at least, don't you think?"

"I'll let you know in the morning, after I've slept on it." She applied perfume to her neck and wrists, then got up from her vanity table.

"Very nice," he approved as she went to the door. "The shoes are especially good."

"You're teasing me."

"Hardly," he claimed. "A mere observation. Spies are taught to be observant."

"Well, thank you, whatever your reason," she said as she let herself out; a few seconds later he came flowing out through the wood. "Ye gods, that's unnerving."

He chuckled and floated along beside her until she reached the foot of the stairs. "I'll be about, but you won't see me."

"Maestro will," she told his fading image.

ELEVEN

In the hours after dinner, Chesterton Holte drifted about the rooms, slipping through walls, hanging just below the ceiling, observing the occupants closely, flickering lights as he went. It was a bit after midnight, and now most of the living were asleep except for a small group of mice now scurrying about the kitchen, making the most of the bits and scraps of dinner. He had watched Stacy reading in bed — Antic Hay — half an hour before, and Derrington working a crossword puzzle and attempting to postpone sleep. He had heard Josephine say her prayers before she turned out the light, and had watched as Missus Boudon left the house, wrapped in an old cloth coat, the collar raised against the damp. He had followed Missus Flowers through the house as windows were checked, their draperies drawn, doors were closed, and those giving access to the outside were locked before she went off to her cottage. Before she retired for the night, she drew a hot bath for herself; Holte departed before she got into the steaming water. At Poppy's door, he found Maestro rolled into a ball, his tail over his nose. Holte's approach roused him enough for the cat to open his eyes in a baleful stare and hiss.

Withdrawing from Maestro's immediate vicinity, Holte took himself along to the library. It had been, he thought, a most frustrating day. The various developments had so far led to little news, and he could see that Poppy was doing her best in what was turning into a difficult situation. There was definitely more to the Moncrief and Poindexter deaths than anyone suspected or acknowledged, and this was increasingly troubling to him. So many questions were either unanswered or half-answered. He hoped that the coroner would soon have test results to announce, and that whatever they revealed, the investigation would swing into high gear at last. He debated with himself about going to the dimension of ghosts to gain more information from Moncrief and Poindexter, and after a few minutes, he turned sideways as only those without bodies could, and found himself in an expanse that was undefined by objects or limits, populated by figures without form. For what seemed a short time, he felt disoriented, but gained his bearings and concentrated on what he had come to do. He summoned Moncrief through a shift in attention, and was almost at once aware of the presence of Madison Moncrief in his vicinity. "Madison." It wasn't thought as such, or conversation, for there was neither the capacity nor the need for speech, though it most certainly was communication, for the energetic identity of Moncrief became fully apparent to Holte, as he was to Moncrief, and the speech-that-was-not- speech allowed them to exchange the equivalent of words.

"Chesterton. Why have you come back?"

Holte gathered his thoughts and said, " The questions about your death are multiplying and answers aren't readily come by; I hoped you had recovered some of your memories . . . Have you remembered anything more? about your death?"

"Not much. It comes and goes — you know what it's like."

Holte felt an awkward wince: the four Germans who had summarily executed him were difficult to recall. What lingered most was the sight of Beresford Oliver Thornton, his body crumpled in a spreading pool of blood from three wounds in the head and neck; his own death was less distinct, a quicksilver flash and an enormous pain that ended before it began. "Yes. I know."

Moncrief went briefly out of focus, then he sharpened. "I think I must have been groggy before I had my nightcap. I've tried to recall the details, but it's as if I were under water, or out of phase with my body. Once in a while, something comes into sharp focus briefly, but it fades rapidly. I must have been more impaired than I was aware of at the time, or I would think that I would recall it more readily."

"Your nightcap was cognac." The lingering impression of a taste passed between the two.

"Yes. But that wasn't all. There was a sharpness about it, or it seems that way to me now."

"Are you sure?" Holte urged him.

"Pretty sure."

"How long before you had your cognac had you eaten dinner?"

It took Moncrief a bit of nonexistent time to say, "It's hard to say now. Time isn't like it used to be." He made an effort to reconstruct the events that led to his dying. "We sat down at seven; I'm almost positive it was seven. Louise was tired and wanted to go to bed early, so dinner was served early. I said we should cancel the party on Friday. I remember that. She said no, she couldn't coddle herself, and that the sooner she was back to entertaining, the sooner she would be through her grief. I couldn't disappoint her, could I?" Their contact wobbled, then reestablished itself. "We must have finished up a little after eight, it had grown dark by the time we sat down, I think, and we left the dining room to our cook about an hour later."

"Then you left the dining room before all the china, napery, and silverware were removed?"

"We usually did. Louise went upstairs. I went to the study, to review the accounts of Beaman Beaman Trevillian and Cooper. You know them, don't you? A company associated with oil brokering. It's an international corporation, the main office is in New York, with the accounting division in Philadelphia; it's got nine branch offices here in the United States and another seven abroad. It looks solid and growing. It's tied into International Business Associates." A twinge of uncertainty twisted between the two ghosts. "I took the account over from James Poindexter soon after Hadley hired me."

"Clients of yours — Beaman Beaman Trevillian and Cooper?"

"Important ones. They bring in close to half a million in fees per year. The books were complicated — they usually are in such businesses — and I was worried that there might be irregularities in their accounts. Hadley had been most insistent that I resolve a few questions about a number of foreign contracts they had and the methods and schedules of payment. It takes a lot of concentration to resolve issues in such dealings, and I'd spent a considerable amount of time in preparing my review. I was trying to do this up until the night I died."

"Did you ever discuss these things with your wife?"

"Not often. Louise didn't find my work interesting in that way. Figures and contracts bored her — you know how women are. She liked the idea of foreign travel. Before she miscarried, she had suggested that we go abroad to visit the foreign offices of Beaman Beaman Trevillian and Cooper as well as those of Sansome and Company and International Business Associates, those being accounts I had been assigned. She said I could get some work done that needed my personal attention, and she could visit all manner of places she longed to see: she had had a tour planned for 1914, but it had to be cancelled when war broke out. She thought the Great War" — an inaudible groan went up through much of the emptiness around them — "had been over long enough that there would be a good chance that much of the damage had been repaired, or at least swept away, and we could enjoy our travel without unpleasant reminders of what's in the past. I told her I'd ask the senior partners what could be done."

"And what did they say?"

"They said they would need time to decide: the cost of such a trip, and the time it would require might be prohibitive, or so I was told."

"Did they explain?"

Moncrief took care in honing his answer. "I began to think that the company wanted to keep me away from our foreign offices, and not just on account of the cost of such a journey."

"When did this happen? How long ago?"

"A week or two before I died, maybe three weeks." He was a bit apologetic. "I've forgotten a lot."

Holte considered this. "They say you were uneasy, not yourself, upset in the days before you were hanged. Is it true?"

"I was worried about some tariff problems, and what I had found out about Poindexter bothered me. I didn't think that our records were complete, and that rankled with me. And I was distressed for Louise, as any man would be. The miscarriage had taken a toll on her, and I was afraid that she might be falling into despondency, which was one of the reasons I thought perhaps a visit to Europe was in order, business or not. Our doctor warned us about that possibility — the despondency — and recommended a change of scenery for Louise. We had started making plans when I died."

"You said the delays in approving your foreign travel piqued your curiosity. What in particular made you assume that something might be amiss?"

"There were a number of notes tucked into the ledgers that Poindexter had made, nothing extreme, but they added up to the likelihood of fraud. The lack of complete information made it difficult to determine if there had been deliberate deception, or mere oversights. It made me wonder about him — about Poindexter — but I felt it wouldn't be good to ask too many questions — you know how that is."

"Tell me some more about Poindexter." Holte found his own curiosity piqued.

"Why not ask him yourself?"

"I plan to. But I need to know what you discovered and what you were told about him." Holte felt a soundless buzz in his noncorporeal ears, and realized that James Poindexter was near by.

"Is this about our supposed suicides?" this new haunt wanted to know; there was a definite New England twang about his non-speech.

"Yes, in part," Holte informed him.

"Suicide. Impossible. I didn't kill myself; I had no reason to do so — in fact, I had a good many reasons not to do away with myself, not the least of which was the question of professional ethics," Poindexter declared with as much volume as a soundless voice could produce. "Had the police or the coroner or my own physician investigated more thoroughly, they would have found a small injection site behind the base of my left ear. The needle was angled up into my brain, and something was" — he nonphysically acted out the pushing of a plunger and the sudden paralysis that had spread through him — "and I was hoisted up, the knot on the rope rubbing the little pinprick from the needle so that there was almost no trace of it."

"Are you haunting anyone?" Holte asked, surprised that Poindexter's recollections were so clear.

"No one," Poindexter replied, his demeanor suggesting that he was somewhat sad that he wasn't. "As far as I know now, I just have to stay around here" — he did something that might have been sad laughter —

"until I receive a correction for the error made about my death, and justice is done. Once that's done, I assume I'll move on. I'm glad you've got that girl working on it. If she has the courage to stick with it, it could make all the difference for me." There was a bunglesome hesitation. "I want to go on from this place." He began to dissolve, dissipating through the busy emptiness of the dimension of ghosts.

"What accounts did you handle at Hadley and Grimes?" Holte inquired, trying to hold onto Poindexter for a little longer, but without success.

"Ask Moncrief. He took over the accounts. There were three of them that concerned me. Moncrief'll know." The impression of a person was unraveling; he seemed to have gone some distance away.

"Beaman Beaman Trevillian and Cooper, Sansome and Company — "

"And International Business Associates," Moncrief finished for him; Poindexter had vanished.

"Is there anything you'd recommend we look at?" Holte inquired even as he felt Moncrief pulling away from him.

"If you can get some access to the records in the New York office of Beaman Beaman Trevillian and Cooper, there might be something not quite on the up-and-up. I tried to review the terms of acquisitions and trades in their overseas branches, but nothing came of it." He was hard to make out, like a radio being heard through static.

"Do you think that your death might have been a way to stop your inquiries?"

Moncrief sounded even more remote. "If that was what they wanted. But it's nothing I can prove."

"Would stopping your investigation at work be worth killing for?"

"I'm dead, aren't I?" This was hardly more than a whisper. "Someone killed me." He was almost gone, then added, "Old Hadley might know something. He's still alive. Retired to a place in Vermont, I think. Or Delaware."

"Thanks." He didn't allow himself the luxury of sarcasm. What he had learned, he admitted to himself, was better than nothing, and slipped sideways again, finding himself outside Poppy's bedroom door, in the pre-dawn gloom, facing a growling cat.

"It's just me, Maestro," said Holte to the outraged cat, then floated away to make his rounds through the house. He discovered both Stacy and Derrington still in their rooms asleep, Stacy calmly, Derrington less so, if his disarranged blankets and sheets were any indication. Tobias was snoring. While Holte did not actually look in on Josephine, he listened at her door, and determined that she had passed an easy night. Satisfied that all was as well as it could be, Holte made his way downstairs, trying to decide how he would present what he had learned to Poppy.

TWELVE

AT THE LAST MINUTE, POPPY REMEMBERED TO CARRY HER UMBRELLA; SHE LEFT
the house after a hurried breakfast while her brother, her cousin, and his
guest remained in bed. She had exchanged a few words with Aunt Jo, who
had insisted on getting up well before dawn and having breakfast with her.
Over poached-eggs-on-toast, Poppy promised to call around noon, and
rushed out to catch the streetcar, the early morning still lit by street lamps.
It was drizzling, a clammy kind of dampness that sank into the body and
made the bones hurt. Her new, lower-heeled pumps would be most welcome
today, she thought as she stood and waited for the streetcar to come. In five
minutes she was aboard and bound for the center of the city. She took a
seat across from the rear doors and put her mind to working out what, if
anything, she should do about Poindexter, or Hadley and Grimes. She was
mildly surprised that Holte had not attempted to speak to her this morning.

Coming into the Addison Newspaper Corporation building — the
Clarion on the second and third floors, the Constitution on the first and
fourth; presses were in the basement — through the large rotating door,
she encountered Carlotta Upshaw, whose call had initiated her work on the
Moncrief case; Carlotta Upshaw was on her way home. Poppy raised her
hand in greeting, and the other woman paused.

"Good morning, Miss Thornton?" she said with that question-like
upward lilt; she smiled a bit uncertainly. "It looks like the assignment panned
out?" She had circles under her large, expressive eyes, and her thirty-nine-
year-old face was drawn, but her manner toward Poppy was warm and
generous.

"I hope so," said Poppy. "Thank you for your interest."

"We have to stick together, we women, don't we?" She said it pragmatically as she pulled on her gloves. "Is Lowenthal still trying to wrap you in cotton batting?" Startled to hear such sentiments from a secretary, Poppy could only nod. "I think Lowenthal is afraid I'll get scared, or swoon, or — "

"They all think that about us, don't they? even the copy-boys," said Carlotta Upshaw, glancing at the men coming and going through the lobby. "But what truly frightens them is that they're afraid that we'll be as good at their jobs as they are, or better. Listen to how they talk about Phyllis Ackersley at the Tribune when they think she isn't listening. She hears every word, and she's careful to give them no call to think she's that sort of woman." She looked at her locket-watch. "Sorry; I have to go. Mister Upshaw will be awake shortly, and we like to breakfast together. He goes to work at nine-thirty. But perhaps we can talk one day? There are things that we ought to discuss."

Puzzled but encouraged, Poppy said, "Yes. I'd like that." She watched Carlotta go out through the turning doors, then went up to the Clarion's floor and hurried to the cubbyhole that was her office. Opening her briefcase, she brought out the pages she had typed up after dinner the night before. Two of the pages had what would become three inches, probably below the fold on page four of five, on the current stalemate in the Moncrief case. She had worked in a few lines about some of the questions that remained unanswered; she doubted that Lowenthal would keep any of them, but at least it showed that she was being diligent. She took these along to Lowenthal's office, walking in five minutes before she was expected, and found Dick Gafney handing in his column on the arson investigation he was following; Gafney's cynical bloodhound countenance looked more world-weary than usual, and it appeared that he had slept in his clothes. He had a cigarette in the corner of his mouth and the lenses of his glasses were hazy.

"I just need a couple more minutes, sweetie pie," he said as he caught sight of Poppy.

Poppy muttered an apology and stepped back into the city room, horrified at herself for her gaffe. I should have knocked, even though the door was open, she thought.

"And why should you have done that?" Chesterton Holte asked her; one of the overhead lights flickered as if to emphasize his question. "Lowenthal told you that knocking wastes time — that's why he leaves the door open."

"That he did," Poppy whispered. "The door isn't closed."

"Why such chagrin for such a minor infraction?"

"Minor to you, maybe; not to me."

Holte buzzed in the nearest lamp. "Can you tell me why?"

"I . . . I don't know." She noticed Lowenthal's door swinging wide, and she made herself collect her thoughts. She nodded to Gafney as he came out, and wished she could slap the smirk off his face.

"Thornton!" Lowenthal bawled out.

"Coming," she responded, and ducked through the door, her pages clutched a bit too tightly in her hands. She took a deep breath as she faced him across his desk. "Here's the latest. What would you like me to do today?"

There was an approving glint in his eyes. "Good to see you're prepared to work. Pace yourself, though; pace yourself. We don't want you running out of steam in the middle of this, now that it looks like there's more to the story than we thought." He glanced at his desk calendar as if he were just now deciding on her assignment. "First off, I'd like you to get over to Hadley and Grimes. Quentin Hadley is expecting you at nine. Nose around the office if they'll let you. Find out what accounts Moncrief was handling. If it looks like there's big money tied up in his death, then we need to find out about it."

"What if they won't tell me about that? Big firms like Hadley and Grimes put great value on maintaining the confidentiality of their business."

"So they do, but you're a reporter. You'll think of something. Most people want to talk after this kind of a shock; if they don't, that means something. Do what you can, but don't get yourself thrown out if you can help it." He took the papers she proffered, gave them a cursory read-through, saying as he did, "I'll trim this a bit. Still, you present the facts well, and you make the police inquiry sound reasonable."

"I thought you might want to trim it," said Poppy, feeling less rattled now than she had after her brief encounter with Gafney. "I'm planning to go to the coroner's office and try to get an interview with Wyman; I have a contact there — an old friend of my father's. I could do that after Hadley and

Grimes, unless I get caught up there; I'll assume you're putting a priority on Hadley and Grimes?" She saw him nod and pull at the curl on top of his head. "If I do get to see Wyman, I should have my story done by three. That's pushing it, but — "

"Do as much as you can, so long as we don't have to chase the paper." He waggled an admonitory finger at her.

"All right." She studied him, trying to discern what it was that he was hoping she would find out.

"Yes. Then you can start on Moncrief's friends, their view of him, and any reminiscences that might make good copy. You said you can get to the widow?" He saw her nod. "Good. Heavy on the sorrow and how good a man Moncrief was, unless you find out something juicy that says he had a double life or a shocking secret. You know most of them, and they should open up to you." He considered her, once again tugging at his thinning hair. "You can work from your desk, if you think that would be better, but I want some face-to-face interviews, not just 'phone calls."

"You want that for the weekend or before?" Poppy asked. "It may take a day or two to set up interviews with the Moncriefs' friends."

"I want the opportunity to keep the story alive for now. If Houghton wants to use some of your work for the Saturday edition, well and good, but keep in mind that you will have a couple inches waiting for you in Monday's early edition, and you work for me, not Houghton. You'll turn in your work this evening, to Pike. He'll handle it from there. And I'll want you in at seven-thirty on Monday, unless Wyman or the cops announce that it's a case of suicide after all, in which case, I'll need a short summary on the resolution of Moncrief's death." He clapped his hands. "Chop-chop."

"I'll get right on it, sir," said Poppy, preparing to leave.

"Oh. Westerman is going over to the Informer as of Monday, and Harris will need a new backup. Just keep that in mind." He waved her toward the door. "On to Hadley and Grimes, then the coroner." As she was about to step into the city room again, he nodded. "I like the shoes.""Thank you, Mister Lowenthal." She went back to her cubbyhole and gathered up her purse, briefcase, and umbrella. As she stepped out of the building, she discovered that the drizzle had increased to a steady, sullen rain. So much for spring, she thought. She brought her umbrella up and decided to take a cab to the offices of Hadley and Grimes, though they were only six blocks away, and ordinarily it would have been a pleasant walk, but not in the weepy rain that washed over the city. She stepped to the edge of the curb and lifted her arm, feeling a rivulet of chilly water slide down her hand and into the sleeve of her coat and blouse. The spreading wet seemed to her to be the theme for the whole day ahead. As a cab pulled up in answer to her raised arm, her shoes and silk stockings got splashed. "Damn," she muttered as she opened the door and furled her umbrella as she climbed inside.

The ride was uneventful but for the congestion near the newly completed Benjamin Franklin Parkway, which was still clogged with the automobiles full of the curious and proud. The cabbie swung through the confusion with expert skill, pausing only once to allow a heavily laden delivery wagon, drawn by two straining Belgian Drafts, to pass. Poppy kept waiting for Holte to speak up, but eventually concluded that he was not in the cab with her, and stopped listening for him.

Hadley and Grimes was located in a twenty-eight-year-old four-storey building that was a stunning example of Art Nouveau; stylized acanthus twined around the four pillars in the front, and provided a handsome fanlight over the double glass doors. More acanthus in low-relief carving and mosaics covered one wall of the lobby, and formed the design of the bannisters on the main staircase, the stairs being of polished rosy-veined marble. The bronze elevator doors were fronted with etched water lilies. According to the lobby directory, Hadley and Grimes had the whole of the second floor. Poppy went up the stairs and into the lobby, which had a black wreath over the receptionist's desk. There was no one else in the lobby but the receptionist, and the place felt unnaturally quiet.

"May I help you?" asked the woman behind the desk, a well-turned-out red-head in a very dark green suit.

"I'm P. M. Thornton of the Clarion; I have an appointment with Mister Hadley." She looked up at the wreath. "Sorry about the loss of your Mister Moncrief."

"That's why you're here?" the receptionist challenged her. "For your appointment?"

"Yes."

The receptionist depressed the call button on her desk. "Miss Thornton to see Mister Hadley."

"Send her in." The voice was male, which surprised Poppy; she had assumed all the secretaries in the company were women, for this firm was known to have a policy of hiring female secretaries.

The receptionist used her pencil to indicate the way to Hadley's office. "Turn left here, take the first right you can, go past the two cross-corridors around this side of the atrium, then take the left to the suite at the end of the hallway." She made no effort to smile. "We're on half-staff today, out of respect for Mister Moncrief, so if you get lost, it'll take a while for someone to find you."

"Thank you; I'll be careful," said Poppy, and found her way through the maze to the oaken door with the elegant low-relief carving of stylized water lilies following the arch of the lintel. Quentin Hadley was etched on a small plaque of dark marble in the frame of the sinuous flowers located at about eye level. Poppy knocked, not too forcefully, but enough to draw the attention of Hadley's secretary.

"Enter," called the same voice she had heard at the receptionist's desk.

Poppy let herself in and found a desk on her immediate right, with a typewriter, a 'phone, and a lamp on it. Behind the desk sat a tall, lissome young man with slicked-back dark hair, dark eyes, in a suit that was not quite black. His shirt was pristinely white, his tie a subtle black-and-grey stripe, and he wore glasses with the thinnest of wire rims; a narrow black band circled his right arm above the elbow. He rose from his chair. "If you'll take a seat, Miss Thornton, I'll ask Mister Hadley if he'll see you now."

Before she sat down, she looked at the name-stand on his desk: Clifford Tinsdale. She made a mental note of it as she took her seat on the upholstered window-seat where she watched the rain bead and slide down the glass. She found herself thinking that she might have come on a fool's errand, for she felt no hint of helpfulness, or even interest, at Hadley and Grimes.

A few minutes later, Tinsdale reappeared. "He's ready for you. But I'll have to interrupt you in twenty minutes. Mister Hadley has a client arriving." He gave a kind of automatic smile with nothing to it but a flash of teeth.

"Thank you, Mister Tinsdale," she said, and went into Hadley's office.

It was a splendid room, one of elegance and dignity, with Art Nouveau valences over the four tall windows, which were partially covered by amber-colored velvet draperies. A fireplace with more Art Nouveau tiles supporting the mantle dominated the western wall. A large rosewood desk in the same Art Nouveau style of the room faced the door from the embrasure of the largest window. Quentin Hadley sat behind it, a black armband barely visible against his dark-Prussian-blue suit; his face was so neutral in expression that it was difficult to see what a handsome man he was, with a profile a Barrymore would envy, a wide brow, and remarkably sensual lips. His folded hands lay on the clean blotter on his desk, almost as if in prayer; only by the merest flicker of his eyes did he reveal that he realized Poppy was actually in the room with him. Between the door and the desk was what appeared to be a pond of water lilies, an expansive carpet in the same design style as the rest of the chamber, which, given Hadley's demeanor, seemed as impassible as the pool it represented.

Taking her courage in her hands, Poppy looked directly at the forbidding figure behind the desk and stepped onto the carpet, half-expecting to find her new shoes dampened again. "Mister Hadley, I'm P. M. Thornton of the Clarion. Thank you for seeing me on this difficult day." She walked up to the desk and extended her hand to him, which he studied as if it was an unfamiliar object, which he did not deign to touch. "My condolences to you and your colleagues."

"Thank you, Miss Thornton," he answered, sounding either aloof or bored; his voice was higher than she expected, and nasal, at odds with his elegant appearance.

When he ventured nothing more, nor offered her a place to sit, Poppy waited for almost half a minute, then said, "I know Madison Moncrief hadn't worked here for very long, but I would imagine that you will find it hard to find someone of his caliber to replace him."

"Sadly, yes," said Hadley, and went silent again.

"His death must have been a great shock to you."

"It was." He turned to look out the windows on his right, as if mesmerized by the rain on the glass.

"Do you share the opinion that he . . . he may have been responsible for his own death?" It was the most delicate way she could think of to ask the question about suicide.

"I'm in no position to say."

"Do you approve of the way the police are handling their investigation?" This was a stronger question than she had planned to ask, but Hadley's refusal to offer her more than minimal responses was becoming nettling.

"This company has had little contact with the police. We aren't that kind of firm."

"But you will participate in their investigation?" It took an effort not to raise her voice.

"That remains to be seen."

"Why is that?" She asked, in as unchallenging a manner as she could.

"I'm afraid that I cannot say anything about a matter that might impinge upon our clients' confidentiality."

"Do you believe speaking about Mister Moncrief in any way would do that?"

Hadley looked at her, then turned his gaze back toward the window. "I have to consider that possibility."

She decided to come at the matter from a slightly different angle. "Well, have you been contacted by the police for an interview? That's standard procedure, isn't it."

"I have no idea."

Poppy knew this was hedging the truth at the least, for there were few attorneys in the country that did not know how police conducted their investigations, but she hesitated to confront him on that point for fear he would throw her out; she went on cautiously. "Then would you accept that the death was something other than suicide?"

"We must wait for the coroner to answer that; it's useless to speculate." He directed his gaze in her direction but seemed to focus his eyes three feet beyond her head. "I'm sorry that I made this appointment: under the circumstances, I should not have agreed to see you."

Poppy was growing more exasperated. "I realize confidentiality is an important part of your work, but can you tell me a little about what sort of duties Moncrief had here? He was a fairly new employee; he'd worked here what? eighteen months or so? What sort of accounts did he handle for you? Nothing specific, if you feel it's inappropriate."

"I don't believe I should answer that," he said.

Poppy had expected that kind of an answer and was ready with a follow-up. "Perhaps you could give me some idea of his duties, then? The police already have that information, so it isn't a confidential matter."

"I can tell you that he kept the books for three corporations, and handled appropriate negotiations for them," Hadley answered, a suggestion of a frown marring his impassive features. "I doubt you need to know more about that."

"It's probably not necessary, no, though it might be of interest to our readers, if this turns out to be a more complicated . . . misadventure than it seems at present," she said, and knew she had made a mistake; Hadley glowered at her. She attempted to frame another question. "Were you aware of Mister Moncrief being . . . unlike himself in the last few months? Were there any indications of anxiety? Did he seem disturbed or worried?"

"He hadn't worked here long enough to have impressed me sufficiently with his personality that I would have been able to detect such changes, as I have already told the police. His clients were satisfied with his performance, and that was sufficient to me. I don't make a habit of becoming friendly with employees, no matter how well-connected they may be." If he was aware of his slip, he gave no indication of it as he went on smoothly. "They — the police — accepted my assurance that there was little I could do to aid them, and have turned their attention to other persons."

"But if you hired Moncrief — " She stopped and began again. So he has talked to the police, she thought. He confirmed it, apparently by accident, but perhaps it had been a clever ruse. Rapidly she reviewed what she had asked that he had avoided, and realized he seemed to want to side-step any question of what he had said to the police. "I know it must be difficult to discuss anything about one of your firm's personnel, given, as you say, the circumstances," Poppy began, and was interrupted by Hadley.

"That is very true, Miss Thornton, and for the sake of his widow, and the rest of his family, I don't think I should say anything more."

"Is there anything you think the police should look into regarding his death?" It was a bold tactic, one she hoped would jar him from his mask of impassivity.

"That would be between the police and me, wouldn't it." He stared past her at the door. "I'm sure you understand my position: my first responsibility is to our clients."

Determined to get something more from Hadley, Poppy pressed on. "Don't you find Moncrief's death puzzling? Doesn't it strike you as odd that two of your accountants have . . . died in the last year?"

"That is not a matter for the public, Miss Thornton."

"Why not?" She was baffled and nettled by his intransigence, and was about to question him about this when Hadley unfolded his hands.

"I'm sorry, but I have a meeting to attend shortly." He pressed a button on the base of his 'phone; a buzz sounded in the outer office. "If you will excuse me." He rose and nodded toward the door, which opened, as if on cue, revealing Clifford Tinsdale, not quite bristling with annoyance. "Good day, Miss Thornton."

Nonplused, Poppy uttered a disjointed thank you as she retreated from Hadley's inner sanctum through the door Tinsdale had opened for her.

"Do you remember how to find the reception desk, or shall I describe it to you?" asked Tinsdale as he took his seat again, watching Poppy as if he expected her to purloin the fixtures; his smile was as artificial as the carved wooden flowers over the window.

"No, thank you. I'm sure I can find my way out," she said, all the while wondering how she would explain to Lowenthal the reason for her failure to cajole information from this senior partner of the firm. Retracing her steps to the front of the offices, she was surprised when a man about forty, wearing thick glasses and carrying an equally thick ledger, emerged from one of the offices and, without speaking to her, handed her a note on a file card as he passed her. Since he gave no sign of having done it, or even of being aware of her, Poppy took the file card without comment and slipped it into the hip pocket of her raincoat, planning to read it as soon as she was safely out of the building. As she reached the ground floor, Poppy realized she hadn't had any opportunity to ask about James Poindexter.

THIRTEEN

RAIN SLOWED THE TRAFFIC AND FRAYED THE TEMPERS OF THOSE CAUGHT IN IT;
Poppy spent most of her cab ride in deep and restless thought; she put off
reading the note she had been handed, almost afraid of what it might say.
Little as she liked to admit it, she found herself entertaining suspicions
about Quentin Hadley, for it was hard to believe that his truculent treatment
stemmed from bad manners alone. When Hadley had told her that he
shouldn't have set up the appointment with her, she had been shocked: if he
hadn't wanted to see her, why had Hadley agreed to the appointment in the
first place? she wondered. She decided to spend some time in the Hall of
Records to see if she could turn up anything about the corporations Hadley
hadn't wanted to name, but that would be after she called upon the coroner.

Handing a dollar forty to the cab driver, she reminded herself that she
needed to stop by the bank. It being Friday, she would need cash for the
weekend, especially with Eustace in town, for he would want to spend time
out on the town, one way or another. She opened her umbrella and trudged
off toward the morgue. Once inside the door, she closed her umbrella and
went to the first of three 'phone booths, slipped in her nickel and gave the
operator the number at Aunt Jo's. "I'll speak to anyone there."

Missus Flowers answered the 'phone, and upon hearing Poppy's voice,
said, "We're quite busy here, Miss Poppy. Eustace has managed to arrange
a dinner here this evening. Your aunt is out with Mister Eustace selecting
some lilies for the centerpiece, so that it won't appear too festive, but will be
more than a black wreath on the table. They're also going to the butcher for
a dressed baron of beef; it will be a task to have it properly roasted in time
for the dinner."

"Oh, dear," said Poppy. "And I'm afraid I'm going to be late. That's why I'm calling."

"I'll tell Missus Dritchner and Mister Eustace that. Given that this is such short notice, we should be able to accommodate your tardiness. It's good of you to call."

"Thank you, Missus Flowers," she said, and hung up. She extricated herself and her umbrella, briefcase, and purse from the 'phone booth and went along to the double doors that were the official entrance to the morgue.

Doctor Emily Kodaly admitted Poppy to the chilly, evil-smelling basement beneath Philadelphia's Central Hospital where Doctor Wyman held sway. Doctor Em, as she was called by everyone who knew her, was forty-three, the wife of a geologist — that crazy Hungarian rock-hound I married she often called him — working in the burgeoning oil business, and mother of two teen-age children; she was a good friend of Poppy's Aunt Esther, and had known Poppy since she was in high school. She greeted Poppy with a serviceable smile that revealed teeth yellowed by coffee and tobacco; her white lab coat had a frayed cuff, but otherwise was the neatest thing in the office. "Good to see you, Miss Thornton. Poppy. How's everything at the Clarion these days? How're your reports on the Moncrief case coming?"

"They're coming along," said Poppy. "And you? How's everything at chez Kodaly?"

"Busy. Geza's out in the field again, and the kids are rapscallions. Not that I don't adore them all." She let that suffice for an answer. "You're here to see Archie about the Moncrief murder, aren't you? Of course you are."

"Murder? Are you certain?" Poppy felt her whole body come alert; so Holte had been right all along. "Did something come back from New York?"

"Oh, yes. The messenger arrived with results over an hour ago. I'll let Archie explain it to you. He's itching to tell someone about it, and I don't think he can wait until noon to make his finding official." She took a cigarette from the silver case on her battered desk and reached for her box of matches. "I've got a day laborer to autopsy shortly. It shouldn't take long. He's got all kinds of obvious indications; all I have to do is confirm them."

"I'll gird up my loins and look in on you when I'm through with Doctor Wyman, unless you're busy," Poppy told her.

Doctor Em struck her match and touched its flame to her cigarette, squinting as the smoke wreathed around her head. "You know where his office is?"

"I think so. Next to your cold storage room." She had a sudden appalling rush of memory of the Influenza Epidemic, when bodies filled the morgue beyond capacity, and pallets stacked with corpses lined the corridor on both sides, so that the living had to turn sideways to make their way through the dead to identify loved ones. Poppy had come here then with Aunt Jo to identify Reginald's remains and to make arrangements for his burial in the family plot instead of the mass grave that was becoming as overcrowded as the morgue. A few of the returning soldiers had said it was worse than the trenches. The smell now was nothing like the sweetish-metallic odor that had hung on the air then, a potent, invisible fog that clung to the clothes and hair and the roof of the mouth for days after the visit; rather now it was redolent of carbolic acid and bleach, with a suggestion of mold or decay beneath. Poppy gave herself a mental shake and a stern reminder that Reginald had died almost five years ago and that the past was over.

"Try not to let the place bother you, Poppy," Doctor Em recommended. "The dead can't do anything to you."

"Are you sure of that," said Poppy with a shaky laugh, looking about to see if any of the lights flickered.

"Go on. We'll talk later." She waved Poppy out of the room.

The corridor was lit by hanging, caged bulbs that provided more glare than illumination, but Poppy kept on along the corridor. How could anyone stand to work here, day after day, in this pervasive stench of death? she asked herself as she knocked on Archibald Wyman's office door, trying not to hold her breath.

"Come in, Miss Thornton. I've been expecting you."

Poppy went through the door into a chamber of stuffed shelves and file cabinets all clustered around an old-fashioned roll-top desk opened to reveal a Corona typewriter, a telephone, a stack of files, a library-style reading lamp, and an overflowing ashtray where a pipe lay across the heap of burned tobacco. Archibald Wyman sat at the desk at an angle, his feet up on a low stool, his hands folded across his waist, blissfully unaware of the extensive clutter surrounding him; his lab-coat was open, revealing a sweater over his white shirt and dark trousers beneath. He was smiling. "Thank you for seeing me, Doctor."

"Thank you for coming. I'd so much rather entertain an attractive young lady than most of your male colleagues. And I think I can reward you with a scoop." He sat up and reached for the file at the top of the stack on his desk. "The results from the tests. The stomach contents are particularly interesting."

Poppy took the file, saying as she did, "I didn't realize you'd sent stomach contents — I thought it was just blood."

"You know how we are in this work: we often hold things back until we have reason to reveal them." He grinned at her, his face impish and self-satisfied. "And the time of revelation has arrived."

"I know the police do that occasionally. I didn't know coroners did, as well." She scanned the four sheets in the file, glad that she had paid attention in her college chemistry classes so that she didn't feel entirely lost. "This residue they mention. What do you make of it?" she asked, holding onto the file.

"I make it out as deliberate poisoning, administered in the evening meal, probably in the dessert, or the coffee" he said. "I haven't run across it before, not in this context."

"Is the poison identified?" Poppy asked.

"Page three, second graph, a poison rarely seen on this side of the Atlantic, a botanical compound, with deadly nightshade as a primary ingredient, along with raw opium and an herb I don't recognize, all reduced to a tincture," said Wyman. "So it is murder, and a deliberate, clever, planned one, and . . . um . . . executed so efficiently that it could easily have passed for suicide if the chandelier hadn't broken and dropped the body on the floor." He clapped his hands once and refolded them.

"Are you planning to announce your findings today?" Poppy asked, trying to decide if she should return to the Clarion at once, in order to make sure the story got above the fold on page one.

"In two hours or so. I've got to brief the cops first; I'll call Commissioner Smiley as soon as you've left." He leaned back in his chair again. "You don't look surprised."

"I'm not, not really," Poppy said, adding hurriedly, "It just seemed to me that there were a lot of loose ends in the case that didn't allow for suicide, particularly the assumption that he had chosen the weakest part of the chandelier to hang from, something he would have known not to use, and not just because it couldn't hold him, but because it is a valuable antique, and the old gas fittings were still in place. The break might have released gases that would have been dangerous. That didn't seem like Madison Moncrief at all. If he were going to kill himself by hanging, I'd expect him to do something more . . . more private." As she said this, Quentin Hadley's evasions on the subject of Madison Moncrief's death seemed more sinister than when she had heard them half an hour ago.

Wyman nodded encouragingly, and launched into what Poppy suspected was trial run on what he would tell the police. "Even if he did hang himself, what killed him was the poison, or would have if he hadn't been put in the noose, which must have been arranged to conceal the murder. Nothing else makes any sense at all. The hanging was a diversionary tactic, that's clear now, intended to mislead and confuse, so that the finding of suicide would be unavoidable. Moncrief had no reason to both poison and hang himself, not that he could have done so; he was more than half-dead when he was hanged, and he couldn't possibly have managed getting the rope around his neck, let alone rig the noose on the chandelier. He was probably semi-conscious at best, unaware of the danger he was in. He might not have known what was happening to him until — " He looked toward the door as if expecting an interruption. "Well, you get the picture, don't you? The hanging was a ruse to conceal the poisoning, planned, by the same person or persons." He cleared his throat, and changed his tone. "That's all I can tell you for now. You may use everything I've told you: it's a pleasure to talk with you, Miss Thornton." He glanced at his watch. "You can run the information about the poison in tonight's paper, but don't mention that you had an early briefing."

"Did Doctor Em ask you to do me a favor?" Poppy asked.

"It's possible," he said, and winked. "She wouldn't have asked if she didn't think you were worth it."

"Thanks," said Poppy. "I think," and left him to continue his review of the test results, organizing his thoughts for the police briefing.

Doctor Em was in the second autopsy suite, a drape over all but the face of the body of the day laborer, a man who looked fifty and was probably thirty-five. She lit another cigarette. "Filthy things. Your Aunt Jo's right not to allow them in the house."

"She doesn't mind pipes, or the occasional cigar, provided it's a good one," Poppy reminded her. "Thanks for letting me in on this a little early. I'll have to do a page for Lowenthal before I go to lunch."

"Duty calls?" She rubbed Vaseline into her hands. "Mine's calling me. It's likely to be messy." She looked at the instrument tray waiting beside her. "I don't think this will take too long. From the hospital report, it's probably a stroke of some kind, or a sudden heart attack. He has significant joint damage and I don't think he's ever seen a dentist. He's been dead about two days by the look of him. And the smell."

"Poor man." It was an automatic response; Poppy realized she had no idea about the life of the corpse on the zinc-topped table.

"Given the scars on his face and his hands, I'd also say he did more than his share of fighting. He's missing five teeth, and his left hand shows signs of being broken some time ago, which is why I don't think he'd ever consulted a dentist," Doctor Em told her, then raised her voice. "Hey, Layton. Get in here."

A harried young man about Poppy's age bustled through the inner door. "I'm here, Doctor Em." He stopped as he caught sight of Poppy.

"Are you ready?" Doctor Em asked him, as if she were unaware of his flustered state. "I don't want to be all day about this. We have three more to do before six."

"Give me a minute or two," he said, going to her tray of autopsy tools and setting it in order.

Her assistant stared at Poppy. "Is it all right to have an observer?"

"This isn't a court case with this fellow, Ben," said Doctor Em, pulling her smock over her head, adding briefly. "Benedict Layton, P. M. Thornton of the Clarion. Now hand me my scalpel."

Layton stared at Poppy. "A reporter? And you say this isn't a court case?

If it's not, what's she doing here?"

Doctor Em sighed. "She came to thank me, and to talk to Doctor Wyman. She's with the Clarion. She won't be staying. But she could if I asked her to." This was so pointed that Poppy blinked at such language.

Layton reached for the scalpel and handed it to her; his face was stiff with outrage and he was struggling to keep from upbraiding his boss. "Have I laid out your tray to your liking? Do you want the tray moved closer, or is it satisfactory where it is?"

"Oh, stop being such an officious toady, Ben. It's unnecessary and irritating. I know the law, and I'm not going to abuse it." She stubbed out her cigarette, and turned to Poppy. "If you don't mind, you'd better go."

Glad for an excuse to leave, Poppy said, "Yes. Well, thanks, Doctor Em. I'll give your regards to Aunt Jo."

"And your Aunt Esther, when you have the chance." She was about to begin her incision, but stopped. "Where is she, by the way? Do you know?"

"I just had a letter from her, from Vladivostok." She realized with some surprise that she had yet to read the letter. I'll read it at lunch, she thought.

"Sounds like her," said Doctor Em, and waved her away.

The corridor seemed to have dimmed while Poppy had been in the autopsy suite. She looked up and discovered one of the lights had burned out. As she left the morgue, she caught sight of Gregory Swindon of the Pennsylvania Ledger coming her way at a good clip. She decided not to avoid him.

"Still on the case, I see," he said as he came up to her. His smile was not friendly.

"You, too," Poppy countered.

"Yeah." He studied the wall beyond her. "Anything worth my time? I'm guessing you were talking to the coroner."

"You'll have to decide what's worth your while," she said.

He smirked, knowing he had rattled her. "I got a call that the test results are back." He raised a speculative brow.

"Yes. They are." She started to move past him, but stopped as he moved to block her. "Step aside, please."

"Tell me what you found out."

Now she looked directly at him. "You'd better ask the coroner. Anything I tell you is hearsay at best, and no use to you."

Swindon chuckled and stepped back. "Your daddy trained you well, kid." He continued on the way she had come.

When she reached the sidewalk, Poppy was upset enough to feel like crying, telling herself she could blame her wet face on the rain. Nursing her indignation, she signaled for a cab, and sternly ordered herself to gather her thoughts for Lowenthal. A 'bus rolled by, sending a cascading bow-wave of water onto the sidewalk and all over her legs. "Ye gods!" she exclaimed. Her wet skirt was instantly dank on her skin. She stamped her foot in vexation while fighting back tears. This was her first important story, a real test of her skills, and those who were her colleagues were treating her like an amusing novice, a complete tyro. No, she told herself, worse than a novice — someone without any credibility at all, a laughing stock. She wanted to scream, but only allowed herself a miffed snort. Chagrin burned in her like new lava.

It took almost ten minutes to flag down a taxi, and in that time her hair became wet and droopy in spite of her umbrella, and when she climbed into the taxi, she was thoroughly disheartened. As she pulled the door closed and told the cabby to take her to the Clarion, she almost hoped that Chesterton Holte would speak up next to her, but that did not happen. The taxi ride to the office was uneventful, but for a newspaper boy who darted out into traffic to hand the latest edition of the Tribune to a motorist, and almost getting run over by a Rambler. The resultant eruption of horns and shouts jarred Poppy out of her morose thoughts and directed her attention to the traffic around the cab. Once the confusion ended, she turned her attention back to what Wyman had told her. She would have to consult the encyclopedia about poisons, she told herself.

Back at her desk at the Clarion, Poppy quickly wrote up the revelations of the coroner, then pulled out the note she had been given as she left Hadley and Grimes. The file-card on which it was written had nothing unusual about it except the message written on it:

Stay away from Hadley and Grimes. You're already in danger.

FOURTEEN

"YOU SAY SOMEONE JUST ... JUST HANDED THIS TO YOU?" CORNELIUS LOWENTHAL asked as he held the card up to the light. "Did you recognize the man who gave it to you? Did he say anything?" Increasing rain spattered on the window in the north wall, and an impatient finger of cold wind probed the office.

"No, to both. So far as I know, I've never seen him before. He went past me quickly, didn't so much as look at me. I think he wore horn-rim glasses, but that's about the only thing I noticed. Aside from passing me that, he ignored me." Poppy felt a chill that had nothing to do with the weather or her damp clothes. Whoever had slipped her the note knew who she was, and why she was at the office of Hadley and Grimes.

"It'd be a good idea to learn who's warning you, and why," Lowenthal said, waggling his eyebrows for accentuation.

"I know it would," said Poppy with a worried frown. Where was Holte, she wondered, when she had something she wanted him to do. She realized that Lowenthal was still speaking, and gave him her attention.

" — send Brandenburg over to Hadley and Grimes, to see if he gets the same treatment. They know him from his column, of course." Micah Brandenburg covered financial matters for the Clarion, not with the depth that Jonathan Wheelwright or Thomas Payton did for the Constitution, but with knowledge and good sense, and most of the financial community respected him. "You can deal with Moncrief's friends for now. Be sympathetic. The police don't have any suspects yet, do they? So for now, keep your ideas about who killed him to yourself. If you can pick up any gossip about Hadley and Grimes, make a note of it, but don't go searching for it. Once we know whether it's just you or reporters in general that worries Hadley and Grimes, we can decide how to handle it."

Poppy could not conceal her dismay. "But this is my story."

"And it's going to stay that way. Obviously you're on to something, and you can move around in that level of society without attracting attention. Maybe you should talk this over with your Inspector friend? He might make some recommendations."

Worse and worse, she thought, but managed to say, "I'll think it over and let you know if I bring it up with Inspector Loring." Just the idea of being hemmed in by protection made her slightly ill; such special treatment would surely put her back on the Society page for the next decade once this case was over. She got up from her chair, saying, "If you'll give me the note?"

"Take it down to the photo office and have one of the men take a picture of it, so we can have a record. This isn't the kind of thing we ignore here at the Clarion." He pulled at his hair. "This is the damnedest tangle; I don't want you caught in it if it turns vicious."

"All right," said Poppy, struck by how seriously Lowenthal seemed to be taking the threat. "Right now, or do you want me to do it before I leave?"

"You're leaving late, remember. Best to do it now. And I really would bring it up with Loring, little as you want to. He can tell you how to take precautions, and the first precaution is for you to stay away from Hadley and Grimes. You don't know who gave it to you, or why, or who's behind it, so let the experts find out." He leaned forward, big arms on the desk like battlements. "That's an order. Until we can discover why you're being threatened, you're not to go near that building. Keep clear of people from that office, too."

"Yes; I will. I understand." She picked up her briefcase, hoping that Lowenthal could not see her frustration. "Where are you going to run my story about the coroner's finding?"

"Front page, at or above the fold." He clapped his hands. "Get back to work. I want to hear from Moncrief's friends and family, as many as possible: five's a minimum. Get the usual. Distress. Shock. Disbelief. How could it happen to such a man? You have a couple hours' lead on the other papers; your calls are likely to get some information, so make the most of it. After two or three reporters phone, those people won't answer."

Poppy offered a casual salute. "Sir, yes, sir," she said, as she had heard soldiers back from Europe respond to orders.

She walked down to her office, thinking as she went that she really didn't want to spend hours making calls to acquaintances to discover their reaction to Madison Moncrief's murder, that she'd rather go to the Hall of Records and find out more about Madison Moncrief's accounts at Hadley and Grimes, but, she reminded herself, the calls are the job right now. She had drawn up a list of people who were friends of the Moncriefs, and decided to begin with them. Picking up the 'phone, she gave the switchboard the number for Walter and Isobel Montgomery, and waited while they put the call through. The housekeeper answered the phone and told Poppy that Missus Montgomery was out and was expected back after three. The housekeeper did not suggest that Poppy leave a message.

Before the housekeeper hung up, Poppy said, "Please, tell her that I'll try to reach her later. I'm Poppy Thornton." She didn't add that she was a reporter for the Clarion. She put a star next to the Montgomerys names on her list; her next call went to Bertram and Geraldine Chapman; this time things went a bit better.

"Chapman residence," said the voice on the other end of the line.

"Geraldine Chapman?" Poppy asked, recognizing her voice; she pictured the pretty, slender Geraldine in one of her elegant dresses, the hem eight inches above her ankles, the drape of the fabric revealing hints of what lay beneath. No doubt her dark-brown hair would be up in a sleek knot on the crown of her head, and she would have at least one rope of pearls around her neck, and a cigarette in her hand. "Missus Chapman, this is Poppy Thornton here. I'm calling to ask you some questions if you could spare — "

" — about Madison Moncrief. Yes, of course. I've heard already: murder. What a dreadful thing to have happened. Louise must be devastated." She took an unsteady breath. "She's been through so much."

"I would think she has, and this would be more than enough on its own; to lose her husband so soon after she lost a child must be devastating," Poppy said. "That's why I'm calling friends of the Moncriefs rather than Louise herself." She knew she would have to speak to Louise sometime, but she wanted to have Stacy with her when she did.

"That's quite considerate, for a reporter," said Geraldine, warming a little. "What would you like me to tell you?"

"Oh, your view on the case. I don't mean accusations of guilt, but what you know about Madison's state of mind recently. Did you notice anything that seemed out of character for him? Did he seem worried? Had he said anything about any difficulties?" That's always a good place to start, she told herself.

There was a short pause, and then Geraldine said, "Well, the miscarriage was terribly upsetting to both of them, as you must know. Louise really isn't over it yet, and I think Madison was more troubled than he wanted to admit; he was more stoic about it than she — as you might expect — but I know it must have been shattering. Still, that might have explained a suicide, but not murder."

"How recently did you see Madison?"

"Just over three weeks ago, at the Sheridans' party for the symphony. Louise wasn't with him, and he seemed a bit at loose ends. He came with Christopher and Isme Greenloch, as I recall; they left early." She hesitated. "After the Greenlochs went, Madison spent a fair amount of time with the Fairchilds — Humphrey and Mildred?"

"Mildred and I were at school together," Poppy said, to reinforce her position; she added the Greenlochs to the list of people to 'phone. "I'll have to give her a call, as well."

"I thought Madison seemed out of sorts, but under the circumstances, why shouldn't he? He was so looking forward to being a father, and the loss of the baby was a burden to him. And he mentioned that he had things on his mind, beyond the miscarriage, but who knows what those things were." Geraldine went on to describe her lunch with Louise a few days after the symphony gala, and then to express her concern for Louise. "She won't find it easy without Madison. She's depended upon him so much."

Poppy felt this was an odd observation, considering how little time Madison and Louise had spent together for the last two years. "How do you mean?"

"He was so devoted to her, and not demanding or jealous, and how many women can say that about their men? He was willing to tolerate Julian Eastley's hanging on Louise's sleeve, and encouraged her to have their male friends be her escort when he wasn't free to accompany her to events — but you know that. Your cousin Stacy took her to horse shows on several occasions, didn't he. And the symphony once or twice. They say the two of them are great friends, don't they? Not many husbands would be so lenient with their wives, or would only be so because they themselves were straying."

"You mean Louise's rumored affair, or something else?" Poppy dared to ask, knowing that Geraldine could stop talking to her at any moment.

"It all came to nothing, you know, that affair business. At the most she had a flirtation, nothing more serious than that. I never thought the story was credible — the identity of her supposed lover kept changing, and that usually means more gossip than substance." She coughed delicately. "Bess Rymer told me that it was all a conflation of tales, nothing more, and she's quite close to Louise."

"Apparently you agree," said Poppy, wondering how often she would have to listen to variations on this report today.

"Look, Poppy, I liked Madison, and I feel for Louise. What do you expect me to say?" She stopped herself. "Why not talk to Bess?"

"I will. And to Milly. And Isme. There are a few others on my list as well." She was about to mention the rest of the names, then changed her mind; she didn't want Geraldine alerting her friends about newspaper interviews — that would come soon enough.

"Well, I don't envy you the task. But I'm relieved you'll be making the calls, not one of those ham-handed reporters who barge right in with inappropriate personal questions the way they did after James Poindexter . . . um . . . died."

"Thanks, Geraldine. I'm glad someone's aware of how difficult such calls can be."

"Yes. Well, say hello to your aunt for me, and to Stacy; I hear he's in town." She paused briefly. "Good-bye." Then she hung up without waiting for Poppy to say the same to her.

Poppy looked at her notes and decided it was going to be a long afternoon. She checked off Geraldine, and prepared to make her next 'phone call.

It was almost eight by the time Poppy left the office. By then Cornelius Lowenthal was gone and Matthew Pike ruled the city room. She nodded to Carlotta Upshaw who was just arriving, but did not stop to speak with her; she was too tired, too worn out from talking, and she needed to get home. Aunt Jo had been annoyed to learn she would be later than originally expected, and further delay would only add to her umbrage.

The rain had slacked off, but was still persistent enough to make her umbrella necessary to Poppy as she stood at the curb and signaled for a cab, telling herself that perhaps she should buy her own automobile rather than spend her time standing on the curb waiting for a cab, or a streetcar. After almost ten minutes, one pulled over, took her destination address, accepted the dollar-seventy-five she paid him, and drove off into the wet, shiny night.

Poppy had dozed on the way home, the voices of the eight people she had interviewed ringing in her head loudly enough to shut out anything Chesterton Holte might try to say to her. She knew there were more 'phone calls to come, and didn't look forward to another two or three hours of interviews.

There were four automobiles pulled up in front of Aunt Jo's, Warren Derrington's Lincoln, a Doble two-seater, a new Pierce-Arrow, and a three-year-old Locomobile. No wonder Aunt Jo had been displeased that Poppy would be late.

Hawkins let her in with a warning look as he took her coat and umbrella. "They've gone into dinner, Miss. I served the soup not ten minutes ago, and there's a salad to come after. That can be delayed a little if I open another three bottles of wine. If you'd go up and change right now, you can join them for the main course; I'll let Missus Boudon know you're here. Fortunately, the Smiths arrived late, and that slowed things down, or we'd be getting ready to serve dessert. As it was, they sat down almost twenty minutes later than Missus Dritchner would have preferred. Mister Tobias isn't with us, incidentally; he is dining with his student and the boy's grandparents. You will make thirteen at table." He shook his head in disapproval.

"Ye gods. Aunt Jo must be having convulsions. Thirteen. Do you think I'd better take my dinner in my room?"

"No, I don't. If you want my opinion, I think Mister Eustace planned this party of his to have thirteen at table, just to tweak his mother."

It sounded like the sort of thing Stacy would do, Poppy thought. "Thanks, Hawkins. I'll be down in twenty minutes." Her estimate allowed a little time to repair her hair and do something about her face as well as change into more appropriate clothes; the rain had smudged her make-up beyond tolerable limits, she was certain of it, and she'd need something to put a little color into her cheeks. Maestro was curled on the bottom stair, the end of his tail, as usual, over his nose; Duchess was sprawled at the top, snoring loudly. Poppy managed to make the climb without disturbing either animal, and was almost as far as her room before Duchess set up an alarming howl that brought Hawkins running in dismay. Poppy suspected she knew the cause, for the light in the nearest sconce flickered; she looked over her shoulder and saw Chesterton Holte there, hovering, a bit off the ground, offering an abashed shrug. "She's seeing spooks," she said to Hawkins. "You might want to put her in the music room."

From his place halfway up the flight, Hawkins called softly to the elderly dog, and waited while she gave up her baying and tottered down the stairs to be led off. "I'll see she gets her dinner, Miss. You go along and change."

Poppy hurried toward her bedroom, wanting to accost Holte before she dressed for dinner. "Don't say anything until we can be private."

"I looked in on you at the office around five, but you were so busy, I didn't stay," Holte said, and went through the door before she opened it.

Partly relieved to see him, partly vexed at his long absence, Poppy went in, turned on the lights, and sat down at her vanity, studying her face as if it were an antique in need of major repair. "I have to go down to dinner shortly so if you have anything to tell me, it'll have to be later; I've got too little time for discussion right now," said Poppy, feeling out-of-sorts as she began a careful repair of her make-up. "Where have you been all day?"

"Various places. Most of the time I was at Hadley and Grimes. You certainly stirred up a hornets' nest there." He seemed unusually pleased. "Whatever was bothering Moncrief, it wasn't a figment of his imagination."

Poppy took a damp make-up sponge from its bowl, thoroughly wiped her face with it, and returned it to its place. Devoid of what little powder had remained, she saw the circles under her eyes and the vertical line between her brows. "Oh, dear."

"You have good reason to be troubled," said Holte.

"How kind," she remarked as she reached for her complexion emulsion. "I'll look better in ten minutes."

"Not your face; Moncrief's murder." He became a bit more visible. "There is something going on at Hadley and Grimes. I've spent half the day trying to find out what it is."

"Why don't you ask Moncrief?" Poppy asked, only a bit sarcastically.

"I did. He said one of the accounts he handled was not proper, possibly more than one."

"Not proper how? What account?" Poppy asked, selecting a light foundation and some rouge. "Was it accidental or deliberate?"

"He didn't go into particulars." He moved back from her, out of her line of vision. "If you like, I'll try again."

Poppy was using mascara to darken her eyelashes. "Do you know the names on the account?"

"Of the business, yes," he said. "There are three accounts that may be involved. He wasn't specific about which of the three was bothering him."

"I'll want to get those from you later," Poppy said. "But right now, I'm going to change."

"I'll join you back here after your guests leave, if you don't mind."

"They're Stacy's guests, but yes, let's talk then."

"Would you like to be alone?" His tone implied that he was not quite comfortable watching her do her face.

"Yes, please." She rose and went to her closet. Something fairly impressive, she thought, but somber in color.

"The dark-turquoise silk evening dress should do," Holte recommended, as he began to fade from the room. "You can wear your new shoes."

It was aggravating to agree with him, but the dress was elegantly understated and surprisingly comfortable to wear, both of which were irresistible to her this evening. She began undressing, putting her clothes in the cleaning hamper before she took the dress from its hanger and worked it over her head. This, she told herself, then her hair and lipstick, then her shoes, a touch of scent, and she would go down to dinner.

FIFTEEN

CHESTERTON HOLTE DIDN'T MIND WAITING: HE DRIFTED INTO THE LIBRARY AND looked over the many titles on the shelves, stopping at one by B. Oliver Thornton, *Changing Hopes*; not a very original title, he thought, but he might have liked it better if he had been able to turn the pages to read it. He wished he could pull that one out, but his noncorporeality made this impossible, and he decided to ask Poppy to read him some of her father's work at a later time; he felt he owed B. Oliver Thornton that much. He decided to wander down to the dining room and laze along the ceiling, the chandelier flickering a bit as he settled in. The dining room was looking splendid, he decided, the oak wainscoting newly polished, the silver and china gleaming on the mahogany table that had been lengthened with the insertion of two leaves to accommodate the thirteen places set around its graceful curves. The evening appeared to be going well.

Arriving in the dining room some fifteen minutes before Holte did, Poppy made her excuses for being late. "I'm very busy at work just now. Thanks so much for understanding."

"You may sit down between Henry and Grace," Josephine told her in her best entertaining-at-home manner. "It's a pity the table is so unbalanced, but there's no hope for it, though why Eustace decided on this seating arrangement, I can't tell you. How inconvenient of Tobias to be away tonight."

Poppy took her seat and repeated the demands of work had made her late.

"Do you mean your efforts at the Clarion?" asked Stanton Fernald, an old friend of Stacy's who now worked on The Monthly Story Bag, a periodical for grammar school students that encouraged good behavior, respect for elders, admirable personal habits, honesty, cheerfulness, and Christian values, all wrapped up in moralistic little adventures in which virtue always triumphed and misconduct inevitably came to a sticky end.

"I'm afraid so," Poppy answered and was immediately peppered with questions from the ten other guests about the murder. "Since I'm working on the . . . the death of Madison Moncrief, which I suppose most of you know."

"Isn't it a bit ghoulish to talk about it tonight?" asked Josephine, her demeanor quelling. "Most of you would have been at their fête tonight if this terrible thing hadn't happened. Let us all respect the dead, and not do anything to remind us of what happened."

"It worries me," said Warren Derrington. "How did it happen?"

Speculation was rife about who could have done such a terrible thing, which Aunt Jo eventually ended by announcing that murder was hardly a suitable topic for dinner table conversation. "And it's rude to Franklin," she added, addressing another of Stacy's fraternity brothers, the second son of Paxton Grimes, of Hadley and Grimes.

"Nothing to do with me, Missus Dritchner; that's father's and Emory's business, not mine. I have no reason to be involved with Hadley and Grimes, much as it might appear otherwise." He saw that Poppy was staring at him speculatively. "It's the diplomatic corps for me, when I finish my doctoral degree. Emory will replace father at the firm."

"You can't blame us for being curious, Mother," Stacy protested, smoothing over the awkwardness, leaning a bit to look around the centerpiece. "Had things turned out differently . . . " His words trailed off.

Derrington nodded to second this, and said, "Not a good thing, though; your mother's right about that."

"Then in the sitting room, over brandy, later, after all this unpleasantness is settled; tonight would be too early," Stacy predicted with a wink. "You know how we all want to speculate, and we have Poppy to guide us, though she may be constrained by ethics." He said ethics as if it were some sort of mental aberration.

"Stacy," Poppy warned him.

Eleanor Croaton, one of Josephine's oldest friends who had been a kind of spare aunt to Stacy through his youth, the widow of a prominent banker, made her contribution to shift the subject. "I was interested to see that Charles Dawes has announced that the commission on the dreadful German inflation is making progress on arriving at a plan that can bring it to an end and to stabilize the economy there."

"Yes, he has," Warren Derrington said, his expression suddenly brightening. "My company is very pleased that Dawes is on that commission, of course. Everyone is, I think. They need some good, old-fashioned American common-sense on that panel, and Dawes is the very man to provide it. The Europeans are still too caught up in issues of the Great War to be able to arrive at a reasonable solution."

Poppy studied him, for he had spoken without shyness or hesitation, which she had never known him to do. She determined to help him out. "I can understand why you might think so; the financial men at the Clarion have great hopes for him. He's supposed to have a real understanding about using money as a means for creating social change."

"Not money, if you please; I'd rather discuss crime, no matter how unpleasant, for in general, I find it less agitating than the matters of finance," Henry Smith interjected; a distinguished professor of philosophy, he had recently published a book on the Enlightenment, and would be spending the summer in Europe, doing research for his next. "There's too much emphasis on money these days."

His wife, Dolores, a third of the way around the table from him, laughed her tinkling laugh. "Oh, Henry. You know that you only think so because you have such a lot of it."

"Inherited, my dear. The best kind." Henry Smith all but crowed.

The guests echoed his laughter with titters and snickers of their own, Stacy adding, "How do you think Henry has time for philosophy? The money makes it possible."

"Eustace!" his mother reprimanded him.

"It's true, isn't it?" Stacy inquired merrily.

"There is something in what you say, of course," Stanton Fernald declared ponderously, ignoring Eliza, who had come in to remove the plates from the second course, a salad of chopped apples, chopped pears, walnuts, and poached, chopped hothouse asparagus, in chilled hollandaise sauce. "Everywhere we see that prosperity fosters the humanities, invention, and the arts, and its lack diminishes them. Education flourishes where there is social stability, and falters where there is inadequate cohesiveness. Nomadic peoples are kept ignorant and nonparticipatory through their lack of education, and their failure to desire to correct that lack."

Warren Derrington squirmed in his seat. "Is that always so?" He avoided looking directly at Fernald, as if to keep from offending him.

"There may be exceptions," Fernald allowed magnanimously, "but they are few, and anomalous."

"What a pedant you are, Ferny," Stacy said.

"Eustace," Josephine said again.

"Well, he is, Mother, and you know it." Stacy beamed at her, and was rewarded with an indulgent smile.

Fernald glowered at his host, his cheeks growing red. "A good education and informed opinions are nothing to apologize for, Eustace."

"Stanton, for heaven's sake," his wife Bernadette said. "No pontification, please; not tonight."

Watching Stacy and Fernald feint at one another, Poppy could only be glad that Tobias had decided not to attend this party, for if he had come, the verbal jousting might well have become rancorous: Tobias had a gift for setting people's backs up. Taking a second look at Franklin Grimes, she decided to have a talk with him before the evening came to an end.

"Hardly that," Fernald said, self-satisfied.

"Of course not; just a little intellectual exercise," Eustace all but purred. "A good education is a wonderful thing."

"Eustace, leave Stanton alone" Josephine told them. "You're not on the playground any more."

Fernald gathered his dignity, looked away from Stacy, and went back to unnecessarily cutting up his salad. "May I have some more hollandaise sauce, please?"

Eleanor passed the bowl to him. "What do you make of the editorial in the Tribune?" she asked of no one in particular.

"You mean that screed that claims Prohibition encourages crime?" Calvin Delacroix asked; he was Josephine's second cousin once removed, a few years older than Stacy, a well-known critic on the arts-and-music scene in eastern Pennsylvania; he and his wife Grace had given up a night of Baroque music for Stacy's impromptu party.

"I think there's some truth in it," said Stacy.

"Well, Madison had been drinking before he . . . died," Fernald said as if the brandy might be to blame. "I would say it has the opposite effect; judge and jury, you might say."

"You would," muttered Stacy.

"Goodness, not at the dinner table," Josephine protested.

Hawkins came in from the kitchen carrying a platter of medium-rare baron of beef, the bone-thick slices surrounded by wedges of Yorkshire pudding. He moved between Stacy and Eleanor Croaton to place it where Stacy could tend to serving it. "Three side-dishes are coming," he said, and went back toward the kitchen.

Primrose North, the seventy-seven-year-old mother of the man of the house across the street, a teacup of a woman, very nearly clapped with delight, and at last seemed interested in the dinner. "Oh, it looks lovely, Josephine. You do have a wonderful cook in Missus Boudon."

"Yes. She is a treasure," Josephine said confidently. "And not a temperamental bone in her body."

This signaled the guests to offer recollections of various erratic cooks they had encountered in their lives. While they each strove to tell a more outrageous story, Hawkins returned with a large silver tray on which sat a ceramic bowl of baked potatoes in their jackets, a small, oval platter of stewed tomatoes and bell peppers, a cut- glass bowl of sweet pickles, and a basket of rolls wrapped in an embroidered towel.

"Butter, gravy, and sautéed mushrooms to come," Hawkins told Stacy, puffing slightly.

The ceiling candelabra flickered; Josephine looked up at it, as if daring the light bulbs to go out. "Not another power failure," she murmured.

"Bring in the Bordeaux next," Stacy said to Hawkins. "Then get the butter and all the rest of it." He studied the centerpiece, a tasteful display of lilies and mums that was not too large for the table. "Should I move this to the sideboard? It's a bit tall for some of us."

Josephine considered the problem. "It might be a good idea," she conceded. "Yes, as soon as he returns, have Hawkins move it."

With the centerpiece out of the way, and the wine poured, conversation blossomed at the table, carefully and unobviously steered away from topics that could prove upsetting to Josephine and provoking to Stacy. Watching from his place on the ceiling, Holte marveled at their skill with small-talk; they were like stage-magicians, concealing their craft even as they used it.

"We'll be putting in another greenhouse shortly," Josephine said to Stanton Fernald. "Something larger than the two we have."

"Flowers or vegetables?" he asked, not particularly interested.

"Fruit trees, I think. Nothing large, but enough to supply the table with something other than winter pears and late apples. We do have a large enough greenhouse, if that's necessary. The Jeffries will tell me." She sighed. "I do enjoy seeing things grow."

"Yes," said Fernald, and cut the last bit of beef from the bone.

Dolores Smith and Eleanor Croaton were asking Franklin Grimes about his dissertation, and he was lapping up their flattering attention.

"It's almost done. My thesis defense is coming up." He shuddered dramatically. "I'm trying to prepare for it."

Eleanor gave him a curious look. "What is your topic?"

"It's pretty dull, you know. It deals with the history of trade between eastern and western Europe from the Middle Ages to the French Revolution, and its effect on return from a service-based economy to a money-based one. I got the idea for it when I was in France, toward the end of the Great War; I joined up just after I finished my four years at Yale, you know, and my officers' training took a few months, so I wasn't there as long as some of the boys." He achieved a kind of smile. "I'm doing the doctorate at Cornell."

Around the rest of the table, it was much the same: Eustace and Warren Derrington were making plans for the weekend that included visiting Louise Moncrief; Bernadette Fernald and Henry Smith were engaged in a light discussion of the influence of myths and children's stories on culture, and its impact on theatre and film; Poppy and Grace Delacroix were taking about the emerging opportunities in the workplace for women and cordially disagreeing as to how long it would take for these opportunities to become securely established.

As the conversation struck one of its occasional lags, Primrose North stated quite loudly, as if responding to something that had been said, "Denton — my son, you know — says they're all criminals."

"All prosecutors think that," said Stacy in his most calming voice, in a tone that said he agreed with what she was talking about.

"Denton says he'll prove they're criminals." She clutched her napkin as if she were hanging from a cliff and it was her only salvation.

Poppy wondered who they might be, but said nothing, as all vestiges of conversation came to a halt.

"No doubt they are," Josephine soothed Primrose.

"He'll convict them all," Primrose said, her assertiveness deserting her. "He's going to clean up the business." She huddled down in her chair.

"Cal, you're next to her; pour her some more wine," Stacy recommended.

Calvin Delacroix complied, saying, "Have a little more, Missus North."

She blinked, and chirped, "Why, thank you, young man," and took her glass; three dainty sips later, she set it down again.

Delacroix put the wine bottle back on the coaster, one of four on the table for that purpose, as Eliza came in to clear away the main course; slowly the buzz of conversation resumed.

After dessert and coffee, the party moved into the sitting room — at Josephine's request, Hawkins had escorted Primrose North across the street to her own home and the stewardship of her son — where bottles of brandy, bourbon, and Benedictine had been set out, with beautiful cut glasses on the coffee table, next to a jar of candied violets.

"We also have fresh-squeezed orange juice. Florida oranges," said Josephine as she took her place in her preferred chair, though most of the party remained on their feet as Stacy poured out the requested drinks.

A flicker from the nearest wall-sconce told Poppy that Holte had come into the sitting room. She asked for Benedictine in a very small glass, lifted it in what she guessed was Holte's direction, and moved away toward Franklin Grimes, who was leaning on the arm of the sofa, a glass of brandy-and-soda in his hand.

"It's been a long time, Frank," she said, holding out her free hand to him.

He took it. "It has. I can't quite place it — after the Great War?"

"And before the 'Flu struck in earnest. The victory celebration at the Signers' Club; the old building, in the Grand Salon," she said, pleased that she had been able to recall that meeting. Then he had been thin and nervous; now he was sleek and confident. She estimated his age at twenty-eight or twenty-nine.

"That's right," he said, his narrowed eyes sizing her up. "You were in college then, weren't you?"

"My sophomore year," Poppy told him, and trying to encourage him to say more, added, "Did I hear you say that you're completing a doctoral degree?"

"I hope. My faculty advisor is pressing me to turn in my dissertation before the end of May. It's the defense that's bothering me." He touched his glass to the rim of hers. "So, Poppy, here's to reacquaintance," he said with the kind of automatic smile that meant nothing.

"Oh, yes," she said, then added, "This must be a particularly difficult time for your family. My condolences."

"If you mean Moncrief, that's Hadley's side of the business. Father's keeping well out of it. Murder's such a tawdry crime, isn't it?" He flashed another smile, one that was supposed to be charming but on him seemed callous.

"It is an unfortunate one," Poppy said carefully.

"That's what we're all supposed to think," Grimes said. "But there are times it's impossible to see it that way." He drank, taking a generous amount of his brandy-and-soda. "I don't mean Moncrief's case is one of those, but I do think this insistence on mourning everyone who comes to a violent end is much overdone."

Poppy kept her expression neutral; perhaps, she thought, he was a little drunk, or he was more upset than he wanted to admit. Perhaps he feared he had said too much — but if he had, too much about what? "I suppose it depends on the individual," she said.

He slapped his forehead. "Your father. I forgot. I'm sorry if I sounded . .

. indifferent." Before he could say anything more, Derrington came over to the two of them.

"Don't mean to intrude," he began clumsily. "I need a little of your time, Frank. There are a few matters we need to discuss." Without waiting for a response, he took Grimes by the elbow and pulled him to the other side of the room.

Watching them go, Poppy asked herself, now what was that all about?

SIXTEEN

POPPY SAT ON THE CHEST AT THE END OF HER BED, LEGS TUCKED UP UNDER HER, her bathrobe snuggled around her; her bedroom was lit by the small Tiffany lamp on her nightstand but otherwise it was dark; the house was almost quiet, the guests either departed, or off to their rooms for the rest of the night, giving Poppy a chance to review the party and discuss it with Holte, who appeared to sit at her vanity, his outline as firm as she had ever seen it; in the mirror he showed as a shimmer more insubstantial than a moonbeam.

"I think it went well," she began, her voice low; the evening had been judged a success as far as Aunt Jo and Stacy were concerned, but Poppy had some reservations. "For the most part," she added.

"I'd agree," said Holte. "Your aunt entertains well, and so does your cousin, though his style is different."

"Stacy has a bit of the gadfly in him," Poppy said. "And he is most likely to tweak his mother, unless Hank — his oldest brother — is around. He and Hank fence conversationally for hours. I think they both enjoy it."

"Is Hank the one Josephine calls Galahad?" Holte asked.

"Yes; poor Hank. He's never liked the name. Aunt Jo went through an Arthurian phase when she was first married. My father said she was taken with the whole idea of the Round Table. She bought an old suit of armor for the entry hall. Cosmo was her Greek phase. She was in her Anglophile stage when Reginald and Eustace were born. Her husband left the naming of her children to her."

"Strange. Most men want to name their own sons."

Poppy nodded. "He was something of a cypher, Uncle Alfred was; he spent a great deal of time away from home."

"Doing what?" Holte swung around to face her, rising six inches above the seat as he did. "Or was that part of what made him a cypher?"

"He dealt in antiques and fine art, fairly large scale. He was recognized as an expert in several fields of antiquities. As I recall, his doctoral degree was in history with an emphasis on art and architecture, or so says Aunt Jo. He often worked on commission from universities and museums, authenticating their acquisitions. They relied on him to verify the provenance on questionable pieces. When he got older, he opened a shop, dealing in mostly European antiques, though he also handled Chinese pottery from time to time: very successful, very exclusive. Percy Knott took over his business; he's made quite a success of it." She shook her head. "Aunt Jo adored her husband, in a distant sort of way."

"Did he ever work for one of those international companies, the kind Moncrief worked with?"

"Not that I know of," said Poppy, suddenly very careful. "If he did, it wasn't directly."

"What about Percy Knott?" Holte asked.

"I don't know; there weren't very many of those international businesses before the Great War, not the way there are now, and the antiquities market wasn't nearly so active," said Poppy. "I think it unlikely that Uncle Alfred did, except as orders from customers at his shop who wanted good antiques for their offices and homes." But even as she said it, she wondered. "He might have had commissions from businesses from time to time. He made a good living, in any case. Aunt Jo once said that he often earned over twenty-five thousand dollars on his transactions, but I have only her word for it; she may have been boasting. It wasn't the sort of thing he talked about."

"How well did he know Knott?" Holte asked the question as if it came out of the most idle curiosity.

"It was more professional than social, but they were often in contact with one another," Poppy said, trying to decide what he was fishing for.

"Men with business in common — that sort of thing?"

"Yes; all those dealers do that, I think, like all manner of other professions. Like Knott, Uncle Alfred was pretty tight-lipped. I think that's why Uncle Alfred was willing to sell to him."

"Nothing like Stacy."

"Not very much, no." Poppy smothered a yawn with her hand. "But Uncle Alfred was never very much involved with his sons."

"By the way, what is it that Stacy does, exactly?" Holte waited for her answer.

"I don't know, exactly. It has something to do with real estate or commercial ventures — funding, I think — and he has interests in the petroleum industries. He's part of International Business Associates, which deals in antiques and antiquities, among other things. He doesn't like to talk about his specific business when he's home; he's like his father in that way, at least, and looks more like Uncle Alfred than Aunt Jo. By the way, she encourages Stacy not to let his work interfere with his family life, which he regularly disregards." Her face grew more somber as she strove to keep herself from indulging in guesses about her cousin. "I know he uses a great many of his university contacts in his work. He often jokes about it."

"I think I should follow him when he goes back to New York, just to get that settled. I don't like having so many unanswered questions about him." He smiled. "Spying, you might say."

"Just to keep your hand in?"

"Of course," he answered, and floated a little closer to her. "You're tired. You ought to get to bed."

She considered this. "All right," she said, then stopped him. "Wait. You said you'd found out something at Hadley and Grimes, about the accounts Madison Moncrief was handling."

He came back toward her. "There were three, just as he and Poindexter told me. They had been James Poindexter's accounts before Moncrief died."

"That's . . . upsetting." She was only half-listening now, sleep more enticing than talking about her relatives.

"It is. The accounts are Beaman Beaman Trevillian and Cooper, International Business Associates — "

"Warren Derrington's company?" Poppy sat up, no longer dozing.

"The same, I believe. And Sansome and Company. All very important accounts at Hadley and Grimes, according to what I've been told."

Poppy mulled this over. "Why, then, did Quentin Hadley assign them to a new member of the firm? Madison Moncrief was new there, and although he was good at what he did, and had excellent social connections, he was a novice in the company. I would have thought Hadley would have given it to one of their established partners. If nothing else, assuming those accounts were so important to the firm, you'd think they'd be in the hands of someone who had been with them for some years, not a newcomer, no matter how capable."

"That occurred to me, as well," Holte said, his form growing sharper than before. "Though what you can do with it, I'm not sure. Not yet."

"Nor am I." She stared at the far wall, her mind going over everything she had learned. "Saturday's a half-day for me, or it's supposed to be; so's Sunday. I'll call in tomorrow morning to say I won't arrive until ten; I'll do my story here and take it into the paper when I'm done. That should suffice, if the story lives up to expectations. Houghton ought to run it. If not, Lowenthal will use it for Monday's edition." She sat up very straight. "Ye gods. I forgot to ask Stacy when he'd be free to talk to Inspector Loring."

"You'll see him at breakfast, won't you?" Holte asked, adding innocently, "Stacy, not Loring."

Poppy scowled at him. "Who knows? Stacy's pretty unpredictable."

"Then warn Loring. You don't want Loring to think Stacy's avoiding him when he's only being spontaneous."

"Do you think he would?" Poppy asked in surprise. "Suspect him?"

"Police suspect people; it's their job." Holte slipped toward the door. "Don't hold it against him."

"Why do you go in and out doors like that? You don't open them, do you? Can't you pass through walls if you want to?"

"It's a habit, I guess, and it keeps anxiety in the household to a minimum. If I only passed through opened doors, the residents might think the house is haunted," said Holte, and left her alone with her thoughts and her dreams.

Poppy awoke from a fading nightmare the following morning at seven-thirty, yelped when she saw the time, and rushed out of bed to take a quick bath and then dress; her call to the Clarion was mercifully brief, and satisfactory to both Poppy and Elias Houghton, who said she wouldn't have to report to Lowenthal until noon, provided she had pages to turn in then.

She reached the breakfast room at five minutes past eight, dressed for work in a handsome spruce-green suit with an ecru blouse of crepe; she found Josephine lingering over coffee and a half-finished bowl of oatmeal; the room was filled with limpid sunlight that brightened everything in it, and there were a symphony of wonderful smells coming from the kitchen.

"Goodness, you're up late," she remarked as Poppy came to kiss her cheek. "Tobias ate and left almost an hour ago. He said he was sorry he missed dinner last night."

"Apologies, Aunt Jo. I was more tired than I realized," she said as if admitting to a flaw in her character. "Yesterday was a hectic day."

"I shouldn't wonder," said Josephine a little stiffly, ringing for Missus Boudon. "You'll need to have a substantial meal if you plan another such day."

The cook appeared promptly, favoring her left leg a little. "Finally! I was afraid no one would want food until lunch, except Missus Dritchner and your brother."

"Sorry, Missus Boudon. I overslept. And I'm hungry." Poppy sat down in her usual place.

"You want more than coddled eggs, then," Missus Boudon guessed aloud.

"If you please."

"I've made popovers for Mister Eustace," the cook announced. "Would you like a couple? There're plenty. I made a double batch."

"Eustace and his popovers," sniffed his mother.

"That would be wonderful. With cream cheese and your ginger preserves," said Poppy, "and a pot of tea, and if you have them, some of those duck-and-pork sausages." Just saying the words ignited her hunger and she had to stop herself from asking for more, knowing she would be unable to eat such a large breakfast."

"Tea will be in in five minutes, the rest in ten," Missus Boudon pledged, nodded to Josephine, and left the room.

"She's limping, though she tries to hide it," said Josephine as soon as the cook was out of the breakfast room. "I keep thinking that there ought to be something someone could do to protect her from that lout she married."

"Yes," Poppy agreed.

"He's not worthy of his wife." Josephine reached for the copy of the Constitution lying open next to her place at the table. "Eustace and Mister Derrington are still abed."

"We all had a late night, thanks to your planning," said Poppy, feeling a faint pang of guilt. "Except Missus North."

Josephine drank a little more coffee, and reached for the tall pot to refill her cup, her eyes focused on the middle distance. "Primrose has these spells from time to time. It comes with her age, you know. She's seventy-seven; she admits to seventy-two, but she's seventy-seven. What can you expect."

"Is she that old?" Poppy asked, a bit shocked. "I hadn't realized. I knew she must have been getting along in years, but seventy-seven!"

"Her son told me at Christmas that he's thinking of hiring a practical nurse for her." Josephine pursed her lips, indicating that she thought the plan was a necessary one.

"It's probably a good idea," said Poppy, unfolding her napkin and putting it in her lap.

"I believe I told Denton that," said Josephine, and would have enlarged upon her remark when the hall door opened and Stacy came in, perfectly groomed in a navy-blue suit, a white shirt, and navy-blue a silk tie. "Eustace. You're up."

"Warren'll be down in fifteen minutes." He went to kiss his mother good morning. "You're looking spritely today."

"No thanks to you," she said, trying to sound severe and instead sounding besotted.

"In my own defense, I have to tell you that I didn't expect the party to last so long. The Smiths were here until close to one."

"Do you have anything scheduled for today?" Josephine asked as she reached for her coffee cup again.

"I thought I might go 'round at the Moncrief's this afternoon; Warren'll come with me. Do a sympathy call, you know. Best to get it behind us. I don't want Julian Eastley to be the only man to show concern for Louise." He glanced at Poppy. "Care to accompany us, Coz?"

"Yes, please, if it's after two-thirty. I'll be back from the Clarion by then, and wholly at your disposal," Poppy said at once, so pleased with the invitation that she didn't ask herself why Stacy had extended it.

Missus Boudon brought in a small tray with a round crockery pot and a cup-and-saucer on it. "Here it is, Miss Poppy. Cream and sugar are on the table." As she set the tray down in front of Poppy, "And before you ask, Mister Eustace, there are popovers aplenty in the kitchen. You've only to tell me what you want with them, and how many. I have some of those duck sausages you like, and some thick-sliced bacon as well as fresh-delivered butter."

"You're a darling, Missus Boudon. I'd like four popovers to start with, with soft butter and honey. Can I have some of your blueberry jam, too? And four rashers of that thick-sliced bacon. There's coffee here already, and I can take a cup from the sideboard."

"Mind you take a saucer as well. I don't want to have Missus Flowers spending the day rubbing heat rings out of the finish, and complaining about the extra work. And there are coasters in the far left drawer of the buffet. If you want more than eight popovers, tell me now so that I can make more batter and get the pans in the oven." Her scolding was as dire as his mother's attempted reprimand.

"Word of honor, Missus Boudon," he said as the cook returned to the kitchen, and crossed the room to collect the cup and saucer. He chose the place on Josephine's right, sat down, and reached for the coffee pot. "Do you mind?" he asked as he was pouring. "I don't know how you can function in the morning without coffee."

"Please," said Josephine.

He reached for the sugar bowl and creamer. "Thanks so much for indulging me last night, Mother. Throwing such a dinner together on short notice can't have been easy, especially at a time like this."

Josephine beamed at his praise, but said, "It's Missus Flowers and Missus Boudon you should be thanking, you wretched boy. They did the bulk of the work. All I did was make 'phone calls. And thank Eliza while you're at it."

"Oh, I will," he promised, and grinned. When Missus Boudon brought Poppy her breakfast, he rose in protest. "Hey, how does she get popovers before I do?"

"She was here first, and I offered them," said Missus Boudon, doing her best not to be charmed by him.

"That's no excuse," Stacy said. "Poppy, give me one of your popovers; I'll give you one of mine when mine arrive."

Missus Boudon shook her head, smiling at Stacy's antics. "I'll be back directly," she said as she went through the swinging door to the kitchen.

There was a muted sound of the 'phone ringing in the front of the house; it was ignored.

"I know you," Poppy accused him jokingly. "You'll claim you never made such an offer and you'll keep all your popovers."

"I probably will," he agreed, then his eyes narrowed and for an instant there was something very unpleasant in his face. Then the genial smile returned.

"All right. Have one." She handed it to him, using her napkin. "I can always ask Missus Boudon for another dozen, so you won't have to part with any."

"Clever, clever, Coz," Stacy said, and winked at her. "Thanks." He picked up his knife and reached over to scoop a dollop of cream cheese from the small bowl that Missus Boudon had brought Poppy.

"No fair," Poppy said.

"Don't be greedy, Eustace," said Josephine, looking up from the pages of the Constitution.

"I'm not greedy, Mother; I'm hungry, and the butter in the ramekin is hard; my honey-and-butter isn't here yet." Stacy pulled the popover apart and spread the cream cheese over half the interior. "Heaven," he declared.

Poppy wanted to offer a rejoinder, but decided against it; Stacy was having too much fun.

"It says here," Josephine announced as if she hadn't heard the last, "that Judge Stephanson is retiring. About time."

"Oh, Mother, I didn't mean anything slighting by asking for — "

Josephine overrode him. "This isn't the kind of behavior I expect from you, Eustace, and it troubles me when you don't behave as you've been trained. Please try to be courteous while you're in this house."

"Sorry, Mother," said Stacy, just as Missus Boudon brought him his popovers. "Thank you, thank you, Missus Boudon," he said. "We were about to come to blows."

"Eustace!" his mother exclaimed.

"I'll make it up to you, Poppy," he said without a hint of remorse.

Poppy was about to express her doubts when Hawkins came to the breakfast room door. 'Sorry to interrupt. There's a 'phone call for you, Miss Poppy."

SEVENTEEN

Poppy sat down on the stairs next to the 'phone table in the entryway, hoping to have a little privacy while the conversation played out. "Poppy Thornton here."

"Miss Thornton, it's Inspector Loring." He was speaking softly, as if he were trying to keep from being overheard; there was an irregular buzz of conversation in the background of the call. "Are you free to speak?"

She found his tone of voice disquieting, but said, "For the moment, yes. Should I get my notebook?"

"Am I interrupting anything?"

"Stacy, my cousin," she said. "Making plans for the day."

"Would he eavesdrop?" The bluntness of the question suggested that it was an important issue.

"He might," she said, providing no other clues that a listener could follow; she listened for static on the line, and heard none. She decided that Holte was not about, and felt both relieved and regretful that he was not with them.

"Then perhaps we should meet somewhere where we can discuss this more privately," he said. "The walls might have ears where I am and you are."

"Where would you like to meet?" asked Poppy, greatly intrigued.

"Do you know the Viennese Coffee House? It's about four miles from your place. If you like, I could pick you up." This last was suggested as if it had just occurred to him.

"I know the place; if you're in a hurry, it might be best if you come by for me, otherwise I'll have to beg a lift from Stacy."

The sconce-light flickered and Holte said, "Developments?"

"Possibly," said Poppy, then told Loring, "Sorry; we have house guests as well as relatives staying. You're right. We should talk about this away from here."

"Ten minutes," Loring said.

Maestro appeared at the top of the stairs, back arched, tail flouffed, his whiskers abristle, muttering imprecations.

"Yes, I know," said Poppy.

"You know?" Loring asked her.

"I'm talking to the cat; he's taken umbrage at something invisible. Appropriate apologies." She sighed. "Ten minutes."

"I'll be there," he said.

With more optimism than certainty, she said, "I'll be ready." As she hung up, she wondered what it was that had Loring so willing to speak with her, but not, it would seem, with anyone else. She hurried up the stairs and to her room, pulling out a spring-weight coat — a new one with a dropped waist and a fur collar — and her larger handbag. She made sure she had pencils as well as her notebook, and then hurried to go downstairs to depart. She had a momentary twinge of ruefulness at not getting to finish her popovers, but that passed almost at once.

"Whither away, Coz?" asked Stacy from the door to the breakfast room, where he had been standing for a minute or so. His expression was ambiguous, half-smirk, half-suspicious.

"I'm going to have coffee with a policeman," she said. "The same one who wants to talk to you later on this morning."

"What fun for you," Stacy said flippantly. "Why in the name of everything tasteful, would you rather spend time with a policeman than your nearest and dearest?"

"My nearest and dearest is Toby, and well you know it," she said. "Do you want to spend time with Toby?" She had the satisfaction of seeing him flinch.

"Given that choice, I'd take the policeman," said Stacy. "Why does he want to talk to you, or you to him?"

"It will help me in my job, and him in his," she said, offended that he should denigrate her work because he knew it would annoy her. "It pays for reporters to stay on as good terms as possible with the police, especially when covering a crime."

"Then by all means, go off with your cop." He executed an ironic bow and went back into the breakfast room.

Hawkins, who had been watching this exchange, came to open the door for Poppy. "When shall we expect you back, Miss Poppy?"

"Probably before noon, since I'm pledged to make a sympathy call with my cousin after two-thirty," she said. "If I'm going to be later, I'll call." She smiled to show she was not bothered by Stacy's needling, then went out onto the front steps and looked about for a police car.

What arrived was a year-old Hudson, the windows partially rolled down; there were no police markings on it, or other paraphernalia to distinguish it from any other car on the street. Inspector Loring waved to her, pulled to the curb, set the break, and got out to go to open the door for her. "Thanks for doing this."

"I haven't done anything yet," she said as she got in. "But you're more than welcome; you're helping me, too, you know. Tell me what this is all about."

"Let's get underway first." He closed the door and went back around the car to get into the driver's seat. As they pulled away from the house, he said, "Do you know anyone named Percy Knott?"

"You mean the antiques dealer? Yes, I do." She paused, thinking that Holte had asked about Percy Knott the night before — one of those odd coincidences that made her skin crawl if she thought about it. "Not very well, of course, but well enough to talk to at parties. Knott bought my Uncle Alfred's business some years ago. A . . . friend and I were talking about him just last night." She managed an uneasy chuckle. "What about him?"

Deflecting her question, he asked one of his own. "What do you know about him, beyond his decorating business?" He double-clutched as he moved into third gear.

"He's somewhere between thirty-five and forty. Poor eyesight kept him out of the Great War, or so he claims, though there are rumors about him. He did something for the Department of State during the Great War. He wears very thick glasses. In spite of that, he's reckoned to be a good athlete.

He sings second tenor in his church choir. He's a Presbyterian. I've heard he is temperamental, which wouldn't surprise me, but I've never seen any sign of it. He's single and has always been. He travels a lot, mostly for his business. He moves in the best social circles and dines out frequently. Why?"

Loring didn't answer her, which was an ominous sign. "Do you know how business was going for him recently?"

"Business? No. There's no reason I would know. But it couldn't have been too bad; he had acquired some Egyptian chairs, and he had a pair of very fine Louis XV pieces that have been on display since January. They've attracted a lot of attention."

"What about Egyptian chairs? I assume they're antiques, but what makes them special?" Loring asked, sounding confused.

"You know; thanks to Howard Carter and King Tut everyone is mad for ancient — and not so ancient — Egypt. Everyone wants something with a Rameses or a Thutmoses on it. There's a lot of junk floating around out there, but Knott has some authentic pieces and is proud as a — " She stopped. "Has something happened to Percy?"

"I'm afraid so," said Loring.

"Not another so-called suicide?" she burst out, feeling offended.

"No; this time it's clearly murder. I'm just trying to work out the connections — if any — to the Moncrief and Poindexter cases, or case, if they're actually tied." Loring honked his horn at two large trucks. "You've got to admit that three murders in your stratum of society is pretty strange."

"Ye gods, yes," said Poppy quietly. "Put it that way, and it's damned odd." She made no excuse for her language. "What's happening?"

"That is what I hope we can work out together; nobody in the department knows much about the antiques trade," said Loring, slowing to a crawl to make his way through a cluster of delivery vehicles, half of them horse-drawn, that lined the street. "They have a parking lot in the rear," he said as he caught sight of the Viennese Coffee House.

Poppy nodded, watching while two muscular men wrestled large barrels down a ramp angled from the rear of their van. "They really work hard, don't they?" she asked inconsequently.

"Until their joints give out," said Loring. "My grandfather was a stevedore;

built like a bull, but rheumatism got hold of him, and he was finished a year later."

"You mean he died?"

"Yes. Nine years ago." He shrugged, extending his arm out the window to signal his right turn. "If you don't want to go into the coffee house, we could talk in the car."

"Oh, no, Loring," she said, wagging a finger at him. "You took me away from my second popover and I expect compensation for such a loss," she said as he parked his Hudson. It was tempting to let herself out and remind him that way that this was a business conversation, but she sensed he would be offended by such a gesture, so she waited for him to come to help her. She got onto the running board and took his hand for the step down to the graveled lot.

As his fingers closed on hers, he said suddenly and bashfully, "I want you to know I'm really grateful to you for all your help, though I probably show it badly. You see, usually when something happens with you high-class types, you close ranks and we can't get through the barriers to find out what really happened, try as we might. This time, we may actually be able to solve these crimes, thanks to you, and get the culprit instead of some poor schnook who gets thrown to us so we can save face."

Poppy blinked in astonishment. "You're welcome, I hope. But I don't think of myself as a high-class schnook."

"No; high-class schnooks don't," he said, releasing her hand and starting toward the restaurant, not bothering to see if she was coming with him.

Holte spoke in her ear. "I told you he liked you," he reminded her in a smug tone.

"He's got a strange way of showing it," she said softly, and frowned as she added, "If you're right."

"Just think of him as a six-year-old boy — if he wants to make friends, he comes up and punches you on the arm." Holte laughed reminiscently.

"Hey! Thornton!" Loring was holding the restaurant door open for her, looking perplexed.

"Sorry," she said. "I had a little pebble in my shoe." As improvisations went, she thought, this wasn't half bad.

The restaurant was more than two-thirds filled, though this was not a busy time of the morning. The waiters moved busily through the place, handling trays with the practiced grace of matadors handling capes. Clusters of lamps hung from the ceiling, looking very much like the gaslights of the last century, as did most of the decor of the place. The aroma of baking bread, vanilla, and nuts hung on the air in a warm, mouth-watering fog.

"Do you have one of your booths free?" Loring asked the maître d'.

"Of course, Inspector," he said with a supercilious gesture. "Follow me."

"You've been here before," Poppy observed, not expecting an answer.

They threaded their way through the tables to a booth tucked into an alcove; the tables on either side of the alcove were vacant. The alcove itself was a handsome little place: the walls were padded and tucked, the table was glossy, the napery was pristine ivory, the flatware was shiny enough to be sterling.

"Thank you, Claude," said Loring, as he helped Poppy to slide into her bench; the maître d' nodded and went back to his reception desk. "Do you want anything more than coffee, Miss Thornton?"

"Do I? With the pastries they make here, of course I want more than coffee," said Poppy with the assumption of indignation.

"We're going to be talking about a pretty brutal murder: you sure about wanting something to eat? Murder is never pretty, and this one was brutal. Not a very good sauce for breakfast." His eyes were looking old and tired again, so Poppy took his inquiry seriously.

Poppy hesitated. "We'll start with the coffee. I'll have a cheese-puff later, perhaps." She chided herself inwardly for being cowardly.

"Okay," he approved and looked up as the lamp above them flicked off and back on. "Bulb's going."

"Or needs to be tightened in the socket," said Poppy, thinking that it was very like Holte to include himself in this meeting; she wondered where he was: hanging from the light-fixtures? sitting on the table like the caterpillar in Alice in Wonderland on his mushroom? floating above them like an invisible cloud? She brought herself to attention, removing her notebook from her unfashionably large purse, and taking out a pencil. "So tell me what happened to Percy?"

"Last night, sometime between midnight and six a.m., someone broke into his house, bludgeoned Knott to death with a blunt instrument, and it would appear, stole a number of valuable pieces of furniture from his basement storeroom."

This news was shocking, and she made no effort to disguise her astonishment. "Are you sure?"

Inspector Loring shrugged. "There are places where there is no dust on the floor."

"Is that why you say it would appear that pieces were stolen?" she asked as she spread her napkin on her lap.

"Dust circles on cabinets, as well as the floor," said Loring. "The dust was minimal, but there was enough of it to show that until very recently, something was there that isn't there now. We have a couple guys over there comparing Knott's inventories to what actually remains." He signaled to a waiter. "Coffee for me, and for — "Deciding at the last moment to splurge, Poppy said, "Hot chocolate for me, and a menu."

"Yes'm," said the waiter, and sped away.

"Hot chocolate, not coffee, or even tea?" Loring mused. "I wouldn't have thought a tough girl reporter like you would like that." He very nearly smiled, but it did not last. "Are you sure you want something so sweet?"

"Yes; I don't drink it often," she said. "But it seems right for today." She leaned forward to speak softly. "About Percy?"

"Well," Loring said, getting back to the business at hand. "There was a lot of blood, all over the place, sprays and spatters and smears. There was even some on the ceiling. By the looks of it, Knott went down hard. Bruises on his forearms and abrasions on his hands show he put up quite a fight."

She steadied herself, reminding herself that this was why she was here. "Do you know anything about the attacker? Where did the attack take place? I gather it was in his home, but where in his home?" Before he could answer, she went on, "I know you're supposed to ask the questions, and I'm supposed to answer. I'll do what I can to answer you, but I can't not ask, now can I?"

He chuckled. "No, I suppose not. So tell me what you know about Knott, and I'll try to give you some information."

"Percy's . . . was a very private person, good socially, of course, but secretive. His private life was very private."

"What kind of secretive?" Loring watched her consider her answer.

"How do you mean?" she countered.

"Was he mysterious, or sneaky, or all gloss and no substance? You say he kept his private life private — does that mean his business and private lives were separate, or that he made a point of not allowing his associates to know what he did in his spare time?"

"Well, when it came to business, he kept confidences, the way most antique dealers do. I've been told he was tough in his dealings, but always provided value for money. He didn't haggle very much. You paid his price or you didn't get his wares. Uncle Alfred approved."

"Sorry, but he doesn't seem the type, you know what I mean? I mean, you say he sang in his church choir — that's not usually a hazardous thing to do," Loring said. "Can you tell me more?"

EIGHTEEN

POPPY TOOK A COUPLE SECONDS TO THINK WHAT SHE SHOULD SAY, AND BEGAN tentatively, "He moved his antiques around almost every day, changing what was being featured. He wasn't a weakling, in spite of the glasses. He swam regularly. I've heard it said that he was something of an outdoors-man — sailing and fishing — but that's second-hand at best." It was strange to think about Percy in the past tense, she realized, and immediately decided to ask Holte to find out what happened, and just as quickly decided against it. There was too much on her mind already.

"One of those wiry types," said Loring. "He looked to be quite fit. His home is remarkably neat. Most bachelors aren't so fastidious."

She nodded. "He is . . . was very much a gentleman, but there was something about him that made me think that his beautiful manners were a veneer more than with most people. I can't be specific, because he was polished enough to be — "

"You're saying he was slick?"

"More smooth than slick," Poppy told him. "Percy was very intelligent, and classically educated, with an encyclopedic knowledge of his field; he was doing graduate work in Europe when the Great War broke out and the Department of State got hold of him." She sat back a little, concentrating on what she was telling him. "After the war, he gave a series of lectures at All Souls Methodist Church on the histories of individual prized pieces in his collection, explaining how he was able to establish provenance for them. I went to one. My Aunt Jo attended them all."

"Do you think she'd talk to me?" Loring asked. "Maybe after I talk to your cousin?"

"I'll ask her when we get back. Why don't you come in with me? I'll introduce you and you can find out then if she'll talk to you." Poppy paused, then continued, "It'll be harder for her to say no if you're standing right in front of her."

The waiter appeared with his expertly balanced tray, deposited the two cups on the table, handed Poppy the menu, and went off.

"To your good health, Miss Thornton," said Loring as he picked up his cup.

"And to yours," said Poppy, doing the same. Her hot chocolate smelled wonderful, and although it was quite hot, she drank it enthusiastically. When she had consumed half the large cup, she put it down and said, "For someone in his position, there was very little gossip about Percy."

The light over their table flickered again.

This time Loring paid no attention. "The man who works for him — Miles Overstreet? What do you know about him?"

"Less than I know about Percy," Poppy replied. "He has a Masters of Fine Arts. He comes from Delaware, or perhaps Maryland."

Loring regards her skeptically. "Perhaps?"

"I told you I don't know much about him. I don't think I've met him more than twice, both times at Percy's shop when Aunt Jo went there; she used to call in every few months, as a kind homage to Uncle Alfred. She likes . . . liked Knott in spite of his reticence. He's not one . . . was not one to encourage conversation beyond a discussion of the pieces for sale." She had a little more of the hot chocolate. "Miles Overstreet usually worked in the office and didn't have much to do with commissions and customers. I don't want to mislead you, Inspector."

"Thanks; I don't want to be misled." He added a little cream to his coffee and took a sip. "Do you think Overstreet might have reason to attack Knott?"

"Ye gods, no," she exclaimed. "Miles Overstreet's probably the last man who would want to do Percy an injury."

Loring gave her a bemused stare. "Why do you say that?"

"Well, for one thing, Percy paid him very well," Poppy said.

"Did they get along, or don't you know?"

"I think they must have — Percy left the business in Overstreet's hands when he went on his buying trips. That suggests trust, if not affection. Do you mind if I make notes?"

"For the moment you may." He let her get herself set up and then asked, "Might there have been affection between them, beyond the usual sort that happens with associates?" He asked without any show of emotion one way or another, and he studied her response to his question.

Poppy took a little time to weight her answer. "People always think that about a bachelor who is cultured, don't they?" she countered, trying to maintain her aplomb. "I never saw any indication of it, but that isn't unusual for such persons, is it? Such alliances are against the law, aren't they?"

"That doesn't stop them from occurring," Loring remarked, once again watching her closely.

"What's your sense of those two?"

"No, it doesn't stop them, but — How do I say this? My cousin is of the opinion that Knott . . . was a ladies' man, but prefers . . . preferred . . . ladies of the evening. No need for emotional ties." Now Poppy felt awkward; to cover this, she opened the menu and read through the extensive list of pastries. "That's Stacy's opinion, not mine. He tends to assume that everyone keeps secrets, you see, and likes to discover those secrets. If you want to know more about that, you'll have to ask Stacy."

"I might, at that," said Loring. For a short while he said nothing more, his manner distracted, then, "The body was . . . messy. He'd been bludgeoned and stabbed. Blood was everywhere. I said that already, didn't I?" He looked away from Poppy. "I can't figure out if Knott knew his killer or not. Wyman is going to have a look at him this afternoon and let me know his primary impressions tomorrow morning."

"Is that going to be difficult? the autopsy?" She assumed that it would be, but wanted to draw him out some more.

"It isn't going to be easy. The injuries are too extensive." He looked away from her. "The whole thing is about the worst I've seen in a homicide, and that's saying a lot. It was almost as bad as the trenches were." He put one hand to his eyes, which was more distressing to Poppy than anything he had said.

"When you can tell me what Wyman says, will you?" She knew she could be pushing her luck, but it was important to make the most of her opportunities.

He stared at her. "I'll tell you whatever I can, so long as I can keep some of it off the record."

The sincerity of this pledge took her by surprise, and she faltered. "Oh. That's good of you, Inspector. Thank you." To cover her sudden awkwardness, she signaled for the waiter and asked for a cream-puff, although she was not sure she could eat it — Loring had been right about that.

"And bring me one of those twisty doughnuts," Loring added to the order as if to make this easier for her.

The waiter nodded, picked up the menu, and hastened off to bring their selections.

"I hope the pastries are as good as this place smells," Poppy said, wanting to make their discussion less troubling than it had been.

"Oh, better. You'll like the cream-puff, I'm convinced of it." He did not quite smile, but his eyes crinkled.

A silence fell between them, and when it stretched out too long, and Poppy decided to venture a new topic. "So, will you want to come in and meet my aunt and my cousin when we're done here?"

"It's a little irregular, but so's this meeting," Loring answered. "It could be useful to talk to your relatives; it could even provide me an entré to the upper crust, so I guess I'd better. I hope I make a favorable impression." He drank more coffee and then held it out for a refill as the waiter returned with their pastries.

"I think it's likely that you will," said Poppy, pleased that he would be so sensible.

He shrugged. "Not everyone wants to deal with the police. We'll see how it goes."

"Do you want to know anything more?" Poppy asked, as the waiter set a salad plate in front of her with a cocoanut-sized cream-puff before her, whipped cream atop it as well as within.

"Yes, but just now, I want to have breakfast." His doughnut was the size of a pie plate and it glistened with a sugar glaze. He used his fork to cut a wedge out of it.

Poppy took her cue from him, and used her fork to cut into the cream-puff; the filling oozed out in several directions; she scraped it up with her fork and tasted it. "Marvelous," she said as the sweetened, vanilla-flavored whipped cream spread over her tongue.

"Better than your breakfast popover?" Loring asked, glancing up at the flickering light once again.

"I wouldn't say that, but this is excellent, and different from breakfast pastries at home." She bit into the morsel she had cut away, and tried to think of what to ask. By the time she swallowed the piece of cream-puff, she was ready. "May I file a story on Knott as well as your current investigation of Madison Moncrief's death?"

"Not yet. But I'll give you the go-ahead before nightfall." He concentrated on cutting up the doughnut.

She realized he would not be worn down with questions, so she had some more of the cream-puff. "May I be present while you talk to my aunt? She's more likely to cooperate with you if I join you."

"Let me think about it while we eat," he said, and turned his attention to his doughnut.

"All right," said Poppy, and dug into what remained of her extravagant cream-puff.

By the time they left the Viennese Coffee Shop, a certain camaraderie had been established between them; the drizzle had slacked off and there were patches of sky showing through the clouds. They went out to his car; he let her in the passenger door then went around to the driver's side, let himself in and prepared to engage the engine. "It's good of you to help me on this case. I don't know how I would be able to get through the social tangle without you." As he drove out of the parking lot, he turned to her before he went onto the street. "No matter how things go with your family, I want you to know that I'm grateful to you."

"I'm glad to do it," Poppy said, doing her best to sound confident.

"And if you'll promise you won't interject questions, I'll let you be present while I talk to your aunt — assuming she is willing to talk to me at all." He double-clutched down as he neared the intersection ahead. "That should reassure your cousin."

"We'll see," Poppy said after thinking over his offer.

"You've got to do better than that, Poppy," Loring said.

"You haven't met Aunt Jo, and although you're clever, Stacy will take pride in outmaneuvering you." She folded her arms and stared out the window at the cloudy day, and the passing traffic, trying to make up her mind about her planned call on Louise Moncrief that would happen in the afternoon, and how much she should tell Lowenthal in advance.

"Penny for your thoughts," Loring said as he turned onto Poppy's street, and began looking for an open place to park.

"I'm just trying to sort out a couple of things. I need to turn in a story today." She looked at him, and saw a fixed look in his eyes. "What is it?"

"That story of yours — you'll have to be careful what you say in it."

"I understand that. I'll be heedful."

"Okay. But there're a lot of things that you've heard that you shouldn't report yet." He drew up in front of the Dritchner house and parked.

"Well, I'll do my best," she said, and prepared to get out of the car as he set the hand brake. "But Aunt Jo can be very protective of her youngest son."

"How do you mean?"

Poppy sighed. "She doesn't want anyone to speak the least ill of Stacy, or even to question his activities. If she thinks that's what you're doing, she'll be difficult."

"I'll keep that in mind. Let me get the door," he said, and opened his. "I don't want your aunt to think that I'm a complete barbarian."

Poppy smiled, and waited until he had opened her door to say, "That's probably past praying for. She thinks all policemen are barbarians." She took his proffered hand and got out, holding onto her purse. "I'll make sure Aunt Jo knows that you're trying to solve a crime that was committed on one of her social circle. That may help."

As they went up the walkway, Poppy was aware of someone watching them from the front parlor; after looking at the size of the figure behind the curtains, she assumed it was Stacy and felt a twinge of upset. She used the knocker instead of the doorbell, which had been on the fritz for the last few days, and waited to see who would open the door.

NINETEEN

"GOOD MORNING, MISS," SAID HAWKINS AS HE PULLED THE FRONT DOOR OPEN. "It's good to have you back." He glanced at Loring and raised his brows.

"This is Inspector Loring, Hawkins. He's investigating the circumstances of Madison Moncrief's death. I've asked him to come with me so that he may speak with my aunt and my cousin." She stepped into the entry hall ahead of Loring, and looked about. "Would you tell me where my aunt is?"

"She's in the music room," said Hawkins, so neutrally that Poppy wondered what had happened while she had been out. "Would you like me to escort you and your . . . guest to her?"

"I know the way," said Poppy, stating the obvious.

"Of course, Miss," Hawkins said, and stood aside.

"I assume my cousin and Mister Derrington are still in," Poppy added over her shoulder as she started toward the corridor that went toward the east wing of the house.

"They are. Mister Derrington is in the study; I'm not sure where Mister Eustace is." Hawkins nodded and moved off in the direction of the dining room.

A wall-sconce light in the corridor flickered as Poppy approached it, and she winced. What was Holte up to now? she wondered. "The music room is at the end of this corridor, and takes up the whole of one side of the wing to the other." It had occasionally been the setting for private concerts, as well as small dances, but they had not had one of either since the 'Flu had struck. "It isn't used much, these days."

"Have you had trouble with the power?" Loring asked as he followed her down the corridor.

"Hasn't everyone?" Poppy responded, trying to discover what Chesterton Holte was up to now. "The house is old; that probably has something to do with it."

"It's all this late rain," said Loring, and paused a step behind Poppy as she knocked on the door on her left.

"Aunt Jo? May I come in?" Poppy asked, hearing some soft, inexpert strains of Haydn coming through the door.

The playing stopped. "Certainly you may," Aunt Jo called out.

Poppy turned the doorknob, and motioned to Loring to come with her. "I have someone with me," she said as she entered the music room, moving slowly and quietly.

There was a Chickering square grand piano on the north wall, and Josephine was sitting at it, a dull-red silk shawl around her shoulders over a Prussian blue woolen dress with a broad lace collar and cuffs; the room was somewhat chilly, and the floor heater had not been turned on. Duchess was curled up on a near-by footstool, snoring gently. "Who have you brought here, Poppea?" her aunt asked without turning. Since the room was large it echoed a little, making her voice sound hollow.

"I have Inspector Loring of the Philadelphia Police Department with me, Aunt Jo. He would like to . . . talk to you about the Moncrief — "

"Oh, dear," said Aunt Jo, turning on the piano bench enough to be able to see her niece and the policeman.

Poppy went over to the ornate heating grate in the floor. "I'm going to turn on the heat," she announced, and knelt down to turn the key. "How can you stand to have it so cold, Aunt Jo? I don't see how you can play."

"I haven't paid attention," she said grandly, then sighed. "But you're probably right. A little more heat wouldn't hurt us." She turned to Loring. "I suppose I should welcome you to our home."

"Good morning, Missus Dritchner," said Loring, coming forward, and waiting for Aunt Jo to offer her hand. When she did not, he took a moment to remove his notebook from his inner jacket pocket, and with it, a Parker fountain pen. "I hope you will not object if I make a few notes."

"I imagine you'll do it whether I agree or not." She gave him a baleful stare and folded her arms.

This was not a very promising beginning, Poppy thought, as she pulled up a pair of upholstered chairs. "Why don't we all be more comfortable? The room will be a bit warmer in a matter of minutes."

Loring kept his eyes on Josephine. "Do you mind, Missus Dritchner?"

"If you must." Aunt Jo turned to Poppy. "Is that necessary?"

"For me, it is," said Poppy brightly. "It's sit or pace."

Aunt Jo sighed, and nodded her permission. "Is this going to take long?"

"That is more up to you than to me," said Loring respectfully as he went to sit down. "I know this is unpleasant — violent death always is — but with your help, we can have an opportunity to solve this mystery with as little upset as possible." He sat down, sitting very straight in his chair.

"What is it you want to know, Inspector? I will do my best to give you a complete and truthful answer. I know my civic duty." Aunt Jo sounded very put-upon but condescendingly willing to help. "I'll do my best, provided that you do not ask anything of a personal nature."

Loring gave a slight nod. "Thank you, Missus Dritchner." He paused, in case she wanted to say something more. When she remained steadfastly silent, he shook his head. "I don't want to offend you with any question I may ask."

"Then, Inspector, we are doomed from the start. I would prefer not to have to answer anything in such distasteful matters." She made her most depressive stare.

"Well, unfortunately, I have to pursue the case — it's my job, I'm afraid." He cleared his throat. "The sooner we begin, the sooner it can be over. You have known the Moncrief's a long time, I understand."

"Madison's mother and I were close friends right up until the day she died. At one time, we hoped that Poppea and Madison might make a match of it when they were children, but it wasn't to be; once Madison met Louise, it was obvious that he had eyes for no one else. Eustace introduced them, you know." She said this as if she were reading from a pamphlet on gardening.

"Did he?" Poppy asked, feeling acutely self-conscious after hearing her aunt speak about the plans Aunt Jo had once had for her.

"Oh, yes," said Aunt Jo, warming to her subject. "It was shortly after you left for college, so you did not have to face any mortification because of it. I asked Eustace not to say anything about it to you. I hoped to spare you the embarrassment."

Poppy wanted to pursue this, to ask Aunt Jo why she had been so hesitant, but she remembered what she had promised Loring back over their pastries, and kept silent.

Loring made a couple of notes, and asked, "How long ago was that?"

"Seven years ago. They — Madison and Louise — married six years ago . . . six years and four months, more or less. It was a New Year's Eve wedding. Their engagement was very short." Aunt Jo made a fussy gesture with one hand. "It was Madison who wanted to marry quickly; his courtship was very determined."

"Why was he so insistent?" Loring asked.

"I don't know." Aunt Jo sighed again, and reached out to stroke Duchess. "No one did."

"Can you tell me anything about his circumstances when he married? I understand that Madison Moncrief had a generous inheritance by then, but I'd like a confirmation, if you can provide one. I found an article on the inheritance in the Constitution; it was very informative." His manner was so deferential that Poppy almost laughed.

"Yes. He had almost a million-and-a-quarter dollars from his grandfather when he was twenty-one; a considerable sum for any man to inherit. Many young men would not handle so much money wisely, but Madison was no fool, at least where money was concerned. He met Louise when he was twenty-three . . . almost twenty-four. Everyone thought him a good catch."

Loring made some more notes. "Do you know how much money he had then?"

"Heavens, no." Josephine pulled her shawl more closely around her. "Only vulgar persons care about such things. He didn't have to work, you know. He was well-provided for, and had enlarged his legacy by a considerable amount: that is the totality of my knowledge."

"Do you know about any of his investments?" Loring inquired at his most deferential.

"My son Eustace might; I have no such information." Aunt Jo almost sniffed. "He is out just now, Eustace is. He left about twenty minutes ago."

There was a knock on the door, and Missus Flowers asked, "May I bring in some tea and coffee, Missus Dritchner?"

Aunt Jo looked up, remembering her responsibilities as a hostess, no matter how reluctant.

"I suppose so. Come ahead, Missus Flowers."

The door opened and Missus Flowers carried in a tray with a coffee pot and a teapot along with a creamer and a sugar bowl filled with cubes; there were cups for three and a plate of shortbread cookies. "Where would you like these, Missus Dritchner?" she asked.

Josephine motioned to the coffee-table on the south wall of the room. "Over there, if you would, Missus Flowers," she said with sublime indifference.

"Thank you, Madame; I knew you would want to offer something to your guest," said Missus Flowers as she set her tray down on the cabinet on the west wall; it contained music manuscripts and part copies.

"Very good, Missus Flowers. I will send for you if I need you." She waved her dismissal.

Missus Flowers gave a nod and left the three people alone in the music room.

"Would you like me to pour you a cup of tea, Aunt Jo?" Poppy offered, getting up from her chair.

"I suppose it would be prudent," Josephine replied in her abstracted way.

"And you, Inspector? Coffee, with a little cream?"

Loring almost smiled. "That would be very nice; thank you." He glanced at Poppy to gauge her response to his self-deprecating manner.

Poppy tried to ignore him; she went to the cabinet, and placed one of the cups on the stack of saucers. She poured out the coffee and added a dollop of cream; this she brought to Loring and set on the broad arm of his chair. "And what may I get for you, Aunt Jo?"

"Tea, of course, one sugar."

"And would you like one of the shortbread cookies?"

Josephine straightened up and gathered her shawl about her with formidable dignity. "I would like two of them, and well you know it," she said, and added a mollifying, "It's good of you to do this, Poppea."

"No problem, Aunt Jo. You've been kind enough to speak with Inspector Loring, and that deserves my gratitude." She returned to the cabinet to prepare a cup and saucer to her aunt's order, all the while hoping that there would be something useful gained from this most disconcerting interview.

"As an old friend of the family, do you know if Madison was happy in his work? You said he didn't need the job, so I've been assuming he must have been." He lifted his cup and took a cautious sip.

"He liked having something useful to do, and he had a skill for investing. Although the last time I saw him — it was at Eulalle Kinnon's Christmas party — he seemed worried. I thought it was about Louise's expecting, which had just been announced, but now I'm not so sure."

"Why is that?" Loring said as he wrote another note. "What made you change your mind?"

"His dying, of course," said Josephine.

"One sugar?" Poppy asked, as much to fill the silence that followed her aunt's answer as to confirm her request. She took two of the shortbread cookies and set them in the saucer before she poured out the strong English variety that Aunt Jo preferred during the day.

"That will be fine," said Aunt Jo in her best lofty manner.

Poppy took the cookies and tea to her aunt, setting them down on the side of the music stand. "It's hot."

"Well, of course it is," said Aunt Jo, and glared at Inspector Loring.

Poppy knew that when Aunt Jo started of coursing it meant she was put out, so Poppy went silently back to the cabinet to prepare her own cup of tea; she did not hear the first few words of Loring's next question.

" . . . Madison's view of becoming a father?"

"What on earth has that to do with his death?" Aunt Jo answered.

"Perhaps nothing, but it could be important," said Loring patiently.

Josephine shook her head. "I haven't a notion of his view of fatherhood. It's not the sort of thing I ask men."

"Was he pleased?" Loring waited for her answer. "Was he boasting, or proud, or — "

"Louise was very happy," Aunt Jo said, making no excuse for interrupting him. "I assumed that Madison was equally so. He did open the good

Champagne to celebrate, Louise told me, and that shows you he wasn't displeased. But he was anxious about her pregnancy; so many men tend to fret about it when their wives are expecting."

Poppy came back to her chair and sat down, her tea, like Loring's coffee, balanced on the arm. "I think Stacy could tell you more about Madison's feelings."

"I'll bear that in mind, Missus Dritchner." Loring scribbled in his notebook, then once more addressed Josephine. "Did the marriage seem happy — as an old friend of Madison's mother, had she told you anything about problems that she was aware of? Anything recently?"

This time Aunt Jo answered at once. "Not recently, but when they decided to marry. His mother was upset by the short engagement; she felt it looked peculiar."

"In what way?" Loring followed up.

"Well, it looked capricious, of course, and they — Louise and Madison — didn't know each other very well when they wed. A long engagement allows for second thoughts, doesn't it, and, of course, a more splendid wedding, both of which his mother was hoping would happen — he would reconsider, and if he did not end the engagement, at least there could be a glorious wedding, as any mother would wish." Aunt Jo took one of the shortbread cookies and bit into it delicately, pursing her lips as she chewed.

"And do you think Madison had second thoughts?" Loring prompted.

After she had swallowed, Josephine said, "Not yet. But in time, I think it would have been likely: Louise is a very . . . vivacious young woman, and enjoys being in society more than Madison does . . . did. He — Madison — was willing to have her go about with men who served as her escort — my son Eustace was one of them — and while everyone knows that Julian Eastley is harmless, there have been a few others she had been seen with who are not. I do not include my son in those numbers."

"Do you think that Madison was jealous?" Loring spoke levelly, no hint of disapproval in his manner.

"I would not be surprised if he were." It was plain that was all Josephine was going to say on the matter.

Loring drank more of his coffee. "Did Madison have any enemies that you know of?" He held up his hand to stop Josephine from answering yet. "Or did anyone question his probity? Was any part of his life under scrutiny?"

"None that said so out loud, or not where I could hear them." Josephine sniffed to show her dismissal of such an absurd notion. "I know that he and Ralph van Rijn didn't get along, but, of course, Ralph doesn't get along with most people."

"What was the problem between them — do you know?"

"They disagreed on financial and political issues, and Ralph wrote a harangue about it." She made a tisking sound.

"What does van Rijn do that his opinion would attract attention — if it did attract attention? From what you just told me, it must have led to some discussion."

"He's a critic, of course. He publishes regularly in the Philadelphia Review — not that anybody pays him much attention," said Josephine, appearing unimpressed by that distinguished monthly magazine.

"Why did he dislike Moncrief?" Loring's pen was poised over his notebook.

"Ralph doesn't approve of obviously successful men under the age of forty," said Josephine with a gesture of disapproval. "And he doesn't have a much higher opinion of successful men less than fifty."

Loring looked down at his notebook, closed his pen, nodded once, and said, "Thank you very much, Missus Dritchner; I realize this has been unpleasant for you, and I apologize for that. You've been most helpful. And thank you for the coffee." He put the pen and notebook back in his pocket, rose, and took his cup and saucer back to the tray on the cabinet. "I would not have pressed you as I did if it didn't involve a death." His countenance was sympathetic.

"You must do your job, of course," said Aunt Jo, her frostiness thawing a trifle. "I'm happy to do anything I can to help discover why Madison died."

Poppy took her cup and saucer back to the tray, a faint smile curving her lips; she was amused by the way Inspector Loring had buttered her Aunt Jo up, and how successful that buttering had been. "Thanks, Aunt Jo," she said as she turned away from her aunt and prepared to leave with Loring. "It was very kind of you to speak with the inspector."

"He's very good," Holte said from behind her right shoulder. "He could have been a newsman."

"Ye gods! Don't do that," Poppy whispered, concealing her jump of surprise by rattling her cup.

"My apology," said Holte.

"You ready, Miss Thornton?" Loring asked from the door.

"Yes," Poppy said, and went to join him, going through the door he held open for her; in the corridor, she found Hawkins waiting for her.

"Mister Eustace asked me to tell you and the inspector that he has had to go out. It couldn't be helped; it's urgent. Something to do with Mister Derrington. He will pick you up in an hour, when you'll visit Missus Moncrief. He wants you to be ready on time." He ducked his head as a sign that was all he had to say.

Loring closed the door behind them, and turned to Poppy. "Then I'll arrange to talk with him later. I'll let you get on with your day, Poppy." He seemed unflustered, but the fatigue was back in his eyes.

"I'll call you after we see Louise." Poppy went with him to the front door and opened it for him. "I hope you will forgive my aunt her conduct."

"She thinks the police are beneath her," said Loring, and chuckled. "I think she's charming." With this surprising announcement, he went out the door and down the steps whistling, at the curb he stopped, and turned back toward her. "Tell your cousin I'll see him tomorrow."

"I will," Poppy called out before she closed the door.

TWENTY

"Then what the devil is going on?" Lowenthal demanded, his voice loud enough to be heard by Josephine, who had left the music room and now was in one of the large chairs in the sitting room, away from the telephone table in the entry hall; she was knitting, with Duchess curled on the floor at her feet.

"As I've told you, I don't know, boss," said Poppy, keeping her voice low, not wanting to have to explain the conversation when she hung up. "I've arranged with Loring to get a briefing on Knott's death after he interviews my cousin, which he is planning to do tomorrow. He told me the basics while we were at the Viennese Coffee House, but I'll try to find out more. And I'll do what I can to learn more about Moncrief this afternoon."

"So what did you worm out of the Inspector over your chocolate and coffee? And is that all he was willing to buy for you?" He laughed ponderously, then got back to business. "Do they see any connection to the Moncrief murder? Knott isn't quite the same, but there are enough things in common about both men that you can mention them in your report, at least that's what Constable Bachus told me half an hour ago."

Constable Bachus was known to be a primary source for most police cases, and was well rewarded for his dependability; Poppy was not surprised to learn that Lowenthal had already spoken with the cooperative constable. "I'll ask Loring," she said.

"Well, see what more you can get him to tell you. After all, you're doing him a favor, aren't you?"

"What would you like me to include?" Poppy asked, trying not to sound tired.

"Anything that seems to be the same about the cases. Not just in the deaths themselves — those are different — but there may be some commonalities that we can hang a group of articles on. For example: were there some missing objects at the scene? If so, what? What about the state of the body? How much did the cop tell you about that?" Lowenthal asked. "By the way, how was the food?"

"The cream-puff was the size of a cantaloupe, and yummy. I was just sorry we had to talk about murder while I ate it." She took a more serious tone. "As to the murder, I have nothing concrete so far; the autopsy hasn't been done yet. Percy Knott was found dead in his home, bludgeoned to death, nothing about it suggestive of suicide, which was the case with Moncrief, though it's clear that Madison didn't kill himself. The police are searching for clues to determine how he was killed. He may have been drugged, but that hasn't been confirmed. When Loring questioned my aunt, he confined himself to background on Madison Moncrief; neither of us said anything useful to either of us about Percy Knott, or if we did, I'm not aware of it. And before you tell me to try to find out more, Inspector Loring wouldn't be more specific than I've already told you. The coroner hasn't been much more forthcoming. Inspector Loring has assured me he still needs my help, so I should have something more concrete later today, after my cousin and I call on Louise Moncrief. I'll try to make the evening edition if I get anything worthwhile. If I can't get anything tonight, I'll have something tomorrow."

"Pity, with two ts," said Lowenthal.

"Dreadful business," Josephine sniffed as she stopped to count her stitches; she had been listening to Poppy's side of the conversation. "I don't know whether you should be involved in any part of it."

Poppy resisted the urge to respond to her aunt, and said to Lowenthal. "Do I report to you on this, even though it's the weekend?"

"You report to me," he snapped. "You get some kind of solid information to me, and I'll make sure it's posted, so no one else gets assigned to the story. But you've got to perform for me. It's hard enough to keep the owners from ordering one of the regular crime reporters on the case without you skimping on material. If you don't turn in a piece I can use, I'll have to hand the story off to someone else."

There it was: the threat of being sent back to the Society page. Poppy swallowed her indignation as best she could, and concentrated on trying to keep her assignment. "Why do that, when I already have my foot in the door with the people involved. So far I've been able to talk to people most of your reporters can't reach. I think I can run with this, if you don't keep me on too close a leash."

Lowenthal grunted. "You got a point there, Thornton. You're right. Stay on your story, but keep me informed at every turn. No wildcat ventures. Your advantage cuts both ways: if anything happens to you, your entire upper-crust will slam the doors against us. You got that?"

"Thank you, boss," She said, keeping her sarcasm in check; then she paused, not wanting to rouse Josephine's indignation. "So you do want a piece for Monday morning in addition to the story for this evening? By the way, thank you for the extension of my deadline. Once I talk to Louise, I'll have a better story for you. I should be able to have the Monday story to you by tomorrow afternoon. If nothing else, this evening I can do a couple hundred words on Louise's state of mind in the wake of Madison's death."

"Yes, I want something as soon as you can get it to me — say, about five hundred words, if you can get enough information out of the police to fill up the column with substantial information beyond the widow's grief. Make sure you confirm as much as you can. Two sources, always. People like the Moncriefs will sue if you get anything wrong, so keep your speculation to a minimum, and identify it for what it is. If you can find anything on the money factor, that should help. People like to read about money; don't go looking for scandal unless you have impeccable sources for reporting it." He said this in a calmer voice, and added almost appreciatively, "I hate to make you work on Sunday, with family and all."

"I don't mind," said Poppy, noticing the table lamp trying to sputter on; she wondered what Holte might be able to find out about Beaman Beaman Trevillian and Cooper, or Sansome and Company, or Hadley and Grimes. She wanted to find a way to get Stacy to talk about International Business Associates.

"When do you see the police again?" His question was sharp.

"Later today, or at least we're supposed to talk. Tomorrow we'll probably meet when he comes to talk to Stacy."

Aunt Josephine sighed, and began another row of knit-one-purl-two. "I wish you didn't have to talk to that dreadful man."

Which dreadful man, Poppy asked herself: Inspector Loring, or Lowenthal? "Sorry, boss," she said to the receiver. "I didn't hear that last."

"I said, are you certain that this guy is being square with you?"

"I believe so, since he's looking for information from me as much as I am from him. He knows if he isn't forthcoming with me, I won't be with him." She rubbed her eyes, feeling frustrated by the whole morning.

"Call me after you talk with Moncrief's widow, and after you talk to Loring; I'll want to hear everything you find out," Lowenthal told her. "Between her and the cop, you should have something useful by then." He made a kind of growl, meaning he was thinking. "We'll work out how to take the next steps."

"Yes, sir," Poppy said, "I'll call you before four."

"Damn right you will," he said, and hung up.

Poppy set the telephone back on the table, then turned to her aunt. "Sorry."

"I suppose it can't be helped. But what a rude man he is." She sniffed and once again took up her knitting.

"He certainly can be," said Poppy, and got up from her chair.

"I don't understand why you put up with his behavior."

"He's my employer," Poppy explained. "And I like working for him, in spite of his manner."

"But you don't have to — "

Duchess got to her feet, growling softly at an empty place in the room, her hackles rising.

"Oh, lie down, you foolish creature," Aunt Jo told her dog. "There's nothing there. You're as bad as Maestro."

The lights flickered again, this time near Poppy's aunt. Duchess woke up and began to bark and bounce on her front legs.

"I don't know what's got into her. She's been on the verge of hysterics for nearly a week, barking at nothing and carrying on. I suppose I should take her to the vet — she probably needs worming." Aunt Jo went back to knitting. "Pets can be such a trial."

Poppy could not help but feel embarrassed on behalf of Duchess. "She isn't doing this to annoy you — she's protecting you, Aunt Jo. Do you think she could be hearing something we can't?"

"Hearing what?" Aunt Jo asked, sounding perplexed.

"I don't know. I can't hear it. But dogs have keener hearing than we do." Poppy was doing her best to sound rational. "Cats, too," she added, thinking of Maestro's response to Chesterton Holte's presence.

"Duchess! Lie down," said Aunt Jo to her spaniel; Duchess continued to growl at the empty air. "I don't know why I bother — she never minds."

"You could let Noah Bemis train her," Poppy suggested. "Missus Collier swears by him, so does Lydia Gradissen."

"Iona Collier has an Italian cook, and as for Lydia — well!" Aunt Jo declared, dismissing the idea of a trainer for Duchess.

Duchess calmed down, made a yap of satisfaction, sniffed the air, then toddled back to Josephine's chair and curled up again at her feet.

"Whatever it was, it's gone now," Poppy said, and gave her aunt a faint smile. "I have to get some work done before Stacy gets back — he'll probably want to leave at once."

"He probably will; he's always been impatient," Aunt Jo declared fondly, then sighed. "Of course, if you must, you must."

"Sorry, Aunt Jo," said Poppy. "But, yes, I must." She blew her aunt a kiss and left her to her knitting. As Poppy climbed the stairs, bound for the library, she heard Holte speak in her ear, his voice so low she could not make out the words. "What do you want?" she whispered.

"I'll wait until we're alone." The voice was a bit louder, but still hushed.

"You tell me no one can hear you but me," she reminded him.

"That's true, but once the library door is closed, we can talk more readily, and a little louder." His voice faded.

"Have it your way," Poppy said as she reached the top of the stairs and made the turn toward the library. She knew she should begin work on the piece about Louise Moncrief, filling in the basic information about her before the coming visit, but she wanted to find out what was on Holte's mind, so as soon as she opened the door to the library, she went toward one of the three occasional chairs near the fireplace rather than take her place at the desk. She selected the wing-backed one, and sat down, addressing the room as she did. "All right. What do you want to tell me?"

Gradually Chesterton Holte materialized, more or less sitting in the nearest of the other two chairs. "It's about the Knott killing. It looks like you've got yourself into a situation."

"What kind of situation?"

"A dangerous one," said Holte somberly. "You could be poking a hornets' nest, Poppy."

"Oh." Poppy was startled, as much by his demeanor as by what he was telling her. "What do you know about it?"

"A fair amount, but I don't know how much will be useful to you." He stared at the stove. "This is a very tangled problem, far more than I originally supposed."

"You mean the Hadley and Grimes connection — if there is one?"

Holte faltered. "That's part of it. Those three companies are . . . troublesome."

It was going to be one of those conversations, Poppy thought. "How do you know this? Is it one of your dubious sources again?"

"If you want to call them that, since I can't provide any confirmation in any form that your editor would accept, but that doesn't lessen the risk you're taking; there are higher stakes emerging than I anticipated," he admitted, then launched into his news. "James Poindexter told me about doing business with Knott, and not in antiques, or not directly."

"How was it indirect, then?" she asked him.

"The antiques were tangential to his real work," Holte said.

"What is that supposed to mean?" Poppy asked, becoming intrigued.

Holte looked over his shoulder as if he expected someone to interrupt them. "It was the nature of Knott's work that he traveled with a fair amount of money, in cash, and occasionally he did this for some of his friends as well, under circumstances that won't tolerate close scrutiny. Your cousin is one of those who has used Knott's accesses to make deals with some of the men in the oil business and the covert antiquities trade in the Middle East. There are other transactions we're starting to check out. His antiques business was legitimate, but it wasn't his only occupation. The same might be said of your cousin."

"Stacy, involved in something shady?" Poppy asked, more curious than alarmed.

"Do you think it impossible?" Holte asked with more sympathy than Poppy had expected. "I don't know the extent of his activities, but Poindexter swore it was true. Knott admitted as much, as well, in general terms."

"And what would he — oh, yes, the financial records, and contracts." Poppy made a gesture of her understanding. "He would have access to such things, wouldn't he? Poindexter would."

"And so would Knott," Holte concurred.

"Is Stacy deeply involved, or on the fringes?" Poppy made herself ask.

"I'm not sure. Neither was Poindexter. Moncrief wouldn't discuss it."

"Knowing Stacy, he would regard the whole thing as a game; he sees most of life that way," Poppy said, giving a tight little nod.

"That wouldn't astonish me. He strikes me as someone who likes matching wits with others," Holte said. "Your cousin would make a good spy."

Poppy tried to smile without success. "You would know."

"Yes, I would." His admission was more morose than smug. He dropped a little lower in his chair, his arms floating above the arms of the chair like a water-strider on the surface of a lake. "According to both Poindexter and Moncrief, Knott always found ways to account for the money: the antiques market is volatile, and there are number of ways that documentation can be altered without raising many questions for doing it."

"And you say Poindexter told you this? Moncrief, too? In the dimension of ghosts?" Poppy inquired, trying to decide what credence, if any, that she should give to these revelations. "How do I get confirmation on this? Where do I start?" She waited for him to answer, trying not to chafe while she did.

"Poindexter and Moncrief. Moncrief may have discovered some irregularities in Knott's records that troubled him. Poindexter had done so." He frowned. "Knott did some things for your government during the last days of the Great War, and he maintained many of the contacts he made then after the war was over, not all of them above-board."

"Yes, I assumed that was what you meant. I suppose that ought to surprise me, but I don't think it does," Poppy said, wondering how she would confirm what he was telling her, and what — if anything — she should tell Lowenthal. "Stacy has always liked getting the advantage over others. Knott doesn't seem the type to do such things, at least not as a game."

"From what Poindexter said, there have been questions about Knott for some time, but most of them expressed in hints and whispers; he had been a very dangerous person during the war." Holte stared up at the ceiling. "I should probably advise you to get out of this."

"You already have. But I don't care if this is dangerous — I'm already risking my career on the story." Poppy looked at him with strong purpose in her eyes.

"Will you let me try to find out how far the corruption goes before you push any further?" Holte asked.

Before Poppy could answer, Hawkins knocked on the door. "Miss Poppy? Mister Eustace is waiting for you downstairs."

Poppy stood up abruptly. "I have to go. We're making a condolence call on Louise Moncrief this afternoon."

"Please think about what we've talked about," Holte pleaded, as he followed Poppy out the door.

"I'll try," she said, and hastened down the stairs.

TWENTY-ONE

POPPY HAD RETRIEVED HER PURSE BEFORE RUSHING DOWNSTAIRS TO FIND STACY in the entry hall, tapping his fingers on the telephone table. "Sorry to keep you waiting, Stacy," she said as he glanced toward her.

"Busy on your story, or so mother told me," Stacy said curtly. He was still in his navy- blue suit with a navy foulard-silk tie over a scrupulously white shirt. He offered her a too-smooth smile and a wink. "At least you haven't changed clothes. That spruce-green should be dark enough for a condolence call."

Poppy would have liked to have given him a sharp retort, but knew this was not the time to wrangle. She took up his bantering tone. "Good. My dark-grey dress with the satin collar is being cleaned, and my dull-red suit is too bright." She had worn the dark-grey dress to funerals for the last four years and by now had no other purpose for it than that. She was glad that she had on her new, sensible shoes and that she was carrying her over-sized purse, so that she would not appear too fashionable for such an occasion.

"Touché." Stacy laughed, a certain quality of meanness in the tone. "You're always good with a comeback, Coz; that's refreshing in our family," he said as he opened the door for her. "Warren's loaned me his Lincoln for the afternoon, so if you will come with me, we can get under way." He bowed slightly.

"How nice of Warren," said Poppy, moving quickly down the walkway. "I thought he was planning to come with us."

"He was, but something came up. Business." It was obvious to Poppy that Stacy would not explain more than that.

She took a quick look around, noticing that the clouds were fading away;

only scraps of them remained, like bits of tissue against the sky. The new green in the trees now shone a bright, pale shade; a few leaves were coming open, and there was good reason to hope that winter had left the city at last. As she reached the Lincoln, she prepared to open the door, saying, "Thank him for me when you get the chance."

"I will," said Stacy, stepping between Poppy and the door.

Nonplused, Poppy asked the first thing that came into her mind. "Will he be staying here, or will he go back to New York?"

Stacy opened the passenger door for her and held it while she got into the car. "How should I know?"

"He's your friend. I thought he might have said something." She settled herself as the door closed, trying to decide if she should have worn a hat to make this call. "Since we're not going to be in church, I decided it would be all right to — "

"Don't fret about it, Coz; it's not like the death was expected, or has a full diagnosis yet; Louise won't expect you to be in mourning mufti," he said as he depressed the starter on the Lincoln and was rewarded with a mechanical purr. He rolled down the window and signaled with his arm, then pulled out into the street. "Warren has good taste in cars."

"If this is any example, he certainly does," said Poppy, and smoothed her skirt. "I appreciate you taking me with you, Stacy."

"So you've said," was his rejoinder. "Just promise you'll leave me out of any articles you write. I don't want to have to answer any questions beyond the ones your inspector friend is going to ask me tomorrow."

"All right," Poppy said, making a bargain that she knew Lowenthal would not approve of. "So long as you don't keep anything back from me."

"It's a deal," he said, and turned toward the street that would, in six blocks, bring them to the Moncrief's house. They covered most of the distance in silence, but as they neared the house on Hamilton Place, they saw a number of cars parked near the house. "Friends of yours, Coz?" Stacy asked pointedly.

"More likely friends of yours; the society-page press have staked out this house since they heard about the death. So have the cops, I understand," Poppy countered, looking around for an open space at the curb, and noticed that two of the cars were from the police; there was no trace of Inspector Loring's car.

"I'll park in the driveway," Stacy said, and gave the arm-signal for a left turn. "Louise won't mind."

"You're driving," Poppy said, trying to decide how to approach Louise Moncrief; she knew it would be useless to seek Stacy's advice on that; he would be his usual impertinent self, and that would be no help at all.

Stacy parked, set the brake, and got out to come around to open the door for Poppy. "I'll be there in seconds, Coz, just hold on," he called as he came around the front of the Lincoln, pausing a moment to look over the cars in front of the house. "You'd think watching this house would be a waste of time," he said as he approached. "It's hard enough for Louise to manage everything that's on her plate now: to have to do it under constant scrutiny is making it much worse for her."

This time Poppy opened the door before Stacy reached it, and got out of the Lincoln. "You don't need to do the pretty with me, Stacy," she said, trying not to sound too critical. "Most of my colleagues don't."

"Do you give them the opportunity?" Stacy asked, and closed the door behind her, then took the lead going up to the front door.

Marian Haas, the Moncriefs' middle-aged housekeeper, opened the front door; she was dressed in black, and her eyes were red. "Mister Dritchner," she exclaimed as she recognized Stacy. "Missus Moncrief will be pleased to see you." She opened the door more widely. "The black wreaths will be here tomorrow," she added, as if chagrined by this lack.

"I'm sure it's been a trial for you, Missus Haas," said Stacy with an unusual air of sympathy. "No one expected this."

"No, no. Certainly not," said Missus Haas. "Who would ever imagine that such a thing could happen?" She stepped aside to allow Stacy to enter, Poppy coming behind him.

Stacy turned as soon as he was in the entry hall. "This is my cousin, Miss Thornton; she asked to come with me to extend her sympathies to Missus Moncrief."

Missus Haas nodded once, as if Poppy's presence was a breach of courtesy. "The house is still in disarray. The police haven't finished their work here, and until they do, we must leave everything the way it was when Mister Moncrief . . . died," she said with great dubiety. "I'm informed they will be finished tomorrow."

"How inconvenient for you," said Stacy. "Will Missus Moncrief see us?"

Recalling herself to her household duties, Missus Haas indicated the sweeping semi-circular staircase to the upper floor. "She and Mister Eastley are in the conservatory. They're expecting you. I'll arrange for some refreshments to be brought up. I'm sure you know the way, Mister Dritchner."

"Yes, Missus Haas, I do," Stacy assured her, and signaled to Poppy. "This way," he said as he started up the stairs.

Poppy took a firm hold on her purse and began the upward climb, admiring the entry hall as she went; when she had been in the house the day before yesterday, she had not had a chance to look at this place, and the few times she had been here before, it had been lavishly decorated. The entry hall, like most of the house, was a later-Federalist style, with a large chandelier with a lavish display of cut crystals to enhance its brilliance hanging in the adjoining drawing room, throwing a host of tiny rainbows into the entry hall. There was an elaborate fanlight over the front door, and above, in the ceiling, a Tiffany skylight lent its many-hued splendor to the entire entry hall.

"That replaced the old dome back in 1887," Stacy informed Poppy as he reached the gallery. "Take the corridor on the right."

"It really is a lovely house," said Poppy. "I've only been here four times before, and the time before this doesn't count."

Stacy chuckled softly. "Had other things on your mind, did you?" He entered the corridor and went along it at a brisk walk. "I don't know how Louise will be, so wait until you get a sense of her state before you pepper her with questions."

Stung, Poppy said, "Thanks for the warning, or I might have begun at once."

"So earnest," Stacy said, obviously amused. "You do always take the bait." He was almost to the end of the corridor; the conservatory glowed ahead, a large, high-ceilinged room with slightly milky walls of windows and a great number of plants on shelves and tables. Wicker furniture in the center of the room was painted as white as the shelves and the cabinet of what Poppy decided must be for gardening supplies.

There were two people in the room: on a Mayes Brothers chaise lounge, a beautiful woman with a mass of loosely dressed blonde hair and an extremely fashionable dress of layers of black organza reclined, like a woman in one of Degas' paintings, every lineament of her posture expressing sorrow; in the chair beside her, a tall, lean figure of a man with an eye-patch and a moustache was rigged out in a black three-piece suit, a dove-grey shirt, and a black tie, his whole demeanor somber, which for him was not unusual.

"May my cousin and I join you, Louise?" Stacy asked from the door, a suggestion of mischief in his voice.

Louise Moncrief glanced up, and her face transformed with a smile. "Oh, Stacy! Yes, please, come in. And your cousin, too." She rose gracefully from the chaise and drifted toward him, her widow's weeds fluttering around her. "These last two days have been so ghastly."

Stacy took her hands in his, kissing first the left, then the right. "I can't imagine what you must be enduring."

"It's been dreadful. Everything has been melancholy, until you arrived. I depend upon you to lighten the gloom." She sighed, then glanced at Poppy. "Oh, yes. I remember you. You were at one of our parties, weren't you?"

Poppy decided not to take Louise's hands. "Yes. Two, in fact. I had a lovely time." Even to herself, this sounded inane, so she tried again. "My sympathies, Missus Moncrief. This must be a most difficult time for you."

"That it is," Louise said, turning back to Stacy. "That's why it's such a pleasure to see you, my friend. Thank you so much for coming."

Julian Eastley had risen from his chair, and now made his way toward Stacy. "Dritchner. How kind of you to come. Louise has been looking forward to seeing you for the last hour and more." His voice was low and hoarse, a reminder of the gassing he had taken during the Great War. "And your . . . cousin?"

"Poppea Thornton. Poppy," she said, holding out her hand to him. "It is a pleasure to see you again, Captain, although this is such a sad occasion."

"Oh, no more captain. I'm Mister Eastley now." He hesitated, then shook her hand. "Yes, this is a most sad occasion. I don't know that I've encountered anything so distressing since the Great War." He turned to Louise. "Won't you sit down again, my dear? You are not to exhaust yourself."

"Oh, Julian, I won't. Stacy quite invigorates me. He's so much droller than you are." She punctuated this by laying her hand on Stacy's arm. "You must help me to my chaise, Stacy, if I become faint."

"Of course, Louise." He grinned briefly. "Missus Haas said that she will have some refreshments sent up, so Poppy and I will linger a while."

"That's sweet of you," she said, floating back toward the chaise. "Is there any news, beyond Madison, that is?"

"Hasn't Neva kept you abreast of the gossip?" Stacy inquired lightly.

"All her gossip is from Baltimore and Washington — isn't there anything local?"

"There's nothing nearly as engrossing as Madison's death, I'm afraid, and you've already said you don't want to talk about that any more." Stacy gave Louise an arch look. "Would you like me to make something up?"

"It's tempting," Louise admitted as she sank back down on the chaise, leaned against the back cushions, and lifted her legs in a single, graceful motion, onto the extension of the chaise. "But it probably wouldn't be very tactful."

"No, probably not," said Eastley with a lugubrious shake of his head. "It would be attributed to a lack of grief, not an expression of it."

"Don't be a wet blanket, Julian," said Louise petulantly. "I've been weeping for two days solid, and I need to stop. You have no idea how fatiguing it is to grieve." She gave an artful sigh. "It's not that I didn't adore Madison, and I'm desolated that he died, but I can't end my life because he ended his."

"No, you can't," Stacy said with more genuine compassion than Poppy had ever heard from him. "But you can't drop sorrow like an old pair of shoes, Louise. It doesn't work that way." He sat down on the end of the chaise lounge, just beyond her feet. "You'll feel better if you let yourself cry some more, when you want to." He patted the thick cushions that upholstered the chaise. "You can't remain in seclusion forever, but it would be fitting that you do for now, at least until after the funeral."

"You always think of me, Stacy." She stared up at the shining ceiling. "I know you're right, but just now, I'm so weary of it all. It's bad enough that Madison is dead, but having the police here makes it so much worse. I feel as if I were an animal in a zoo, and everyone is peering at me. And all those reporters!"

"They're all doing their jobs, Louise," Stacy reminded her; Poppy, who had sat on the most distant of the wicker chairs, winced at how Louise would feel if she remembered that Poppy was a reporter, and at that moment, intercepted an ironic glance from Stacy.

"Once the police finish their investigation, you'll have a private life again, Louise," Eastley promised her.

"And when will that be?" Louise demanded, and began to cry.

"You could go to Baltimore, stay with Neva and her family; most people would understand," Stacy said soothingly.

Louise shook her head, using her lace-edged handkerchief to wipe her eyes. "I can't stand it. I simply cannot stand it," she sobbed.

"Louise," Eastley exclaimed, and came to her side to clasp one of her hands in both of his, his face rigid with emotion.

Stacy was more bracing. "Missus Reedly will be coming up with refreshments in a couple minutes, unless Missus Haas deigns to bring them herself. Do you want her to tell your staff that you're coming apart at the seams?"

Poppy resisted the urge to squirm, and hoped that no one would pay her any attention.

"Dritchner?" Eastley challenged him. "What are you doing? Can't you see you're distressing Louise."

"Whatever it is he's doing, I wish he would do more of it," Missus Moncrief said.

"I'm sympathizing. If you don't think that the staff is talking about Louise's state of mind, and Madison's death, you're more of a dunce than I think you are. At least they know to keep it in the household," Stacy told Eastley in his most blighting manner. "Louise doesn't need her people telling everyone that she is a perfect wreck, and you can be sure that that's what her staff will be saying among themselves if they aren't already; Madison's death is too juicy to be ignored. Do you understand what I mean, Louise?" To Poppy, this last sounded almost threatening, but it served to bring Louise back under control.

"I do know," said Louise faintly. "You're right. I'll do my best to maintain my decorum."

"That's wise of you," Stacy approved.

"Yes," said Eastley, in sudden agreement. "You're a brave girl, Louise. You'll silence all the talk, I'm sure you will."

Louise had a black-edged handkerchief in the hand that Eastley was not holding, and she was using it to wipe her eyes. "Speaking of those observing my grief, what must your cousin think of me?" she said a bit wildly to Stacy. "You told me that she works for the Clarion, didn't you? She could say . . . anything."

"Don't worry about her. She won't talk out of turn, will you, Coz?" He turned toward Poppy, a warning look in his eyes.

Poppy shook her head. "No; I'm not one to gossip," she said, reminding herself that there was a difference between gossip and reporting — or she hoped there was. "I'll respect your privacy," she added, knowing that she was fibbing again, but promising herself not to expose Louise Moncrief to more rumor-mongering than was absolutely necessary.

There was a tap on the door; Louise blotted her tears and stretched out on the chaise again; Eastley released her hand and took his place in his usual chair; Stacy got up and went to the largest set of shelves and looked at the plants in the pots there. Louise called out, "Come in, Jeanine."

Missus Jeanine Reedly, Louise's personal maid and household cook, was a colored woman in a black uniform with a black apron, and bearing a tray with pound cake, coffee, utensils, cream, sugar, and a bowl of strawberry preserves. She carried this to the low coffee table and set it down. "Is everything all right, Missus Moncrief?"

"Yes, Jeanine. Thank you for bringing this. It looks wonderful." Louise motioned to Stacy, her eyes still welling with tears. "Would you be willing to pour? And Julian will cut the pound cake. Perhaps Miss Thornton will hand the plates around?"

"I included a plate and a cup for Missus Plowright; she's supposed to be back from the funeral parlor shortly," Jeanine ventured.

"That's very good of you," said Louise. "I'm sure Missus Haas will send Neva up as soon as she returns."

Jeanine did a curtsy-like bob and left the room.

"Let's have some coffee and pound cake," Louise said, a touch too enthusiastically. "I don't think I can take any more sympathy just now, Stacy."

"Whatever you want," said Stacy, and signaled to Poppy to move closer. "Nothing but small-talk for now."

Poppy hid a sigh and did as she was told.

TWENTY-TWO

❧

POPPY HAD BEEN HOME FOR TWENTY MINUTES BEFORE SHE HAD DECIDED HOW TO report what she had observed at the Moncriefs' house without disappointing Lowenthal or aggravating her cousin. She went to the library and sat down at the desk, then rolled a sheet of paper into the typewriter, striving to organize her thoughts. She half-expected to hear Chesterton Holte speak from behind the draperies or the top of one of the bookcases, but the room remained silent. She began to type, choosing her words with care.

Missus Madison Moncrief has been in shock since the death of her husband two days ago from as yet undetermined causes. Police are conducting an examination of the site of the death, and the coroner, Dr. Archibald Wyman, has ordered more tests on Madison Moncrief's body as part of the official inquiry. During this difficult waiting period, the young widow has been receiving the consolation and support provided by friends and family, who have come to her aid in her mourning. Missus Moncrief is hoping that the coroner will be able to establish the cause of her husband's death within the next few days, for that knowledge will be as great a consolation as the company of her sister, Missus Theodore Plowright of Baltimore, and her social companion, the Great War hero, Julian Eastley, have been in this unhappy time. They ask that Missus Moncrief's seclusion be respected until the funeral has taken place. Those wishing to express their sympathy are asked to delay making condolence calls until the day of the funeral is announced.

Poppy read through it, thinking it was a fairly soggy first paragraph, and tried to decide on how to make it more compelling than what she had written; there had to be a more intriguing way to present the information that did not actually intrude on anything she had seen or heard while visiting at the Moncrief house, which was all true, but lacked excitement. Lowenthal would not be pleased with such a lackluster opening, but anything stronger would incur Stacy's wrath and put an end to his help at a time when she was depending upon it. She leaned back in her chair, and noticed that there was an unaccountable shadow forming at the edge of the heavy window draperies. "Is that you, Holte?" she asked in an undervoice.

"You look dejected, Poppy," Chesterton Holte said, becoming more visible. "I gather the case is getting . . . difficult."

"That's one word for it." She pinched the bridge of her nose to keep from weeping with vexation. "Sorry; the harder I search, the more confusing this whole thing becomes: Hadley and Grimes, Sansome and Company, and all the rest, on top of murder. But I have to make this work, or it will be years before I have any opportunity to report on crime again." She tugged the paper out of the typewriter and slapped the carriage return. "I need to make this better, before there's another body."

"Do you think there is going to be another body?" Holte asked.

"Don't you?" She did not wait for him to answer. "What do your ghosts tell you? Or don't you talk about it?"

"I haven't talked to them today." He faltered, and slid away from her side. "Would you like me to?"

Poppy smiled broadly, thinking that she was probably certifiably insane, but keeping on so that she would be able to pursue her story. "Would you? Ask Knott what happened to him, and who did it, and what — if anything — his getting killed has to do with Madison's and Poindexter's deaths, or Hadley and Grimes." Listening to herself, she felt an utter fool. "And if you run into my father, tell him I miss him, if you would." This last left her a little giddy, for she realized that she had come to accept that Chesterton Holte was real, and just what he claimed to be.

"So you truly haven't given up the ambition to complete the story," said Holte, moving nearer to her.

"Ye gods, no. How could I? If you were in my position, would you?" She almost stood up to express her indignation at such a question. "I have to do this right, to make sense of it all." After taking a deep breath she went on in a less strident tone. "Don't you see? I have to follow the story as far as it goes, and find out all the ways in which the Poindexter's and Knott's deaths tie into Madison's, which isn't going to happen if I can't turn up a few real clues. I have an obligation to the Clarion to do the best I can with my investigation." Just saying this out loud made her feel tired, but she did her best to mask the extent of her sudden weariness. "I need to show them — the other reporters and the police — that I won't flinch from gruesome cases. And besides, to me there is nothing more gruesome than the Society page."

"So I've assumed," said Holte. "Which is why I want to do what I can to help you, and to" — here he hesitated — "guard you to the extent that I can."

Poppy heard something perturbing in these words, and said, "Guard me?"

"What you're investigating is dangerous; I've warned you already, that you are taking a great deal of risk in this."

"You've made that clear. But what kind of a reporter would I be if I wouldn't take a chance or two?" She knew this was more bravado than courage, but she would not take anything back. "You've told me that you want to help me, and now I think there's a way that you can actually do that. I need to find the connections in the case and show how Poindexter and Moncrief are part of the same larger threat. Are you going to refuse to help me do that?"

"No," he confessed. "But there are limits on how much more risk I'll expose you to. I'll do what I can, and I'll tell you what I find out." Holte moved away a little farther, then swung around toward her. "Will you give me your word that you will not leave the house until I get back?"

"If you have a time when you could return?" She was feeling a little steadier now, and she concentrated on her task at hand.

"How do you mean?"

She reminded herself to be patient. "You keep telling me that your take on time as a ghost is different than mine."

"I'll try to be back in two to three hours," he said, starting to fade.

"I have to call Inspector Loring and my editor; I'll do that while you're gone," she told him as he vanished. "Damn," she muttered, and decided she ought to start with Lowenthal, and rolled another sheet of paper into her Remington typewriter and took a new run at the piece he was expecting from her, and as she did, she hoped that Holte would return with more answers than he had provided so far.

Now that Holte was no longer visible, he slipped away into the dimension of ghosts, doing his best to ignore the worry that was growing within him. What if Poppy had been right, and her lack of information was adding to her peril? It was possible, but he did not like to have to consider it. What bothered him more was that he had not been able to discourage her, and he was convinced that he would not be able to now that she was committed to her assignment. These nagging questions slowed his progress from the corporal world to that of noncorporeality. When he arrived in the dimension of ghosts it was its usual, slightly faded, foggy reality. Ghosts eddied like whirlpools in a river and clustered together at the edge of an invisible, limitless current that washed throughout the dimension of ghosts. The place was continually shifting, its nature too fluid to remain constant in anything but its discrepancy, and that made locating specific ghosts difficult. It took Chesterton Holte an unmeasurable passage of time to come upon Madison Moncrief in the company of James Poindexter in a small whirlpool of cloudiness, and he made his way toward them.

"Where's Thornton?" he asked in the ghosts' soundless language. "Has he been here? I need to talk to him."

"Gone on," said Moncrief when he had deliberated the question. "Or gone elsewhere."

"I need to speak to him — get his advice." Holte insisted. "For his daughter." Holte flung up one non-physical hand in consternation. "Is there any way to find out where he has gone?"

Poindexter drooped in resignation. "Not that I've discovered. I may learn specifics in the future, but for now, I cannot help you."

This was not very encouraging, but Holte would not let that deter him. He summoned up as much force as he could, minimal though it was. "If he should return, would you let him know that I would like to talk with him?"

Moncrief nodded vaguely. "If I remember."

"He is gone on," Poindexter remarked without interest, sidling away from Moncrief and Holte. "I hope you can find him."

"He may know something about a murder," Holte persisted.

"Murder, suicide, accident, disease, and age, one of them eventually brings everyone here. Why is this so unusual?" Moncrief asked.

"It is part of my remaining tasks among the living, and it concerns one of you — " Holte began.

Moncrief interrupted. "You mean Knott."

"No," said Holte. "I mean you."

"Oh," said Moncrief, and shifted where he was.

Holte felt his hope waning, but made another sally. "What about you, Poindexter? There's a chance that your death is connected to Moncrief's, through your professional dealings. The police may not have made the connection, but your old firm has closed ranks. Do you have any useful recollection about who killed you?"

"I haven't thought much about it," Poindexter admitted, non-sounding slightly bored, "You don't, after a while. It is part of moving on. For me, I'll have a great deal of time to recall; when my murderer comes here, I will know for sure."

"But there is nothing that you have . . . called to mind?" Holte wished it were possible for ghosts to shout; he would be shouting now if he could.

"It was someone I knew, I recall that much. Not Grimes, I'm fairly certain. I will know who he is at once, when he arrives here, as we all do who were murdered. I can wait until then." Poindexter did something that was very like an expression of unconcern.

"But that may be too late," Holte exclaimed. "There is danger for one of the living at this moment."

The two ghosts did something that might have once been laughter. "All of the living are in danger at this moment," Moncrief said. "But most of them don't know they are because it's so remote to them. They think that death is far off, not as near as their next heartbeat."

Poindexter made a dreamy kind of nod. "I don't think it crossed my mind that someone might want to kill me until it happened."

Moncrief added his support. "Most of the living don't like having to think about such things. Dying seems far away to most of them."

"But it's not for some of them, including Louise, and Poppy Thornton," Holte insisted, his non-voice roughening.

Poindexter seemed to lose his train of thought, and in a moment or so, he asked, "Have you seen Myrna Freemantle? Light-haired, and fey. She wasn't the same after the 'Flu, but she still had something special about her."

"No," said Holte. "I'm sorry; I don't know who she is."

"That's sad for you," Poindexter wafted a little farther away, caught up in his reverie. "She was charming."

"Charming?" Holte inquired, knowing there was nothing useful to be gained in trying to find out why this had come to Poindexter's thoughts. "I gather you were fond of her." Then something occurred to Holte, and he tried a new approach. "If Myrna Freemantle were in danger, wouldn't you want to do something to mitigate it?"

"If I knew anything about it, I reckon I would, if Douglas — her husband and a complete bore — were nowhere about." Poindexter started to fade once more.

Moncrief suddenly came back into focus. "Has anything happened to Louise? I was sure that Julian Eastley would take care of her, but now that I muse about it, I'm not so sure."

Holte did his best to remember what he had heard Stacy say about Louise Moncrief, and made an answer he thought Moncrief wanted to hear, and that was close enough to the truth that it would pass muster with her husband. "She misses you, and the inquiry into your death is taking a great deal out of her. She has been trying to remain in seclusion; her sister Neva has come to be with her. But the press is everywhere because the coroner believes that you were murdered, and the police have been told to look for evidence." Holte studied the other two ghosts, doing his best to discern their emotions; he said nothing about his own doubts about Louise. "The living young woman I am trying to help has been assigned to the story for her paper. The more that is learned about this cluster of deaths — meaning yours, and perhaps Knott's — the greater her danger is."

"Knott has just arrived; he's disoriented."

"Weren't we all," Holte remarked, and anticipated something similar to a chuckle from the other two, but nothing came.

"You're spending a lot of time with the living," Moncrief remarked distantly.

"I have a few things to do among them before I move on," said Holte, striving again to give his non-words emphasis, without success.

"Oh, that's right," said Moncrief in his soundless voice. "Something to do with Thornton's daughter. Or was it his son?"

"If you knew his son, you wouldn't ask." Holte felt a spurt of hope; it was possible that he might get something useful, after all.

"Tobias is a bit of a stick, isn't he?" Moncrief said unexpectedly.

"A self-important stick," Poindexter agreed.

"Then it's the daughter Holte's talking about," said Moncrief. "I was hoping to see her cousin before I came here. He was planning to do some work for me when he arrived from New York. If he'd arrived a day early, matters might have turned out differently."

"Her cousin has been providing some service in her inquiries, out of respect for you, and as a gesture of friendship for your . . . widow. He took Thornton's daughter with him when he made his sympathy call on Louise," Holte elaborated now that he had stirred a little interest among these ghosts.

"Louise always liked Stacy; he introduced us, you know." Moncrief's non-shape became slightly more visible.

"I remember Louise — a vibrant young woman." Poindexter became increasingly engaged again, seeming to move closer to Moncrief. "Eustace Dritchner dealt with some of my clients, although I was never quite certain in what capacity. I haven't had to deal with him directly very often, but his business acumen is keen. He struck me as a clever man on those occasions when I encountered him."

Holte found this observation perplexing. "Clever in what way?" He had his own opinion of Eustace Dritchner, which he kept to himself.

Poindexter gave a movement that was almost a shrug. "A trifle cynical, intelligent in educated terms, ambitious, glib, personable, a little too facile for my taste, but generally liked and trusted. There are a few who seem to think that he's not completely on the up-and-up; one hears rumors. He's well-known in the art-and-culture crowd, but I'm not entirely certain that he cares that much for — He warned about inflation in Germany." His demeanor changed and he moved in on Holte. "Damn you, Holte. You're making me remember. I do not want to remember."

"I apologize," said Holte.

"Yes. Well." Poindexter was turning huffy.

Not wanting to become involved in a dispute with Poindexter, Holte gave his attention to Moncrief again. "Have you seen much of Knott since he came here?"

Moncrief shook his noncorporeal head. "Not much. He's still adapting to this place. You know what that's like."

"Has he talked to you about his business? Any problems with clients, perhaps? Or trouble with his assistant, Overstreet?"

Poindexter wafted a short distance away. "Overstreet. He's an odd one."

"Knott has said nothing about Overstreet. He still hasn't entirely grasped what happened. I doubt he was expecting his death. If he has any coherent opinion of his condition, he probably still thinks he's unconscious. As I said, not prepared for what happened." Moncrief might have been amused, or he might have been puzzled. "But then, neither was I."

"I hadn't that luxury," said Holte, recalling the firing squad that killed him behind a roadside inn on a glorious spring afternoon near Liège.

"At least you knew how you got here when you did," Moncrief sniffed. "And you knew why you were here."

Holte tried not to be distracted by Moncrief's remarks, but conceded, "Yes, but I wouldn't recommend it."

Poindexter made a strange movement in the swirling eddy, and said, "All right. I'll do what I can to help you if I can keep it in mind. If, in exchange, you will find out who killed me, and why."

"I'll do the same," said Moncrief abruptly, moving out of unseen shadows. "And if you will leave us alone when you're done we'll call it equal."

It was a binding agreement, and all of them knew it. Holte held up his nonexistent hand. "I swear." With that, he slipped back into the world of the living, and went looking for Poppy, still hoping to provide her some information that would not only be useful, but be enough to convince her to keep out of the investigation.

TWENTY-THREE

ON LOWENTHAL'S SUGGESTION, POPPY TOOK A TAXI TO HIS HOUSE, HER STORY tucked into a file in her briefcase. All the way there, she thought over what Inspector Loring had told her when she had 'phoned him upon her return from the Moncriefs' house: there was no new information on the Moncrief case, but talking with Stacy might change that, and the Knott case was just getting underway; the coroner had not yet released any details other than it was a homicide, which, Wyman had said, was obvious to a blind man. This had brought her nothing more than a grunt from Lowenthal, the demand that she present her story and herself at his home as soon as possible, and added the expectation that she would have more for Monday's edition, with the unspoken warning that there had better be some kind of break in one of the cases.

"Sure, boss," she had told him; sitting in the taxi, she felt she was treading on very thin ice, and by the time she arrived at Lowenthal's house, she was nervous. This would be a test that she was not confident that she was prepared for, and she had so much at stake. As she paid the cabby, she gave him fifty cents extra, and asked him to wait for twenty minutes at the most.

The cabby squinted up at her, taking his measure of her and the nature of the neighborhood around him. "Make it a dollar and I will," he said, speaking around his cigarette. "Twenty minutes, but not one second longer."

"That's fine," Poppy said, taking her briefcase and her purse before getting out of the cab, and approaching the house in the fading afternoon light.

The porch was small, railed in decorative cast iron from seventy years ago, and painted a dull-red; Poppy surmised that this was the house bought by Lowenthal's immigrant grandparents, an example of family ties that she found unlike Lowenthal at the office. Taking stock of the rest of the house, she saw that it was carefully maintained, with red shutters on the windows, and relatively recent paint of a dark-buff shade. The door was the same red color as the shutters, and boasted a large, brass knocker, which Poppy used, mentally rehearsing her explanation of what she had written.

"You made good time," Cornelius Lowenthal declared by way of welcome as he opened the door; he was in a lounging jacket that was a bit too small for his barrel chest, and for a moment, Poppy was apprehensive; Lowenthal's next order stilled her worries. "Come in and let me have a look at your piece. I don't want to be late for the deadline. I've told them to hold three inches for you." As reassuring as this was, there was an air of skepticism about him that drained most of her closely held courage.

She stepped into a small entryway, and noticed that the parlor on the right had two lights shining already. "Where would you like me to go?" From her two previous visits, she knew that the front parlor was off to the left, but she thought that a smaller setting might be Lowenthal's preference this afternoon. He had spoken about a study, but she had no notion as to where it was.

"In to the parlor, of course; on the right. I've got a fire going in there, and no one will disturb us," said Lowenthal, and did not enlarge upon what he meant by no one. "Eunice will bring you coffee, if you want. She's working on the leg of lamb in the kitchen, for our dinner."

Poppy knew that Eunice was his wife — they had met at the last Christmas party — but she shook her head. "I think I'd like to get this settled before I have anything. " She tried to summon up a smile, but could not quite manage it; the taxi was waiting outside, and she did not want to have to 'phone for one and then wait for it to arrive. She held up her briefcase. "I have the file in here. Three hundred twenty-nine words. There isn't much about the police investigation because there isn't much progress to report."

"Yes, so you said," Lowenthal agreed, half-escorting Poppy into the parlor; it was a medium-sized, L-shaped room with a tile-fronted fireplace in the west wall where three cut logs were burning in the grate behind a linked-metal screen. The draperies had not yet been pulled over the windows, and the soft purplish afternoon light suffused the room. "Take the occasional chair. I'll use the loveseat." These two pieces of furniture, matchingly upholstered in dark-blue damask, were set at right angles to each other, with a round mahogany coffee table in front of both.

"Whatever you like," said Poppy automatically, a little disconcerted by this display of polite regard; she went to the chair Lowenthal had indicated, and sat down, crossing her ankles next to her briefcase. "Before I wrote the piece for you, I spoke to Loring earlier. I'll see him again tomorrow, and — "

"Yes, yes; call me after you talk to your Inspector; just keep in mind that he's going to be pumping you as much as you're pumping him; don't be too obliging unless he's helpful," said Lowenthal impatiently, going to the loveseat and plunking himself down in it, settling back against the cushions. "So where are your three hundred twenty-nine words? I want to run my eyes over them." He held out his hand.

Poppy moved her briefcase onto the flowered carpet and opened it in order to bring out the manila file, which she offered to him. "I've tried for a more-to-come tone, as — "

Lowenthal waved her to silence as he opened the file and took out the two wide-margined pages. "Hush up, Thornton."

She obeyed, only nodding before going still as well as silent, and focused her attention on the nearest lamp, and was almost disappointed when it did not flicker. So, she thought, I'm on my own. She folded her hands on top of her purse and stared out the front window; she followed the progress of an airplane across a swath of thin clouds, and thought about her Aunt Esther, who, according to her letter from Vladivostok, had recently learned to fly.

Lowenthal continued to read carefully, frowning from time to time, and occasionally pausing to reread small portions of Poppy's work while he twiddled his hair. Finally he put the pages down on the table. "It'll do," he announced, which, for him, was high praise. "I'll make a few minor cuts in it and messenger it down to the Clarion." He leaned back. "You're skimming the rim on some of what you have here, but it isn't enough to have the mouthpieces put the kibosh on it, or that's my take on how it looks. You won't get spiked." He showed her a vulpine smile. "There may be a future for you in crime, after all, Thornton. I got to admit, I didn't think so when I put you on the case, but you're rising to the challenge."

Poppy was startled by his remarks, but she only said, "Thank you, boss."

He smoothed his hair. "So where do you go from here?"

"That depends on the cops, doesn't it?" Before he could start to lecture her, she went on, "I think it would be best to be open to all possibilities, since the police don't have any likely suspect yet. We don't want to get the public in an uproar for no good reason. The courts don't like it when someone is wrongly convicted of a crime in the press."

"No," said Lowenthal. "That they don't." He coughed gently. "I like the way you rolled in the Knott murder, making it another part of the pattern, not necessarily connected to Moncrief, but an unhappy coincidence through Hadley and Grimes. And you're right: high society has been rocked by the violent deaths happening in a matter of days. I know I've told you to keep your eye out for a scandal, but make sure you have solid proof of one, if it crops up. For now, we'll keep you on Knott as well as Moncrief, but how long will be up to you and what you can uncover to show a link. High society isn't like the gangsters — they kill each other all the time — but the upper crust doesn't go in for slaughter. Having your by-line on the pieces gives us a degree of protection from suits, and you know it's possible that we could get sued if we don't back up everything we print."

"I remember the trial. The Clarion did step over the line then, and Richman was right to resign over it," Poppy said in as mild a voice as she could; she did not add that Lowenthal's promotion to his present position was one of the results of Vincent Richman's miscalculation.

"That was during the Great War. Things were different then." He shifted on the loveseat. "But Richman went too far. Saying a man is an enemy spy without rock-solid evidence is irresponsible, and having German relatives isn't good enough. It muddies the water too much."

Poppy shook her head, then took a chance. "It's still not that different. And, boss, you really did dodge a bullet with the Boorsten incident."

Since Lowenthal had been at the center of that crisis some three years ago, he pulled at his lower lip as he thought. "You got a point there, Thornton. The Board wouldn't tolerate another blunder like that one. So check all your sources and make sure of the details. It's safer to print when there are details; and don't rely on relatives — no matter what they promise you, in the end they'll circle the wagons and throw you to the wolves."

"That's why I'll be doubly careful," Poppy vowed.

"And you understand the ground rules. That's good. Get to work on it this evening." Then he raised his voice. "Eunice! Coffee and a couple of your fresh doughnuts."

A swinging door opened at the end of the parlor's L-shape, and Eunice Lowenthal came in with a laden tray; she was in a neat, flowered house-dress with an old-fashioned full skirt that fell to four inches above her ankle. She gave Poppy a wide smile as she set down the tray directly in front of her husband. "It's good to see you, Miss Thornton."

"Thank you, Missus Lowenthal," Poppy said, realizing for the first time that Eunice Lowenthal must have been a very pretty, soft-faced young woman, but the softness had sagged and left her with an uncomfortable facial resemblance to a Basset hound; to add to the decline, she now had a stout-bodied figure, a testament to her skills as a cake-and-pastry baker, all developments that she took on with patient dignity, meticulous attention to dressmaking, and careful haircuts to minimize the loss of her beauty. "Would you like me to pour?"

"You go right ahead," said Lowenthal for Poppy. "She takes one sugar and a little cream."

"Is that what you would like?" Eunice asked Poppy.

"That would be fine," said Poppy, grateful to Eunice for this courtesy.

Eunice took her good china coffee pot and poured out a steaming stream of it into a Limoges cup, then took up the creamer and added about half a teaspoon of the cream to Poppy's coffee, after which she held out the sugar-bowl and sugar-tongs to Poppy. "Have as much as you like."

Poppy used the tongs to take one cube. "Thank you; this will be fine." She used the very small spoon in her saucer to stir the coffee, thinking that Aunt Jo would approve of Eunice Lowenthal's hostessing skills.

The nearest light flickered.

"Electricity!" Lowenthal exclaimed. "Well, it's great when it works. Eunice, I'll have a little imported sugar in mine; the sugar that was delivered last Tuesday, from Ireland. And then break out the kerosene lamps, just in case."

"Yes, I will," said Eunice tonelessly, filling another Limoges cup, but leaving a more space. "I'll be right back — with your sugar."

It was at moments like this that Poppy wished she were more like her Aunt Esther, who would lambaste Lowenthal for treating his wife in such a way; but since Poppy had a job to protect, she offered Eunice an understanding smile.

"Would you like any . . . sugar, Miss Thornton?" Eunice asked.

Knowing that the sugar in this case was whiskey, Poppy shook her head. "What I have is fine, thank you."

"You should have some," Lowenthal encouraged her. "To celebrate. It's excellent sugar."

"I'll celebrate at home, later. After I get some more work done." She closed her briefcase and picked up her cup-and-saucer. "So I'll leave as soon as I've finished my coffee, and one of these doughnuts."

Lowenthal signaled with his hand. "Chop-chop, Eunice."

Poppy bit back a sharp remark, sinking her teeth into the powdered-sugar-and-pastry of Eunice Lowenthal's justly famous doughnut; the powdered sugar held to her lipstick, and Poppy reached for a napkin to wipe it away. "Boss," she began hesitantly. "You have a housekeeper and a cook, don't you? Why does Missus Lowenthal always serve your guests?"

Lowenthal lifted his caterpillar eyebrows as if he had never noticed this. "I don't know. She always has, from the time we got married, and I was a reporter, just like you."

Not just like me; you were never female, Poppy thought, but said, "But she doesn't have to now, does she?" She heard a car start outside and realized that her cab was leaving. Returning her attention to Lowenthal, she wondered if she should change her mind about the whiskey.

"See if you can convince her of that." He sighed. "I keep telling her, let Missus Waters serve, or hire Waters' niece to do it when we entertain, but she won't hear of it. She takes her own doughnuts and cakes to the Veterans' Home every two weeks, and plays pinochle with the men there. She's a dynamite pinochle player. Beats me six times out of seven. And she's a Quaker; you wouldn't think she'd go in for playing cards." His obvious pride in his wife's talents startled Poppy, who found her disapprobation in her boss' conduct fading. "You know, the Great War was a real eye-opener. As all the Doughboys went off to war, a lot of their sisters and wives took over their places in industry — well, you must know that: your Aunt Esther organized whole companies of them, just as she trained many nurses during the 'Flu. During the Great War, your aunt had women driving the dairy trucks, and delivering the mail, and manning the telephones for the police, and distributing public support to the poor, and setting the type for the newspapers. Between the Great War and the 'Flu, we lost a lot of those women, along with the men who died in the epidemic and in battle. My mother pitched in, did her part." He paused thoughtfully. "She was fifty when she started her work, a grandmother, and with a crippled husband at home, but she took on dispatching ambulances for Pittsburgh — that's my hometown — from 1916 to 1921."

This was news to Poppy, and as she listened to Cornelius Lowenthal go on, her opinion of him continued to change. "Do you have any brothers or sisters?" She realized that she had never heard him speak of brothers or sisters.

"Used to have five, but the 'Flu got the oldest of us — Augustus — and my sister Lorelei died in childbirth in '15. I'm the fifth of six. Lorelei was the second. My brother Thaddeus, the third, is in Washington, one of those behind-the-scenes men in the Justice Department. My sister Celeste, the fourth, is married and lives in Montpellier with her four kids; her husband is a civil engineer. My brother Everest, the youngest, is in a veterans' home in Florida; he's not right in his head. He had Trench Fever, and it damaged his brain. "

"Oh." Poppy tried to think of something appropriate to say, and came up with "I'm sorry about your brother."

Eunice came back through the swinging door, a small pitcher in her hands. "Your sugar, Mister Lowenthal." She extended the pitcher to him, and gave him a satisfied smile.

Lowenthal took the pitcher and poured in a quarter of a cup of his Irish sugar. "Thanks, sweetheart," he said.

"I'll leave you alone for now," Eunice said. "Call me if you need anything.

Nice to see you again, Miss Thornton."

"Thank you, Missus Lowenthal," said Poppy to the retreating Eunice.

"She's a gem; I'm a lucky man." Lowenthal said with a brief grin that was so lopsided that Poppy wondered if this was the first time he had had recourse to his imported sugar this afternoon, or was it that he had a hidden streak of sentimentality. "So, Thornton, how soon can you turn in your Monday story tomorrow? You'll bring it to me, like today, unless I tell you otherwise. I don't want you getting into trouble. That doesn't look good for anybody."

The lamp flickered again.

"Damn!" Lowenthal took up his cup of coffee now laced with whiskey. "I hope we have enough kerosene for the night."

"It may just be something on the line; our lights flicker regularly." Poppy took another bite of her doughnut, and again wiped her mouth.

"You live farther out. I'm not surprised you have trouble. But young Ben Franklin walked by this house from time to time. You'd think our service would be more reliable. There's an electrical station two blocks away, right next to the fire station." He had more coffee and took his doughnut from the plate. "As soon as I'm done, I'll call the messenger, and then a cab to send you home." He chewed vigorously, then had a gulp of his coffee. "I know it's an inconvenience to have you come all this way, but you must see that it's necessary. Don't worry, the paper will pay for it."

This gesture of generosity outside the office made Poppy wonder why Lowenthal was being so helpful. "I can take the streetcar."

"Yes, you can, but Eunice would never let me hear the end of it." He continued to devour his doughnut, making his observations around his chewing. "I don't want it said . . . that I would allow a woman alone . . . to ride the streetcar after sunset . . . Especially not one . . . of my own reporters."

"Then, thank you, boss," she said, and finished her doughnut before drinking the last of her coffee, noticing how the shadows were encroaching on the parlor.

Lowenthal set down his cup and lumbered out of the loveseat, and made his way into the entry-hall where the telephone stand was situated. He spoke curtly to the operator, giving the woman the number of the Clarion. As soon as he finished ordering a messenger to come to his house, he rang off and then placed a second call to the Liberty Taxi Company, requesting a taxi at his address in ten minutes. Then he hung up and trundled back into the parlor, closing the draperies before returning to the loveseat. "The taxi will come shortly. You might as well add a little more coffee to your cup and have another doughnut."

"Thank you, but I'll pass," Poppy said, and noticed the lamp fluctuating rapidly, and concluded that Holte was doing the ghostly equivalent of laughing.

TWENTY-FOUR

AUNT JO WAS IN THE MUSIC ROOM AT THE PIANO, MEANDERING HER WAY through a Mozart Sonata, humming the melody-line as a kind of guide for her fingers; two floor-lamps provided the illumination for her instrument, and three wall-lamps imparted a gentle glow to the area beyond the piano. She looked up as Poppy came into the room, and used that as an excuse to stop playing. "So you're back at last." Anticipating dinner, she was dressed in a puce dinner-dress, one with a beaded belt and bead-edged bolero.

"I am," said Poppy. She pulled up a chair and sat down. "The cab was cold. I should have taken a coat rather than a jacket."

"Did it go well, dear?" She accented her question with a languid arpeggio.

"Better than I feared," Poppy admitted. "Has Stacy come back yet?"

"No, not yet." Josephine reached up and closed her sheet music. "Eustace can be the most aggravating boy."

"That's nothing new," said Poppy. "He's been up to antics of this sort since he was child; I remember those days well: he'd make plans and then do something else entirely. But this time he has the excuse that his friend has been murdered."

Josephine shuddered. "Would you please not use that word? Killed is bad enough, but murdered! Are they sure Madison was killed by violent means?"

"They are. Doctor Wyman himself told me. Poisoned and hanged."

"I don't know how you can bear to talk to such persons."

This stung Poppy. "Ye gods, Aunt Jo: you talk to Archibald Wyman at the Symphony Gala every year, and at the July Fourth Croquet Match."

Aunt Jo summoned up all her self-regard and declared, "Well, of course I do, but never about his work. Those are charity events."

Poppy shook her head. "If you say so," she remarked, thinking of the many guests at those events would seek out Doctor Wyman to learn all the juicy details that he was willing to reveal. Then she saw a movement in the corner, and stared, in case Holte had joined her, but it was only Maestro, who had been curled up on one of the upholstered chairs lined up against the wall. "When do you expect to sit down to dinner?"

"How should I know?" asked Josephine. "Whenever Eustace and Mister Derrington come back — that is, if Mister Derrington hasn't decided to return to New York." She made a gesture expressing hard use. "The way young men act these days. I just don't know."

"Would you like me to go up and change?" Poppy asked.

"You might as well remain as you are. Sometimes I wonder why I bother." She held out her hand to Maestro, who recognized the offer of affection for what it was, and came over to the piano, his tail in full plume, his purr growing louder as soon as Josephine's expert fingers touched his ruff. "There, there, my sweet."

Poppy sighed, but kept her thoughts to herself. "What do you plan if Stacy doesn't return? He and Warren may well dine out tonight."

While she continued to pamper her cat, Josephine thought for almost a minute. "I think I'll order dinner for eight-thirty, whether or not Eustace is here. You're right, Poppy — he and Mister Derrington may dine out, and it would be just like Eustace to forget to call me to let me know."

"Then I'll join you in the sitting room at eight." Poppy rose from the chair.

"I'll order drinks for us. I'll have sherry, and you can tell Hawkins what you'd like before you go up to work." Her voice went cold on the last word, but she achieved a slight smile, and added, "You truly are your father's daughter."

To Aunt Jo's astonishment, Poppy said, "You're sweet to say that," as she went out the door. Baffled by Poppy's remark, Josephine resumed bedeviling Mozart, pausing now and again to stroke Maestro, murmuring endearments to the preening cat.

Hawkins was in the dining room, and looked up when Poppy slid the left side of the pocket-door open. "Has Missus Dritchner decided how many to set places for?"

"So far as I know, it'll be just the two of us. At eight-thirty. Drinks in the sitting room at eight, if you please. My aunt will have sherry, and I'll have cognac, the choice of the finger-food can be made in the kitchen." Poppy saw the dejection in Hawkins' eyes. "If you hear anything from Stacy, will you tell Aunt Jo? She's worried about him."

"Of course, Miss Thornton," Hawkins said.

"I'll be upstairs, trying to pound out a couple of pages." Poppy stepped back and slid the door closed once more; she lingered a moment, wondering if the lights would flicker. As she reached the top of the stairs, she noticed that Duchess was pawing at the library door. "What now?" she asked the air, and twisted on the lights along the corridor before going into the library, feeling reluctant to enter so dark a room. The spill of light from the hallway provided enough illumination to help her find the way to her desk and turn on the lamp behind the typewriter.

"You handled yourself well with Lowenthal," Holte said from the alcove behind her. "Accommodating, but not subservient." His voice, which had sounded distant at first, was now loud enough to cause Duchess to whine.

She kept from jumping, but she swung around and stared into the darkness. "Ye gods! Can you stop doing that?"

"Doing what?" he inquired politely as he glided toward her.

"That!" Poppy almost yelled. "Just coming out of nowhere."

"What would you rather I do?" He sounded genuinely interested.

"I don't know," she said in exasperation. "Announce yourself, or materialize in the same spot, or make a sound . . . no, that won't work. You'd upset Duchess and Maestro. I gather Duchess was aware that you were in here?"

"Probably," Holte admitted. "She was aware of me when I first arrived."

"Well, at least we've established that." She pulled out the chair and sat down. "I'm going to do some work so I don't have to scramble tomorrow." Removing the cover from the typewriter, she opened the second drawer down on the right side and took out ten sheets of paper and two carbons, sandwiched the carbon between two sheets and rolled them into the typewriter. Without waiting for Holte to speak, she began typing.

"I didn't get much information from Poindexter, Moncrief, and Knott." He hesitated. "I wish I had something of substance to offer you, Poppy."

"When you say you didn't get much information, what do you mean?" She stopped typing to stare at him.

He gathered his thoughts. "This may be a little demanding; words don't exist that really describe the state, so bear with me." With that, he made a noise that might have been a clearing of his noncorporeal throat, and began. "Ghosts who don't deal with the living on a regular basis often forget what they were like before they became ghosts. Poindexter is a little more forgetful than Moncrief, but he's been dead longer. And Knott is still in shock, from what the other two said; I didn't get to speak with him. I hope he realizes what has happened soon, so that I might be able to learn who killed him. He must know, or be able to describe his murderer."

"That would be useful, though I don't know how to account for having that kind of information." She typed a line.

"Policemen don't much sympathize with talking to ghosts," Holte agreed. "You need to maintain credibility with them, for your own sake."

"I'm glad you understand," said Poppy, a bit surprised that Holte realized the awkwardness of her position.

"I'll try to learn more in a day or two." Holte sought out the sofa near the fireplace and extended himself over it and appeared to prop his heels on the arm.

"Are you resting?" Poppy inquired.

"In a manner of speaking," said Holte. "Ghosts don't sleep, but we do run low on energy. Just keeping partly visible takes concentration and stamina. I'll vanish in a few minutes, and will work to restore myself."

"Then you might as well make yourself comfortable. I hope my typing won't bother you."

"Type away." He appeared to close his eyes, and hovered an inch or so above the sofa seat; on the rug in front of the fireplace, Duchess whimpered in her sleep. "Don't worry, old girl," he said to the dog.

Poppy began typing, working as steadily as she could. She found Holte's invisible presence a bit of a distraction, but would not disturb him, for fear that she would not get sufficient work done before dinner if they started talking again. By the time the mantle-clock chimed eight, she left her pages in the typewriter, put on its cover, turned out the lamp, and went to the door, where she whistled quietly to Duchess, snapping her fingers to summon the liver-and-white spaniel. "Suppertime," she called softly, and waited for the old dog to toddle over to the door and out into the hall before Poppy closed it, reminding herself that Holte could pass through it when he wanted to leave the room. She went ahead of Duchess down the stairs, and nodded to Missus Flowers, who was just going into the kitchen. "Good evening," she said, and mustered her thoughts for apologizing to Aunt Jo for being tardy; Aunt Jo was a stickler for punctuality, and would expect some kind of expression of regret for this lapse in courtesy.

Josephine was in the sitting room, a glass of straw-colored sherry in her hand, and a plate of crackers topped with baby clams in cream cheese, pickled onions, and celery sticks stuffed with paprika-flavored mayonnaise. She gave Poppy an impatient glance, and said, "Your cognac is on the sideboard in a thistle-glass. Hawkins suggests that we dine in the morning room, and I agree."

"I'm sorry for being late, Aunt Jo." Poppy went to get her cognac, then settled on the other end of the sofa, well within reach of the appetizers. "And I may give Stacy a piece of my mind when he finally shows up."

"Let me attend to that," said her aunt with an air of great indignation. "It may be that this is Mister Derrington's doing; he doesn't know much about the way we manage things in this household."

"Stacy does," Poppy observed.

"I'm sure Mister Derrington is over-riding Stacy's good manners," Aunt Jo announced in a tone that brooked no opposition. "Eustace is many things, but he is never rude — Mister Derrington is."

Unable to see how either of these things could be possible, Poppy tried to change the subject; she lifted her snifter, and said, "To your good fortune and good health, Aunt Jo," before taking another sip. "I know you'd never drink your own toast."

"That's nice of you; no, I would never drink a toast to me — it's such dreadful luck to do so, and such abominable manners," Josephine said, a little vaguely, her eyes distant. "That son of mine. Why does he have to be so secretive? I'm not inclined to gossip, particularly about my own family. Eustace refuses to understand: I don't want to intrude in his life, but I would like to know where he's been."

Poppy did her best to soothe her aunt. "This is hardly something new, Aunt Jo. Everyone knows it."

"He's lively and easily bored, so he thinks up tricks," said her aunt with great conviction, wanting to come to her son's defense. "But it occasionally causes him to be inconsiderate. I don't doubt that Mister Derrington encourages him in this."

"It seems to me that Stacy doesn't need much encouragement," said Poppy, a bit more acerbically than she had intended. "I'm not saying anything against Stacy, just that he's been prankish and secretive his whole life."

"Do not disdain your cousin, Poppea. Have a little compassion." She finished her sherry and reached for the crystal bottle to refill her glass. "He felt the loss of his brothers very keenly."

This remark was so wholly unlike what Poppy had experienced with Stacy from the time they were in grammar school that she took a little while to summon up something to say that would not contradict Josephine's vindication of her son. "He . . . he doesn't always think about the consequences of his actions, Aunt Jo, no matter what else he may do — except, I gather, in his business dealings. There he's as canny as an owl."

"That may be," Aunt Jo conceded. "It's the dare-devil in him, don't you know." She had another sip of her sherry. "He's not irresponsible."

"I suppose," Poppy said, and took a cracker from the platter. To her amazement, she discovered she was hungry.

"Are we going to have that policeman here in the morning?" Josephine asked abruptly.

This sudden change in topic startled Poppy, until she mentally reviewed Aunt Jo's train of thought: Stacy to the Moncriefs, the Moncriefs to the murder, the murder to Inspector Loring, or, she told herself, something along those lines. "That's my understanding. Inspector Loring told me that he does need to talk with Stacy, to help him fill in some of the gaps in Madison's personal background." Poppy finished her cracker and took another.

"I don't see why that should be necessary. The poor man's dead — let him rest in peace." She finished her sherry, and once more refilled her glass. "Least said, soonest mended."

This troubled Poppy, who rarely saw Aunt Jo drink so much before dinner. Taking another judicious sip of cognac, Poppy realized that her aunt was worried, but could not bring herself to admit it; Aunt Jo, being Aunt Jo, could not accept that she was troubled, and so was masking her worry with sherry. "The police are doing their best to find out what happened to Madison; they're sure to have an answer in time."

"In time," Josephine echoed with scorn. "Those sorts of men! No grasp about people of quality. But how could they grasp our way of life, dealing with scoundrels and hooligans as they must do every day." When she refilled her sherry glass once again, she almost spilled it as she carried it to her lips.

"Have a cracker, Aunt Jo. They're quite good." Poppy watched her uneasily, realizing that her aunt was getting drunk. "Or the celery. I know you like stuffed celery."

It took Josephine several seconds to answer. "I don't have much of an appetite," she said indistinctly, and then added, "In fact, I'm tired. I believe I'll have my dinner in my room." She put down her glass, shoved herself to her feet, and tottered from the room, Duchess following after her.

Poppy watched her go with mixed emotions; she admired Aunt Jo's conclusion that Stacy was still the high-spirited boy he had been in his youth, but it bothered Poppy that there was more to Stacy's behavior now than a simple desire to amuse himself. In the last ten years he had become cynical and manipulative, and both those traits troubled her. She took another sip of cognac, then set the glass aside, got up from her chair, and made her way into the morning room to have her solo meal accompanied only by her unrewarding thoughts.

TWENTY-FIVE

ᘉᘉᘉ

STACY CAME DOWN TO BREAKFAST HALF AN HOUR LATER THAN WAS HIS HABIT IN an unusually surly mood, his robe on over pyjamas instead of shirt and trousers, his hair negligently combed, and his eyes slightly red. He glared at Missus Flowers when she asked him if he preferred tomato or orange juice. "What I'd like is two aspirin and a cup of strong coffee, if you can manage it. I'm afraid I indulged myself more than usual last night."

Josephine, who was in her dressing gown gave her son a look of umbrage that only Maestro could improve upon, for though she was willing to defend him to others, she reserved the right to disapprove of him to herself. "You came in very late, I understand. Another sign of over-indulgence, perhaps. Perhaps we should both go to the one-o'clock service at Holy Family?" She had departed from her usual breakfast and was having poached eggs on a bed of corn-meal mush, and she would have a baked apple to follow; there was hot chocolate in her cup instead of tea. She, too, was looking a little haggard, a silent testament to a largely sleepless night.

"Spare me the demands of piety," Stacy declared. "Warren and I had a . . . dispute about the way I'm handling his dealings with . . . well, that's not important. Business confidentiality, you know. We argued during dinner, and he went to a hotel for the night, or he said he would. I haven't spoken to him this morning. I don't know if he's going to remain an associate of mine, and he said he would take his business elsewhere before I left. We were both a little . . . indulgent, and I think it likely that he will reconsider once he is himself again." He sniffed as if he had encountered a noxious odor.

"What time did you arrive?" It was clear that Josephine expected an answer.

"I'm not sure," Stacy answered, and added, "It was some time after three, maybe as late as three-forty." He yawned hugely and suddenly. "If he keeps to what he said last night, Warren will be by later, to pick up his things — unless he changes his mind, and stays in Philadelphia for the whole weekend and into Monday, which I hope he will: he's an intelligent man, and there was nothing we disagreed upon that can't be negotiated." With a slow shake of his head, he fixed his mother with a stare. "We dined late, at Henry's, in the upstairs room, and parted company about midnight."

"How did you get home? Did you call a cab?" his mother asked as she poked at the yolk of her eggs with a fork.

"Couldn't find one. I walked most of the way." He coughed. "There were a couple of sprinkles during my walk, and my coat got soaked. I hung it in the mud room so it wouldn't drip all over the house."

At once Josephine was distressed. "You didn't get wet, did you? It would be horrid if you took si — "

"I won't take a cold, Mother," Stacy assured her, sounding bored. "The 'Flu is long gone and no one catches it because of a little rain."

"You know best, I'm sure," Josephine said in a tone that implied the opposite. She drank a little more chocolate.

Stacy gave a tired chuckle. "Don't be such a goose, Mother. You know I'm rarely ill." He looked up as Missus Flowers came into the morning room. "Will you be good enough to bring me some strong, hot coffee, black? And then will you bring me French toast and sausage? Thanks, Bertha."

Unfazed by Stacy's cavalier behavior, Missus Flowers put down a small pot of hot chocolate for Josephine. "Directly, Mister Eustace."

"What an admirable servant you are," Stacy went on as if he had not heard her. "I marvel, I truly marvel."

This was more than Josephine could endure. "Oh, Eustace, stop it. I am sorry you had a fracas with your friend, and that you had to walk home in the rain, but I'm tired of your petulance and sarcasm. If you're displeased, don't take it out on the servants." She made a moue of distaste. "You're not a child any more, and these displays of temperament are no longer diverting." She shook her head, then picked up her cup, drank the last of the cooling chocolate, and poured more from the pot.

"I'm sorry I've disappointed you, Mother," Stacy said in a chilly voice.

As Stacy intended, Josephine melted. "Nothing of the sort, Eustace. You know I'm very proud of your accomplishments, and I will defend you to the death in any endeavor you undertake. Yes, it's apparent you're successful, but that's hardly sufficient for your erudition or position in society. Whatever it is you do, it doesn't give you the opportunity to live up to your potential."

"Please, Mother," Stacy said at his most pained. "You've stated your case before. I know you'd prefer that I become a professor or a judge or a senator, or something equally traditional, but none of those things appeal to me. I'm far more comfortable in the wheeling and dealing of international trade; everything else bores me, Mother, and I won't spend my life being bored." He could see that she was about to begin a long harangue, and so he held up his hand to stop her. "Will you be willing to take my word that I'm not doing anything that might embarrass the family?"

"Of course, Eustace. I understand your reservations, I do, but don't you think you could do better than — " she began, but was silenced as Poppy came into the room, fully dressed for the day: her skirt was grape-colored wool done in box-pleats, and over it she wore a long sweater in a soft lilac shade. She had a printed, narrow silk scarf tied loosely around her neck, and her hair was brushed to a high sheen; she was a fine example of city-casual fashion. "Oh, Poppea, I'm so pleased you decided to join us. I don't believe you're bound for church this morning."

"Good morning to you both, then, and no, I am not going to church. I haven't done so since Christmas," Poppy said as she pulled out a chair for herself. "I hope you both slept well."

"Please, Coz, no cheeriness," Stacy said with a dramatic gesture. "It's much too early."

"It's a clear day, and it's beginning to feel like spring is finally here," Poppy announced, undaunted by Stacy's posturing.

"It's unendurable at this hour," Stacy said in pained accents.

"You're being foolish, Eustace," his mother admonished him. "Yes, Poppea, I slept very well, thank you, once I got to sleep. I had to resort to veronal, but it was precisely what was needed."

"You and your veronal," Stacy complained, largely for the fun of nettling Josephine. "I wish you wouldn't use it as often as you do."

"Doctor Morrow says that I require it," Josephine declared, and went silent as Missus Flowers returned with Stacy's coffee in a large china mug.

"Hot and black, as requested," Missus Flowers said, and set it before him.

"You are an angel, Bertha. Word of honor." Stacy smiled.

"Whatever you like, Mister Eustace," she said crisply, and turned to Poppy. "What would you like, Miss Thornton?"

"Scrambled eggs on hash, if you would, Missus Flowers, and coffee." Poppy glanced at Stacy. "What's on your agenda today, Stacy? after you talk to Inspector Loring at ten-thirty."

"Will you be joining us?" Stacy asked. "Since you know the time, perhaps you should sit in, to observe." He punctuated this with a mirthless smile.

"It wouldn't be proper for me to do that," Poppy admitted, and added, "I'd like it if I could."

"So would your editor," Stacy said with an expression remarkably near a sneer.

Josephine intervened. "Yes, Eustace, what are your plans for the rest of the day? It's a reasonable request, isn't it."

Stacy picked up his coffee and had an experimental sip, and set it down. "I promised Louise I'd drop by later; she's still having a rough time. And I have a business meeting in the evening, so I won't be here at dinner. I think I'll take the train back to New York tomorrow morning, unless I find out that the current deal I'm working on needs my attention here. I'll be back for the funeral, but that won't be for a few more days. The coroner informed Louise that he won't release the body until Wednesday, or so Louise tells me; it will have to be closed casket. After so long, he's bound to be a little . . . ripe. That means Thursday at the earliest, or maybe Friday. Louise would not like to have it on the weekend — too many gawkers about."

"Eustace!" Josephine exclaimed. "Not at table, I beg you."

Stacy gave a low chortle. "Madison is dead, Mother. It won't matter to him."

"You don't have to be outrageous because you're hung over," Poppy chimed in.

Stacy glared at her. "And you a reporter, Coz."

"You're upsetting your mother," Poppy said, refusing to rise to the bait. "Ye gods, Stacy: you're doing it deliberately."

Josephine made a little gasp. "Surely you don't mean that, Poppea."

"Well, Aunt Jo, yes, I do." Poppy sighed. "You've protected him all his life, and you will not let anyone but you speak against him. He's taken advantage of that since he was four."

"You are aware, aren't you, Coz, that I'm sitting here, listening." Stacy took another sip and then a gulp of his coffee.

"I certainly am," said Poppy, and glanced at her Aunt Jo. "I apologize if I'm offending you, Aunt, but Stacy's being horrid this morning, and it's time he stopped."

Stacy made a face at her. "Goodie Two-Shoes."

"Grow up, Stacy," Poppy said bluntly.

"Poppea! This is most unbecoming of you," Aunt Jo admonished her, and glowered as Missus Flowers came into the morning room with a baked apple in a bowl, smelling of maple syrup and butter, and another mug of coffee.

"Your scrambled eggs and hash will be ready shortly, Miss Thornton; I'll bring it in within the next ten minutes," said Missus Flowers.

"Thank you, Missus Flowers; I'll be glad of a little sustenance," Poppy said, and added a bit more cream to her coffee; she picked up her spoon and stirred the contents of the mug, her gaze fixed on a distant spot.

"You're welcome, I'm sure," she said, and again left the room.

A tentative silence fell over the morning room. Josephine finished her eggs and moved the plate aside to make room for the bowl with the baked apple, which she carefully cut into with a spoon. Poppy added a little sugar to her coffee, stirred it once more, and blew on it to cool it. Stacy drank down more of his coffee and set the mug aside, giving a sigh of ill-usage and directing his abstracted gaze toward the south-facing windows. There was a clatter in the kitchen, and the oven-door banged.

"Is the paper here yet?" Stacy asked languidly.

"I don't know," said his mother, her sensibilities still offended.

"Do you mind if I go and look?" he rejoined, satisfied in the knowledge that he had got under her skin. "Hawkins is at church, isn't he? And this is his day off."

"You know he is, and it isn't church, it's meeting house. And you are aware that he has Sundays off; it's been the same since you were in grammar school," Poppy said. "Stop needling your mother."

Stacy chuckled and got up from the table. "I'll be back in a tick." He made a suggestion of a bow and left the room.

As soon as the door was closed, Poppy turned to Aunt Jo. "Why do you let him behave like that?"

Josephine shrugged. "I can't do much about it, dear," she said; when she used the word dear in a response, it was useless to pursue the subject.

But Poppy refused to be deterred. "He just keeps getting worse. The next thing, he'll be undressing in public."

"Poppea, you mustn't say such things about your cousin." Josephine was sitting very straight, revealing her umbrage. "You know he doesn't mean half of what he says. You're being unfair to him."

"Unfair? How is it unfair?" Poppy countered, and would have gone on, but Missus Flowers appeared in the door.

"There's a 'phone call for you, Miss," she said.

"Did the caller give you a name?" Poppy asked as she rose.

"No. It's a gentleman, though," Missus Flowers said, and was about to leave the room when Josephine stopped her.

"I'll have another pot of chocolate, I think. This one's nearly empty."

As Poppy left the room, Missus Flowers went to retrieve the pot, saying, "Five minutes and you'll have your chocolate. Do you mind the wait?"

"Of course not," she said, and finished the chocolate in her cup.

Poppy went into the entry hall where the 'phone was located and picked up the receiver from its stand. "Hello? This is Poppy — "

" — Thornton, yes, I know," said Inspector Loring. "I'm calling to ask you if you might have some time free this morning? If you're busy, I'll understand, but I'd really appreciate it if you would agree to give me thirty to forty minutes, as soon as I'm done with your cousin."

"If that would be helpful, of course I would be glad to be of assistance;

you know I have to maintain source confidentiality, but if that won't be a problem . . . " She had begun speaking before she had thought about the implications of what he was asking. "I'll be working on my next installment on the story. I have to turn it in this afternoon to make tomorrow's paper, and I may have more to write about by our Monday deadline." Listening to herself, she realized she was babbling, and made herself go silent.

"Thank you," he said. "So, I'll see you later?"

"I should hope so," said Poppy, and wondered if that sounded too cooperative, too eager. "I'm counting on hearing what's happening with your investigation, since it appears to parallel with mine. If you have any information you can pass on to me, I'd appreciate it," she added, trying to keep her tone professional.

"You mean, trade information again?"

"If you're willing, I am," she said, and wanted to bite her tongue in case he should interpret this the wrong way.

"We'll see," he responded. "Until then."

She heard the click as he hung up, and thought that the operator might have been listening, for there was a soft pop on the line immediately after.

An instant later, Chesterton Holte spoke from behind her; he was barely visible, like a faded sketch in pastel chalk. "I told you he likes you. You can hear it in his voice — at least, I can." He wafted around her, a place in the air that seemed denser than the rest. "By the way, I apologize for eavesdropping."

"Ye gods! That was you?" She moved as if to take hold of him, but discovered only a patch of chilly air. "You were listening?"

"Yes — you know how I can make lights flicker, and I can also tap into an active phone line, but only while it's in use." His shape wavered and he slid across the wall like an image from a movie.

"Stop that," Poppy said, then added, "I'm on edge."

"With excellent reason," said Holte. "You're under pressure and that cousin of yours is not helping."

It bothered Poppy to hear him; defending Stacy was more than she was up to just now. "I need to get back to the morning room. I haven't had breakfast yet."

TWENTY-SIX

ॐ

"Go ahead," said Holte, and faded away to a pale smudge.

WITH THE HEAVY DAMASK DRAPERIES OPEN THE LIBRARY WAS AWASH WITH LIGHT; the floor-to-ceiling oak bookcases were glossy with polish, the fireplace had been swept yesterday, and the tiles on the hearth were shiny. On the sofa in front of the fireplace, Maestro was dozing, his tail twitching occasionally. Poppy sat at the typewriter, rolling in her fourth page in an attempt to put together as much information as she had to hand. She had a small stack of fresh pages, another of onion-skin second sheets, and three sheets of carbon paper laid out at her left elbow; so far all she had done was roll three aligned sheets into the platen.

"You're dawdling," Holte said to her out of the empty air. "It isn't like you to dawdle."

Poppy did not jump at the sound of his voice; she made a gesture of exasperation, then said, "You're right. Yes, I am marking time because I think I ought to wait until I've had a word with Inspector Loring in order to do an article that's really worthwhile. As it is, what I have is pretty thin. I can pad it out, but Lowenthal would probably cut those parts."

"Are you planning to mention anything more about Knott, or just Moncrief? Or anything else connected with this case, or these cases?"

"I won't know until I hear what Loring has to say, and he only arrived ten minutes ago — he's with Stacy, in case you didn't know, so I'm left to what I have on hand already." She tapped on the desktop, revealing the high level of her impatience. "Unless you have something to add, of course."

Holte became a bit more visible. "Not yet. But I have a feeling that

Overstreet may also be among the missing — not dead, necessarily, but missing."

"You mean that he is afraid, and has left?" she asked.

"It seems likely, don't you think?"

"Have you learned anything more concrete than that?" Poppy could see him falter, and she leaped on that. "What is it? What do you know?"

"Nothing specific, but after what happened to Knott, it makes sense that Overstreet might want to get out of range."

This caught Poppy's attention. "Did Knott tell you so?" As she listened to herself, she decided she might need to consult an alienist when this whole matter was finished: thinking that she was getting information from a ghost — hooey! would be the usual response. She was an educated, intelligent, modern woman. Yet she could not help but listen to what he told her.

"No. He's still somewhat . . . unsettled." Holte moved about the room, almost disappearing as he skidded through the bars of light from the windows.

"How long will that last?" Poppy demanded, her frustration getting the better of her.

"Who knows?" he answered.

She stopped the sharp retort that rose to her lips, reminding herself that she would be doing the very thing she condemned in Stacy. "It's one of those ghostly things, isn't it? The way you reckon time when you're noncorporeal?"

"Or don't reckon it," he agreed. "Sooner and later are very much the same to us."

She would have liked to rub her eyes; they were itching from lack of sleep, but she was wearing mascara and knew it would smear, so she laced her fingers together. "What do you mean about Overstreet? Why should he . . . um . . . get out of range?" she asked.

"If he saw what was done to Knott, he must be frightened. Overstreet ought to put some distance between himself and the crime if he has any sense at all, what with the police trying to find him, as well, I suspect, as the killer or killers." Holte became slightly more visible.

"Put it that way, and I see what you mean."

"Since police haven't found him, it's troubling, under the circumstances."

"You know this because you've watched them? the police?" Poppy waited for his answer. "Or have you learned something you aren't telling me."

This time Holte chose his words carefully. "I spent a little time with the police yesterday afternoon. From what I can surmise, they're beginning to think Overstreet did it — that he killed Knott, I mean."

"Just to be clear about it," Poppy said, "what do you think?"

Holte grew first brighter, then dimmer. "It doesn't seem likely, not given how bloody the scene was. Ask Wyman about it, when you get a chance. If he'll tell you."

"But do you think Stacy knows more about it than he's telling?" Poppy asked. "Stacy?"

"It seems likely, unless he having fun playing games with the police," said Holte.

"I wouldn't think he'd try to make a game out of a friend's death." She got up from the desk and began to pace. "But I wouldn't think he were capable of that kind of violence, or even participating in it indirectly. Stacy's a gadfly, not an assassin."

"You think he would draw the line at Knott, you mean, or anyone?" Holte moved toward the fireplace; Maestro raised his head and hissed, his eyes narrowing and his tail lashing.

"Anyone. He doesn't seem the type to kill an associate, does he?"

Holte gave a single laugh that had as much despair as amusement in it. "What type is that?" He waved his barely visible hand. "I don't believe there's a type of murderer. But no, I don't think he would; as you say, it doesn't appear to be his style. Extortion or embezzlement, maybe forgery, but not murder." He slid along beside her. "I could be wrong, but I think Overstreet has fled not from guilt, but from fear of whomever killed Knott."

"Which means that Overstreet knows who the killer is?" Poppy pursued.

"Or thinks he does," Holte cautioned. "Take it from a spy — people often don't know as much as they believe they do. And those who know more than they admit to are not apt to share it with you."

Poppy let this pass unchallenged. "Is there a way you could find out about Overstreet? though your ghostly connections." Poppy was astonished at what she was asking; she was amazed at what Holte was telling her, that he was not some kind of trick that Carter the Great invented to astonish his audiences.

Holte regarded her so keenly that she could almost make out the inquisitive gleam in his eyes. "I can make the attempt; that's the best I can offer. Would you like me to?"

"Wait until I talk with Loring." She was beginning to feel encouraged. With help from Chesterton Holte, she might be able to bring her assignment to a good conclusion, and with a little luck, she could establish herself as a crime reporter.

"All right. I will." He drifted toward the end of the room and the tall windows that overlooked the rear garden. "Someone in the dimension of ghosts should know where I can start looking, assuming that he or she is willing to tell me, or cares about Moncrief's or Knott's death." He began to disappear, but halted when he was little more than a wavering place in the air. "Don't get your hopes up, Poppy."

"You mean you intend to do this now?" asked Poppy, and not wanting to appear too eager to learn more, added, "Given your ghostly view of time, that is."

"As soon as you have your tête-a-tête with Loring. He may have something useful to say about what's happened to Overstreet, or tell you if there is some kind of trail he can follow. If you can get it out of him, that is; I'll listen in, and hope to discover something new from him." He shimmered a little in the bars of light.

"If it will help you get information, I'll think of something to pry with; we need to have some solid answers," Poppy said, making it a promise.

"That sounds . . . like a good possibility." Holte said, mildly distracted as he weighed various scenarios in his mind. "This whole investigation — if that's an appropriate description — has been a tangle: every new discovery leads to many more questions. I wish I knew what kind of business dealings your cousin had with Knott. Has he ever talked about that?"

Poppy shook her head. "Stacy doesn't discuss business in general, and when he does, he avoids specifics and once in a while, he resorts to outright evasion. He says it's professional confidentiality, but in the last year or two, I've had some doubts — he knows bootleggers, you see, even Aunt Jo admits it — and he's not one to reject an opportunity. But I can't see how any of this case ties into arranging for the covert importation of wines and spirits." Saying this aloud bothered her, and she stared up at the ceiling as if to separate herself from her anxiety.

"If it is about bootlegging. I'm not sure that it is."

Poppy spoke up at once. "Stacy might take pride in being able to work his way around a law he doesn't approve of, but I can't see him conspiring in anything so violent as murder, not even at a distance. That," she added, "doesn't mean that he is unaware of who might be. Involved. I think that he would keep compromising knowledge compromising for others to himself. That's one of the things I almost admire about him."

"Almost?"

Poppy considered her answer carefully. "I think he could withhold crucial information for the sheer mischief of it, if he thought it would be . . . amusing."

"Including information about murder," Holte said, for clarification.

"Yes, if it's to his advantage, he could very well keep back what he knows about a murder, especially if it involves friends of his," she admitted, and wished that she could fall through a sudden hole in the ground. "He's as fastidious as a cat, and murder is — "

"Sodding ugly," Holte finished for her, startling her with his blunt use of language.

"Yes, and that's not at all like Stacy," she said a bit too quickly.

"But where is the tipping point?" he mused. "How much would he conceal, and what would be enough for him to reveal what he knows?"

Poppy took more time to answer. "It would depend upon what would happen to his business, that's my guess." She frowned. "And he's a snob, and that could turn out to be a problem. He would do almost anything to avoid besmirching his reputation among his peers."

"In what way?" Holte inquired.

"He might not want to speak against anyone who is part of his class, friends or not," she said, worried that she was saying too much, admitting too many of her reservations about Stacy. "Still, I don't think he'd withhold information on murder." She felt a bit ashamed of herself for not being more stalwart in her cousin's favor.

Holte said nothing.

"You don't agree?" Poppy ventured.

"Let's say that you know him better than I do; you're smart and observant, so I'll accept your assessment even though he's your cousin, and you're biased in his favor." He quivered in the sunlight and rose toward the ceiling. "It's best if he believes you two are alone against the world — I don't want interfere with that."

"Why?"

"Because it strikes me that your cousin Stacy is a much downier character than you give him credit for being, and that bothers me; I'm a bit bothered that his connections to shady groups hasn't alarmed you, since you're a reporter. I want to make sure that he suspects little about my inquiries, which I hope he wouldn't believe if you informed him of them at breakfast." With that, he whisked away to the far corner of the room and lay back against the ceiling.

"Do you imagine that Stacy suspects that I'm being haunted?" Poppy challenged, and was met with silence. Heaving a sigh of aggravation, she went back to the desk and sat down at the typewriter. In the space of ten minutes she managed to get no more than her heading on the page, and then sat staring at the swath of blank paper. She was about to get up and go downstairs to ask Missus Flowers for more coffee when there was a tap on the door. "Come in," she responded automatically, and stood up as Inspector Loring entered the room. "Good afternoon, Inspector — I trust it is afternoon by now."

"Barely, and it's going to be a long afternoon," said Loring as he closed the door and looked around him; he was in dark-brown slacks, a dull-blue roll-neck pullover under a Scottish tweed jacket. "What a nice place this is," he declared once he had taken the whole thing in. "No wonder you enjoy working in it."

"Thank you, Inspector," she said, surprised by his interest. "I like it, too." She gestured to the sofa and the two chairs that framed it. "If you'd sit down?"

"Thanks." He chose the chair on the far side of the sofa; Maestro opened one eye and glared at him before draping the end of his tail over his face as if to shut out his human interlopers. "That's quite a cat you have there."

"He certainly thinks so," said Poppy, coming to the other chair at the end of the sofa.

"Is he yours or your aunt's?" Loring inquired in a tone that assured her it had nothing to do with his investigation.

"Aunt Jo's, of course, like Duchess. They're both royally spoiled in their own way." Poppy sat down and faced Loring, meeting his eyes as forthrightly as she could. "If it isn't impolite to ask, how did things go with Stacy?"

"I'm trying to figure that out," said Loring, giving a quick shake of his head. "He's a conundrum, no two ways about it."

"Was he uncooperative?" Poppy asked, dreading the answer.

"Not obviously so, but he didn't actually tell me anything I hadn't found out already, and he wouldn't be lured into saying more than a few remarks that appeared casual but I doubt were. The one thing I truly couldn't get out of him was what kind of business he was doing with Moncrief. He kept citing professional — "

" — confidentiality," she finished with him. "He often uses that to keep from revealing the things he wants to keep private, and there are many things he wants to keep private."

Loring nodded. "I told him that his deliberate obfuscation made him seem less than candid in his responses not concerned with his work, and he said that I could be suspicious of him if I liked, but there was no reason to be."

Poppy laughed, a bit nervously, and said, "How like him."

"He's a slippery rascal, I'll give him that, but he's not doing himself any favors with such tactics. He's raising more questions about what he's doing than if he had been straightforward with me. Unless he's breaking more laws than the Volstead Act imposes." He tried to make this sound reassuring and succeeded in doing the opposite; he leaned forward, as if to touch her across the empty carpet. "I'm not calling him a suspect, Poppy. I haven't sufficient information to do so, and certainly none from him. All I am certain of is that he's withholding some things from me, and that they may or may not be connected with Moncrief's murder; he might be doing it for pleasure."

Poppy rubbed her forehead. "As I've told you, he's always liked having secrets."

"That much is obvious," said Loring, sounding tired. "He was enjoying himself all through my questioning."

She regarded him in a way that she hoped was neutral enough to hide her anxiety. "Did he mention that he has been spending time with Louise? They were friends before she married Madison."

"He said he introduced them, that they were old friends."

"That they are. They met about fifteen years ago, and have been close ever since." Saying this made her worry again, in an ill-defined way that made her fret.

Loring went on, "He said she asked him to visit her often while he's in town." He coughed once. "I don't know why he told me that, except that it was all of a piece with the rest of what he volunteered, like letting me know he and Moncrief were members of the same country club, where they sometimes golfed."

"That's true enough. At university, they were on the sculling team. They also belonged to the same shooting club for a while; Moncrief relied on Stacy to handle his foreign business dealings; Warren Derrington has done much the same thing, but I understand Stacy and Derrington have had a parting of the ways, which wasn't the case with Moncrief. Stacy and Madison spent part of a summer sailing, before the country got into the Great War." She wondered what she should say next to encourage him to provide more material she could use in her story for Lowenthal. "Would you tell me if you do come to suspect him?"

"I'd have to; it would mean an end of conversations like this one," he said. "Where did that come from — asking if I might suspect your cousin in some capacity?"

"Protective curiosity. He's my cousin. My aunt would be devastated if he became a suspect."

"Okay, I understand that." Loring ran his hand through his hair. "It'd be dam . . . dratted awkward for you to cover the story if Stacy were seriously involved."

"You can say damned around me, I won't mind; I hear worse at the paper.

Just don't use profanity or obscenities where my aunt can hear you."

"So you've said." He sat back in his chair. "You're in a difficult position, aren't you? Your work can't be reassuring to the people around you."

She was suddenly feeling that she had been dilatory in their discussion. "How do you mean that?"

"Your friend is dead, your friends are being investigated, and your cousin is playing games with the police. You're expected to cover the story for your paper and not to take sides. That's got to be a difficult stance to maintain."

"Yes, yes, it is, but to be frank, it's exactly the kind of opportunity I've been hoping for since I went to work at the Clarion." It felt strange to admit this so baldly; she tried not to look too chagrined. "Not the murder, of course, but the chance to cover crime."

"I get that," he said. "But it would probably be easier if your friends — and your family — were not directly part of the investigation."

"It is a balancing act. And you're right —Stacy isn't making it any easier."

As if it had just occurred to him, Loring asked, "Do you know what your cousin and Derrington argued about last night?"

"I imagine you asked him that already," she said.

"And he danced around the answer like Nijinsky. I was hoping he was more forthcoming with you."

"Nothing particular, or nothing that he was willing to discuss. Keep in mind that what I'm telling you is second hand."

"What did he say? What did you observe?"

Poppy shrugged. "He came in very late, and Aunt Jo was worried about him. And he was in a foul mood this morning." She wished she had bitten her tongue rather than tell him so much; she added, "He was hung-over at breakfast, and brooding about a business deal he was working on, that much I know. He has been bothered about a problem with one of his ventures since he got here, but whether it was his deal with Derrington or someone else, I have no idea, and I didn't bother to pursue it. He didn't say anything important about this one way or the other."

"Has Derrington come to collect his things yet? I'd like to talk to him."

"Not that I know of." She did not add that she was curious about his absence. "Maybe he's reconsidering whatever he said last night."

"Your cousin gave me the impression that this has happened before; they have quarreled but it has never resulted in a lasting rift." Loring was fishing, and Poppy knew it.

"All I know is that he was disappointed in Derrington."

"I understand that," said Loring. "Stacy's habit of hints without anything substantial must drive you over the top, being a reporter."

"Oh, it drove me over the top long before that," she said, wanting to lighten the mood so that she could pump him about the case. "He was much more annoying when he was ten."

"So I gather; he said you used to yell at him for being surreptitious," he said, taking his cue from her. "Yet you guard him. Why do you do that? Is it family or something more?"

"How do you mean, something more?"

"Ambition, perhaps," he said. "Or one of those complicated family situations that can't be directly resolved. It would be surprising if you didn't feel some conflicts between your family interests and the Clarion's."

"It'll depend on how things turn out," she answered. "If there are any more murders among people I know, I'll probably be taken off the story, so it won't matter."

"Have you any reason to think you might be taken off the story as things stand now?" he said, pouncing on her remark.

"Not really. I think the murder of Mister Knott spooked me." She was pleased with her private joke.

"Are you following that?" He seemed surprised.

"Everyone in the city room is following that," she answered.

"Are you sure about Derrington and your cousin?" Loring demanded, almost getting out of his chair. "That they were involved in business ventures together?"

"I don't have a confirmation, but my source is most reliable, so I'm proceeding on that assumption for now." She glanced up at the far corner of the ceiling, wishing as she did that she knew what Holte was thinking. "Knott dealt with the people in the tri-city region who could afford what he supplied. He dealt only in top-quality antiques and antiquities, for top-quality prices. "

It was an effort of will for Loring to sit back down. "Antiques can be very expensive, as I remember. I'm not on that case, Inspector Tyler's in charge."

"Perhaps you two should talk," Poppy suggested.

"Yeah," he said, sinking into deep thought.

They sat in uneasy silence for nearly two minutes, and finally Poppy said, "Is there anything else we should discuss."

Loring glanced up at her. "There probably is, but for the life of me, I can't think of what it could be. I'll have to 'phone you when it occurs to me. I'll let you get back to work." Saying that, he launched himself out of his chair, strode to her side, took her hand, kissed it, and made for the door. "If you learn anything before I do, you 'phone me. Hawkins will see me out. Get back to the typewriter."

Startled and unexpectedly gratified, Poppy got to her feet and followed him to the door. "Good luck, Inspector," she said as he went toward the stairs.

"Thanks," he said, offering her a grim smile.

She watched him while he descended the stairs; when she turned back into the room, Maestro was puffed out like a bottle-brush and Chesterton Holte was mostly visible and hovering near her desk.

"Told you so," he said with an expression that was dangerously near a smirk.

TWENTY-SEVEN

THIS TIME, CORNELIUS LOWENTHAL CAME TO POPPY TO COLLECT HER STORY, his Dodge Brothers auto looking a bit out-of-place among the other, more expensive autos on the street, and Lowenthal himself seemed a bit deflated as Hawkins let him into the entry hall, where the wall sconces glowed with light as golden as that of the fading day outside.

"Do come in, Mister Lowenthal," Hawkins said as Poppy came out of the sitting room, and shook her boss' hand.

"This is some place you've got here," he muttered as he looked around.

"Thank you — I'll tell my aunt you said so," Poppy remarked, hoping to put her boss at ease.

"I didn't realize you were so . . . grand." He looked around again, his eyes widening.

Poppy motioned him toward the sitting room. "It's not mine, it's my Aunt Jo's."

"You live here — that's what counts," he grumbled, revealing his discomfort; Poppy realized that the house intimidated him.

"Yes, I'm fortunate," Poppy said, trying again to make him feel welcome.

He cleared his throat. "How many servants?"

"Realistically, six," said Poppy, indicating the settee near the sideboard.

"How many rooms, then?" Lowenthal pursued.

"Seventeen, if you count the mud room; Aunt Jo doesn't," she replied, and changed the subject. "Would you like something to drink? I can offer you coffee and tea, of course, or something stronger, if you prefer. We have some very good whiskey, or English gin, or rum. Or cognac." She lingered at the sideboard, standing so that Lowenthal could see the array of bottles and glasses set out on the dark-stained walnut sideboard.

Lowenthal remained standing — a rare courtesy for him — and mulled over the possibilities. "If I might have a wee dram?"

"You may," she said, and reached for the whiskey glass, then the bottle, removing the stopper and pouring out a little more than an ounce of the potent liquid into the squat glass. She set the stopper in place again, and went to Lowenthal, handing him his drink before turning on the central light in the ceiling. "Missus Flowers will bring us some finger-food shortly. Do, please, sit down." She took a manila file folder from the end of the sideboard and handed it to Lowenthal. "I've gone about as far as I can until I talk to Doctor Wyman tomorrow morning." She had set up the appointment shortly after Loring had left, and now she felt that it had been a sensible precaution. "I'll be able to get my story about that interview by press time tomorrow."

Holding his drink in one hand and the file in the other, he sat down on the settee as if he feared it might collapse. He set his glass on the occasional table at his elbow and opened the file, reading quickly, then asked, "Do you think the investigation is stalling? You're not breaking much new ground in this." He tapped the file.

"I'm not sure. The police are playing this close to the vest and — "

"Is your Inspector Loring shutting you out?" Lowenthal asked, less pointedly than he would have done in his office.

"No; from what I can tell, he's as bewildered as anyone." She noticed that he had not touched his whiskey, so she got up, saying, "I think I'll join you," and returned to the sideboard to pour herself a small cognac; she noticed that Lowenthal looked relieved. "I've been thinking that perhaps the investigation got off on the wrong foot. I think that we've assumed that the cops are right, but now I'm not so sure."

"Why is that?" Lowenthal asked, taking a first sip of his whiskey and nodding his approval.

"Well, if we were talking about the gangs near the docks, the cops would treat the killing as rivals fighting over territory. Not just Madison Moncrief, but James Poindexter — whose cause of death is still undetermined: it is tentatively considered a suicide, but it could also be a homicide, according to the coroner — and now Knott. The reason the police think these are different and distinct cases is because of who has been killed, because of the social portion of the victims, not the nature of the deaths as such. If the victims were members not of the upper class but of criminal gangs, the police would be apt to lump the events together."

"But what kind of territory or enterprise would people like your relatives and friends fight over? Embezzlement is one thing for folks like you, but murder is another — they don't execute you for embezzlement. It isn't sensible, is it?" Lowenthal wondered.

"When is murder ever sensible?" Poppy asked, thinking of her father, and Chesterton Holte's claims about her father's death.

But Cornelius Lowenthal was warming to his topic. "You got big houses, big cars, political influence, lots of mone — "

Poppy dared to interrupt him. "That's the same error the police are making, if you don't mind my saying so. They think that upper crust families are above such things, that they leave any dirty work to their underlings, that they don't resort to the kinds of violence that are apparent in this case. But what if they do?"

"They?" Lowenthal inquired. "Aren't you one of them?"

"By birth, yes, but I'm also an unmarried woman of nearly twenty-five, and that makes me an oddity. What's worse, I earn my living in an ungenteel occupation — from their point of view. I think I'm doing something more useful than hybridizing roses and attending lectures. And I refuse to be someone's brood mare." She thought of her recent meal with Mildred Fairchild, and suppressed a wince.

"Is that the only reason you're a reporter?" Lowenthal asked as he had a second sip.

Poppy returned to her chair with her drink in hand. "It's the primary one." She lifted her glass in a polite toast and tasted the cognac.

"Um-hum." It was Lowenthal's version of reciprocation.

Missus Flowers appeared in the doorway, a tray of canapés in her hands; behind her came Duchess, a hopeful wag in her tail. "Where would you like me to put this, Miss Thornton?"

Poppy looked around her. "If you'll bring the larger nesting table and set it between Mister Lowenthal and me?"

Missus Flowers put the tray on the sideboard and went to fetch the nesting table. "Would you like me to close the curtains? It's coming on to sunset." She paused, and added, "Your aunt is planning to dine in her room tonight since Mister Eustace hasn't returned yet."

"Oh dear," said Poppy.

"Yes," said Missus Flowers curtly, then continued more eagerly. "It's Fisherman's Stew — Missus Boudon made it before she left last night, and I'm about to put it on to simmer — and some rolls into the warming oven. What would you like? I can make an omelette or a sandwich if you would rather have a light meal."

"If you'll send a bowl of the stew and a roll or two up to the library in an hour or so, I'll be happy to have it," said Poppy, vexed at her quixotic cousin for providing so little information about his activities.

"And the curtains?" Missus Flowers prompted.

"No need for you to close them, Missus Flowers, thank you; I'll manage it when it's needed." Poppy moved in her chair in order to face Lowenthal a bit more directly. "In the meantime, perhaps a pot of coffee to accompany the stew — I'll be working late tonight."

"Very good," said Missus Flowers, placing the nesting table where Poppy had asked her to, and then went to get the canapés from the sideboard. "If you need anything, I'll be in the old staff common-room; Missus Boudon said she saw mice in there yesterday. If they are in there, I'll have to 'phone the exterminator in the morning." She tried to conceal a shudder. "I hate the thought of rodents in the house."

"Why not turn Maestro loose?" Poppy suggested. "He's been known to present Missus Dritchner with dead mice."

"Mice hide in the walls," Missus Flowers reminded Poppy. "Maestro might enjoy torturing a mouse or two, but I need to find how they're getting in in the first place, and stop them." She nodded once and left the sitting room, whistling to Duchess to follow her; the spaniel paid no attention, but wandered toward the table on which the tray of canapés had been set, a conjectural wag in her tail.

"So places like this get mice," Lowenthal said with the beginnings of a satisfied smile. "Just like the rest of us."

Poppy chuckled. "Mice are no respecters of social position."

Lowenthal took a deeper drink of whiskey. "I guess not." The canapés were small cups of puff pastry filled with smoked baby oysters, cream cheese, and a morsel of candied ginger, all dusted with sweet paprika. Lowenthal reached out and took one. "Looks pretty nice to me, even without caviar and lobster," he said before he ate it.

"Missus Boudon — our cook — does much fancier appetizers. Missus Flowers is the housekeeper, and she has a limited repertoire when it comes to cooking. My aunt prefers it when Missus Boudon prepares the food; she always has a variety of offerings."

"But this is her day off?" Lowenthal guessed, his words muffled by the canapé.

"Yes. Sundays and Wednesday afternoons, unless a formal dinner is planned." Poppy took a small sip of cognac.

He gave this information his attention. "Is that the usual arrangement in establishments like this one?"

"Most servants have one day off — Sunday is the most usual — and a half-day at another time during the week. Missus Flowers has Monday and Thursday off, so that the staff remains fairly constant; she lives in, as the butler does: Hawkins has his half-day on Sunday morning and his full day on Monday, though he occasionally switches them." She would have liked to know why he was asking, but was not willing to make it appear she was denigrating his standing in society.

"Do the Moncriefs have servants who . . . live in?" Lowenthal asked. "You might get some information out of them, if they do."

"They have a housekeeper — Missus Haas, I think — who lives in, and, as I recall, a handyman as well — he takes care of the repairs around the house and looks after their two autos. Their cook — who is also Missus Moncrief's personal maid — comes six days a week — Missus Reed, or maybe Reedly. I don't know the handyman's name, but Stacy should." She slapped the arm of her chair. "Ye gods! You're right. I should talk to them both, shouldn't I?"

Lowenthal shrugged and reached for a second canapé. "You might want to have a word with the housekeeper, at least."

"I'll have a word with Stacy, as well." Her eyes narrowed. "Why didn't he suggest it? talking to the servants."

"He might have a blind spot, the same way the police do, but in reverse; your cousin probably doesn't have a high opinion of servants," said Lowenthal, drinking down the last of his whiskey.

"It's possible. But I didn't think of it on my own, so I need to think about my own blind spots — they're shortcomings, and I ought to be rid of them." She sipped at her cognac, and helped herself to a canapé. "This truly is turning into a complicated story, isn't it?" She gave him no chance to answer. "I think that Missus Reed or Reedly will be inclined to talk to me, but I don't know about the handyman, or the housekeeper. They're likely to keep their talk in the household."

"You going to give it a try?" Lowenthal was watching her intently.

"If I can." If Inspector Loring had spoken to the servants, why had he said nothing about it to her? She had no answer that she liked.

Lowenthal set his glass aside and prepared to rise. "When you turn in your work tomorrow, I'd like to see something from the Moncriefs' servants. Do you think you can manage that?"

"I'll do my best," said Poppy, and got to her feet, reaching for Lowenthal's glass. "Would you like any more?"

"I certainly would," he said, picking up her file, "but I have to get your story into the paper shortly, so I had better leave. Besides, you have work to do, don't you?" This nudge was far from subtle, and Poppy knew what Lowenthal wanted to hear.

"You're right, boss. I'll call the Moncrief house in ten minutes and see what I can arrange for the morning."

"Atta girl," Lowenthal approved. "Give my regards to your aunt."

"I will. You give mine to your wife, please." She walked him to the front door and turned on the porch light. "Mind the third step on the walkway — it's a bit uneven," she recommended, and watched him make his way to his Dodge Brothers sedan; closing the door, she debated going back into the sitting room, but changed her mind and started up the stairs, trusting Missus Flowers to go in and remove temptation from Duchess' reach.

The library was a mass of shadows, and in an hour or so, it would be chilly. Poppy went to light the small fire laid in the fireplace, watching as the kindling winked into flame. She took a notebook from the desk and made notes to herself about calling the Moncrief house. It might be best to wait an hour to call, for that would be time for the servants' dinner, and in the intervening hour, Stacy might come back to his mother's house and provide some suggestions as to how she might best approach her latest assignment. While she waited, she composed the questions that she would ask the Moncriefs' staff, assuming they would speak to anyone from outside the household. When the clock in the corridor struck five, she looked around with a start. "Get to work, Thornton," she said aloud. At last she could demonstrate her perseverance and initiative, she thought, as she prepared to go down to the entry hall to the telephone, and the next stage of her investigation.

TWENTY-EIGHT

MISSUS HAAS, HER RAW-BONED FRAME DRAPED IN SHAPELESS BLACK CREPE, WITH her brown-going-grey hair done in a severe bun at the back of her head, sad eyes, a knob of a chin, and posture that revealed fatigue, gestured to Poppy to come in. She closed the front door before looking Poppy over suspiciously, saying, "You were here with Mister Dritchner." There was no cordiality in her manner; she fixed her gaze on some point three feet beyond Poppy's head.

"Yes, I was; it was a condolence visit. Today I'm here as a journalist." She faced Missus Haas. "I believe I can be of some help."

"Help in what way?" Missus Haas asked.

"My cousin has told me that Missus Moncrief is being dogged by the press. A good story on her situation could help lessen that." She waited a moment, then added, "My cousin asked me to look into it." This was partly true she thought, salving her conscience.

"Your cousin isn't here. He left over an hour ago," Missus Hass said, prepared to dismiss Poppy from the building.

"I'm sorry I missed him; he would explain my intentions better than I can," Poppy fibbed. "But he isn't why I'm here, because I don't want to intrude directly on Missus Moncrief; I would like to talk to you and to Jeanine Reed — "

"Missus Reedly," Missus Haas corrected.

Poppy nodded. "Thanks for telling me. I'd like to speak to you both about the events surrounding Mister Moncrief's death."

"Why speak to us?" She mulled the possibilities, and went on, "And why should either of us tell you anything?"

"Because I believe you may have information that is important to the investigation, and I think you may be able to shed light on what happened to Mister Moncrief on his last days," Poppy said, with more confidence than she actually possessed.

"You're a reporter, aren't you? Missus Moncrief doesn't want us to talk to reporters," said Missus Haas, her manner becoming frostier.

"I understand, and I wouldn't want you to go against your employer's instructions. You won't have to tell me anything you don't want to, but I hope you may have some intelligence that will help remove the suspicions gathering around Missus Moncrief. She has enough to deal with without that, hasn't she?" Poppy kept her tone bland and her demeanor helpful. "It won't take long."

"I don't know . . . I ought to ask Mister Eastley."

Poppy was certain that Julian Eastley would put the kibosh on the interview, so she said, "Do you think that he would be willing to let me talk to him?" as if that would be a welcome development.

"I don't think so," said Missus Haas, but there was a hint of umbrage in her manner that Poppy would prefer to talk to Mister Eastley rather than to her. "He's keeping close to Missus Moncrief, in case she should need him."

"Sadly, his devotion may be contributing to the gossip," said Poppy. "You and I know his conduct never crosses the line, but others do not see it that way."

Missus Haas nodded. "So your cousin has cautioned her. It is a most unfortunate development. When you think about what Missus Moncrief has been through — " She turned a hard stare on Poppy. "Why do you bother with us when you can talk to your cousin? Mister Dritchner must know more than we do."

Poppy did not let this throw her. "He does know a lot, but he isn't aware of the daily atmosphere in the house, as he doesn't live under this roof. You know how it has been here, day to day, and that should tell me a great deal."

"Yes, that's true," Missus Haas said thoughtfully. "We do have a . . . perspective that many others would lack."

"You see? You could help the public to understand how grueling the last few days have been for Missus Moncrief. You can show that she's been distraught, and that she needs peace and quiet in this dreadful time."

Missus Haas blinked. "I hadn't thought of that. I see your point."

Poppy took advantage of this opening. "Could you spare me ten to fifteen minutes, then? I don't want to have to tell my editor that no one here is talking. With so much gossip spreading, and all the attention the press is giving Missus Moncrief, you could do much to silence all of that. I believe my cousin would agree with me on this. He has been most consistent in his condemnation of the way the case is being handled." She offered a sympathetic smile before adding, "My editor might think you had something to hide, or that you've been forbidden to say anything to anyone if you're unwilling to speak with me."

Missus Haas brooded. "I'll ask Missus Reedly if she would have any objection to talking to you, and if she says it's all right with her, I'll join you."

"That sounds reasonable," said Poppy mendaciously.

Missus Haas made her decision and marked it with a small, single nod of her head. "I'll show you into the front parlor. If you'll wait there, I'll have a word with Missus Reedly. She's doing the cooking tonight; Missus Reedly is here on Sunday afternoons. She's a very good plain cook."

"Not surprising," said Poppy, wanting to sound in accord with the dour housekeeper. "Our cook is gone on Sundays. Our housekeeper cooks when our cook is out."

Missus Haas escorted Poppy to the front parlor, although she knew where it was. "There, Miss Dritchner — "

"Thornton," Poppy said almost apologetically.

"Oh, yes." Missus Haas agreed. "Miss Thornton. If you'll take a chair, I'll tell you what we decide in the next ten minutes."

"Thank you, Missus Haas," said Poppy, going to a grandmother's chair away from the door and sinking into it, trying to keep from showing her eagerness for the interview.

"Ten minutes," Missus Haas repeated, and left Poppy by herself in the elegant room.

Being alone, Poppy could not help but think of the next-to-last time she was in this house, with the police looking around the dining room, with the air of subdued hysteria filling the place, with Madison Moncrief's body lying next to the dining table, a sheet over his lower body and a handkerchief covering the upper half of his face, the ruined chandelier dangling above him. The discomfort of the condolence visit of yesterday paled beside that dreadful beginning to this case; the image of Madison Moncrief lying on the floor became uppermost in Poppy's thoughts. She resisted the urge to rise and go into the dining room, to have a look at it now that it was empty. It was nerve-wracking to wait.

"Miss Thornton," Missus Haas said from the doorway. "If you're willing to come to the kitchen, Missus Reedly and I will give you fifteen to twenty minutes; we can't spare much more than that. I hope it will suffice. All we ask is that you do not identify us by name in anything you write."

"That's very generous of you both; I'm very appreciative," said Poppy, and followed Missus Haas to the kitchen.

"We'll do what we can, but there are certain things we will not be at liberty to discuss with you, or anyone," said Missus Haas, a little less formidably as she pushed the swinging door open.

"I appreciate that," said Poppy, alert to the warning the housekeeper was issuing.

"Just so you understand," said Missus Haas, and stepped into the kitchen; it was a very modern place, with all the most recent appliances, from a two-sided toaster, to an oversized refrigerator, and a four-burner range on which a large pot was emittining the aroma of chicken, wine, and herbs. The walls and the counters were clean and shiny, and the cabinet doors were closed, all neat as a pin. There was a good-sized preparation table in the middle of the room, and it was there that Missus Reedly was busy with getting a simple dinner ready. "This is Miss Drit — Thornton, Missus Reedly." Missus Haas went to the tall cupboard next to the refrigerator, and began to take down dinner plates and large soup bowls, setting them on the counter beside the stove, which was lit by a hanging overhead light; it reminded Poppy a little of a hospital's operating theater.

"How do you do?" Missus Reedly looked up from the mound of vegetables she was cutting into bite-sized bits. She was sitting on a drafting stool, facing a large, thick butcher's block set into the end of the counter. A chef's muslin smock covered her black maid's uniform; there were a few small stains smirching the fabric. "I'm almost done with the stew. If you'll bear with me?" She smiled and continued to chop potatoes and carrots, sweeping the results of her labors into a large enameled bowl. "The chicken is already in the pot. I have onions and half a cabbage to go, and then you can have my undivided attention."

"I don't want to interrupt you," said Poppy, trying to find a place to stand that would keep her out of Missus Reedly's and Missus Haas' way.

"I can talk and cook at the same time," said Missus Reedly, taking two yellow onions and cutting both of them in half before beginning to peel them.

"I realize that," said Poppy, and made a show of taking her notebook and a pencil from her purse.

"Would you pour us a cup of coffee, Missus Haas?" Missus Reedly asked. "I want to keep going while I talk."

Missus Haas went to the stove and lifted the percolator off the simmer burner, took three mugs down from the crockery cabinet, and poured coffee into all of them. "Do you take cream and sugar, Miss?" she asked Poppy.

"One sugar and a little cream," Poppy said, and watched while the housekeeper added cream to two of the mugs and sugar to all three. "So, thinking back, had Mister Moncrief been worried about anything recently?"

Missus Haas paused in handing Poppy her mug. "He was desolated that Missus Moncrief had lost their child."

"Yes, so I have heard," Poppy said, "but had he any other obvious worries?" She took the mug and set it on the counter at her elbow.

Missus Reedly took the mug offered her. "He was a businessman, working with other people's money. Of course he had worries. That's part of his job." She worked her cleaver energetically. "There was always something that bothered him. Ever since he went to Hadley and Grimes, he was . . . wound up."

"Do you have any idea why that should be?" Poppy asked.

Missus Haas huffed. "He didn't talk about such things with us."

"Why should he?" Missus Reedly agreed, continuing her chopping. "Missus Moncrief didn't say much about it, but she was more melancholy than he was."

"But you must have seen something," said Poppy, trying to encourage more responses from both women. "I have been told that he had had difficulties with some of his accounts recently. Do you recall him saying anything about them?"

"Missus Moncrief told Mister Eastley that Mister Moncrief had unrealistically demanding clients," Missus Haas conceded. "It troubled her that he took on such persons as he did."

"Do you know why he did? take them on?" Poppy asked.

"Missus Moncrief said it was because Hadley and Grimes required it," Missus Reedly said, pausing in her preparations. "She told me that he did not yet have the advancement to allow him to shift the clients to other members of the firm. Whatever it was the clients demanded, Missus Moncrief thought it might have been about business arrangements that were not entirely legal. She mentioned it to me because she was worried about him, and she was hoping I could find a way to ease his mind. I knew they occasionally argued about the demands of his work."

"You never mentioned that to me," Missus Haas said, offended by this lapse.

Missus Reedly shrugged. "It didn't seem important, not then. I began to wonder about it when he . . . passed on."

Poppy inquired, pencil at the ready. "Did Missus Moncrief explain what it was that upset Mister Moncrief about those clients? What kind of things they wanted?"

"No. But it wasn't my place to ask," said Missus Reedly, going to work on the half-cabbage. "She mentioned it privately, but she has mentioned it to others, as well. It was no secret that he was bothered about his work."

"That's useful," said Poppy, stretching the point.

Now Missus Haas spoke up. "I once heard Mister Moncrief say to Mister Eastley that he was considering resigning his position, but it was after three very long days at the office, and I assumed he was objecting to the extra hours he had been told to put in. He — Mister Moncrief — was uneasy, wanting to decide if it would be proper to go to the authorities about his suspicions."

"Which authorities, did he say?" Poppy was hoping for a direct answer.

"Local police, state investigators, regulatory institutions, the Justice Department?"

"I have no idea," said Missus Haas.

"He mentioned someone in the District Attorney's office once, to a small group of friends, to find out who among them knew the man he wanted to contact." Missus Reedly wiped her eyes between onions.

"Was that the evening that the Ellises were here?" Missus Haas asked, as she offered Poppy her coffee in a white ceramic mug. "With the Greenlochs and the Kinnons?"

"That was the occasion," said Missus Reedly, resuming her work on the onions.

"Missus Moncrief retired early; she was feeling unwell? Mister Moncrief seemed anxious, and I attributed that to his concern for his wife." Missus Haas pulled a small, black-edged handkerchief from her skirt pocket and dabbed at her eyes.

"How long ago was that?" Poppy had wrapped one hand around her mug and nodded her thanks, not wanting to slow Missus Haas' remarks.

"Five or six weeks ago, I think," said Missus Haas. "It was sleeting that night, as I recall, and Mister Moncrief had had a hard drive home. He looked exhausted when he arrived."

Poppy followed up this revelation. "Did he say anything more about resigning after that?"

"Not that I can recall," said Missus Haas.

"Missus Moncrief was unwell during that time," said Missus Reedly. "She was vexed about Mister Moncrief's dissatisfaction, worried that it might mean problems when the baby came."

"In what way? Mister Moncrief didn't need his job to support his family," Poppy observed.

"I don't know nothing about that," said Missus Reedly. "But I do know that Missus Moncrief had a lot of questions about what would become of their children if he lost his job. You see, she was planning a big family, five or six children is what they were aiming for, or so she reminded Mister Moncrief two weeks before he . . . did away with himself." She sighed and looked away. "I don't listen at doors, but as her maid, I occasionally hear things. You know how that is."

"That's no longer what the police think happened — that he did away with himself," said Poppy, and watched the two women for their reaction.

"What do you mean?" Missus Haas asked sharply.

"The coroner and Inspector Loring are of the opinion that there were aspects to Mister Moncrief's death that rule out suicide." Poppy let her words hang in the air.

"Are you sure?" Missus Haas demanded.

"Yes. I had it from the coroner himself." Poppy did not want to extend the truth too far, but she felt she was on solid enough ground. "There was something about it in the paper yesterday." She was not surprised that neither Missus Haas nor Missus Reedly had read the paper, for in most large households, the staff was not encouraged to do so.

"But the chandelier . . . " Missus Haas said.

"Oh, my God," exclaimed Missus Reedly. "Oh, poor Missus Moncrief."

"Murdered? Is that what they think?" Missus Haas asked, shock softening her voice.

"Yes. The coroner has ruled his death a homicide." Poppy forced herself to remain silent, and watch the two servants take this in.

"Does Missus Moncrief know?" Missus Reedly asked.

"Yes, she does," Poppy replied. "Well, no wonder the press has been flocking to this house," said Missus Haas, her indignation making her voice rise three notes.

"The manner of death was not officially announced until day before yesterday," Poppy said, "and the Clarion published it yesterday."

Missus Haas was unmollified. "I think we should have been told as soon as the possibility was recognized."

"It's all of a piece," said Missus Reedly. "God save us all."

"Who would have . . . They're wrong to suspect Missus Moncrief. She isn't the kind of woman to kill anyone, least of all her husband." Missus Haas rounded on Poppy. "You put that in your paper: Missus Moncrief wouldn't hurt a fly, and certainly would not do anything to harm her husband."

"I'll let everyone know that you said so." Poppy pledged.

"How sad," said Missus Reedly, who resumed chopping cabbage. "Do the police think that the troubles in Mister Moncrief's business had anything to do with his getting . . . killed? How could that be?"

"It would make sense for them to consider it, wouldn't it?" Poppy said. "You see why your views are so important."

Missus Haas coughed diplomatically. "Missus Moncrief was worried about Mister Moncrief, as I've told you. I know he was distressed when Missus Moncrief lost their baby, and I didn't realize how much his business contributed to his suffering. The last few weeks, he came home late more nights than not, and he seemed . . . more disturbed in many ways. He was lethargic, disinterested in things that usually pleased him, and fretful about minor issues: the lack of shine on the brass, the arrangement of furniture in the sitting room, the flowers in the entry hall vase, the choice of a coffee pot at breakfast. Little matters."

"Two weeks ago, Missus Moncrief was very troubled by his state of mind," Missus Reedly contributed. "It bothered her that he was preoccupied with his business situation, which is what she felt it was, although she knew he was deeply disappointed in the loss of their child. She told me that he was escaping into work so that he would not have to think about the baby. I believed that the two things together had put him into his slump."

"How much did she know about his business dealings themselves? Did she know what was troubling him?" Poppy asked, hoping for another revelation that she could include in her story.

"In terms of the nuts and bolts of his work, she didn't know very much. She isn't interested in such things," said Missus Reedly.

"But since she was aware something was wrong, did she mention anything about it to anyone? Perhaps to Mister Eastley?" Poppy urged.

"It isn't likely," said Missus Haas. "Mister Moncrief always did all he could to shield his wife from problems. He was determined to spare her any more hurt after her miscarriage. He withheld many things."

"That's very true," Missus Reedly seconded.

"I assumed he was trying to help her to recover from her loss, but now that you ask about it, I can see that more was upsetting him beyond losing the baby." Missus Haas sounded shocked at her own lack of perception. "I should have been aware that it was more than that."

"Don't blame yourself, Missus Haas," said Missus Reedly. "We were both of us blind. Mister Tanner, too."

"Mister Tanner?" Poppy asked.

"Our man-of-all-work. He comes in two days a week — does repairs and general household maintenance. He only said that Mister Moncrief seemed a bit off his feed. That was a keen observation for Mister Tanner." Missus Haas took a generous gulp of coffee.

"That's more than he usually says," Missus Reedly agreed. "And almost none of it to anyone's good."

"I should have paid more attention," Missus Haas said with deep regret, "but Mister Tanner is always deploring something."

"That he is," said Missus Reedly. "He's a sour sort of man."

"Do you think he would talk to me?" Poppy inquired.

"It's unlikely," said Missus Haas, and Missus Reedly nodded.

"Well, then, I won't bother." Poppy wrote Tanner at the bottom of her page, then looked at her notes, and tried to think of a few more questions, but decided she had enough material, as well as a few new leads; she said, "I'm grateful to you both for talking with me."

"We should be thanking you, for alerting us to the truth of Mister Moncrief's . . . death," Missus Haas said firmly. "We will be able to deal better now that we know what the situation is."

"Then we're all better off for this meeting," said Poppy, and added, "If you like, I will see you each get copies of the Clarion when my article with your insights appear. That should be in a day or two."

"That would be very nice of you; Mister Haas and I do not subscribe to a paper," said Missus Haas with far more warmth than she had displayed since Poppy had arrived at the door. "I suppose we should get back to work — all of us."

Taking the hint, Poppy drank most of her coffee, and gathered up her notebook, pencil, purse and jacket, saying, "You've both been a great deal of help." She allowed Missus Haas to precede her; she nodded to Missus Reedly as she went out of the swinging door.

"I had been thinking that the reporters were trying to enlarge on the sensationalistic aspects of the case, and were exaggerating what was being said about the case. Now I understand better their reason for it. To think Mister Moncrief was murdered!" Missus Haas reached the front door. "I appreciate — " She did not finish, but opened the door and saw Poppy out, closing the door before Poppy could thank her.

TWENTY-NINE

POPPY WAS ALMOST FINISHED WITH HER STORY WHEN MISSUS FLOWERS CALLED her to the telephone, saying, "It's Missus Fairchild. She sounds very excited."

"I'll be down in a minute. Please ask her to hang on," Poppy raised her voice so she would be heard as she rose from the chair at the library desk. She wondered briefly where Chesterton Holte had gone, but shrugged the question away. After turning off the lamp, she hesitated before she decided to leave her current page in the typewriter and went downstairs to take the 'phone call, her descent accompanied by the hall clock striking the half hour. Five-thirty, Poppy thought, and decided she would have to push herself to finish the story. She picked up the receiver, saying, "Good evening, Mildred. How are you?"

"Oh, Poppy, it's wonderful. I'm pregnant again. Humphrey's beside himself! I wanted you to know before we make our announcement tomorrow. I'm so happy!" She was breathless with exhilaration.

"That's great news," said Poppy, doing her best to summon up enthusiasm. "I'm very happy for you both, you and Humphrey. You've hoped for this so long."

"The doctor was kind enough to call me yesterday, knowing how hopeful I've been. He's the best obstetrician in all of Philadelphia." She took a joyous gasp. "Can you come 'round for a toast on Tuesday evening? We're going to celebrate. It won't be the same without you." She paused, then hurried on. "Nothing elaborate, just friends and family; a light supper and Champagne. Do, please, say you'll come." This all came out in a rush, and Poppy listened with patience.

"I'd love to be there, Milly, and I hope I can make it," said Poppy, stretching the truth. "What time are the festivities?"

"Seven-thirty. I know it's a little early, but I'm under orders to get plenty of rest. As if I'd do anything else. Humphrey wouldn't let me go gallivanting about in my condition." Mildred gave a little spurt of laughter.

"I'll try to be there. If I can get there I will. But you know I'm on the Moncrief story still, and I may have to come a bit later than seven-thirty. I should be able to get there by eight."

"Eight?" Mildred gave a little shriek. "Oh, please, come before that."

"I have to turn a story in tomorrow evening, and if my editor wants me to do more work on it, I won't be out of the office until after six. By the time I get home and change — "

"Come in your business clothes. It's all right with me. You don't need to change. Come straight from the paper," Mildred urged her.

"I'll try," Poppy assured Mildred. "I can't promise, but I will try." She did not want to injure her friend, so she added, "I'm thrilled for you, Milly."

"You don't sound like it," Mildred said, her tone petulant.

"I am," Poppy said emphatically. "I know this is just what you wanted. You said Humphrey is delighted, and I can hear your happiness in your voice." She took a deep breath. "Are the twins happy about another child in the family?"

"They're more curious than excited. They don't really understand much about this, but they are very interested. They want to know if I'll have more twins, and they don't believe that I don't know. They've put in orders for a brother since each of them has a sister. They're very clever for three." She laughed a bit perfunctorily. "You should hear them: Miranda and Portia are full of questions. Almost as bad as you can be." Her attempt at humor did not quite come off. "That's nothing against you."

Poppy knew she needed to say more to explain her lack of ebullience. "I'm sorry if I seem uninterested, Milly. It's the Moncrief investigation; it's weighing on me. I was putting the finishing touches on my next installment when you called, and it has left me in a somber mood. I apologize. You know I'm having raptures for you, but until I finish the article for the paper, I've got my mind on murder."

"And you wonder why I don't like the thought of you working on such appalling material," Mildred said.

"You're far more capable of mothering and family life than I am, and you do adore your children. I'm overjoyed that you'll have another; it's marvelous that you are getting to have it."

"Oh," said Mildred, chastened. "Well, that's different." She could not help but add, "I don't know how you can stand to work on something so sordid."

"It's important, Milly. People need to be informed." Poppy heard Mildred sniff. "I'm making headway, and that's encouraging."

"But murder . . . "

"It isn't pleasant, but uncovering the truth is satisfying," said Poppy, knowing that Mildred would not understand.

"But murder isn't the sort of thing a lady should have to address. Leave such ugly things to men," Mildred recommended. "Surely there are more pleasant things to report. This preoccupation you have with crime can't be healthy. There must be other events you can report."

"There are, and I've been doing them for two years and I am bored beyond endurance," Poppy admitted.

"But can't there be important events other than murder? Stories that won't bore you?" Mildred exclaimed. "Surely covering the legislature or scientific discoveries would be important, and exciting."

"There are other, more important stories than Great Books and Garden Society meetings, but I want to cover crime, and that includes murder. Think about it, Milly: women get murdered as well as men. We should be aware of how such crimes are pursued," Poppy could not stop herself saying.

"Oh, Poppy! How are you ever going to find a husband if you keep on this way?" Mildred was almost crying with vexation. "There are times I despair of you: there really are."

"Ye gods, Milly, don't carry on so, please. You know what kind of woman I am, and I hope you're willing to bear with me, since I'm not likely to change," Poppy responded, placating her friend. "If it's easier for you, consider me a lost cause. I'm finally doing what I've wanted to do for years and years, and I'm not about to stop now."

"I know," Mildred wailed.

Poppy took a deep breath. "Look, Milly, I'll be at your party on Tuesday night. And I'll be on time."

"No matter what?" Mildred asked tremulously.

"No matter what," Poppy promised.

"I'm so glad! It will be delightful to have you here to celebrate with us."

"Shall I bring a present?" It was the right thing to ask, and Poppy knew it.

There was a brief hesitation, and a sense that Mildred thought this was embarrassing. "Only if you want to. Having you will be a present in your own right," she said, and at her inadvertent pun, and repeated it in case Poppy had not got it. "You being present will be a present." Then she did her best to chuckle.

"I got it, Milly," said Poppy. "Seven-thirty. I'll be there. Word of a Thornton."

"Thank you, Poppy. Truly, thank you. It means a lot to me."

"I'm looking forward to it, Milly. And I hope you have a healthy, happy baby," said Poppy, preparing to hang up.

"Oh, so do I! We've been so lucky with Miranda and Portia, I hardly dare to hope that we do as well again. I suppose it's all in God's hands now." She sighed wistfully, then continued in a more social manner. "You must be about to dress for dinner. I'll let you go."

Poppy had no intention of changing clothes to dine tonight, but she accepted this dismissal gracefully. "I'll see you on Tuesday. Thank you for your good news and your invitation. I'm honored to be included."

"That's so nice of you. Have a lovely evening." Having discharged her mission, Mildred hung up, leaving Poppy to wonder how she would tell Lowenthal that she would not be able to work late on Tuesday. She replaced the receiver in its cradle and went back up to the library with the intention of finishing her story. But when she sat down at the typewriter, all thought deserted her; she stared at the page trying to pick up her narrative thread without success, and realizing that her writing lacked concision; it was all over the place, unfocused and incomplete. Annoyed with herself, she pulled the page out of the typewriter, separated the carbon paper and set up another sandwich of pages, which she rolled into the platen; then she stared at the blank sheet, waiting for inspiration to strike. She got up from the desk and began to pace, almost wishing that Chesterton Holte would manifest himself in some way so that she could discuss this lack of concentration that had come over her. But there was no sign of the ghost, and she had to accept that he would not appear on request. "You're procrastinating," she chastised herself. "Get back to work." She went back to the desk and sat down.

"How is it going?" Chesterton Holte spoke out of the third window embrasure, and became a shiny spot in the air as he approached the desk.

This time Poppy did not jump. "It's not," she answered curtly.

"It didn't go well with the Moncriefs' staff?" He was immediately in front of the desk. "I thought that sounded promising."

"It was, and I think I can get something worthwhile out of it, but it's not coming together well. I'm scattered." This last admission appalled her as she heard herself speak. She decided to change the subject. "When you've questioned Moncrief in your ghostly dimension, has he ever said anything about wanting to resign his position at Hadley and Grimes?"

Holte thought for almost a minute. "Not that I recall. Why?"

"The Moncriefs' housekeeper and Louise's maid seem to think he was talking about it with friends." Poppy reached for her notebook and flipped through the pages. "It was shortly before Louise miscarried. Apparently Madison had been putting in longer hours than usual at the firm, and may have found something that troubled him about one or, perhaps, more than one of his clients."

Holte swung in the air in a way that appeared to be like pacing. "I'll ask him, if you like." He waited for her to answer, and when she did not, he continued. "Have you talked to anyone, other than the servants, who heard him say anything about resigning?"

"I was planning to call some of the Moncriefs' friends a little later this evening, after I've had dinner with Aunt Jo. Lowenthal will want at least two sources on this, and he won't count both servants as independent sources, and he's probably right." Poppy leaned back in her chair, beginning to feel worn out. "I need a short break."

"Not surprising," said Holte. "You've been working quite steadily these last several days."

She nodded. "And I'm starting to get ideas I don't like."

"About the case?"

"What else?" She sighed and straightened up again.

"And what ideas are those?" Holte asked, and before she could answer, suggested, "Proving yourself?"

"That's part of it," Poppy allowed. "But I'm beginning to think that Stacy is mixed up in this more than he has admitted to being." Now that she said it, she felt both better and worse.

"I see," said Holte. "That is troublesome."

"It's necessary," Poppy responded. "If I'm going to do my job, I have to admit that Stacy appears to be part of whatever crime is at the heart of these murders." She stared at the filmy outline that was Chesterton Holte. "If you can learn something from the ghosts that could point me in the right direction, I'd be grateful."

"And that would be good?" Holte inquired, although he knew the answer.

"It would help my career, at a time when a little help could make a difference." She shoved her chair back from the desk. "And I'm ashamed of myself for putting my career ahead of my cousin's interests."

"Why?" Holte asked. "I doubt he would put your interests ahead of his."

"That's a wretched thing to say," Poppy protested. "I'll grant that Stacy has a host of faults, but . . ." She thought of some of the things she had said against Stacy, and suddenly flushed with embarrassment.

Holte became a bit more visible. "Be careful, Poppy."

She heard something in his words that demanded her attention. "How do you mean? Why do I need to be careful?

"You know why," Holte told her. "You're worried that your cousin is involved in at least one of the murders in some way."

Poppy felt her face redden. "And?"

"It's how I've been trained to look at things," he said.

"But why should I look at Stacy that way?"

Holte did not answer directly. "Keep in mind that I was a spy, and I because of that, I have a very untrusting nature: I think you're right about your cousin — that he's somehow caught up in these murders. I'd be surprised if he's the primary miscreant: he doesn't seem the type to get his hands bloody, or to take such risks. It seems more probable that he connects to them indirectly, but I feel he knows more than he's telling you, or anyone else; he's hiding his knowledge behind his claim of professional confidentiality."

Poppy watched him, her expression of shock not entirely convincing. "Thanks," she said, watching him rise into the air.

"You don't mean that," said Holte.

"No, I don't," she admitted. "But I have been thinking that I was inventing trouble where there was none, imagining tigers in the dark. After all, everyone in our class knows everyone else, and we all keep secrets. So I haven't wanted to believe that he is connected to these killings, no matter how indirectly. But it looks much too likely that he . . . might have had something to do with them. " She hesitated. "I don't see what could be the link, or what he could get out of such an association."

"Do you think he is capable of blackmail?" Holte suggested, his manifestation growing a little brighter. "Perhaps he's withholding information because someone is paying him to keep silent?"

"That's a terrible thing to say!" Poppy exclaimed.

"Does he need money?" Holte pursued.

"Not that I know of," Poppy replied, but reminding herself that Stacy did not often discuss his financial affairs, and when he did, it was in the broadest generalities. "He certainly doesn't live as if he needs funds."

"But it is possible," said Holte.

"I guess it could be," Poppy said, feeling increasingly troubled. "People tell him things, and he might — if he were in trouble — take advantage of what he knows."

"Do you believe he might extort money from someone, based on his knowledge?" Holte dropped back down to floor-level, watching Poppy intently.

"I wish I could say no, but I can't. I don't want to suggest that he . . . would take advantage of a friend, but if he looked at it as a game . . . " She bit her lower lip. "If he's really entangled in this mess, I think he should get out of it as soon as he can. But I'd need to talk to him directly, try to persuade him to go to the authorities and make a clean breast of it."

"Would he take your advice?" Holte did not apologize for his directness.

"Or would he do the opposite of what you recommend?"

"He hasn't paid much attention to anything I've said in the past, but then, people he does business with have not been dying violently before now." She shrugged. "I suppose I ought to try to convince him to talk to . . . not the police — he wouldn't do that. But he might talk to Denton North; he's an assistant District Attorney, and our neighbor's son."

"There's one thing you might want to know," said Holte, more slowly. "Knott told me that Warren Derrington's mother is a cousin of Montague Grimes." He paused, then hurried on, "I don't know if this has anything to do with the case, or Derrington's disappearance, but I thought you might find it useful."

"Ye gods, yes, I want to know," said Poppy. "You're right — it may be nothing, but that kind of connection might turn out to be important."

Holte did something that might have been a sigh of relief. "Thank you, Poppy."

"For being willing to suspect my cousin of being part of a capital conspiracy?" She wanted this to sound sardonic, but it came out indignant.

"For being prudent," he said. "If you should end up in danger, there isn't very much I could do to help you."

"Noncorporeal. I know."

"And I want to keep you out of danger, not put you in the middle of it." He wavered, then wafted over to the wing-backed chair.

"You've explained that already," she said, wanting to change the subject.

Holte became a little more defined. "You're full of pluck, but you're delving into some very sinister doings."

"Good of you to say so," she said, her nervousness returning.

"I want to help you keep out of trouble," he insisted.

"So I gather," she responded.

He stretched out his semi-visible legs and crossed them as if his heels were resting on an invisible hassock. "I hope you still think that by the end of this investigation."

She chuckled angrily. "No more than I, Holte, I promise you," she said, and returned to her typewriter. "Lowenthal's sending a courier. I've got to finish this."

"Then I won't intrude on your work," Holte said, and vanished.

THIRTY

⌒♆⌒

POPPY REACHED THE CLARION TWENTY MINUTES LATE ON MONDAY MORNING, the call she had received from Inspector Loring still ringing in her mind; this had come as she was hurriedly getting dressed and had taken almost ten minutes to complete, a delay that threw her off as much as her lingering fatigue. Feeling mortified at this tardiness, she hurried to her desk, put down her briefcase, and removed the file that contained her story for the next day's paper; she had been up past one finishing it, and would have overslept if not for Missus Flowers tapping on her door. Now that she had arrived at the paper, she felt a little groggy, and was sorry she had skipped breakfast; she was irritable and had the beginning of a headache.

Around her, the city room was in full activity — copy-boys walking quickly to and from the composition room where the typesetters labored, reporters pounding on their typewriters or talking on their 'phones in preparation for the evening's edition. Even though she was late, Poppy felt proud to be a day ahead of her assignment, and trusted that Lowenthal would give her credit for her efforts. She dropped her coat over the back of her chair and made her way to Lowenthal's office, her file clutched in her right hand, rehearsing in her mind what she would tell him to account for her late arrival.

The door to Lowenthal's office was open, and the man himself sat behind his desk, scowling portentously at the sheet of paper he held in his hand. As Poppy tapped on the doorframe, he looked up. "So you got here at last," he grumbled. "Come on in and explain yourself. It's not like you to be late."

"Sorry, boss. I missed my streetcar. Hawkins drove me in." She did her best not to sound chagrined.

"Pity, with two ts," he said.

"I've got tomorrow's story for you," she said as bravely as she could.

He looked mildly curious. "It's already done? Does that mean that the case is bogging down, and you don't expect any more news between now and midnight?"

"If there is any, I'll do the story over, or write you another four inches," Poppy assured him. "But the next major event will be the funeral on Wednesday afternoon; the coroner doesn't have the report on the poison used on Moncrief yet. I'm planning to cover the funeral, and to report on the state of the police investigation before they tell the press about it."

"That's thinking ahead," said Lowenthal.

"And I'm in contact with Inspector Loring," she added.

"Even better." He leaned back in his chair and laced his fingers atop his chest. "Anything more from the coroner? Anything we can use?"

"He's going to make a statement about Percy Knott later today."

Lowenthal nodded. "And you're planning to be there?"

"I am." Poppy sat a little straighter in the ladder-backed chair. "I still think there's a connection between Moncrief and Knott, and I'm going to spend most of tomorrow digging into that." She offered him a smile to conceal her doubts. "I tried to get another appointment at Hadley and Grimes, but no luck so far."

"I'll let you have another two days to find the connection, and then, if you don't deliver, I'll hand off the Knott murder and the search for Overstreet to Westerman — he'll be back tomorrow, he tells me." He stared toward the window, not seeing the spring day outside.

"I'll get on it just as soon as I talk to Loring," she assured him.

"So how are you marking time?" Lowenthal gave her a challenging stare.

"I did what you suggested — I talked to the servants, and I boiled down their comments about the Moncriefs. Not just backstairs gossip, but a few observations that suggest that Madison was worried about something more than his wife's health." Poppy took a deep breath. "I'm going to talk to the police about what I've learned."

"Probably a good idea. What a cock-up this is turning out to be. It's never a good sign when the upper crust is in the middle of a case. Too many closed doors." Lowenthal cleared his throat. "You having any trouble with your relatives over this?"

"Nothing beyond the usual; at least not so far," Poppy said, and was not inclined to explain, so she went on more briskly. "I think you'll like what I have for tomorrow's edition." It was the most positive thing she had ever said directly to him, and it left her feeling a little giddy. She handed him the file folder.

He took it from her without comment, but prior to reading what she had written, he motioned her to the straight-backed chair, then opened the file to read the two sheets of typewritten text it contained. "Not bad," he said when he was finished. "You may have a talent for this job."

"Thanks, boss," she said. "I hope you'll like what I'll have tomorrow morning, after I have that meeting with Inspector Loring."

Lowenthal nodded twice decisively. "You're sticking to your guns on this."

Poppy felt color rising in her cheeks. "Thanks," she muttered, and made up her mind to get more information from Loring than she had planned. The more she could turn up, the likelier it was that Lowenthal would keep her on the story. "I'm grateful to you for giving me this chance. I won't let you down."

"I'm counting on that," said Lowenthal.

Poppy tried to summon up a smart rejoinder, but only said, "I'll do my best."

Lowenthal regarded her in his most evaluating way. "So tomorrow is a busy day. What about this evening? You think you could get anything out of your cousin? Something that you can use, that is?"

"I'll talk to him this evening, if he's in. He might go back to New York today," she said, not looking forward to trying to pump Stacy.

"Anything else?" He brought his chair upright.

"Tomorrow evening, I have a . . . an engagement. I'll have to be out of here by four at the latest." She cleared her throat, fighting nerves once more.

"Then go home directly from your interviews and put your story together there. So long as you have it here before you go to the funeral on Wednesday, it should be all right. You can bring in your funeral coverage in the evening, when it's over." He made a shooing gesture with his hand. "Chop-chop."

Feeling relieved, Poppy got to her feet and started toward the door. "Thanks again, boss," she said as she went out the door and returned to her desk; she was a bit light-headed now that she was out of Lowenthal's office. She sat down and stared at the inkwell under her desk-lamp that stood next to the Royal typewriter. It was a substantial machine, but not quite as formidable as the Smith on the desk in her Aunt Jo's library. There was a ream of paper in the lower drawer in the left-hand side, and she opened it to remove a sheet, and then took carbon paper and onionskin second sheet from the central drawer. She set them up and rolled them into the platen, and told herself to type something. But after two minutes, when no words had come, she got up and went to the lunch room for a cup of coffee. She was almost alone in the room which smelled of coffee and bear-claws set out on the service table; the keeper was on the far side of the room, wiping the table-tops in an automatic way, and paid no attention to Poppy's arrival.

Poppy went to the service table, took an ironstone mug from the shelf, and poured out coffee from the coffee samovar, then added one cube of sugar and a teaspoon of cream, and went to the nearest table to sit; she pulled a small paper napkin from the dispenser on the table, and took one of the tin spoons that sprouted from a greenish glass. She took a little time to stir the coffee, preoccupied with what she would be doing later that day. She was about to take a first sip when she saw the lights flicker, and she set her mug down and looked around for the shimmer in the air that would announce Chesterton Holte's presence.

"I hope I didn't startle you," he said, as if he were sitting in the chair across the small table from hers.

"Don't speak so loudly," she whispered. "Missus diMaggio will hear."

"Not me," he said, not lowering his voice. "Only you can hear me."

"And why is that?" She took the mug and sipped the coffee.

"Others can't hear me unless I remain entirely visible, and even then, most of the living aren't aware of ghosts. My voice goes along with my body." A spot of air glistened where his eyes might be, but other than that, she could not see him.

Poppy did not stop whispering. "Is there some reason you're here?"

"There is," Holte said. "I've had another chance to talk to Knott, and he said that the night before he was attacked, your cousin warned him about Warren Derrington; came to his house and swore Knott to secrecy. He thought that was strange, that Stacy should warn him against Derrington. Knott doesn't remember most of it, not yet, but he said that he recalled that the warning seemed . . . unexpected."

"Did he happen to tell you what Stacy said about Derrington?" Poppy asked, and saw Missus diMaggio glance at her in a disapproving way. She raised her voice and said, "I'm trying to straighten out my grammar. Number and tense. It helps if I do it aloud; I hear the errors better than I see them."

Missus diMaggio resumed her polishing, and paid Poppy no more attention.

"He said it probably had something to do with counterfeit antiquities," Holte answered. "There's been a spate of them in Boston and New York, and he was worried some might crop up in Philadelphia. He seems to think Hadley and Grimes knew about it."

"Do you want me to find out from Stacy what he told Derrington?" Poppy hated to ask, for it once again tied her cousin to the terrible killing.

"If he's willing to talk about it, and assuming that he will tell you the truth. You might see if he knows where Derrington has gone," Holte responded. "Don't push him, though. He might turn obdurate."

"I'll try — that's the best I can promise." Poppy drank some more coffee, and then quietly asked Holte, "Anything more?"

"Knott still can't remember who killed him, or exactly when, but he said it might have been someone he knew, or someone from one of his clients, because he doesn't think he was surprised to see him." Holte paused. "He's fairly certain there was only one person."

"That's better than nothing," Poppy murmured, wanting to encourage him. "What about Overstreet? Any news on that front?"

"Well, he must still be alive," said Holte. "He hasn't turned up in the dimension of ghosts, so that means he's not dead."

"Small comfort," Poppy said softly.

"It means that you aren't looking for a body," Holte pointed out. "That should be useful to the police."

"I'll have to think of some way to explain that to Inspector Loring,"

Poppy said, a little more loudly than she had before. She finished off the coffee with a deep gulp, then got up to pour herself some more. Taking her time, she poured a second cup, added her sugar and cream, and returned to the table. "Did Knott have any idea where Overstreet might be?" she muttered as she sat down.

"No," Holte admitted. "Neither did Moncrief."

"Did you ask Madison about Overstreet?" Poppy looked askance.

Holte seemed to shrug. "So long as I was there, I though I might as well find out if he had brought anything more to mind."

"Such as who attacked him," Poppy whispered, and glanced up as Tony Milligan, one of the older copy-boys, came into the lunch room. "Good morning, Tony."

"Miss Thornton," he responded, going to the tray of bear-claws and using a paper napkin to take one of them. "Slow day?"

"For another hour or so, then it goes into high gear," said Poppy, doing her best to sound at ease. "What about you?"

"Busy," said Tony, and took a large bite of the pastry. "I'll leave a dime for this," he added to Missus diMaggio before he tossed a coin into the jar set out for that purpose, and then sauntered out of the room.

"He's a weasel, that one," said Missus diMaggio.

"He's fifteen," said Poppy, and went on in an undervoice, "What did Moncrief say?"

"He said he'd talked to Warren Derrington that afternoon, and whatever he was told upset him. That was one of the reasons he was tippling more than usual." Holte's face became a little more visible, but it faded away like a puff of smoke.

"Any idea what Derrington told him?" Poppy leaned nearer to where she guessed that Holte remained.

"Not really," Holte admitted. "But it does suggest that there was something odd going on with Derrington."

"And maybe Stacy," Poppy added. How could her cousin be caught up in anything so dreadful as murder? Poppy asked herself, and made herself listen to Holte.

"Perhaps after the fact," said Holte. "All we have now is a collection of guesses," he warned her. "You admit that he isn't forthcoming about his business dealings, and it could be that there are things going on beyond his control."

This did not seem like Stacy to Poppy, but she seized upon it, saying, "That's possible."

"If you'd like, I'll try to learn more." Holte sounded as if he were farther away now, and preparing to leave.

"Let me talk to Loring before you do anything more," Poppy said, this time loudly enough to earn a sharp look from Missus diMaggio.

"I'll talk with you again tonight. Will that do?"

"Sure. Later," said Poppy, and drank down her second cup of coffee before returning to her desk, concentrating on what she would put on the pages waiting in the typewriter.

THIRTY-ONE

"I APOLOGIZE FOR BEING LATE," INSPECTOR LORING SAID AS HE SAT DOWN NEXT to Poppy on the bench near the edge of Constitution Pond. "It couldn't be helped. It's one of those things I can't say much about. I trust you understand." There was enough of a breeze to riffle the pond, and it frisked between him and Poppy, carrying a frisson with it.

"Un-huh." Poppy continued to follow the progress of a flock of ducks out on the pond and paddling for the far side. "It's a shame that this will be gone next year," she said after a perfunctory glance in his direction.

"That it is. I'm going to miss it." He rubbed the lapels of his tweed jacket, and attempted a quirk of a smile. "And now that we're agreed on this, and that the mayor has made a mistake to have it drained, shall we get on with our business?"

"As you like," she said, and resisted the urge to take her notebook out of her purse. "You go first."

"That's good of you," he said, but did not continue.

"Do you have anything new to tell me?" she asked, and was shocked at how snippy she sounded.

"One or two things," he replied cautiously. "What about you? Have you learned anything that will help this investigation?"

"I have a few leads, and you may want to follow them; I'm going to," she said, not turning away from the ducks.

"Okay," he told her. "Are you certain about any of them?"

"No — that's why I said they were leads," she countered, wondering why she was treating him this way. You want his help, she reminded herself. Don't antagonize him. "There is one thing that looks like it might be useful:

apparently Warren Derrington's mother is related to the Grimes'."

"Huh," he said.

"I haven't confirmed it, but Aunt Jo will be able to tell me. I didn't get much of a chance to talk to her this morning." She decided to say nothing of her hectic scramble to get to work — it would sound unprofessional — and might lead Loring to think less of her as a reporter.

"I'll see what I can do with it." He ran his thumb along his jaw. "Is that your only lead?"

Poppy wished she felt more confident about the things Holte had told her. "No, but it's the easiest to check out. The others are more . . . indirect."

"But you think they're promising?" Loring pursued.

"I wouldn't want to follow them if they weren't, not the way things are going." She took a deep breath and moved slightly to put a few more inches of bench between them. "I've had some information that Miles Overstreet is probably alive and has gone into hiding. He might be able to tell me if there truly is a connection between the Knott murder and Moncrief's."

Loring heard her out, then asked, "Is your source reliable? About Overstreet?"

"He has been right about other things so far," said Poppy, adding impulsively, "And just now, I'm trying to find out where Warren Derrington has gone. I can't help thinking that he's tied into the murders." The alternative, she added to herself, was to think that Stacy was.

"Doesn't your cousin know?" Loring was startled; he turned to watch her more closely.

"If he does, he hasn't mentioned it," she replied.

"Have you spoken to him about any of this?"

Poppy disliked being under scrutiny, but she knew it would be unwise to say anything that could be shown to be wrong. "Not in any detail; I haven't had much of an opportunity," she answered. "Stacy's closed-mouthed about what he's been doing."

"I know what you mean. He was the very dev . . . dickens to interview. Whatever is going on with Derrington, he doesn't want to talk about it." He looked across the pond to the stand of cattails where the ducks had taken refuge from a yappy dog on a leash on the far bank; the dog's owner was attempting to pull his pet back from the brink.

"No, he doesn't," Poppy said.

Loring was silent for a moment. "So what do you think? Is your cousin involved in any of these deaths directly, or is he simply on the fringes?"

"I wish I knew," Poppy admitted. "I'm fairly sure that Derrington is involved, but I don't know about Stacy, which could be because we're related, and I don't want to suspect him of anything illegal, but I haven't seen anything concrete that would seem to implicate Stacy in an overt wrongdoing."

"At least you're aware of that," said Loring, by way of expressing sympathy.

"I can't help that. It isn't as if he's going to confess to me," she said, and added, "I don't always like Stacy, but — "

"Blood is thicker than water. I understand that. And you're both upper crust, so you probably wouldn't speak against him, no matter what." Loring sighed. "Anything else?"

"I still think Knott's murder is tied to Moncrief's, and to James Poindexter's supposed suicide," Poppy said boldly, wanting to regain her position as a disinterested reporter. "They had a number of things in common — and not simply their social stratum, but their employments overlapped. These commonalities are beyond the bounds of coincidence, in my opinion. And with Derrington's being part of the Grimes family, it complicates things even more."

"You mean that Poindexter and Moncrief worked for the same firm? I agree that I find that suspect, but that's not enough to make direct charges. Still, we're trying to get more information on Hadley and Grimes. We know that Poindexter and Moncrief had a few accounts in common, Moncrief having taken over some of Poindexter's clients. We know that for a fact — it's been confirmed. And we know from bank records that they had both purchased goods from Knott in the past, but at that level of society, such connections aren't unusual. They are factors, not facts, worse luck." He shaded his eyes to look at the far side of the lake. "Since there's still no sign of Overstreet, we're putting more men on finding him. That's not for publication."

"All right." Poppy made a mental note to keep this to herself for now. "But if anything turns up, you'll give me an exclusive?"

"If I can." He gave her a sheepish smile before he once again gazed across the pond. "That's the best I can do."

"Then I'll have to accept it," she said, not quite as affably as she wanted. "I have a theory I'd like to discuss with you. And for now it is simply a theory: I'm not planning to use it unless I can find some evidence to support it, but," she continued, rushing to address the matter before she lost her nerve, "I think that Moncrief knew the person who killed him. He let someone into the house, and I don't think he would do that without actually knowing the person. Same with Knott. That's one of the commonalities I mentioned. It's one of the reasons I think they're connected, no matter how different their deaths. Work might not be significant in this case, but hospitality might be."

Loring thought this over, then hesitantly asked, "Would either or both of those men admit your cousin if he called unexpectedly?"

"They would, but the same can be said of a great many men, not just Stacy. They would let Denton North in, and he's investigating their firm in some way," Poppy replied at once. "You keep insisting on talking about my family's position in society: we're not the only ones in our station, and anyone among the so-called upper crust would reasonably be expected to be received by Moncrief or Poindexter or Knott."

"I get your point," said Loring, "and I'll keep it in mind. I hope we find Overstreet soon — I have a hunch that he could explain a great deal."

Poppy wanted to yell at him, to tell him everything that Chesterton Holte had told her, but knew she could prove nothing, and some of what she had to offer would seem implausible at best, so she only remarked, "I'll try to keep a decent perspective on the case, so long as you give me your word that you will do the same."

He turned to look at her. "You drive a hard bargain, Miss Thornton."

"It's my job, Inspector Loring," she reminded him. "As yours is yours."

Three boys, newly out of school, came running along the path, shouting as they went; a woman pushing a baby-carriage glared at them. The boys yelled more loudly and kept going.

"Do you really think that draining the pond will stop another 'Flu epidemic?" Loring asked her inconsequentially.

"I think the authorities hope so; they need to demonstrate that they are taking precautions beyond talking to doctors," said Poppy, feeling strange about discussing the 'Flu so directly. "They have to do something visible to quiet the fear of the 'Flu, and this will be an obvious change, something people can point to."

"That's true," Loring allowed.

"Though I suppose the draining of the pond is more aggravating than beneficial."

"Is there anything else that can be done?" Loring stared at her, waiting for her to answer.

"There probably is, but it may be politically or financially too expensive. I don't know if anyone in a position to make changes would take the time to explore the matter."

"But what do you think will happen?" he pursued.

"I have no idea," she said. "But we can't afford another epidemic, so I think it makes sense to do everything that might work to prevent another outbreak, however minor."

Loring thought this over, then nodded slowly. "Cover all bases, in other words? Just in case?"

"So long as the proposal is reasonable. Burning down the old parts of the city isn't sensible, no matter what Reverend Towers may say, and what people in the city government endorse him." She had read the transcript of his latest sermon, and had decided that his plan was untenable, designed more to drive out poor immigrants than to eliminate the 'Flu. "Coolidge won't address the issue; he's leaving it up to mayors and governors."

"There we agree," Loring said, sounding relieved. "Tower's a fool, he likes to frighten people, and he doesn't like newcomers."

"No, he doesn't," Poppy concurred, curious to find out where this all might be leading.

"There is a group of important men here and in New York and Boston who want to tighten the requirements for immigrants entering this country. Do you happen to know how Moncrief felt about such things?"

"No, I don't. If you want me to ask Stacy, I can, but I doubt he'll give me an answer," said Poppy, wondering if she should ask Holte to ask Madison about this.

"And what do you think about immigrants?"

His question took Poppy by surprise. "Well, I know all my ancestors were immigrants, and as my father used to say, the standards that were good enough for then should be good enough for now. I know we've had an influx since the Great War, but it's hardly the first time that a crisis in Europe has brought more immigrants to this country."

"Nothing against the Irish, or the Eye-Ties? Or Polacks?" Loring's questions had turned sharp again.

"Nor Russians, nor Jews, nor Chinese," said Poppy. "It's that wretched refuse from your teaming shores promise. I don't want to have us renege on something so basic."

"How do you mean?"

She thought about her answer before she spoke. "I haven't met many immigrants, but those I have, have been unexceptionable. That doesn't mean I will always approve of all immigrants — I don't like everyone I know now, so I reserve the right to take personal dislike to individual immigrants, but not whole masses of them." She waited for him to say something, and when he did not, she asked, "Why these questions? Do they have anything to do with your investigation?"

"Not as such; I'm curious, that's all. Police are curious," he said, a trace of amusement in his expression.

"So are reporters," she told him.

"I've noticed." He stared off into the distance, then said, "You've helped me out, so I guess I owe you a lead or two."

"I guess you do," she said. She hoped he would supply her with information she could pursue the following morning.

"There's one thing that might interest you: we're trying to locate the warehouse where Knott kept his most valuable imports. There have been questions about their authenticity, and we want to turn them over to the Smithsonian to settle the question once we find them. If Knott was dealing in forgeries, then it puts a very different slant on the motive for his murder."

Poppy heard him out, trying to think of a question that would keep him talking. "Does the District Attorney agree with you?"

Loring shrugged. "He doesn't disagree. We're supposed to get a court order to open it as soon as we locate the warehouse, but those things take time. When we find the place, I'll let you know."

"What about what you discover inside?" Poppy asked.

"That depends on what that, or those, may be," Loring responded.

"All right." She straightened up a little, her feeling of awkwardness returning. "Is there anything more?"

He became almost bashful, not quite looking at her. "I gather you're going to the funeral day after tomorrow?"

"Yes. Are you?"

Loring took a deep breath. "It's part of my job. I need to see who attends." He looked across the pond again, as if searching for the ducks. "Would you be willing to have lunch with me afterward?"

She was a bit startled. "To compare notes?"

"If you'd like to. Or we could talk about the weather, if you'd prefer." There was a glint in his tired eyes.

Poppy blinked in astonishment. Could Holte have been right? she thought; Loring was interested in her as more than a reporter. "I'd like that," she heard herself say, and wondered why she had agreed, since the last thing she wanted to do was to make her reportage subject to charges of biased judgment.

He smiled, but then his manner changed. "That's assuming nothing significant happens at the funeral, of course."

"Of course," she echoed.

"Okay." He stood up abruptly. "I'll look forward to seeing you."

Poppy watched Loring striding away, and wondered what she ought to do now.

THIRTY-TWO

"STACY WILL BE IN AFTER WE'VE DINED, PROBABLY FAIRLY LATE; HE DECIDED against going back to New York until after the funeral. He's joining Louise Moncrief and Julian Eastley for dinner at The Town House tonight, something to do with her investments, and the opportunity to cheer Louise --- she's been so dejected, and the Town House is her favorite restaurant. Some may think it unseemly for Louise to appear in public so soon after her husband's death, but Stacy assures ne that it is in Louise's best interests. " Aunt Jo informed Poppy as she arrived shortly after five in the afternoon; the day was closing in, and Hawkins was busy turning on the lights in the entry hall and the stairwell. "You and I will be served in the library at seven. I want to talk to you about your work." She was occupying the largest chair in the sitting room, Duchess lying at her feet, snoring. Josephine had the butler's tray on its cart in front of her, six bottles of illegal European spirits out in plain view; the gin bottle was more than a third empty.

Poppy halted in the doorway into the sitting room. "All right," she said, trying to conceal her alarm. What on earth could Aunt Jo want to know? She had given her coat and her briefcase to Hawkins when she had come through the front door, and had a panicky moment that left her feeling a bit tipsy as she tried to make up her mind if she should ask for her briefcase in order to show her aunt what she did. "I didn't realize that my reporting interested you, Aunt Jo."

"It doesn't, as such, but Primrose North told me this afternoon that Denton is looking into Eustace's business activities, in case there may be some remote connection to Madison Moncrief's untimely demise. I'd like you tell me what you know about the whole dreadful affair." The sniff in her words told Poppy that her aunt was greatly displeased and much troubled. "You may have learned something useful that we could pass on to our attorney, in the unlikely chance we will need to consult him."

Poppy faltered in reacting, and when she did, she felt that she had disappointed her aunt in some indefinable way. "I'm following leads, Aunt Jo, and there isn't much I can tell you, beyond what the Clarion has published. So far my leads are just leads, and that means little more than gossip; you know how outrageous rumors can be. So I'm sorry, but since I haven't very many hard facts to work on, I don't know that I can be much help to you."

"I still want to know as much as you can tell me." For once, Aunt Jo seemed formidable, and Poppy did not want to have the evening end in confrontation. "I realize you have an obligation to the public, but I would think you have more responsibility to your family."

Poppy mulled this over. "I'll tell you what I can, Aunt Jo, which isn't very much, but right now, I need to put on something more comfortable. My feet are killing me, and I know my hair is a mess. Let me put on my lounging slacks, and a loose blouse and get out of these shoes. And I don't mean anything . . . off-color."

"Certainly not." Aunt Jo sighed in a spirit of ill-usage. "Do what you must. I will expect you to return here in . . . shall we say, twenty minutes. I'll pour you a cognac, as a restorative. You do look a trifle bedraggled." She reached for the bottle of gin and topped off her glass with more of it. "Go on, then."

"It's been a difficult day," Poppy reiterated, knowing that Josephine was not entirely attentive. She withdrew from the sitting room and made for the stairs, doing her best not to trip on Maestro, who accompanied her, stropping himself on her shins as she climbed, ignoring her protests and threats to fall on him if he dared to trip her. As she entered her room, she turned on the lights only to have them blink. "So you're back," she said to the empty air even as Maestro laid back his ears and hissed.

"Briefly," spoke Holte from the top of the chest of drawers. "I have something I want to look into."

"Pressing business among the ghosts?" Poppy asked as she peeled out of her wool-crepe jacket. "Or is there more you're working on?"

"I believe there is more that I can learn," he said.

"My, aren't we oblique tonight," she marveled, feeling too harried to be minimally polite.

"You're being brusque, which is unlike you," he said without any indication of having taken offence. "I learned something that might be germane to your story, and I want to follow it up. I'll tell you what I find in the morning." He hesitated. "Would you like me to turn away while you change clothes?"

"If you would, please," she replied, unbuttoning her heavy linen blouse; this she threw into the hamper at the edge of her closet. "It may be silly, but I'd prefer you do not look."

"Of course," said Holte, his voice fading a bit.

Poppy hung her jacket up and unzipped her skirt, stepped out of it, and secured it to another hanger. Then she pulled her slip over her head and put it into the top drawer of her chest, and went back to her closet to take down a long, drapey blouse in pale lilac silk; she shrugged into it, and removed the charcoal lounging slacks from the clipped hanger and tossed them onto her bed, then bent over to remove her shoes. That done, she drew on the slacks, and zipped them up. "All right. You can turn around now."

Holte became something like a pencil sketch on the air as he complied. "That's a very nice outfit," he remarked as he almost reclined on top of the chest-of-drawers. "The silk is particularly flattering."

"It's comfortable, which is more important than fashion right now," Poppy informed him as she took a pair of low-heeled slippers from the rack at the end of her bed. "So what have you come to tell me this time?"

"Overstreet is in Montreal, at a hotel under the name of Morris Otterman. The name is close enough to his own that he will be able to respond to it quickly, and the initials will match his new name, and the brand on his luggage." He drifted a bit nearer to her, watching as she combed her hair back into a kind of order. "Knott searched him out, and summoned me to inform me of what Overstreet has done."

"Why did he do this?" Poppy wanted to know. "I mean Knott."

"Because he thought I might be interested," said Holte blandly. "He would like to have his murder solved, and who can blame him for that. He is of the opinion that Overstreet knows the identity of his killer."

"And are you — interested? in what he may tell you?" Poppy inquired as she studied her reflection in the vanity mirror. "I guess this will do," she said, tweaking a wayward tendril on her cheek. She reached for a pot of lip-rouge and its brush, and restored a bit of brightness to her mouth. Satisfied with her efforts, she took a tissue and blotted the color. "There."

"Your aunt will approve," Holte assured her.

"That's the general idea; she's pretty discomposed just now," said Poppy, bending down to scratch Maestro's ruff; the cat was vociferating his disapproval of Holte's presence. As she straightened up, Poppy looked toward the place in the air where there was a shiny haze. "I'm sorry — I'm tired and I'm worried, and that makes me snippy. I shouldn't take my annoyances out on you."

"I do understand," said Holte. "I used to be a bear if I went more than five hours without eating. It was inconvenient in my work."

"Thank you," Poppy said, and saw the shine vanish. She shook her head once, and looked down to address the cat. "Come on, Maestro. The fun's over for now."

Maestro yowled, but went toward the door, his tail lifted, his whiskers fanned out as if he expected to find Holte's scent somewhere in the room.

Poppy closed her door behind her, and went back down to the sitting room, two stairs behind Maestro. As she reached the bottom step, Missus Flowers appeared, and said, "Good evening, Miss Thornton. Did Missus Dritchner tell you that dinner is going to be served in the library this evening?"

"Yes, Missus Flowers, she did. Thanks for the reminder," said Poppy.

Missus Flowers glanced toward the sitting room, saying to Poppy in a lowered voice. "If Missus Dritchner should need a little help up the stairs, you may call on me. I'll be in the kitchen with Mister Hawkins for another hour, having our supper."

"That's very good of you, Missus Flowers," Poppy said. "How long has she been . . . tippling?"

"Since about three this afternoon, just after Mister Eustace went out," said Missus Flowers. "I suspect he said something that upset her."

"Oh, dear," said Poppy. "That's unfortunate." She wanted to say that it was typical of Stacy to be so insensitive, but kept silent.

"And sad," said Missus Flowers.

"True," said Poppy, and steeled herself to deal with her aunt as she went toward the sitting room. At the door she paused to give herself the opportunity to size up Aunt Jo's state of inebriation, then she coughed gently. "How are you this evening, Aunt Jo?" she inquired calmly.

"I am well enough, thank you," said Josephine, her words a trifle too crisp. "That color is quite becoming on you. Come in. I have your cognac poured." The room was sunk into shadows as the last rays of sunset lit the wisteria trellis outside the windows. "Will you be good enough to turn on the lights?"

Poppy did as her aunt bade her; when the room was lit again, she pulled the draperies across the windows and went back to the settee. "How kind of you," she said, indicating the snifter after sitting down, smiling brightly so as not to disturb Josephine; she reached for the small snifter and lifted it toward Aunt Jo. "Your health."

Josephine raised her almost empty glass in response. "To yours."

Maestro had taken up most of the hassock in front of Aunt Jo's wing-back chair, and now dropped his front paw over his eyes and pretended to sleep; Duchess was lying on the rug in front of the fireplace, snoring audibly.

"How has your day been, Aunt Jo?" Poppy asked after she tasted her cognac.

"Oh, you know how a day goes. I had a light luncheon with Primrose North around one in the afternoon — all she could talk about was Denton's current case, you know, the one involving some kind of massive fraud in the importing market — and afterward I played in the music room for an hour or two." She took a last drink and refilled her glass. "Eustace was here for a little while, and told me about his evening plans. He promised not to be out past midnight." She sounded desperate at this last.

"I'm sure he didn't mean to be a bother," said Poppy mendaciously.

"No doubt, but I had planned to . . . " She dabbed a lace handkerchief to her eyes. In the next moment, she pulled herself together. "I apologize, Poppea. I'm not quite myself just now, and every little thing upsets me."

"I'm sorry you've been disappointed," said Poppy, setting her snifter down; this looked to be shaping up for a tricky evening.

Josephine gave a shaky laugh. "You know Eustace: always concerned for his friends."

"Um-hum," said Poppy, who knew no such thing.

"It is kind of him to help Louise Moncrief with her plans for Madison's funeral; it can't be easy for her so soon after her loss of a baby. She has unexpected fortitude, but she is still a woman, and in need of a stalwart man to support her through this difficult time." She stifled a yawn. "I can't imagine that Julian Eastley is much help, he's such a lapdog. Eustace has a keen sense of what is appropriate on such occasions as this one, and what will suit Louise. No doubt Louise is depending upon him in her current ordeal." She put the stopper back in the gin bottle and took hold of her glass with unusual tenacity.

"It's good of him to help her," said Poppy, wanting to ease her aunt's distress.

"Yes, it is; she has always been a special friend of his," said Josephine, and added with a version of acquiescence with what Stacy was doing, "It is my duty as his mother to respect his decisions."

"It's to your credit that you do," said Poppy, knowing what was expected of her.

"Missus Flowers will bring us some finger-food shortly," Josephine said abruptly. "Missus Boudon made crab puffs."

"That should be lovely," said Poppy, trying to decide how to find a way to bring up Warren Derrington before Aunt Jo lapsed into incoherence.

"I know you like them, as do I," Josephine went on before taking a generous sip of her gin.

"It's one of the niceties of a well-run home, to have delicious finger-food." She daubed at her eyes again. "If only Eustace were here to enjoy them."

"I'm sure he'll be sorry to have missed them." She put down her snifter and rose. "If you don't mind, I'll light the fire. This room is a bit chilly, don't you think?"

"By all means, do," said Josephine, with a wave of her handkerchief for emphasis. "Now that I think of it, the room does feel — " She stopped speaking in order to have a little more gin.

"It will warm up shortly," Poppy said, smoothing the front of her blouse.

Josephine raised her glass. "This will warm me up."

Poppy went to the fireplace, taking care not to disturb Duchess, who had moved there from Josephine's feet, and selected a wooden match from the box on the mantle, struck it alight on the small iron rasp provided for that purpose, and bent to move the fire screen. She gathered her thoughts and ventured a question as if it had only occurred to her at this instant. "You haven't mentioned this: has Mister Derrington come by to pick up his things?"

"No," said Josephine. "I've had Hawkins put them in the hall closet."

"Probably a good solution for now," said Poppy, setting the lit match to the crumpled newspaper that served as kindling. "One of the things I heard about Mister Derrington is that his mother is related to either Hadley or Grimes. If this is true, it may have something to do with my current assignment," she remarked, shading the truth. "Can you clear this up for me?"

Josephine thought this over, then said, "I seem to recall that she was a Grimes, either by birth or marriage; her mother was widowed young, as I recall." She frowned with concentration. "I believe she was a Grimes by birth, now that I think about it." After taking another sip of gin, she went on, "Her name was Samantha. She died of the 'Flu."

Poppy would have liked something a bit more certain, but she knew she could not count on Aunt Jo for more than she had volunteered. "Samantha Grimes. I should be able to check that out," she said, and went back to the settee to have a little more of her cognac before Missus Flowers arrived with the crab puffs.

"How long do you anticipate being involved in this investigation of yours?" Aunt Jo asked as Poppy sat down.

"As long as there is a story to report, assuming my editor keeps me on it," said Poppy, picking up the snifter and swirling the cognac within it.

"Does that mean more irregular hours?"

"I'm sorry, Aunt Jo, but it might. I can't anticipate where the leads will take me." She saw Josephine shake her head in disapproval. "But I'll be spending the evening with the Fairchilds tomorrow. Mildred is going to have another child, and she wants to celebrate their good fortune. They're having a small dinner party."

"Very appropriate. Congratulate Mildred for me, will you? I know her family must be very proud," said Josephine, with elaborate courtesy.

"I gather you have a better opinion of how Mildred is living than how I am," said Poppy, challenging her aunt's tone although she knew it was unwise.

"How could I not, Poppea? You should have married at least four years ago." She drank again. "It may not be my place to say it, but I am convinced that your parents did you a disservice in sending you to college, as they did. A finishing school would have been more useful. You wouldn't be wasting your youth struggling for that paper, caught up in matters no decent woman would want to pursue." She fumbled with the gin bottle to remove the stopper.

Poppy knew it was useless to contradict Aunt Jo in her present state, but between the frustrations of her day and her general fatigue, she allowed herself to object. "I don't think what I'm doing is wasting anything. I want to report the news, to inform the public. You're disappointed: you've made that clear any number of times. But, Aunt Jo, I can't live the life you want for me unless it coincides with the life that I want for me."

"So you've said, but I can't conceive of why that is." Josephine splashed a generous amount of gin into her glass, spilling a little in the process. "Esther has a lot to answer for."

Whatever Poppy might have responded to this was silenced by the arrival of Missus Flowers with the tray of crab puffs and a wedge of white cheddar. Poppy smiled gratefully up at her. "Oh, thank you, Missus Flowers. This looks delicious."

"Good of you to say so, Miss Thornton. Dinner will be ready in thirty minutes," she said, and glanced at Josephine. "I'll brew up some tea for dinner, shall I?"

"It might be best," said Poppy, and watched while her aunt did the unthinkable and snagged three crab puffs from the tray without so much as a nod to Missus Flowers. "We'll go up in twenty minutes, then. How does that sound, Aunt Jo?"

Josephine had taken a bite of the first of her crab puffs, and so did not answer at once. "Whatever you think is wise, Poppea. I find I'm quite hungry."

Missus Flowers ducked her head and left the room.

THIRTY-THREE

It was twelve forty-eight when Stacy finally let himself in the front door; he was tiptoeing, and had almost made it to the stairs when Poppy spoke to him from the parlor. "Good morning, Stacy. I'm glad to see you found your way home at last." She emerged from the gloom of the parlor into the low light in the entry hall.

Stacy froze two steps away from the stairs, then swung around and smiled. "Good morning to you, Coz," he said at his most charming. "I didn't think anyone would be up."

"If you mean your mother, Aunt Jo went to bed at ten, when she ran out of gin; I don't think I have seen her so under the weather before," said Poppy with a sternness that she rarely used with him. "She was desolated when you didn't arrive by nine, in spite of knowing that you had told her that you would be in before midnight."

"Things took longer than I anticipated," he said glibly.

"You could have 'phoned when you realized that," Poppy said, refusing to be beguiled by him.

"It's well past that now, isn't it? I would have had to call after ten, and, as you are well aware, mother does not like to answer the 'phone after nine. Do you want to give me a piece of her mind, or shall I wait until breakfast, to experience it directly?" Stacy lifted one eyebrow; in the half-light, he had the look of a carved demon in a medieval church.

"I'm not even going to give you a piece of my mind. You really are a thoughtless rogue, aren't you?" Poppy came a step nearer to Stacy, staring at him with a measuring look that unnerved him. "Do you have any idea how much you distress Aunt Jo?"

"I'm sorry if my mother was worried — all right?" He came a step nearer to her. "She thinks I'm still seventeen."

"That's because you often behave as if you were still seventeen," said Poppy.

"She wants to keep me as young as possible," he persisted.

"Whether she does or not, the least you can do is show her some regard. It would mean a lot to her." Poppy folded her arms.

"Oh, please, Poppy, don't start with the familial obligation speech. I've heard it ever since I was nine." He took a quick look toward the stairs. "You have to get up early, don't you? And yet you've stayed up to berate me, in spite of having to get up early. Because you have a job. If my mother wants an example of rectitude, it's you, Coz, not me."

"You, too, have a job, or so you claim," she said, refusing to rise to the bait. "That's something we have to talk about, you and I. Tomorrow morning."

"My, my, my, aren't you the stern one?" He chuckled, and wagged a finger at her. "Tisk, tisk, Coz. I'm afraid I'm busy tomorrow morning. Do you think you might be free in the afternoon for your inquisition?"

Because she had expected equivocation from him, she was nonplused by his frank question. "Do you have a specific time in mind?" she managed to inquire.

"You're asking a lot of me, Coz. I may not be able to tell you until I talk to Louise in the morning."

Poppy made an exasperated gesture. "You can try to dodge me all you like, Stacy. I have an assignment, and it involves you and whatever-it-is that you do. Starting with what you know about Warren Derrington's present location."

"Warren again?" Stacy glowered at her. "I wish I knew where he is. I have a few questions I'd like to ask him."

"As would many others," said Poppy.

"If I tell you as much as I know tomorrow afternoon, will you let it alone?" Stacy asked, for once sounding serious.

"Why wait until then?" Poppy inquired. "I'm glad to stay up now."

"I have a meeting with a mutual business associate tomorrow at lunch, and I might find out more than I know now. Besides, I don't know about you, but I'm tired."

Poppy considered this, and decided it might be better to trust Stacy for the time being; if he failed to show up in the afternoon, she would have to reveal her vexations to Inspector Loring. "If that's what it will take to locate Derrington, I'll wait."

Stacy grinned. "Thanks, Coz. I'll make it worth your while — you'll see."

"That depends on what you'll have to say." She glanced at the mantle clock in the parlor. "What time tomorrow afternoon, and where do you want to meet?"

"Not here," said Stacy promptly. "Where are you going to be?"

"At the Clarion, doing some research in the morgue." She was not looking forward to reading through back issues of the paper to see if she could find confirmation about Warren Derrington's mother being connected to the Grimes, or explaining to Cornelius Lowenthal why she was not out chasing down leads. "In the morning, I have an appointment with Doctor Wyman, the coroner."

"I know who he is," said Stacy. "Why are you consulting him?"

"I'm following up a lead," she said, making no excuse for being evasive.

"About Madison?" Stacy asked, for once appearing to be surprised.

"No," she said, and volunteered nothing more.

Stacy shrugged. "All right, keep that to yourself." He stared at her, then sniggered. "You win. I'll play your game. What if I pick you up in front of the building at . . . shall we say three? Louise has loaned me Madison's car; Eastley will drive her in his if she needs to go anywhere." He offered her a boyish smile. "It's a Duesenberg."

The automobile was as much a temptation as was the promise of information. "Three o'clock. On the dot."

"I'll be there." Stacy sounded unusually earnest, and went on to elaborate, which made him appear deceptive again. "I want to know what happened to Warren as much as you do, Coz."

Poppy gave him the benefit of her doubts, and chalked his sudden cooperation up to his need to find Derrington. "Three o'clock," she repeated. "Sleep well. And make sure you apologize to Aunt Jo in the morning."

"If you insist," said Stacy before he turned away and went up the stairs.

Poppy watched him go, wondering if she had made a mistake to let Stacy go without questioning him thoroughly, but his assurance that he would provide her with more the next afternoon reminded her that she wanted to find out about Derrington as much as Stacy did, and that single aspect of his bargain stuck with her, convincing her that it was better to wait than to insist on guesses and half-truths now. She went to the stairs, looking around to make sure that Maestro was not under-foot again; after she turned off the entry hall light, darkness engulfed her, and it took almost twenty seconds before her eyes adjusted enough to allow her to climb the stairs without feeling her way along the bannister. By the time she reached her room, she was drowsy, and when she had undressed, she almost stumbled into her bed. As she fell asleep, she briefly wondered where Chesterton Holte was, then gave herself over to her dreams.

While Poppy slept, Chesterton Holte was moving about in the dimension of ghosts, seeking out Moncrief and Poindexter, trying to locate them in the swirls and eddies of noncorporeality, hoping against hope that he would be able to find out what had become of Warren Derrington, and what he had been involved in.

"Is that you, Holte?" The presence that was less than a shadow approached, bringing the hint of another presence with it.

"Moncrief?" Holte ventured.

"Yes. Poindexter is here somewhere." Moncrief seemed vaguer than before, and less focused. "What do you want now?"

Holte realized that he would have to be rigorous in sticking to his purpose. "What can you tell me about Warren Derrington?"

"Who?"

"Warren Derrington," Holte said again. "He's with International Business Associates. He was one of your clients. His work has something to do with international financing, apparently. He's supposed to be a friend of Stacy Dritchner's."

"Supposed to be?" Moncrief echoed. "That's a strange way to put it. They've been thick as thieves for years. Ask anyone."

The other presence grew clearer, and it startled Holte to recognize Percy

Knott.

"What do you have to add to this?" Holte asked.

"I've remembered a little more about the incidents surrounding my death; I thought you'd want to know." Knott did something that seemed like a sigh. "I do want my murderer arrested."

"Not unusual," said Holte. "What's on your mind?"

"I had a 'phone call about twenty minutes before my killer arrived," said Knott in a hurried non-voice. "I think it was from Stacy Dritchner, looking for Warren Derrington, but it may have been the other way around. It was one or the other of them — I'm certain of that. I may have been expecting one of them to come to talk with me. I don't know if either of them came."

"Do you happen to remember what the reason was for the call?" Holte asked, aware that Moncrief was listening closely to this silent exchange.

"It must have had something to do with the antiquities they've been bringing into the country," Knott said slowly. "I can't think what else I would have had to discuss with either of them. Derrington is the more knowledgeable on international finance, but Dritchner is better with the practicalities, at least that has been my experience." He did something that suggested a hitch of his shoulder if he had had a body. "I'd had a visit from a customs agent the week before; he was checking on the provenance of the antiques I had in the shop — nothing older than sixteenth century, and all papers in order. He also wanted to know about the antiquities I kept in my warehouse; that was the rare stuff. I had museums waiting for half of them, and serious inquiries from some very wealthy collectors. My treasure was an Eighteenth Dynasty Egyptian chair, covered in gold leaf, with inlays in turquoise and fulminous glass; you know, the kind made from lightning striking sand. A man in Chicago had offered me over a million for it. We were still negotiating when I . . . was murdered."

Chesterton Holte heard Knott out, and weighed up his response. "Do you think your Chicago buyer might have had something to do with the killing? A treasure like that would tempt a great many people."

Knott simmered with emotion. "It's possible, especially if it could be proven that what I had was a forgery. He was expecting the real thing, no questions about it, and had put a considerable amount into an escrow account while we worked things out. I was satisfied that the chair was genuine, but with the kind of rumors that were running rampant, my buyers had been more demanding on documentation." He paused, then went on more slowly, "I thought the gossip came from one of my competitors trying to get a lead on me, but now I'm not so sure. I certainly paid authentic prices, and everything I've learned about that period was present in the nine pieces I bought. Getting them into the country took more . . . adaptability than I had originally expected."

Now Holte was deeply interested. "What did you do?"

"I brought half the load in through Canada with bootleggers, the more valuable half. The rest I declared and paid the tariffs on at Boston. I didn't want the Philadelphia authorities tracking my inventory too closely." He was speeding up his flow of information, as if he wanted to rid himself of its burden. "I hadn't done anything wrong, aside from dodging customs, but I was getting worried that someone would make the connection between me and Hadley and Grimes. They were the ones who came up with the way to avoid the heavy import tariffs, and I didn't want to get caught in that mill."

"That's interesting," said Holte, hoping that Poppy could find some way to use it, since she would have to find a secondary source in order to publish. "Who else knows about this?"

"Moncrief figured it out, after he got here. Same with Poindexter, unless it was his idea to begin with." Knott stared around the vague space of the dimension of ghosts.

"It wasn't," Poindexter interjected from his location in the whorls and eddies. "I was warned off my examination of the records in the files. I told both Hadley and Grimes that I thought they were making a mistake, but Grimes told me the amount of money this meant to the firm, and I decided to keep silent, at least until I was completely retired and could approach the Justice Department anonymously."

Holte felt a spurt of alarm. "How much money are we talking about here?"

Poindexter hesitated, but answered, "At the time I died, I figured the income since the end of the Great War, for the firm, was at least six million dollars. More since I died."

"That's a huge amount of money," Knott observed.

"They could build a new bridge for that amount." Moncrief made an unnoise of agreement, and spoke to Holte. "The three of us have been talking since your last visit about what we suspected was going on at Hadley and Grimes."

Poindexter took up the topic. "I had largely forgotten my worries about the money — it was hidden in a number of accounts, including International Business Associates, Stacy's and Derrington's company, and I hadn't realized how large the sum was that was involved."

"Money doesn't mean much here," Moncrief said, not so much as an excuse, but an explanation. "It doesn't seem that important any more, not when we're all noncorporeal."

There was a thickening of the atmosphere around Poindexter, Moncrief, Knott, and Holte as more of the ghosts in their area grew curious about the unusual degree of distress that was being generated by the exchange the four were sharing.

"How soon after you started examining the finances did you get killed?" Holte asked, taking care not to reveal his burgeoning fear.

"I'm not sure," said Moncrief. "Several weeks, I think, but perhaps sooner."

"I didn't say anything about what I had found, not until I was certain of how extensive it was, and then, I double-checked my calculations before I brought it to the attention of my superiors, and I was dead in just under a month, if I'm remembering correctly." Poindexter shimmered in the swirl. "Until we discussed this, I hadn't made the connection."

Holte asked, "Did it ever occur to you that you were in danger?"

Since this was the dimension of ghosts, all three shades shuddered in sympathy. "The firm will do all it can to protect its profits, I know that, but I didn't see that I was exposed to . . . retribution for what I had discovered," said Poindexter. "I'm the unliving proof."

"And I," said Knott.

"All three of us are." Moncrief did his best to summon up more of his memories. "When I realized what was going on, I tried to cover my tracks, as it were, but I had already been discovered. I had decided I ought to resign; Louise did not want to move, and I didn't want this problem hanging over me. It seems strange that I would not remember an important thing like that, but it had slipped away, along with a number of other things. Something Knott said brought that back. You know how it is. Bits and pieces drift away, and there's comfort in having them gone. But you've been so persistent, I've been doing my best to recall as much as I can, and this is what I've come up with. It's something that your young lady might pursue."

"She's not my young lady, not in the way you imply," Holte said testily. "I'm responsible for her father's death, and to recompense what she lost when he died in my place, I'm haunting her."

"No disrespect intended," Knott said dimly. "It's unfortunate that you couldn't forget those circumstances, you might have moved on by now if you hadn't remembered."

"Moved on to what, to where?" Holte countered, and felt a jarring around him as other ghosts heard his response to Knott. "When I move on, I want my slate clean."

"When will that be?" Poindexter asked, as if seeking the definition for an unfamiliar word. "How will you know?"

"I'll know when the books are balanced," said Holte "I have a number of things to work out — being a spy does that. This is my first step in that direction, and it is just that: a first step."

Knott had almost vanished, but he said, "I imagine there are things I should do, and I will remember in a while. The Great War was . . . difficult."

"When will that be — that your books are balanced?" Moncrief was more troubled than the other two as he addressed Holte.

"I wish I knew," said Holte. "What you've told me may be very helpful, and I appreciate how difficult it was to face what the memories brought back."

"Do you think it might speed up our moving on?" Knott asked, a bit wistfully.

"I don't know," said Holte. "Perhaps it will."

A soft kind of moan went through the ghosts who had surrounded them, and their non-presence lessened.

"Will you let us know how it turns out?" Moncrief asked. "While we still remember."

"If I can," Holte promised.

A kind of soundless hum passed between the four, and then Holte slipped away and found himself in the darkened music room of Josephine Dritchner's house in time to hear the hall clock strike three.

THIRTY-FOUR

❧

THE MORNING HAD BEEN A FRUSTRATING ONE FOR POPPY: DOCTOR WYMAN HAD cancelled their meeting, saying he was being called out on a suspicious fire in an old hotel, and then Henry Dermott, who ran the Clarion's morgue, was unable to find the relevant files on the records of marriages in the Grimes family; she was trying to decide if she should go to the Bureau of Vital Statistics to pursue the matter, or if she should wait for Dermott to locate the missing clips, when she was called into Lowenthal's office.

"How's it going?" the editor asked as Poppy came through the door. He pointed to the chair in front of his desk.

As ordinary as that question sounded, Poppy was not fooled; she sat down, and asked, "You tell me, boss. Is there anything wrong with my story?" She made an effort to compose herself, wanting not to appear out of her depth. "Have you got anything more you want me to cover, beyond the funeral tomorrow?"

Lowenthal gave a mirthless chuckle. "To borrow your phrase, you tell me. You're implying a connection between the deaths of James Poindexter, Madison Moncrief, and Percy Knott, based on an unknown source. You haven't revealed your informant, saying he believes he would be in danger if he made himself known, which could be true — so you'll have to find someone who can vouch for what you have here, because if you're right, this is explosive. If you can back it up, it's a great story." He mauled his forehead lock, an expectant smile widening. "So: can you back any of this up?"

"That's what I'm working on, boss." She smoothed her trumpet-cut skirt as she gathered her thoughts. "My source is good, but, as you know, he doesn't want to be identified, for fear of reprisals." This was not accurate, she thought, but the explanation made more sense than to reveal that she had a ghost for her source.

"Given what you have here, I'll take your word that your man has good reason for his decision to remain unknown," said Lowenthal, "but I can hold off on his identification only for forty-eight hours. Either you find some printable confirmation, or I'll have to put someone else on the story with you, to help you uncover more cooperative informants, and leave out the parts of your story that include your guesses — because that's what they are without verification — when we go to press." He could see that she was shocked, and so he offered his version of a soothing assurance. "I'm going to cut the last three paragraphs of your story until you can supply me a recognizable source, or offer some other hard evidence. Same as I do for the rest of the reporters here."

Poppy swallowed. "I'm working on that, boss." It was true as far as it went, but she knew it was not enough. "I know my source is good, and that I can't reveal him. I've tried to get back in to Hadley and Grimes, but no one will book an appointment with me. And, remember, I've been warned away from there; at the time, I thought it might have been a little melodramatic, but after all that's happened in the last week, I'm not so sure. And I have to tell you that my cousin and his friend aren't about to tell me anything that might be compromising for their business, or distressing to their families, most of whom I know. If it turns out that Moncrief was killed because of his discoveries, you said yourself that I could be in danger. That note I was given — "

Lowenthal was nodding. "And putting someone like you at risk could have nasty repercussions. I know that." He steepled his fingers. "Look, I'm going to have Jonathan Mullen have a look at your information. If anyone can find something askew in the financials, it's Mullen. I think the money aspect of this story — if there's anything to your speculations — should come from one of our money reporters, and Mullen knows more about the international markets than anyone else at the Clarion."

"You're working to convince me about Jon Mullen," said Poppy. "You don't have to. I agree he knows his stuff."

Lowenthal almost sighed. "Good. That's sensible. If Mullen finds any fire in your smoke, I'll tell him to pursue it, and give you a partner to follow up what you uncover. To get more solid commercial information, I'll have to borrow someone from the Constitution, assuming we can't turn up anything in the next thirty-six hours." He gestured to demonstrate how unlikely that was. "So if you can give your notes to Mullen, I'll have him dig into it."

Poppy sighed. "If that's what you want, boss." She wanted to scream, but she kept her voice level. "I'm going with my cousin Eustace this afternoon. He tells me he has information that has to do with all this, and that he's willing to tell me what he has learned, as soon as he's got enough to substantiate his suspicions. I'd like to wait until then before giving anything to Mullen. To avoid rumors."

"Well, that sounds encouraging." Lowenthal twiddled his hair again. "Tell you what: I'll give you until tomorrow morning to hand over your notes, but I expect them to include whatever useful you learn from your cousin, and if that breaks the story open, you and Mullen will share the by-line. How's that?"

It was better than anything she had dared to hope, but she masked her relief, saying, "That sounds fair to me."

"Good girl." Lowenthal smiled ferociously. "I'll tell you again — you've surprised me."

"Even though I'm a woman?" The words had come before she could stop them.

"Like your Aunt Esther; it must run in the family," Lowenthal countered. "Oh, yes. I know all about her. The National Geographic Society has a treasure in her." He laid his hands flat on his desk. "Go get your lunch. It sounds like you're going to have a busy afternoon before you head off to your . . . engagement."

"Thanks, boss," she said, rising. "Do you want me to say anything to Mullen before I go?"

"No," said Lowenthal. "I'll call him in a little later. But on your way out, tell Miss Stotter that I need her in here in ten minutes."

"Ten minutes it is," said Poppy, and left Lowenthal's office feeling not vindicated but at least granted a stay of execution, a final chance to prove herself. She went to the work-stall where Miss Stotter sat, sorting through a stack of memos and 'phone records. "The boss wants you in ten minutes, Miss Stotter."

Miss Stotter put a paperweight atop the largest of the stacks and glanced at the clock on the wall. "Ten minutes. Minus two."

"Sounds likely," said Poppy, and went to her desk to retrieve her jacket; she was a bit sorry not to find Chesterton Holte hanging about her desk, but she did her best to shrug this off, and went off to lunch.

Sitting at the counter at the Liberty Bell Café, a block away from the Clarion, Poppy found Denton North devouring a roast-beef-and-cheese sandwich, a cup of coffee at his elbow. He was formidable in his pin-stripe navy-blue suit and regimental tie; even his horn-rim glasses gave him an air of importance. Glancing up as Poppy started toward a table, he said, "Good afternoon, neighbor. Why not join me?" He patted the empty stool on his left.

Poppy considered, then put down her briefcase and sat on the stool next to Denton. "Thanks. Don't mind if I do."

Denton offered her a smile. "I've been following your work in the Clarion. Interesting stuff. You've got your teeth in this, don't you."

Poppy studied Denton for a few seconds, wondering if this meeting were wholly coincidental, and concluded it must be; Denton was clever and ambitious, but not psychic, and had no way of knowing she would be here, since she had only made up her mind five minutes ago. "How are you, Denton?" she asked politely, neither thanking nor questioning his praise of her work. "I haven't seen you since . . . was it Thanksgiving?"

"Some time around then, I think. We've been busy at the District Attorney's office. You probably know that." He took another predatory bite of his sandwich.

"Your mother's mentioned it, and so has Aunt Jo," said Poppy, and took the menu card from behind the salt-and-pepper-shaker stand. "I don't think I've seen you here before. Not that I'm here often." She read through the menu, and decided on the chicken salad sandwich, and a cup of the beer-and-cheese soup.

His lunch muffled his response. "I could say the same of you." He took a swig of coffee and swallowed. "I just gave a briefing to Edward Daly at the

Constitution, about the current state of our investigation into the importing fraud case, and its international implications — as much information as I'm at liberty to provide, that is." This last sounded more smug than apologetic.

"That must have been a brief meeting," said Poppy with just enough of a vocal jab as she could without offending him.

He chuckled. "A hit, a very palpable hit." He took another bite, and went on as he chewed. "From what I've read, you've stumbled across some of the same people we're investigating. I can't help but hope if you discover anything that needs the District Attorney's attention, you'll report it."

"If it involves criminal activities, and if I can prove it, I know my obligations." Poppy signaled to the counter waitress and gave her order to the harried woman, then turned to Denton, "Leads can take reporters strange places, just as they can for Assistant District Attorneys."

Denton raised his brows in amusement. "You're getting fast on the uptake, Poppy."

"Part of the job," she said, and nodded her thanks to the waitress, who brought a mug of coffee to her.

"Un-huh," said Denton, and set down his sandwich. "Anything you can pass on to me now?"

"Not really," she said, adding a little sugar and cream to her coffee. "Not yet, anyway."

"Well, keep me in mind when you're free to talk. Things are getting pretty hot in the office, and we'll remember the people who help us." He drank most of the coffee remaining in his mug and signaled for a refill. "For ten cents a mug, they should give at least one free refill," he said with a smile as the waitress poured out a mugful.

There was an outburst of laughter from a nearby table; both Denton and Poppy looked around.

"They're from Mayes' Brothers," said Denton, referring to the fashionable fabric-and-furniture store in the next block. "I took mother there last week; she likes expensive, high-quality things, and the staff caters to her. You know salesmen." He took another swallow of coffee. "They come here frequently, or so I understand."

"Oh, yes; this is conveniently located for them, as it is for me, though I usually do lunch in our cafeteria," said Poppy, wondering why Denton should be here, his interview at the Constitution seeming to be a tenuous explanation, now that she had a little time to think about it; she took a napkin from the dispenser; the fabric was flimsy and there were hints of old stains on it, but it was clean and its folds were neat. "Speaking of information, do you have any that you could pass on to me, about Hadley and Grimes? It might have a bearing on Madison Moncrief's death, and I'm covering his funeral tomorrow."

Denton shrugged. "Nothing specific. They have clients we're looking into, but nothing's concrete yet." He tasted his coffee and set the mug down again. "Too hot." He was studying Poppy out of the tail of his eye.

"Better than too cold," said Poppy, and saw the waitress approaching with her cup of soup, a broad spoon in the saucer under the small bowl.

"You got that right." Denton went back to demolishing his sandwich. "At least they aren't stingy with their portions."

"A good thing, if they're going to charge eighty-five cents for a sandwich, they need to make it a substantial one, or offer pâté and caviar," said Poppy.

"Yes. And they have a captive audience for lunch, though not so much for supper." He offered her as much of a smile as he could while he chewed. "Still, they're open until midnight, so the night shift has a place to come."

"True enough," said Poppy, and smiled at the waitress as she set Poppy's sandwich next to the cup of soup. "Thanks."

"Pleasure," the waitress said automatically. "Anything else, counselor?"

Denton shook his head. "No, thanks, Hilda."

This exchange startled Poppy, who had been under the impression that Denton North rarely ate here but if he were on familiar terms with the staff . . . She kept her reflection to herself as she began to spoon out her soup, trying not to eat so fast that she spilled any of it onto her pebble-crepe suit. She finished the soup and set the saucered bowl aside in order to bring her sandwich nearer to her. "They make their own mayonnaise here," she remarked. "Every morning; it's very good."

"Yeah, and horseradish sauce, too; they use heavy cream." Denton dropped fifteen cents on the counter as he rose, picking up his briefcase in the process. "I'd buy your lunch, Poppy, but with you writing on what may be an aspect of my present case, well, you understand."

"Yes, I do," said Poppy.

"Perhaps when this is all over?" The offer was more conciliatory than ardent.

"Don't worry about it, Denton," said Poppy.

Denton nodded. "I'll see you around? My regards to your aunt."

"And mine to your mother," said Poppy, watching him as he went to the cash register to pay for his meal. She decided that she might ask Lowenthal if she ought to talk to Denton about his case, since it might touch on whatever was going on at Hadley and Grimes, but would wait until she covered the funeral, tomorrow, when she could link the request to those attending the service. Her sandwich was tasty enough, but she paid little attention to it, her thoughts on what it might be that Stacy was going to tell her. She left fifteen cents for Hilda and paid her seventy-five cents to the young man at the register before she returned to the paper to continue her hunt through the maze of files in the paper's morgue.

At ten minutes to three, she gathered up her things, donned her jacket, and climbed the stairs to the ground floor. Poppy went out to the curb to await Stacy's arrival. To her amazement, he was already drawn up in front of the Addison Newspaper Corporation building, the engine of the Duesenburg idling, the suggestion of a satisfied smile on his handsome face. Poppy went to open the door herself, and settled herself on the passenger side.

"Good afternoon, Coz. I hope you're having a good day," he said, engaging the clutch and putting the auto into first gear, his arm extended out the window to indicate his intention to enter the flow of traffic.

"It's going well enough," she said, putting her briefcase between her calves to keep it from sliding.

"How dreary that sounds," he said, glowering at the hoot of a delivery van's horn. "I don't know how you endure it. That ten thousand a year your father left you could keep you comfortably enough."

"I like what I'm doing," she said, prepared to argue if necessary.

"Well, I think it's a waste," he said, and signaled for a left turn. "You'd be a treasure to any man worth his salt. You could get your husband into the

Senate, if you set your mind to it."

"I'd rather get myself into the Senate," said Poppy.

Stacy laughed. "If anyone could do it, it would be you, Coz," he said, jockeying the Duesenberg through the turn, narrowly missing a massive delivery vehicle pulled by a hitch of four straw-colored Suffolk Punches. As he slowed to turn into the next street, he said, "I'm going to be away for a couple of months. One of our clients has a new venture in the rubber trade, and he wants International Business Associates to handle the on-site negotiations. It is a service we provide, but it's not my cup of tea; one of the reasons I'm worried about Warren is that he usually handles those sorts of things. I do somewhat better with the antiquarians and customs folk. If Warren doesn't turn up, I'll have to do the job for him. Mother won't like me being gone for any length of time, and she'll be worried because she won't know where I am; I hope I can rely on you to keep her from becoming overwhelmed on my behalf. She'll need you to steady her."

"Thanks for the warning," said Poppy, not completely sincerely. "What kind of negotiations are we talking about?"

"Just what I told you, Coz: the rubber trade. And that's all you need to know." He squeezed the Duesenberg through a century-old arch and onto a cobbled street fronted on both sides by warehouses. "Warren was scheduled to take the Orient Express to Belgrade at the end of next week; I'll have to wire Hiram Buel if I can't find Warren before Friday."

"Hiram Buel?" Poppy asked.

"Our representative in Brussels. He's our primary man in western Europe. He handles the contracts, but once in a while, he has to work on a project for us." He made another turn into another cobbled street; this one was almost dark, the westering sun blocked by more warehouses.

"So where are you taking us?" Poppy asked, not wanting to let him get off on one of his disparaging tirades.

"There's a warehouse about ten minutes from here where there's supposed to be a shipment of antiques that Warren Derrington brought into the country not quite legally." He coughed gently. "I want to be certain they're there, so I can send the documents to the Justice Department. I've had enough egg on my face. I'm tired of being the one taking the heat on this.

I don't mind shaving the law very closely, but we've gone well beyond that now. And, frankly, I want a witness, in case anything unexpected should happen to the shipment in question." He passed the Harding building and changed lanes to turn toward the wharves. "You're the best witness I could think of."

Poppy was alerted by this remark; she had been puzzled at Stacy's frankness, and now she began to suspect that he was not offering her his candor without an agenda: he needed someone to support his story when he approached the Justice Department, someone who could back up his statements. "So have you found out anything about Warren Derrington?"

"In a manner of speaking," he said, reverting to his habitual allusive responses.

All her journalistic instincts awakened, she sat up a little more erectly, and resisted the urge to pull her notebook from her purse. "Where is he? Has he left the country?"

"I think so." He turned right into another alley, and lifted his right arm to shield his eyes from the afternoon sun. "Mother said you're going to the Fairchilds this evening?"

"I am." She felt steadied by this simple commitment. "Mildred's expecting."

"How nice for her," said Stacy, using the horn to encourage a heavily laden flat-bedded truck to move aside. "Can you believe the traffic?"

"I don't know. I don't get down to this part of the city very often," she said, looking around with curiosity. "Which warehouse are we going to?"

"The Mayes Brothers, the old one. Warren and I have an arrangement with them — did I mention that? We have access to the basements; they're not using them any more, and they're glad to get a bit of rent for the place."

"You didn't say much about your involvement in the arrangement." She could see the waterfront cranes now, their structures rising above the warehouses. The air smelled of salt and tar, and gulls screeched overhead. "Do you actually know where the warehouse is?" She was beginning to think that he was deliberately finding the most indirect route to their destination, probably in the hope that she would not be able to lead others to the location.

"I have the address. We should be there shortly." He began to hum Whispering, his manner becoming far calmer than he had seemed when he picked her up. "We'll go in the side door. I have the key for that one." He resumed his humming, and Poppy decided that she had no reason to interrupt him.

After another seven minutes, and three repeats of Stacy's hummed version of I'll See You in My Dreams, he drove the Duesenberg into an alley with the dubious name of King Charles Lane — which suggested it was named before the Declaration of Independence — guiding it between the high walls of two large, blank-sided, brick buildings, finally drawing up to a stout fence with a small gate that opened from the warehouse loading stage onto the alley; the Duesenberg was the only auto from one end of the alley to the other, and no trucks or vans were in evidence. "You should have room enough to get out of the car without banging the door on the wall. I'll unlock the gate." He smiled as if he knew he ought to. "This shouldn't take long."

Poppy quieted the qualms that had been building within her, and let herself out of the Duesenberg, taking care not to scratch the car door on the bricks of the next warehouse. After a few seconds' hesitation, she left her briefcase in the auto — after all, Stacy had said this would not take long. She closed the door and came around the front of the Duesenberg, admiring it in spite of her uneasiness.

There was an audible click as Stacy got the gate open; he stood aside so that Poppy could step into the parking area near the loading dock. "The door is on the left, up the half-flight of stairs."

"I see it," she said, mildly surprised that there was no one around at three-thirty in the afternoon.

"Relax, Coz. We're not intruding on anything. Nothing's being loaded in or out today, or tomorrow," Stacy said behind her. "No one's here but us."

She was about to turn around when a sharp odor claimed her attention just as the chloroform-laden handkerchief was clapped over her face; she struggled against it, but in less than a minute she sank into unconsciousness.

THIRTY-FIVE

FOR MOST OF THE AFTERNOON, CHESTERTON HOLTE HAD DRIFTED AROUND THE various places Poppy had visited recently. He had spent almost an hour at the Clarion, listening to Cornelius Lowenthal address five different reporters on their current progress on various assignments. Holte had half-expected to see Poppy back at her desk before leaving to go home to change for her evening with the Fairchilds, but as the day waned and she did not appear, Holte faded away from the Addison Newspaper Corporation building, en route to the Dritchner house, hoping to have a word with Poppy before she left for Mildred Fairchild's dinner. He searched through most of the house, watching Josephine idling her way through some Scarlatti while Duchess slept on the footstool next to the piano; in the library Maestro hissed at him, but made no attempt to impede Holte's investigation. In the kitchen, Missus Flowers was having a cup of tea with Missus Boudon, the two of them discussing the high price of poultry this spring, and shaking their heads over Derrington being missing. Hawkins was in the sitting room, helping himself to a tot of brandy while listening to the radio.

But Poppy was nowhere to be found, and there was no indication that she had been and gone. She was not expected at the Fairchild's for another two hours. Holte was becoming restless; he remembered that she was planning to accompany Stacy to a warehouse, but that was supposed to be a brief excursion. On impulse, he went off to the Moncrief house, on the chance that Stacy had stopped by there on his way to return Poppy to Josephine's home; he only found Louise Moncrief sitting in the drawing room, with travel pamphlets for a number of cities in South America; she was reading the one for the Peruvian city of Iquitos. By now, Holte was doing the ghostly equivalent of pacing by shifting back and forth from floor to ceiling in the parlor, then rising out of the house entirely and setting his senses to Poppy herself, as if trying to tune into a radio station. Gradually he began to be aware of the one presence that was Poppy out of the hum and static of the city. He took hold of that signal and went toward it, taking care to stay on it in the increasing confusion of the dying afternoon; he was trying to discern what had happened to her that she should be so remote.

"Ye gods." Poppy came to herself in a small, dark, dank room with a steel door in the far wall, and a dirty, clerestory window behind her; she craned her neck, trying to see beyond the frill of weeds that blocked the view from it, but gave up when the muscles in her neck began to ache. She turned her attention the room. There were six large crates in the room, one of them open, its protective packaging spread about on the floor. She was in a small, elegant, wooden chair, apparently covered in gold leaf and inset with polished semi-precious stones; her wrists and ankles were tied with stout cotton rope, the knots under the arms of the chair and on its back legs. She was aware of being thirsty; her thoughts were jumbled, her recollections of the afternoon in disorder. She looked around the room with growing dismay. There was no source of light in the room, so soon she would be in complete darkness. For the next several minutes, she concentrated on locating the crates in the room, as well as the distance to the door; when she was confident that she had a good picture of the room fixed in her mind, she took a short time to summon up her energy. Most of the chloroform was wearing off, and she realized just how isolated she was. As she reviewed her situation, she had to admit she could not be certain that she was in the Mayes Brothers old warehouse; for all she knew, Stacy, or an accomplice of his, might have taken her to another building altogether. While all of this was disheartening, she rallied herself, telling herself that if she could free herself from the chair, and the door was locked, she might be able to squeeze out the window. Keeping her intention to escape uppermost in her mind, she went to work with her teeth, trying to loosen the ropes that held her in the chair. Although the rope was fairly soft, the knots were strong and their position under the arm of the chair made pulling at them exhausting, and after the greater part of an hour, when the room had fallen into twilight,

Poppy felt herself begin to lose strength. She stifled a sob, and reminded herself sternly that she needed to get herself out of her bonds on her own. "I'll take a break," she said aloud, as much to reassure herself as to hear a human voice. She sat back in the sturdy chair and did her best to trust that someone was coming.

As the room darkened, she forced herself to remain focused on freeing herself from the chair. Her jaw was hurting from her efforts, but she resumed her biting and pulling, wanting to bring the knots near enough to be able to wrench them open. She imagined that her dentist would be displeased at all she was doing, but she reminded herself that an occasional bridge was better than dying. That stark realization enveloped her, and again she went still. "No one knows you're here but Stacy." She listened to herself, and decided she was right: Stacy would not return. "If he tells anyone where you are, it won't be until he's safe, or, if someone's killed him, he won't tell anyone at all." This last realization shocked her; she wanted to sob, to rail at her predicament, but instead delivered a stern scold: "Poppea Millicent Thornton, you are not the kind of ninny who just resigns herself to die — you're a crime reporter. You have a crime to report. You have to do your best to get out of here." With those bracing words, she once again took hold of the ropes with her teeth and did her best to work them around the arm of the chair and her wrist. She could feel her skin go raw as the rope finally slipped a little; briefly she considered working on her left arm rather than her right to save herself from further damage to her wrist. But that would only delay working the knots loose, so she steeled herself to continue tugging.

After another twenty minutes, the knot eased slightly, making it easier for her to gain more play in the rope. Taking this for encouragement, she redoubled her efforts, and in almost three-quarters of an hour, she had succeeded in dragging the main knot to the inside of the chair-arm, and had felt the first give in its tension as she tugged at it again; the first stubborn twist in the knot gave, and the end of the rope flopped along the chair-leg. Her head was aching and her wrist was bleeding, but for the first time since she came to, she began to hope that she would be able to escape from this improvised dungeon. She did her best to get her hand to work enough to bring the bulk of the knot nearer; this time it took little more than twenty minutes to pull the rope-end through two interlocking loops, but gradually the ropes gave to her steady manipulations. The bonds on her right wrist were almost released; she wriggled her arm, trying to develop enough play that she could pull her hand free. Her concentration was so intent on her bonds that she did not notice a shift in the small amount of light coming in from the window.

"What the devil?" Chesterton Holte's voice came from the window as he went through it into the room. "Poppy. Are you all right?" He slid down from the ceiling and hurried up to her, anxiety in every semi-visible line of his noncorporeal form.

"I will be soon," she said, stretching her fingers to restore feeling to them, although this made the pain in the back of her bleeding wrist worse; she bit back the sudden impulse to lick the blood away, but she restrained herself; she did not want to disgust Holte even as she told herself such scruples, under these circumstances, were absurd. "It's good to see you, whether you're really here or not."

"Oh, I'm really here, as really as I ever am," said Holte. "I'd like to know what you're doing here."

Poppy was pulling the ropes from around her wrist, and then bending over to loosen the bonds on her right ankle. "It wasn't my idea," she said brusquely. "I don't even know where here is." If she had been able to touch him, she would have burst into tears, but since she could not, she maintained her composure. She sighed, and pulled another knot loose, and wiggled her foot before she worked on the next cluster of knots.

"You're on a side-street in the old section of the wharf district. Not a very busy place since the Great War ended, and in decline before then. I didn't see any sign on its outer wall." Holte approached within a few inches of her, studying the knots she was loosening now that she had a free hand. "I wish I could help you."

"So do I," she said with feeling, then, more practically, she asked, "Is this the Mayes Brothers old warehouse?" She tried not to hold her breath as she waited for his answer.

"I think it could be," said Holte, startled that she knew. "How long have you been here, and how did you get here?"

Poppy resisted the urge to scream, and told him, "I think we arrived here about three-forty-five, but I'm not sure. We — Stacy and I — pulled in a bit more than half an hour after he picked me up at the Clarion, and the last thing I remember is a handkerchief clapped over my face with something nasty-smelling on it; that was before we entered the building, so I'm not sure this is the one he drove me to. I can't tell you what time it was when I woke up either, except that it was about sundown. I wish I'd worn my watch, but I didn't think I'd need it."

"Do you know how long you were unconscious?" Holte asked.

Poppy shook her head. "I came to myself a while ago; the sun was still up, but not for very long; I've been trying to get out of these knots ever since."

"Stacy tied you up?"

Poppy took a moment to consider her answer. "I assume so. I didn't actually see it, but I have a few memories of when it was happening, and his was the only voice I heard. I didn't know he was so adept at making knots."

"I think he underestimated your perseverance. You didn't let the knots stop you." Holte nodded his approval. "It looks like you're doing a good job of getting loose. You'll be free in another ten minutes. Then the next step is the door."

For the first time since his arrival, Poppy felt her confidence fail her. "It's steel, and I think it's locked."

"Stacy told you that?"

"I don't think so, not directly," she said, having a hazy impression of a number of things Stacy had said as he was tying her to the chair. "I wasn't very conscious. But I believe he was boasting about how well he had planned all this." She frowned and shook her head. "I have to admit, he was very clever. If you hadn't found me, I don't know when I might have been . . . discovered."

"People must be looking for you," he said, wanting to comfort her.

"But how will they know to look here?" She intensified her efforts with the knots.

Holte accepted that she had good reason to worry about that. "Is there a night watchman in this place? I might find some way to catch his attention if there is one," he said, still hoping to inject a note of encouragement into their conversation.

"According to my cousin, there isn't a day watchman here, so I doubt there's one for the night. Since it was Stacy who told me this, I don't know if we should believe him. I have my doubts about everything he told me." She made a mull of laughing, but Holte gave her credit for her effort.

"Small wonder," he said.

She freed her left leg and went to work on her left arm. "He could have killed me and left me here; I guess I should be grateful," she remarked, and made a complete botch of a smile. "I don't suppose you can think of some way to help me with this."

"Noncorporeal," he apologized. "I wish I could."

"Never mind," she said, pulling several feet of rope through the first loop in the knots under the arm of the chair. A note of misgiving crept into her voice. "I'm assuming there's some way to unlock the door from this side."

"I'll see what I can find out," Holte said, and slid through the door, peering at the substantial lock affixed to the cleat holding the steel brace. The key was in it, and slightly turned so that it could not easily be jarred out, making it impossible to maneuver the lock to an open position. Holte swore comprehensively, then took a rapid turn around the warehouse, finding no one to alert to Poppy's plight, and went back into the storeroom. Little as he did not want to discourage her, he shook his head. "Sorry. The lock is . . . jammed. I can't turn it. And there's no sign of anyone other than you being here."

"Of course," said Poppy, and strove to keep from screaming in frustration, afraid that if she began, she might not be able to stop. "I don't suppose there's a light you could flicker that might draw some attention? Maybe an outside light, something a passing car or truck could see." Before he could answer, she said, "No; I didn't think so."

Holte blinked, and whipped quickly around the room. "Is this the Mayes Brothers old warehouse?"

"I told you — I'm not sure. Possibly." She shivered in the increasing chill. "It would be like Stacy to tell me we were one place when we're at another; he probably thinks of this as some kind of joke," she added with angry sarcasm. "I've tried not to think about it."

"Are there labels on the crates?"

"How should I know? I didn't see any when there was a little light in the room, but they could be turned away from me." Even as she said it, she knew what he was hoping for. "Might there be an address? Or a name?"

"I can look. The dark doesn't bother me as much as it does you." Holte swung around the room. "What's in the crates?"

"How should I know? From their size, I'd guess it's furniture, or statuary. Any luck in finding labels?" She worked the last two knots, and made her numb fingers move. As soon as the rope was through the last knot, she cast it away from her as if it were tainted, then rubbed her hands together as much to rid them of any hint of rope as to restore full feeling to her fingers.

"International Business Associates?" Holte said. "Isn't that your cousin's company?"

"It is," said Poppy, her curiosity increasing. "Where did you find that?"

"On the largest crate, stenciled on the side. Any shipping information has been removed. No addresses." He circled around the other crates but found no additional information except a large stenciled warning in red: FRAGILE. "Statuary you said?"

"It could be," she said, attempting to get to her feet, but not able to stop the trembling in her legs; she lowered herself back into the chair.

"Could it be the kind of thing your cousin helped to import?" Holte asked, and knew he had gone too far.

"How would I know?" she repeated. Hearing how bitter she sounded, she relented and continued in a more propitiatory tone. "He told me he wanted to have someone with him when he removed the contents from these crates. He said he wanted to report the antiques, or antiquities, to the Justice Department. That may or may not be true, but at the time I wanted to believe him."

"That's not surprising," said Holte. He took another swoop around the room, hoping to discover something he could use to help Poppy get out of the room without waiting for help to arrive.

"I could pull this chair over to the window; the seat's kind of low, so it's not as much as I'd like, but it could get me up a way. If I break the glass, I might be able to get out. I wish we had a crowbar. Perhaps it could work the door loose."

"It wouldn't be enough to open the door," said Holte. "You'd have to break the steel beam that the lock is holding in place."

"I wasn't thinking of that side of the door," said Poppy, her dismay returning. "I was thinking we . . . I could open one of the larger crates and use whatever's inside to boost me up high enough to wriggle out of the window. The crowbar could open the crate, and when I got up to the window, it could break the glass."

"So it could." Holte was amazed at her pluck. "All right. I'll see if there is anything you can reach that will serve as a crowbar." He ricocheted around the room, trying to find a tool that would open one of the crates, but found nothing; disheartened, he returned to her side. "I'm sorry, Poppy; I can't find anything."

Poppy was still trying to restore feeling to her legs and feet, and as part of her efforts, she gave the chair as much of an examination as she could in the darkness; her fingers ran over carving on the front of the arms; she felt a few familiar shapes, and for the first time, she was interested in the chair as something more than an object of captivity. "I think this is Egyptian."

"What kind of Egyptian?" Holte asked as he circled the clerestory window.

"Pharaonic," said Poppy. "Or a very good forgery." This last observation troubled her, and she kept her other thoughts to herself.

Holte went back to measuring the height of the window. "The lower sill is almost nine feet off the floor. Even with the chair pulled against the wall, you would still have to reach up about seven-and-a-half feet. You're what? five-foot four?"

"About; a smidge taller," said Poppy.

"So five-foot four and a half, plus eighteen inches or so, for the height of the chair, and then add say fifteen inches for your maximum reach. That's eight feet one inch, meaning you have eight inches for grip, which gives you the length of your hand, more or less, that would require great stress on your hands and arms. With the shape your wrists are in, are you able to pull yourself up to the window?"

"I may have to," said Poppy.

"Not while your wrists are still bleeding," Holte warned her.

Abruptly she rounded on him. "Do you mean I'm stuck here? That there's nothing I can do but die?"

Holte held up his insubstantial hands. "No, I don't mean that. But you're exhausted, and if you fall back, trying to get out the window, you'll be in worse shape than you are now. It isn't a good risk." He moved up near to her. "I have a couple of ideas. Let me try them before you take such a chance."

For the first time since he found her, Poppy visibly sagged. "You mean you're leaving."

"I mean I'm going to try to find someone to unlock the door, and you've given me an idea." Holte moved up to the window again. "Do you happen to know if Inspector Loring was in the Great War?"

She frowned with thought. "I assume he was. I think he mentioned it at some point."

Holte circled the ceiling. "I'll do what I can," he promised. "One way or another, I'll be back in an hour." Without waiting for Poppy to try to stop him, Holte passed through the window, circled the warehouse, and finally found a weathered sign that identified the building as belonging to Mayes Brothers. Satisfied, he flitted off toward the Addison Newspaper Corporation building and the Clarion offices.

THIRTY-SIX

CORNELIUS LOWENTHAL WAS NOT AT HIS DESK, AND MISS STOTTER WAS NO longer at her station; Holte swung through the city room of the Clarion, and found himself unable to gain the attention of any of the reporters at their desks. He made the large light fixture at the center of the city-room ceiling blink, but no one noticed. He considered going to Lowenthal's home, but changed his mind; he was not at all sure he could command the editor's concentration sufficiently to justify the time he would have to expend in doing what he had in mind. Vexed and worried, he went on to the local police station, hoping that Inspector Loring was still at his desk. But the night shift had arrived, and Loring had gone home, leaving Holte at a stand-still. He considered returning to the Dritchner house, but he had no means of questioning anyone there, no matter what he might do to alert them to the situation. It was coming on to eight, and he was aware that the night would be chilly — he wanted to get Poppy out of that basement before she had to fight the cold as well as hunger and thirst. Holte was about to depart for the warehouse when he heard the telephone ring on the duty sergeant's desk in the next room. Intrigued, Holte went in to listen to what was being said, in the off chance that the call had something to do with Stacy, or better yet, Poppy; she had been missing long enough for someone to have noticed, and might have decided to call the police; he could not imagine Josephine doing that, but Missus Flowers might. He floated over the duty sergeant's desk, willing the 'phone call to be helpful to Poppy.

"Fordham here," said the duty sergeant, and listened to what the operator had to say. "Yeah, I'll talk to her. Put her through."

Holte drifted a little nearer to the duty sergeant, paying close attention to what was said, trying to hear everything.

"No, there's been no report of a missing woman tonight. Who are you?" Fordham took out a pencil and a notebook. "How do you spell Fairchild?" He wrote what the caller had said. "Why are you calling?"

Holte could not believe how lucky he was. Taking care not to make too much noise in the process, Holte slipped into the 'phone line and was able to hear both sides of the conversation, although he also caused some static on the line, despite his precautions.

"My good friend has dropped out of sight. Miss Poppea Thornton, who works at the Clarion was expected to attend my party tonight — she gave me her word that she'd be here, but she's not. It's not like her to just vanish; she's not the flight sort. She always keeps her word."

Fordham rolled his eyes, but asked, "Maybe she's late leaving home. Have you tried calling there?" He winced as the line crackled.

"Yes, I have, and no, she's not there," said Mildred indignantly. "I called her house, and the paper where she works, and she isn't in either place. No one has seen her. So I thought you — the police — might know where to find her. That's your duty, isn't it?"

"Sorry, lady. We don't keep tabs on everyone all the time." The desk sergeant twirled his free hand around his ear. "She might be caught up in traffic." He was ready to hang up. "If she isn't around by this time tomorrow, call back and I'll put you on the assignment list, or do it earlier, if you find out anything more substantial than that your friend is late for dinner." Now short of patience, it was an effort for him to keep from cutting the call short. "Thank you for calling us, Missus Fairchild. Sorry your friend hasn't shown up yet."

"There's something wrong, I tell you." Mildred began to cry. "She ought to be here, or she would have notified me. Her aunt's butler told me that she had gotten off work early today in order to attend my dinner, but she didn't go home to change. She hasn't spoken to anyone. Her cousin said that when he went to pick her up at the paper, she never arrived. That isn't like her. Isn't there something you can do?"

Fordham hesitated. "Call back in the morning, if she hasn't turned up. You'd do better talking to the day watch in any case. They handle missing person reports. It sounds to me like your friend just took a day off." He prepared to return the receiver to its cradle.

"She's investigating a case; she's a reporter, I told you. She's been covering a story. The one about the Moncrief murder," Mildred almost screamed.

This caught Fordham's notice. "The Moncrief murder?"

"Yes, you cretin! If you doubt me, call the inspector on the case. He'll tell you that she's helped him. Maybe he can convince you that she's in danger." Before Fordham could respond, Mildred slammed down her receiver.

Desk Sergeant Fordham hung up, and was tempted to ignore the call entirely, but the habits of twenty years would not allow it. He knew, as every policeman in the precinct knew, that Inspector Loring was in charge of the case, and would likely want to know about the reporter. Fordham opened his personnel directory and looked up Inspector Loring's home 'phone number, wholly unaware that Chesterton Holte was watching over his shoulder. While Fordham rang the operator, Holte memorized Loring's address, and hastened off toward William Street, moving as swiftly as he could among the vast network of electrical wires that festooned much of the city. He reached the fifty-year-old building where Loring had the second floor flat, and entered the building through the side wall, where he sensed there was a living person inside; he ended up in what had once been a child's bedroom but had been partially transformed into a den, though the wall paper still was filled with cavorting bunnies and playing kittens. There was a wall of bookshelves filled with all manner of references ranging from medical texts, to catalogues of flowers, to atlases of all kinds, to a massive catalogue of fabrics, to descriptions of all manner of weapons. There was also an old, leather chair by the bookcase; a large, roll-top desk on the opposite wall was illuminated by a library lamp; otherwise the room was dark. Inspector Loring was seated at his desk, an open file in his hands, a worried scowl on his face. The receiver of the 'phone on his desk was held to his ear, Loring listening intently.

"Well, thank you, Mister Grimes. I'm sorry to have taken up so much of your time; I trust you understand my situation, sir," said Loring, and replaced the receiver.

Holte sidled nearer, and reached for the library lamp, making it flicker in an orderly fashion. Pleased at the result, he touched it again, establishing a rhythm, trusting that he would gain Loring's attention: . . . . - - . . . . Holte was hopeful as the light blinked clearly. He did it again, taking care to keep the code clear: . . . - - . . . . - - . . . . - - - . . .

"What the hell?" Loring demanded, looking up from the file, and then setting it aside as Holte gripped out his message.

. . . - - - . . . . - - - . . .

Loring had been about to turn the light off when the pattern became clear to him, and with uncharacteristic bravado, he exclaimed, "Okay. I'll take this for an S O S. You've got an emergency, and for some reason you can't 'phone me directly, or go to the precinct house. Either that, or it's a prank. You better tell me which, and do it right now." He waited, and Holte repeated the S O S three more times, wanting to make it clear that this was a cry for help. "Where are you? Up an electrical pole? Well? If this isn't some kind of freak accident, tell me what this is about." Now that Loring had acknowledged the apparent signal, he was bothered that such a thing could be happening. Still, he felt he had to pay attention. He picked up a pencil and a pad of paper.

Relieved, Holte settled down to tell him. . - - . . - - - . - - . . . . - - . - . - - . - . . - - - - . - . - . - . - . . . . - . - - . - - - . - - . . - - - . . . . . . - - - . - . - . . - - - . . . . .

. . . . .

- - - . . - . . . . . - . . - . . . . - - . - . - At the end, he hoped that he had got it right; it had been seven years since he had had to communicate in Morse code, and he was afraid that he was rusty with his dots and dashes. He had watched Loring taking down the letters of his message with care, and saw that all the letters were correct.

"Poppy," Loring said as he worked out the first word. "Poppy Thornton?" he asked nervously; he had tried to reach her earlier that afternoon and had been unable to. While this was not unusual, it rankled at him most of the rest of the day, so this extraordinary communication — if that was what it was — only fed his foreboding.

- . - - . . . .

"Yes!" Loring sat up and studied what he had put on the page. "Poppy locked in Mayes Bros old warehouse basement." He looked up at the open air. "Is that it? Poppy is locked in a warehouse basement?" As he asked, he told himself that he must be going nuts.

- . -- . . . . Holte squeezed out on the lamp. - - - . - . . . . - . - . - . . . . . .

Loring cut him short. " — warehouse. Okay. I got that. Do you know why she's there?" As he asked, he was trying to figure out where his informant was hiding.

- . - - - - . - . . . . - . - . . . . . - . - . - - . - - - - . . . - - - - . . . . . . - - . - .
. - . - . - -

"Hurry. Okay. I get it," Loring interrupted. "Mayes Brothers old warehouse." He stood up. "How do you know?" He was incredulous that he should continue to question the blank air, but he was too caught up in what was happening to abandon it now.

. . . . - . - . . . - - . . . . - - . . . . Holte was becoming tired, but he wished that he could do more and faster. He continued to squeeze the lamp base . . . . - . - . - - - . - . - . .

"Trapped, and cold," Loring said aloud, and in the next instant he made a decision. "I'll call the precinct. They should be able to find where that warehouse is. Though the Devil alone knows how I'm going to explain this if it doesn't work out." His whole demeanor was abashed, but it was apparent that he was worried about Poppy, and that his worry was escalating. For a moment he stood still, as if trying to make up his mind if any of this was real, or just an illusion borne out of desperation. "This is nuts," he announced. He looked around the room, saying as he did, "I don't know who or what you are, or if you're here, but if we find her, I'll owe you one." He saluted the room, and reached for the 'phone, and gave the operator the number of the precinct secretary's desk. "Hurry, please." As the 'phone began to ring, he tapped his fingers on his desk, not wanting to wait one minute longer than he had to, in case he should lose his nerve. Finally, when the secretary answered, he had to keep from upbraiding her for taking so long. "Shirley," he said. "It's Inspector Loring."

"I recognize your voice; Fordham was trying to reach you a little while ago," said the elderly woman who had managed the night shift information desk for almost as long as Loring had been alive, and was reputed to know the voices of all the inspectors in the Philadelphia Police Department.

"What do you need, Inspector?"

"I need the address of the Mayes Brothers warehouse, the old one, not the new one. Maybe a way to get there, too." He stopped himself from urging her, knowing it would not work. "It's probably in the older part of the warehouse district, but beyond that, I don't know for sure." He would have liked to have had something more solid to give her than what he had been provided, but he was becoming convinced that something had to be done. He could always say that he had a tip from a snitch, and was told that time was of the essence if any of his superiors demanded an explanation for his actions. "Why was Fordham calling me: do you know?"

"No idea," she said. "I'll have a look for that address. About what year would it have been built, do you know?" Shirley would not be rushed, and refused to be bullied.

"No, I don't know. About eighty, ninety years ago would be a good place to start, but it could be older," he said, doing his best not to yell.

"Is this for an investigation?" Shirley asked.

"Yes," said Loring at once. "It's part of the Moncrief homicide." Holding the 'phone in his hands, he started to pace his unorthodox study. "It's urgent, Shirley."

"It always is," she rejoined. "I have your number. May I call you back in ten minutes?"

"Yes; sooner if you can," said Loring, and heard Shirley hang up.

Hovering in the darkest corner of the room, Holte was hoping that Poppy would not have to spend the whole night in the locked room; he could see that Loring was still taking Holte's message seriously enough to pursue his information. He was sorry now that he had not taken time to learn the address of the warehouse before coming to look for help; Loring would not have had to ask someone to find it for him, and in waiting for that information, lose precious time. Watching Loring twitch as he chafed in anticipation of Shirley's return call, Holte was of two minds: should he remain here to help Loring, or should he go back to Poppy? His impulse was to return to the warehouse and offer what comfort he could to Poppy, but he also knew that Loring might falter or be side-tracked; right now, Loring was her best hope for release, and doing all he could to assist Loring seemed more urgent than trying to buck up Poppy's state of mind, yet once Loring was committed to action, Holte would not be able to communicate with him; Loring's willingness to pay attention to Holte's Morse code kept him observing the inspector for now, since the library lamp was readily accessible, and that could be crucial in Poppy being freed. Yet, if there might be more he could do, he could not think of it. At present, he wanted to be certain that Loring could find the warehouse, and so he remained in the corner of the room, wrapped in darkness, and watching Loring fret at the delay in obtaining the address.

Loring picked up his pipe and filled it with tobacco from a pouch. He tamped this down, took a match from a small box on his desk, and lit the pipe, drawing the rum-flavored smoke into his mouth as a distraction from his galling impatience. He moved around the room aimlessly. At his bookcase he stopped to take out a book on fingerprints, which he opened and did his best to read. He had read the same paragraph three times when the 'phone shrilled; he shoved the book back into its slot, then went to answer.

"Loring here," he said, wanting the voice on the line to be Shirley.

For once, his wish was answered, and he heard Shirley say, "I have an address. The building was registered in 1798. If you have a pencil to hand, write this down: Number nineteen, King Charles Lane. On the western edge of the old warehouse district."

"Anything more?" Loring asked.

"According to the file, Mayes Brothers rents out space to a group of importers. The building is largely unimproved, but five years ago, they installed a few electric lights and some steel doors."

Loring was relieved to hear this. "Any kind of guard or watchman?" Perhaps, he thought, there was someone on the premises he could call.

"There's nothing in the file. Sorry, Inspector." Shirley clicked her tongue. "There was a federal investigation of one of the renters back in 1916, but nothing came of it."

"Thank you, Shirley. You're a treasure," he said, and heard the 'phone click as she put down her receiver.

Holte listened to this with tremendous relief. He waited just long enough to see Loring put out his pipe and leave his study for the hallway, and the front door, and then he slipped away, bound for the old Mayes Brothers warehouse, trusting that Poppy would not be more distraught than she had been when he had found her. He went more slowly than he would have liked, for the energy he had expended in sending the coded messages had left him enervated. Coasting along the rooftops, Holte wondered if he had done enough, and told himself that Inspector Loring would be the one who would determine that.

THIRTY-SEVEN

BETWEEN THE DARKNESS AND THE INCREASING COLD, POPPY WAS MISERABLE. IN spite of her best efforts, she was becoming mildly disoriented, and she feared it was getting worse. Now that she was freed from the chair, she had spent most of the time since Holte had left stumbling about in the room, touching all the crates and the chair where Stacy had tied her, doing her best to keep her bearings in the space. A while ago — she had lost track of time — she had gathered up all the packing material that had been strewn on the floor when Stacy, or whomever was working with him, removed the Egyptian chair in order to tie her up; she had been increasingly worried that she might trip on it as she made her regular turn around the space. Three circumnegotiations ago, she had stopped long enough to remove her shoes, for although the floor was cold, Poppy knew she was not as apt to fall if she were barefoot. "Don't cry, and don't despair," she told herself forcefully. "Don't give Stacy that satisfaction. Holte will be back." She resumed her movement about the room, touching the crates and the walls, counting her steps as she went.

The bleating of a tug-boat's horn demanded her attention, and she took a little time to try to determine how near the wharves she was, but gave it up after a while, unable to sort out the original sound from the echoes, so she resumed her moving survey of her prison; if she was to get out before morning, that escape would be determined by her ability to locate herself in the room, no matter how confused she became.

Some time later — she reckoned it to be twenty minutes to half an hour — as she sat down to rub her feet to restore feeling to them, she sensed a change in the room, and she rose from the chair, hoping she wasn't imagining things. "Holte?" she asked tentatively, afraid there was a less welcome presence in the room. "If it's you, speak up; I'm afraid of rats." She was ashamed of herself for this admission.

"I'm here," he said from somewhere near the window that now was almost as dark as the room.

She stood still, waiting for him to do something, all the while telling herself that she better not be hallucinating. When nothing happened, she sat back down, suppressing the urge to scream. "If you're here," she said, "let me know where you are."

The bellow of a truck's engine invaded the room, but died away almost at once. Neither Poppy nor Holte gave more than cursory notice of it.

"I'm here," he said from another part of the room. "I wanted to have a look at the door again."

"You mean you can see? Ye gods." She clutched the arms of the chair as if she were suddenly dizzy.

"Noncorporeality has a few advantages," he said, going to her side.

"Such as being able to get out of this room." The bitterness in her tone was unlike her, and Holte could tell that her captivity was weighing on her.

"That is one," he said, not wanting to wrangle with her. "But I'd trade it for being able to speak and be heard by other people than you alone." For several seconds he remained silent. "I'm sorry I took so long."

"What time is it?" she demanded; she finally saw a wispy outline like a patch of thin fog about five feet away from her, and took tremendous solace in his presence.

"About nine-thirty." It was more of a guess than he wanted to admit, but it was near enough to be accurate that he was willing to stick to it. "It's later than I said I'd be back, for which I ask your pardon. But it was hard to get anyone's attention. I wanted to be sure that help was on its way before I returned."

"How did you manage to do it? Or did you manage at all?" She was cold enough to know that if she remained in it all night, it could harm her; the prospect was disheartening. She did her best to direct her thoughts to a more positive point-of-view. "You didn't happen to bring a blanket with you, did you?"

"I wish I could have," he said sincerely.

She sighed and sagged in the chair. "Then I suppose I'll have to make a nest in the packing material and hope for the best," she said, drawing her knees up and hugging them to her chest, doing what she could to stay warm. "And I need a bathroom."

"I trust you won't have to wait much longer." Holte swooped around the room, wanting to find a place in it that would offer a bit more warmth until the police arrived; he could tell that Poppy needed warmth as much as she yearned for light.

Poppy gazed into the darkness, striving to resign herself to her confinement. "You can stop letting me down easily. I need to be able to make a clear assessment of what I'm up against. Go ahead and tell me that you didn't succeed in your mission. I won't mind." She did not let him speak yet. "I thought it was a long shot, in any case. I'm glad you did your best, but I didn't really expect — "

He cut into her lamentation. "But I did succeed, in a way. Your Inspector Loring paid attention when I made his library lamp blink in Morse code."

This revelation held her attention. "What are you saying?" she asked softly, afraid she had misheard him.

"You know I make electric lights flicker," he said, coming nearer to her. "That, and I can listen in to an engaged 'phone line."

"Yes. A sputtering light usually means you're about; either that, or Maestro hissing and trying to grab at nothing." She tried to discern his form, but in the darkness, the sketch-like outline she could usually see was indistinguishable from the blankness in the room, and the foggy smear was no longer easily seen. "I wish we had a light in here, and not just for you to work with; you might be able to speed up Loring's finding this place. But that probably wouldn't be enough. Maestro's temper tantrums aren't sufficient to make most people pay attention to your presence."

"Well, I told you that you gave me an idea of something I could do," he said, observing her demeanor to determine how she was receiving this news; he decided to tread carefully. "I told you I was going to try it out, didn't I?"

"You did, but I thought you were just attempting to cheer me up, since you were going to leave me alone here." There was no emotion in what she said, so she was astonished to feel tears welling in her eyes.

"Hang on, Poppy. This is almost over," he said as he watched her use the cuff of her sleeve to wipe at her face. "You did give me an idea."

"And what was that? Flickering lights aren't much of a device for communication." She made herself stop weeping, and wished she had a handkerchief so she could blow her nose. "What did you do?"

"I sent a message in Morse code: I made a lamp blink in dots and dashes." He emitted a sound that could be understood as a single laugh. "Quite exhausting — I wouldn't like to have to do it again — but in this case, it was worth it." He let this sink in, smiling a little as he saw her sit up in her Egyptian chair.

There was the screech of the brakes of an auto going by a street or two away, but it did not wholly stop, instead accelerated, and in less than a minute it could no longer be heard.

"That was very clever of you, using Morse code," she said, having trouble believing him.

"Spies learn to improvise," he pointed out, making this sound entirely ordinary. "In a situation like this, improvisation is necessary."

She had managed to make herself stop trembling. "And who had the good sense to comprehend what you were up to? Loring?"

Holte spoke quietly. "As I mentioned, I went to Inspector Loring's flat and made his study lamp blink in such a way that it sent him a message about where you are. When I left him, he was preparing to come here."

Poppy held her breath, in case she had misunderstood what he had said, and summoned up the courage to ask, "Loring is coming here?"

"He was planning to do so when I left his flat." He paused, making an effort to help her wait for Loring's arrival. "I don't know if he's coming on his own, or is going to bring more police with him."

"Ye gods!" She looked around as if this news might immediately transform this storage room in some way. "You're sure?"

"When I left his flat, he was on his way to his auto." He saw her push herself to her feet. "He has an address which is this one, or somewhere nearby."

"Is he going to search the whole building?" she asked, her shivering returning. "That could take . . . hours."

"I told him that you are in the basement. That should make it sooner than later for him to arrive, assuming he begins in this warehouse." He came to her side. "There's little I can do but keep you company, but I'm glad to do that."

"And I'm glad you're here to do it," she said, and sat down again, huddling in the chair. "Is there any news about Stacy?" She did her best to sound only mildly interested, but Holte could tell that she was deeply disquieted about his whereabouts.

"None that I know of," he replied carefully. "Your friend Mildred told the police sergeant when she spoke to Stacy earlier this evening, he said that you had not met him at three."

"What?" she exclaimed, and at once added, "Mildred called the police? What on earth made her do that?"

A loud clanging at least two blocks away, accompanied by the yelp of a siren, announced that help was on its way to a fire. This time both of them listened, and were relieved when the sound faded as the fire truck and the fire marshal's car rushing behind it, on their way to a different destination.

"She was upset because you did not come to her party as you said you would, and no one could tell her why you weren't there," said Holte, pointedly ignoring the sound from the nearby streets. "I was ridiculously fortunate to be in the precinct house when she called; I eavesdropped on her 'phone call — another habit of spies. I think she wanted to talk to Inspector Loring, but she got the desk sergeant."

"How . . . intrepid of Mildred," said Poppy, holding back the laughter that threatened to overcome her. "I may have underappreciated her."

"She was most indignant, and also very anxious on your behalf." Holte moved nearer to her. "That kind of good luck happens rarely, and I know it was a break that was quite remarkable. But if Red Grange can have a miracle, so can I."

Poppy mulled this over, uncertain whether or not she believed him. "A true coincidence, in fact?"

"I know it sounds unlikely, but things do sometimes happen at the same time," he reminded her, seeing her breath as a white cloud in front of her mouth.

"I'll give you that," she said, as much to keep her courage up as to agree with him, but she could not keep from sighing. "No crowbar, the window is too high to climb out. It seems Stacy thought of everything."

"I can look around for other tools," Holte suggested.

"You haven't found one yet, and neither have I. For a while, I thought about breaking up this chair and using the legs to try to get into the other crates, but I kept thinking that if the chair is the real thing, and not a forgery, then I'd be ruining a priceless archeological treasure, and I couldn't bear to do that." She cleared her throat. "At least, I couldn't do it, not yet."

He took the time to smile enough that she could see it. "There is a point where such perspectives can be dangerous, and you're in one of them."

"I trust I don't have to find out, at least not now." She got up and began another circle of the room, touching the crates and the walls.

"Loring is coming, Poppy. He might take a little while to get here, but he will come," Holte said staunchly. "He likes you. He was willing to suspend his skepticism to take down my Morse code about you. He won't leave you in a place like this. He's not that kind of man."

"So you think. I'm gambling that you're right." Her bare feet were once again going numb; she stumbled, and steadied herself against the second-largest crate.

"If he doesn't arrive in the next hour, do you want me to go and look for him?" Holte offered.

"If he doesn't arrive in the next hour, I'll want you to find a way to open one of the larger crates. Crowbar or not, I need to find a way out. I don't care if it means cutting up my hands doing it, I have to get out of here." She flung up a hand for emphasis. "If I don't, how am I going to attend Madison Moncrief's funeral tomorrow? Don't look at me like that," she added. "I'm not crazy yet. After what I've been through, I don't want the story handed over to anyone else." There was an edge of dread in her voice, but her purpose was unshaken.

"I'll do it," said Holte, although he had no concept as to how this was to be done; Poppy had not mentioned changing her mind about demolishing the chair.

"Thank goodness for that," she said, clinging to the necessity of having something on her mind beyond her desperation. "Can you slip into the second-largest crate and find out what's inside?"

"Certainly," he said, and proceeded to do so. The large amount of packing material made for confusion, but taking heed of the various textures and densities around him, he was able to make out a seventeenth century highboy; it was about four-and-a-half feet tall, with three ranks of drawers above two-doored shelves just above the squat, bowed legs. He had to admit that if Poppy could get it out of the crate and over to the window, she had a good chance of getting out of the locked room through the window. He slid out of the crate and told Poppy what he had found. "I can search about for a loose slat on the crate, if you like. It might make a difference."

"If there is one, you're right: it could make a difference." She ducked her head. "I can't just sit here waiting to be rescued, Holte. I have to do something, in case it doesn't happen. And I don't want to be unprepared if my cousin comes back." Looking up toward the filmy smudge of a misty shape near the side of her chair. "I hope you understand."

"Oh, I do," he said, an ironic tinge to his words. "Toward the end of the Great War, I was able to excuse almost anything on that basis." He saw the shock in her eyes. "Not that I hold this against you; the only life you're risking is your own — I risked others' lives." He drifted toward the window, becoming slightly more visible than he was out of the minimal light it provided. "Let me know when you want me to check the slats, and I'll do it."

Poppy frowned, but gathered her thoughts. "The sooner the better," she said, unhappily aware of her increasing fright. "Sorry, but it's this or strong hysterics."

"I know the feeling," said Holte by way of consolation. "Give me a minute or two; it shouldn't take me too long to find that kind of slat, if there is one." With that, he started circling the chosen crate, looking for any sign of looseness or disruption that Poppy might be able to use to break into it. He was a bit more than halfway up the crate when he heard the cough of an engine shutting off; it was close at hand, and Poppy had taken an involuntary breath.

"There's a car in the alley," she said aloud, her voice shaking. "It's Loring, or Stacy has come back to see if I'm still alive."

THIRTY-EIGHT

HOLTE HOVERED IN THE AIR, CONCENTRATING ON WHAT HE HEARD; HE WAS hoping for the sound of one of the warehouse doors opening. "It's just a single auto," he told Poppy. "It could be either man, or someone else entirely."

"That's not likely," said Poppy. Now that her release was at hand, the headache that had been gathering on her forehead was increasing in vividness. She touched her forehead and found a lump the size of a half-dollar.

"No, it's not," he agreed, drifting toward the steel door.

"I don't think it's Stacy," Poppy said dubiously, shaking her head. "Stacy was in a Duesenberg this afternoon. That isn't a Duesy's motor, and so far as I know, that's the only auto he has access to just now. I think it's not in the side alley."

"Is there a door on the front of the warehouse?" he asked, while he realized that the sound of a door being opened might not be loud enough to carry to this basement room, he thought he could go out into the warehouse to see who had arrived.

"I don't know," said Poppy. "We came in by a side entrance, near the loading dock. I think Stacy did that deliberately."

"Shall I go out and look?" Holte offered, hoping to lessen her fright. "If it is Stacy, we can work out some way to surprise him if he enters this room."

Poppy nodded again, more vigorously than before, courage warring with fear within her. "Yes, if you would, please," she whispered.

"Certainly." He floated down from where he had been lingering, and turned himself upright. "I'll be back shortly."

"I'm counting on it," she said, and watched his brumous shape disappear into the heavy steel of the door. As soon as he was gone, she retreated to the chair, sat down in it, and pulled her knees up to her chest in an effort to ward off the cold. She forced herself not to think about why Stacy might be back, as well as not to hope too intently that Loring was actually here; if he had not arrived, her disappointment would be overpowering, and that would be hazardous for her. Pressing her lips together she turned her attention to reviewing the details of her reporting on the Moncrief case, looking for any errors she might have made, or significant detail she could have overlooked, an occupation that served to divert her attention.

Holte came back through the door. "It's Loring. He's got someone from Mayes Brothers with him. I gather that Loring took the time to pick him up on the way here, so he wouldn't waste time once he reached this place, and that accounts for his delay. Your inspector thinks ahead. That's a good thing in a policeman." He made a quick circuit of the room, explaining as he did, "They're just going to the stairs that lead into the basement. Their intention is to open each storage room until they find you." He went to her side. "It's almost over, Poppy."

"Ye gods, I hope so," she said fervently; she stared at the dim outline of his head. "You aren't saying this just to shore me up?"

"No, Poppy, I'm not." He would have laid his hand on her shoulder, but he knew it would only chill her further, and he did not want to do that. "They'll get here in a little while. You're going to get out before long."

She reached out her hand to him. "Holte, I owe you a lot; no matter how this turns out, I owe you a lot." The chair was hard, but she took solace from its sturdy presence.

"No, you don't," he said, suddenly very serious. "I owe you. And I still do."

"What does that mean?" she asked him, her manner uneasy.

"It means that I still haven't vacated my debt to your father; you'll be stuck with me for a while longer." He would have said more, but there was a grating sound on the other side of the steel door; the steel brace was being tested.

"How long would that be?" Poppy asked.

"I have no idea." Holte swung around, sensing Loring outside the storeroom. "You'd better take up your position," he warned Poppy.

Poppy hesitated, then got to her feet once more, squaring her shoulders. "I want to go to the door," she said, a bit giddy with anticipation. "I want to meet them standing up, not huddled in a chair."

"No cowering, right?" Holte asked. "Your father understood you: you're as steadfast as a New England lighthouse."

Poppy's voice shook. "Did he say that?"

"In the dimension of ghosts, yes, he did."

As much as Poppy wanted to know more about this encounter, she set her questions aside, and threw her dwindling energy into preparing for her release. "You said there is a padlock on the steel brace?" She put her shoes back on, and was shocked to feel cuts and bruises on her soles. As a precaution, she tucked the bloody cuffs of her sleeves so that her wrists would not seem as damaged as they were.

"Yes. It's fairly new, so it should ope — " The sharp click of the wards' release seemed like a thunderclap; Holte moved toward the door, positioning himself to see the persons outside before they entered the room. There was a scrape of metal on metal as the bolt was drawn back, as loud as a bugle-call.

Poppy touched her hair, wishing she had a comb to properly restore order to it. But her silk stockings were ruined, and she was fairly certain that there was a bump forming on her brow; Stacy must have banged her head when he brought her into this storeroom, or possibly he struck her deliberately, to keep her groggy until he was gone.

" — and bring up the flashlight," Holte and Poppy heard Loring say as the hinges of the door whined.

"Just a couple of crates in here," said the man accompanying him, preparing to depart.

"We haven't checked it out yet," said Loring with exaggerated patience. "I'm going to have a look around," and with that, he swung his flashlight's beam around, and caught Poppy's exhausted face in it. "Be damned!" he exclaimed, and took four steps toward her. "Poppy!"

"Hello, Inspector Loring," she said, her voice shaking. To her chagrin, she felt her knees tremble; she reached out to steady herself against the second-largest crate. "You can't imagine how good it is to see you," she was able to tell him before she burst into tears. "Ye gods!" she snuffled through her weeping. "Appalling."

Loring went to put his arm around her to steady her. "In your position, I'd probably do the same thing," he said as he played the light over her, taking stock of what he saw. "What in the name of Black Jack Pershing happened?"

Poppy gulped back her tears. "My cousin — Stacy? You know him — picked me up at the Clarion at three." She made herself organize as much of the afternoon as she could remember, and when she was satisfied, she started to report. "He said he had to show me something, that what he would show me would prove his innocence, and would give him a witness to corroborate the report he would make to the Justice Department. I was hoping that he would have some way to show that the suspicions against him were unfounded, and I thought it would help me to flesh out my stories for Lowenthal." She took hold of his arm. "Does he know I'm missing?"

"He must by now," said Loring. "I made some 'phone calls from the police-box before I picked up Mister Wimmering here. I'm grateful to him for interrupting his dinner to come with me." There was an edge in his remark that implied that Mister Wimmering needed some persuasion before he abandoned his meal.

"Good of you to say so," Wimmering grumbled.

Loring was not finished. "I need to take Miss Thornton to the hospital. She's injured. You will have to lock this storeroom as we leave; other officers will return first thing in the morning in order to catalogue the contents of these crates. Have one of your men keep watch here all night: if we're right, and these crates contain contraband items, we'll have to catalogue them before your company can have access to this room again. We apologize for any inconvenience this may be to Mayes Brothers, but we have to make sure that if there are criminal activities going on here, we can bring a case against the perpetrators."

Poppy heard this out with a fair amount of curiosity. "Right," she said as she daubed at her eyes with the end of his tie. "So I guess Stacy's in trouble."

She was not surprised that she was relieved to hear this.

"Stacy is missing," said Loring, "or at least we haven't been able to locate him. He's not the only one," he added, helping her toward the door.

As she went, she heard Holte speak softly, "Go on; I'll see you when you return home," news that left her feeling unexpectedly forlorn. She knew what Loring wanted her to ask, so she said, "I know about Warren Derrington."

"Oh, not Derrington," Loring said, raising his voice as Wimmering pulled the protesting door closed behind them, lowered the brace, and secured the padlock to the large staple, "it's Louise Moncrief who's missing. Julian Eastley reported it an hour ago. He was distraught." Loring guided her to the stairs, and leant her his support up them.

"Louise? Gone? But what about the funeral tomorrow morning?" She had expected to file the usual kind of story about the event, but if Louise did not return for it . . . She listened to Loring fill her in.

"According to Eastley, Missus Moncrief packed up her trunks and bags and took the train to New York at around four this afternoon: your cousin drove her to the station. The Duesenberg was found in the parking lot around six, and both Missus Moncrief and Stacy Dritchner were gone."

"Gone?" Poppy echoed in astonishment. "You mean . . . eloped?"

"So it seems," he said. "Her housekeeper, Missus Haas, said that Missus Moncrief was planning to take a ship to Rio de Janeiro."

"Before her husband's funeral?" Poppy marveled.

"It looks like it." He stopped at the top of the stairs to have a closer look at her. "You've got awful bruises on your wrists, and some new scabs. What happened in that room?"

She had expected the question, but it still rattled her as she answered him. "I think Stacy carried me in, and tied me up in what may be an Egyptian antiquity — a gold-leafed chair. That's where I woke up. I spent a considerable amount of time working loose the knots that bound me. I did it with my teeth." She trembled again, and was reassured when he put his arm around her once more.

Loring started moving again; Poppy went with him perforce. "Do you have a regular doctor?"

Poppy blinked. "Yes. Gideon ter Horst." She did not look forward to the examination that would be coming, but it was clear that her injuries needed care, and the sooner that was done, the better. "I can afford a house call."

"Very likely," he said as he stood aside to permit Wimmering to open the front door for them. "But I'd still prefer that you go to the hospital. We'll need an official record of what was done to you."

"To add to your case against Stacy? that's in case you ever get your hands on him." She paused as Wimmering prepared to close the door. "Is there a toilet I could use before we leave?" Color mounted in her face as she asked.

"The other side of the office, just to the left of this door. It's pretty primitive."

"I don't mind," she said, and stepped away from Loring's supporting arm. She moved as quickly as she could without falling, and when she found what she was seeking, she was ridiculously grateful for it; leaving the room when she was done, she walked more confidently back to the front door, ready to undertake the next phase of her first crime story.

THIRTY-NINE

ON THE DRIVE BACK TO AUNT JO'S HOUSE, THE EXUBERANT EUPHORIA THAT had gripped Poppy when she was released from her intended tomb — as she was coming to think of it — gradually faded, transforming into anxious fatigue. Her answers to Loring's questions grew more terse, and she found her thoughts as hard to contain as a school of fish. Images and insights flickered and vanished. "There's something I ought to tell you," she said as he turned the corner toward her aunt's house.

"There are lots of things you ought to tell me, but after you're rested," he soothed her. "You've been through a lot today, and you're rattled."

She summoned up all her concentration. "No, I'm not. There's just so much to deal with."

"And you should sleep on it. After you see your doctor. Those are some nasty abrasions on your wrists and ankles, and they need to be taken care of. All we'll do tonight is get a bare-bones preliminary report." He could see the porch-light on over the Dritchner door. "Are you certain you wouldn't rather I take you to an emergency room?"

"I am. I don't want the news to get out." She caught her lower lip in her teeth. "I almost had it . . ."

"What?" Loring asked as he pulled into a parking place one house down from the Dritchner house.

Poppy shook her head slowly. "Something about Louise Moncrief, I think."

"If it's important, you'll remember it," Loring said, repeating the old saw that he no longer believed as he curbed his front wheels and turned off the motor. "Stay where you are; I'll come around and give you a hand."

Galling as it was, Poppy nodded her consent, afraid that she would be shaky on her feet. She looked toward the front steps as Loring opened the passenger door. "There are lights on. Someone's still up." She took hold of Loring's proffered arm and pulled herself up. "Thanks."

He would not let her release her grip on his arm. "There are half-a-dozen steps coming up. Keep hold until we're inside."

They made their way slowly to the front porch, and Poppy was looking for her key when the door opened and Missus Flowers gave a little shriek that was compounded of relief, alarm, and confusion. "Gracious, Miss," she exclaimed as she took stock of Poppy's condition. "What's happened to you?"

Before Poppy could speak, Loring said, "That's a long story. We need to get Miss Thornton's injuries cleaned up, her physician summoned, and I need to take a preliminary report from — "

From the top of the stairs there came a cry from Josephine. "Stacy? Oh, Stacy, is that you?"

Missus Flowers provided the answer. "No, Ma'am. It's Miss Poppy and the police."

Aunt Jo let out a wail of dismay, and came hurtling down the stairs, Duchess trailing behind her, moaning in sympathy.

Missus Flowers had turned on the entry-hall light, and was doing her utmost to conceal her dismay at Poppy's state; she summoned up her usual aplomb, and took charge. "I'll get some bandages, and a basin of hot water, and some antiseptic. You take her into the parlor, Inspector."

"Who is going to call her doctor?" Loring asked as he guided Poppy into the parlor.

"I wish I knew what it was I need to tell you," Poppy said as he settled her into the most comfortable side-chair in the room.

"Later," Loring began, and was interrupted by Josephine's arrival.

"Oh, dear Lord!" she exclaimed as she erupted into the parlor, her hairnet pulling off her head, her peignoir in disarray. "What has happened? Poppea, you're bleeding."

"Stacy," said Poppy, and tried to keep from leaving blood on the upholstery.

"No, dear, he hasn't returned yet, and I've been thinking the worst for the last two hours. He drives so recklessly." She moved the coffee-table aside and tried to approach Poppy without actually touching her. After a brief examination of Poppy's hands and arms, she got to her feet, tears welling in her eyes, and announced, "I will call Doctor ter Horst. He'll know how best to attend to this." And with that, she bustled out to the 'phone in the entry-hall and started giving orders to the night operator. "This is an emergency," she announced as she began to wail.

Missus Flowers came in from the kitchen, a basin of hot water in her arms, medicinally scented steam rising from it, a pair of clean white towels over her shoulder. "I suppose I should just try to clean her up?" she said to Loring.

"Yes, if you would," said Loring, drawing up a footstool for Missus Flowers' use. "I'll try to get down some notes while you work, and until the doctor arrives." He positioned himself on the settee and took out his notebook while Missus Flowers began her ministrations.

"I wish I could remember about . . . it had to do with something Stacy and Warren had planned to do with Louise. It had something to do with the party that the Moncrief's were planning . . . something . . ." Her voice trailed off as the recollection faded.

"You're worn out; we'll get to it later."

Poppy fought off the impulse to cry. "But I think it's important," she protested. "I need to remember what it was."

"Not tonight," he said, and reached out to take her hand.

"Stacy and Derrington and Louise," she said insistently.

"We'll get to that later," said Loring, his pencil poised. "For now, tell me about yesterday afternoon."

Twenty minutes later, Missus Flowers left them alone, bearing her implements back to the kitchen; she kept the lights burning so that Loring could continue taking notes.

"The doctor should be here shortly," Loring said to Poppy as he finally put away his pencil and notebook. "I still wish you'd agree to go to the hospital."

"There'd be a record of it, and that could lead to questions I'd like to postpone," said Poppy, and heard the doorbell ring. "Missus Flowers will get it; she's still in the kitchen." She adjusted herself on the settee, feeling as if she were swimming in molasses: every movement was an effort and felt as if it were taking five times as long as it usually would. "Doctor ter Horst knows how to keep his mouth shut."

"That's probably a good thing, under the circumstances," said Loring, studying her with concern.

Missus Flowers paused in the doorway to announce that Gideon ter Horst had arrived in answer to Aunt Jo's semi-hysterical summons on the 'phone some forty minutes earlier. Poppy sighed, overcome by fatigue; she leaned back against the cushions of the side-chair and looked over at Inspector Loring, who was drinking a second cup of coffee which had been hastily prepared by Missus Flowers. It was twenty-nine minutes after two, and the entry-hall clock was about to sound the half-hour. "I hope you'll explain all this to the doctor," she said. "I don't think I'm up to it."

"Small wonder," said Loring, and went to shake the portly, middle-aged physician's hand. "Good to meet you, Doctor ter Horst. As you see, Miss Thornton has had a . . . difficult experience."

Ter Horst raised his caterpillar-like brows. "Something to do with her work, I gather, from what Missus Dritchner told me."

"That, and her cousin," said Loring. "There are a number of injuries, mostly to her wrists and ankles, and a knot on her head. If you'll prepare a full description of what you find after you complete your examination, I'll stop by your office around noon today to pick it up."

"Is this part of a criminal investigation?" ter Horst asked, some of his smooth bed-side manner slipping. "By the sound of it, this is more than an accident. Missus Dritchner said nothing about that."

"No doubt," said Loring drily.

"I was tied to a chair in a warehouse basement," Poppy said, pushing herself upright. "Stacy either did it himself, or arranged for it to be done. I've gone over the whole event with Inspector Loring for nearly an hour."

"Are you certain? I don't mean to doubt you, but that wasn't my understanding when your aunt 'phoned me," ter Horst said, looking about uncomfortably. "Missus Dritchner explained it somewhat differently, but she was very upset. She's afraid something dreadful has happened to Eustace."

Loring set his cup of coffee aside. "That's possible, but not likely."

"What do you mean?"

"I mean that he was the instigator of Miss Thornton's ordeal," said Loring, a bit more tersely than he might have done at another hour.

The doctor did his best to mask his shock. "When did this happen?"

"It began yesterday afternoon," said Loring. "Miss Thornton managed to get out of her bonds on her own, but the door to the room she was in was barred and locked, and it took some hours to locate her." He said nothing about how he came to find her. "She's had a trying night."

Ter Horst nodded three times. "I see that she's been . . . cleaned up."

"Missus Flowers washed most of the blood away and dosed the cuts and scrapes with iodine, as you can see, but that's only good first aid. There may be more hurts that need your attention." Loring glanced at his watch. "I have a preliminary report from her, but I'm relying on you, Doctor, to provide me with —"

"Yes, yes, I understand," said ter Horst impatiently. "It's never a good idea to delay treating deep injuries. I'll let you know if I decide to admit her to the hospital, probably Smithson Memorial, if it's necessary. Whatever happens, for the next few days, she's going to be groggy and easily distressed; when someone goes through something so distressing, it is to be expected that he or she will experience difficulties. Don't force her to relive what happened until she is ready to do it." His demeanor became more officious. "I will keep you informed of how she is recovering, of course."

"I appreciate that," Loring said, in his most professional voice. "Aside from being a member of the press, Miss Thornton is now an important witness in an on-going investigation; the District Attorney will be relying on her testimony once we apprehend the perpetrator, whom I suspect is her cousin."

"Gracious!" ter Horst exclaimed, using the strongest language he dared. "Does Missus Dritchner know?"

"Not yet," said Loring. "I don't think she wants to hear from Poppy about Stacy's role in this. After she 'phoned you, she had Missus Flowers take over Poppy's care, and went up to bed. She refuses to believe that any of what has happened is due to Stacy. Miss Thornton has given me a preliminary report, and based on what she has said, I will be issuing a state-wide bulletin for Stacy's apprehension."

"I can hear you," said Poppy, not nearly as loudly as she would have liked.

"This sounds fairly dire," said ter Horst, rubbing his chin. "You may rely on my discretion, but I must tell you that I don't like the sound of this. It could become a scandal."

Poppy put her hand to her eyes. "Become?" she echoed incredulously. "It already is."

"And it may become worse," Loring said, half-decisively, half-apologetically. "There is an indication that Stacy has left the state, if not the country; it is my intention to find him and bring him here to face justice, or make certain others do it."

"What a dreadful business," said ter Horst.

"Not an easy thing to do, if he has really left the country," Poppy remarked, suddenly fighting off her exhaustion.

"I should be able to discover that tomorrow," said Loring, speaking to her as if ter Horst was not in the room. He took a step nearer to her. "It may take time, but we'll find him. I'll contact the Department of State if it comes to that. We might not be able to bring him here to answer for what he has done, but we'll make sure that we keep tabs on him."

Poppy managed a smile. "Thanks."

Hovering near the ceiling, Chesterton Holte decided he had done as much as he could for Poppy at present, and he had already decided that he should go into the dimension of ghosts to discover if Knott or Moncrief had anything to add to what they had already told him. He wondered if Moncrief had remembered enough to know what it was that Poppy had been talking about: something to do with Stacy, Derrington, and Louise. Gideon ter Horst knew what he was doing, and Inspector Loring would make sure that Poppy had proper care, so he slipped away into the dimension of ghosts, looking for Moncrief and Knott amid the shades and shadows that filled that place. He drifted through a large swarm of what seemed to be new ghosts, a few of them clearly still in shock from their deaths. Wasn't that always the way of it, he thought, sensing the penetration of the bullets that had struck them down, and recalling his own dazed state when the Germans had executed him.

An uncertain while later, Holte found Moncrief in an energetic eddy, a shapeless blot of distress that revealed how troubled he was. "Moncrief," he called out silently.

"Holte?" Moncrief responded, and his agitation lessened. "What's happened?"

"Someone — probably Stacy Dritchner — has tried to do away with Poppy Thornton," said Holte voicelessly; he had decided that directness was preferable to obfuscation.

"Stacy? He tried to harm his cousin?" There was a sense of genuine horror in this question.

"It certainly looks like it," Holte responded.

"And what does Stacy say?" Moncrief seemed wary as he asked this.

"Nothing. It seems he left the country."

"Stacy left the country?" Moncrief repeated, dazed.

"It looks like it," Holte said.

A silence greater than the ordinary silence of the dimension of ghosts descended between the two.

"When did that happen? How did it happen?" Moncrief ventured at last. "What is going on here?"

Although he was shaky on the actual passage of time, for the sake of convenience, Holte answered, "Yesterday evening, some time after four. I don't yet know what the underlying purpose is, but it has something to do with counterfeit or illegal antiques. And perhaps something to do with your murder."

"With my murder? How? What are you talking about?"

Holte took a little time to frame his answer. "I'm not sure, but it may be as important as Poppy thought it was when I left the world of the living."

"We should find Knott. He might know about this." Moncrief sidled in the eddy, his anxiety increasing as he brought his whole focus to bear on his companion. "Damn you, Holte! Why do you always distress me so?"

"I don't intend to," Holte soothed, a bit taken aback by how emphatic a non-voice could be.

"But you do." It was clear that Moncrief was sulking. "Every time you seek me out, you bring me more bad news."

"My apologies." Holte drew back a little from Moncrief; when he became aware of Moncrief's attention once again being directed toward him, Holte resumed his questioning. "Where do you think Stacy would be likely to go?"

Moncrief took a little time to answer. "I have no idea. He has business associates in Greece and Europe, but that's probably the first place investigators would look for him, so if he has committed a criminal act, he isn't apt to go either of those places. It takes a long time to apprehend fugitives in a foreign country, but these days, the government is persistent if the crime is important enough, and there is an extradition treaty in place."

"What about South America?" Holte hoped he sounded casual instead of probing.

Moncrief made a non-sound that might have been a laugh. "Louise must have told you about that — Stacy was always saying that in a pinch, he could run away to Rio." He hesitated. "I suppose he might have done that. What does Louise think?"

"I don't think the police have spoken to her yet." He consoled himself with the thought that it not a lie but a half-truth to say that.

"They should. She can tell them where he's gone. They were always thick as thieves." Moncrief went silent again, then changed his tone. "I guess we should talk to Knott about that, too. If we can find him. He's been keeping to himself; trying to remember. He's determined to find out if he's right about Derrington."

The two ghosts drifted off among the vast crowd of other ghosts, trying to pick up a trace of Percy Knott in the constantly shifting crowd. Eventually they came to an out-of-the-way spot amid the general confusion where they discovered Knott on the verge of slipping back into the world of the living.

"Going somewhere?" Holte made the inquiry as unchallenging as possible.

Knott wavered and then came into greater cohesion. "Sorry. I was about to try to find Warren Derrington."

"So Moncrief tells me. Do you mean you have some idea where he might be?" Holte asked, a bit too quickly.

"No; I mean I think he might have killed me, and I want to find out," said Knott.

"You've remembered?" Holte was surprised. "That was quick."

"No, I mean I've almost remembered, and I want to find out if I'm right. I might see if I can get through to Miles. He may know more than I thought." There was a tinge of belligerence in his remarks, and a firmness in his purpose that Holte had not seen since Knott entered the dimension of ghosts.

"What makes you think it was Derrington?" Moncrief interjected before Holte could pose his own question. "Do you recall seeing him? I wish I could bring back something about how I died, and who did it."

"I believe I can recall his voice. I want to hear him speak, to be certain."

"And how were you planning to do this?" Holte wondered.

"I think I could haunt him, get him to reveal himself — you know, Banquo's trick in Macbeth. You seem to do that well enough yourself," Knott replied.

"It's not quite the same thing," said Holte.

"Not entirely, but it's a step in the right direction." There was a mulishness about Knott that warned Holte that it would be difficult to dissuade him.

"Well, if you find him," Holte said as nonchalantly as he could manage without sound, "would you be good enough to let me know where he is? I understand that Miles Overstreet may have gone to Canada, but I don't see Derrington doing that."

"Or Stacy," Moncrief added.

This had the power to command all Knott's attention. "Stacy? Is he missing, too?"

"He is," said Holte. "It is likely that he left Philadelphia around four yesterday afternoon." He knew better than to bring up the possibility of more time passing among the living than could be reckoned in this non-place.

"Is the law after him?" Knott pursued. "What has he done now?"

Rather than explain about Poppy's imprisonment, Holte said, "That's what they're trying to determine. There is an active case with the police that involves Stacy Dritchner."

"And Derrington?" Knott asked. "That's encouraging."

"So, if you can find him, will you let me know? It could help the police and the District Attorney." He did his best to make his request be a positive one.

Moncrief once again interjected a thought, revealing that he was having trouble concentrating. "Stacy may have left the country, according to Holte. That's going to slow things down, if it's true. You could help speed up the search. That could help all three of us."

"That's assuming I can find Derrington and that I can make him tell me what I want to know." Knott moved about in a way that, had he not been noncorporeal, would have been pacing. "All right. I'll give it a try, and I'll get back to you when and if I learn something useful." And then he slipped away, back into the world of the living.

For a short time neither Holte nor Moncrief moved bodilessly, or spoke without sound. Then Moncrief asked, "Do you think we should follow him?"

"How? He didn't tell us where he was going." He wafted through a sudden influx of Russian ghosts, all in a dazed state of recent arrival. "Right now, I can't decide what more I can do beyond making sure that Poppy is recovering from her — " He could not find an appropriate word to describe her state of mind following her experiences in the warehouse basement.

"From her hours of tribulation." It was not as clear as he had hoped, but it provided a flavor of what she had endured.

"Shock?" Moncrief suggested. "Ordeal?"

Holte did a kind of shrug. "I want to be useful to her."

"So you've said." He began to fade, but summoned up enough presence to plead, "Will you look after Louise for me? She's gone through so much..." The rest was lost in the soundless buzz and rumble that was what passed for conversation among ghosts.

Holte replied, "If I can find her, I'll try." It was the best he could promise, he assured himself as he prepared to return to the world of the living.

POPPY WAS SITTING AT HER TYPEWRITER IN THE LIBRARY, JUST PUTTING THE LAST touches on her story that summed up the whole of the Moncrief investigation so far; it was four nights since she had been freed from the storeroom, and the bump on her forehead was fading from purple to greenish yellow. Her ankles and wrists were still bandaged but no longer painful; the soles of her feet, cushioned by woolen socks, no longer hurt. When he had called the morning after her ordeal, Lowenthal had ordered her to write an account of it, and had given her three days to do it. She would have to deliver it first thing the following morning to meet his deadline, but she could sleep for at least six hours, and that seemed like true luxury. Although she did not want to admit it, she was far from recovered from what had happened to her. Her wrists and ankles still ached and every muscle she possessed complained when she moved, but she was committed to do her work, no matter how much effort it took. She rubbed her eyes and inwardly commanded herself to disregard her fatigue.

Maestro was curled up in the wing-backed chair on the far side of the fireplace, one charcoal paw over his eyes. The rest of the house was quiet, and outside the night was still.

The library lamp blinked, and Chesterton Holte semi-materialized in front of her. "So you've finished your first full day back on the job. How is the work going?" he asked as if they were resuming a conversation instead of starting one.

"Well enough, I hope," she said, unalarmed by his presence. "I'm pleased you're here. I want to thank you for all you did to get me out of —"

"You've thanked me enough. I was doing my . . . job," he responded. "As you are doing yours."

Feeling a bit nonplused, she changed the subject. "You've been in the dimension of ghosts again, haven't you?"

"I have," he said, turning toward Maestro's laconic hiss. "Why do you bother?" he asked the cat; for an answer, Maestro got up, stretched, and recurled himself on the chair with his back to the desk; his tail twitched in disapproval.

Poppy was enough of a reporter that she could not keep from asking, "Did you tell Poindexter and Moncrief and Knott what happened?"

"I did . . . Well, not Poindexter; he's gone on. But Knott told me that he thinks it was Warren Derrington who killed him, but he isn't sure." He moved around to her side of the desk to look over the page in the Smith.

"How can anyone forget something like that?" Poppy removed the three sheets from the typewriter, separated the carbon from the front and copy sheets, then stacked them with the two typewritten pages already arranged next to the typewriter. "I guess I'll find out, one of these days."

"Like everyone else," he said, and asked, "What was it you wanted to tell me about Stacy and Derrington and Louise Moncrief?"

Poppy looked over at him. "What do you mean?"

"You told Loring that there was something about the three of them." He gave her time to gather her thoughts.

She tried to put her mind to what that might have been — that there was some sort of involvement among the three of them. Considering it now, it all seemed absurd; she shook her head. "It was nothing," she told him, but felt doubt niggle at her.

"Well, if anything occurs to you . . ."

"I need to get this done," she said brusquely, and set her mind on the page in front of her.

"Sorry; I didn't mean to distract you," he said, sounding genuinely contrite.

She ordered herself not to be disquieted by Holte until her work was complete, so she took a manila file-folder out of the desk and put the three front sheets into it, then dropped it on the desk. "You've never mentioned women when you go to the dimension of ghosts," she said, her attention drifting again; she inwardly cursed Doctor ter Horst's prescribed medication for muffling her thinking. "I suppose there are some there."

"Yes, of course. Although sometimes it's hard to tell — noncorporealty does that to you." He went to the sofa and stretched out a couple of inches above its seat.

"Then how do you recognize one another?" That question had been bothering her for the last two days.

"Often we don't," said Holte, rather sadly. "Sybil hasn't recognized me since she died of the 'Flu in November of 1919."

"Who's Sybil?" Poppy asked, suddenly very curious.

"My wife." He looked around the room, sorting out his cogitations. "Once I became a spy, I didn't spend as much time with her as I should have. She deserved better."

"Did you haunt her the way you've been haunting me?" She tried to imagine what that must have been like for Sybil, and realized she could not.

"No. She did not want me about; she didn't think badly of me for getting killed." He shifted his posture again. "It wasn't what we had planned, but the Great War . . ." His voice faded.

Fascinated in spite of her remaining work, Poppy pursued his revelations. "Did you do something before you became a spy?"

"I taught European History in Halifax. I'd taken my degree at Brasenose College in Oxford. They call it the Wedding Cake; if you'd seen it, you'd know why. One of my college-mates approached me about getting me into Europe in 1911 — they were worried about war even then — and since I'm Canadian, they hoped I would be less conspicuous than an Englishman would be; Canadians are often mistaken for Americans, and visa versa." He contemplated the ceiling for several seconds. "Sybil said I must go, and, not wanting to appear lacking in her eyes, I did. I don't hold her responsible in any way for what happened."

"You're not blaming her?" Poppy was indignant, and she made herself to calm down; she had been far too mercurial in the last three days, and her concentration had flagged at the most inconvenient times. She determined to pursue what he was telling her, at least for now. "Did she insist that you go?"

"No, of course not," he said at once, with undoubted sincerity. "She and I both had romantic notions about what spies do, and she wanted to help defend the Empire; so did I. I was a bit too old for the Army, but the Intelligence Service took men of my age: I was thirty-two when I signed up, and thirty-seven when I was killed." He regarded Poppy with measured sympathy. "You probably remember what it was like at home: while I was gone, Sybil participated in various war drives, and knit endless numbers of winter vests and socks."

"I know," said Poppy, recalling what it was like, watching her aunts and her instructors filling every empty moment with yarn and needles. "Were you gone for four years?"

"No. I was gone for two, was given a three-months' leave, and went back for another two." He sat up, still not quite on the sofa. "After she died, and I had remembered enough to haunt her, I wanted to apologize for being gone, but she had no memory of me. She still doesn't." There was sorrow in his voice, and he took another few seconds to compose himself. "That not unusual. Once she remembers, she'll move on, unless there are obligations with the living. When those are finished, then ghosts can move on."

Poppy had resisted the urge to take notes, but went ahead with another question. "Move on to where?" She did her best to mask a yawn as weariness threatened to overcome her.

Holte made a gesture that might have been a shrug. "I'll find out when it happens. For now, I am constrained to be here, with you."

"The undiscover'd country from whose bourne no traveler returns?" Poppy ventured. "Is that what comes next?"

"It seems so. Shakespeare got that right, as he did so many other things," said Holte. Then he got up. "You look tired. I won't keep you up."

"You'll be back?" There was a wistful quality to her words.

"I still owe your father, and I like you more than Tobias." He floated toward the window.

She smiled, some of her customary pluck returning. "Ye gods, I should hope so."

— *end* —

During the Great War — which we now call World War I — more combatants died of disease than were killed in battle, as is usually the case in wars. But the Great War ended with a secondary disaster, the Spanish 'Flu, as it was known, which actually originated in Southeast Asia but was first identified in Spain when it reached Europe. It spread with the returning troops more rapidly than any comparable disease since the Black Plague of 1343-1349. It began in 1918 and continued until late in 1920. The worldwide death toll from it was greater than the number of deaths from the Great War.

In America, the 'Flu was first seen in Philadelphia in the winter of 1918, and although there is speculation that there might have been cases in Baltimore and San Francisco before then, it had not been specifically identified. The 'Flu spread rapidly, and by early 1919, hospitals were being overwhelmed by 'Flu victims. The death rate was high, this being in a time before antibiotics, and the most that could be offered was palliative care. Coming as it did, immediately after a catastrophic war, the 'Flu took on an apocalyptic tone to many, and as physicians and nurses succumbed to the disease along with their patients, dread of it led to increasing neglect of those who contracted the disease. In some smaller cities and rural areas, hospitals refused to admit anyone who might have had the 'Flu, for fear of it infecting all other patients. Those who survived the disease — my maternal grandmother was one of them — often suffered long-term health complications because of it.

As the 'Flu abated, the countries of the world struggled to get back to normality at last, with varying degrees of success: in Germany there was horrendous inflation, in France there was regional famine, in Turkey there were political upheavals, in Greece there was an employment crisis, and so on throughout the world. In America, as soon as the 'Flu was gone and the economy appeared to be stabilized, the 1920s began to Roar in a kind of overreaction to the deprivation and death of the Great War and 'Flu. This was the Jazz Age, the rise of the film industry, the beginning of Prohibition, the expansion of the road system, and an increase of immigration from many parts of the world.

From 1922, when America had finally staggered back from those double tragedies, until the crash of the economy in 1929 and the resultant Depression, America was giddily expansive, innovative, and progressive, but there were also a few dark places amid the bright lights and noise: there was an upsurge in crimes and violence, a kind of national paranoia and growing isolationism, a shift in political skullduggery along with corporate shenanigans, and emerging stresses between classes and ethnic groups.

The 1920s were a pivotal time in American evolution, the result of a confluence of calamity and opportunity, and even now, almost a century later, its echoes can be heard in many of the issues that still confront us today.

ACKNOWLEDGMENTS

Since no writing exists in a vacuum, I would like to thank the following people whose participation in various ways made it possible for this book to make it into your hands: Bill Fawcett, Connor Cochran, Wiley Saichek, Pat LoBrutto, Maureen Kelly, Paul Huckelberry, Denise Hull, Mason Brown, Tiffany Usher, Merle Langerton, and Libba Campbell. I couldn't have done it without you.

Coming soon from *Chelsea Quinn Yarbro*
LIVING SPECTRES: A CHESTERTON HOLTE MYSTERY

10

"You know the Pearse family, don't you?" It was not a completely unexpected question, but Poppy could tell that Loring was uneasy about asking it, which puzzled her.

"A bit, yes. Sherman and Isadora were friends of my father's. When I was a child, my father took Tobias and me to their house to have Sunday dinners with the Pearse family from time to time. Why?"

"They have a son — Gameal Augustus Darius, called GAD?"

"Yes. I knew his oldest sister, Auralia, somewhat — she's a few years younger than I am — and his late brother, HOB." She suddenly realized what was going on. "This is about GAD being missing, isn't it? Something's happened to him."

Loring nodded unhappily. "Pearse was in to report his son missing, and filled me and two other senior officers in on what he knows about his son's situation, but asked that the information not be released to the public, or the Federal Bureau of Investigation, to avoid press attention, so the whole matter is unofficial, as I've said. There's no paperwork on file anywhere. Pearse doesn't want people prying into his family affairs. But his wife is afraid that GAD has been kidnapped, which is a possibility, though there's been no real hint of that yet, beyond her dread. Pearse himself is afraid of being barraged by all kinds of claims for money to reveal where GAD is, and what has happened to him if knowledge of GAD's being missing becomes public, not without cause: the man's worth ten million if he's worth a dime. He'd be barraged with demands for money, either offering information or the return of GAD. Pearse is asking us to maintain his privacy until we know more."

"Thus you talk to a reporter?" Poppy asked with a suggestion of a laugh.

"No, thus I talk to a friend of the Pearses, who understands Mister Pearse's reticence." He put his elbows on the table and leaned on his hands. "You know if there are secrets in that family, and you can do some snooping if you catch a scent. I'm not interested in scandal, only in things that might have something to do with GAD's being missing." He stared into his coffee cup. "And if you decide to do any snooping, I hope, you will report to me if you discover anything useful. Later on, you'll have an inside story on the case."

"If anything comes of it," Poppy added in as neutral a tone as she could achieve.

Loring shrugged awkwardly. "It's the best I can offer."

"The same bargain as the one we've made for you to continue telling me, sub rosa, about what you have found out about the Moncrief and Knott murders?" She considered this for a few seconds, then nodded. "All right. You've been a great help to me before and it's only fair that I help you where I can. But if the family goes public with their worries, you'll let me use whatever you find out."

He looked directly at her. "Deal; and if you can pass on anything you might pick up from your guardian angel . . . ?" He let the suggestion hang in the air.

Poppy gave an exasperated sigh. "I don't have a guardian angel," she reminded him, and inwardly chided herself with the thought that while she had been truthful, she had said nothing about the ghost of a Canadian spy who was helping her in various ways. "I'm not aware of any secrets in the Pearse family, beyond the usual gossip. But I'll make some inquiries among my . . . acquaintances — discreet inquiries — to see what's what."

"Okay," Loring said, and visibly relaxed.

Poppy regarded him for a moment or two, then asked, "What have you learned so far? So I can start snooping."

He took a sip of his coffee and put the cup aside. "According to Pearse,

GAD went to Europe in the second week of June, and had reservations to return the third week in August. When he left, he told his parents that he would be going into eastern Europe. He mentioned Vienna and Buda-Pest as places he expected to visit before returning on the 28th of August. Throughout July, he sent home letters weekly, the last two coming from Vienna. In his final letter, he declared his intention to spend the rest of his time in Vienna doing what he could to help the Armenian refugees there — he was distressed at their plight, and the state of their living conditions, as well as the lack of indignation that the Europeans felt for them — and believed that someone should do something about it, so he decided he wanted to be useful before he —"

"Aunt Esther said something about the Armenians. She spent a few days in Vienna on her way home, and was able to see the conditions in which they were living, which she thought outrageous," Poppy interjected. "I'll have a word with her tonight, to see if there's any light she can shed on where GAD might be."

"That's a good place to start; better than anything we have here," Loring approved, and took another sip of coffee. "Anyway, he was scheduled to leave from England over two weeks ago, but a telegram from the White Star Line informed his family the day the ship — I forget its name — sailed that GAD was not aboard, and that he had made no other reservations, at least not with the White Star Line. This was quite upsetting to his family, as you may suppose."

"I don't need to suppose — I've heard Missus Pearse expostulate on the matter," said Poppy, thinking back on Hank's birthday party.

"Then you know that she is certain that something dreadful has happened to GAD." Loring saw her nod. "She's very worried."

Poppy thought a moment, then answered carefully, "I know that Missus Pearse has been clamorous in expressing her worries to anyone who will listen, and that her fears grows worse with each retelling. She was at Aunt Jo's dinner-party last week, and belabored the guests who would listen with her dreads and dismay at GAD's absence. I think she's in a panic, but I wouldn't say so to her face, and she's fueling it by describing her imaginings." Poppy sat back in her chair, her pencil dawdling over an empty notebook page.

"I've also heard rumors that the reason the Pearses let their son travel is that he has been courting a young woman they don't approve of."

"I hadn't heard that," said Loring. "Do you happen to know who she is?" He shot a disapproving glance at the nearer sconce as it went off, then back on at once. "If that happens again, I'll ask for a pair of candles."

"It's working fine now," she said, and before she could stop herself, she added, "It's not blinking Morse code — that's something."

Loring scowled. "Okay. No candles." He tapped his fingers on the table. "So tell me who the unsuitable young lady is."

Poppy could feel herself blush, worried that Chesterton Holte might be up to mischief, and testing the depth of her knowledge. "Merrinelle Butterworth, or so Isadora Pearse claims. I don't know it for a fact, but before she was worried that GAD went missing, she was horrified at the prospect of having Merrinelle Butterworth for a daughter-in-law. The Pearses are wealthier than the Butterworths, and that's saying something, and Old Money besides. Isadora has no intention of letting GAD marry beneath him." Poppy felt a rush of chagrin. "I'm sorry. That sounded awful."

Loring chuckled. "Well, at least Miss Butterworth can't be called a fortune-hunter. The Butterworths are doing quite well for themselves."

Poppy achieved a smile. "Not even Missus Pearse could make that claim, although she's certain that Merrinelle wants to advance herself socially. Isadora's main objections to the Butterworths is that the family is still making its money through business, not inherited investments and land. The thought of a nouveau riche bride in the family was more than she could endure. She might not feel that way now."

Loring fell into a brief, thoughtful silence before going on. "Mister Pearse was quick to warn us about his wife's tendency to bruit GAD's dangers about. He has persuaded her not to go to the press with her fears, and for now, she is in agreement with her husband, but he told us that he doesn't know how long he will be able to keep her from announcing GAD's disappearance to the world at large." He had more coffee. "I'm supposed to call on her tomorrow and explain what the police can do to search for him — which isn't very much, to be honest about it — and that for our work to succeed, her continued silence is necessary."

"Since he's apparently in Europe, I wouldn't think there is much anyone can do from here."

Loring shook his head. "If we don't make this an active investigation, there's almost nothing anyone can do, and that includes the State Department. But during the Great War, I made some contacts among various police forces, and I'll be writing to the men I know, those still in active service, and a few retired, to find out if they have any recommendations for how I might pursue this . . . non-case."

"Is that why you were included by Mister Pearse? That you have connections?"

"I think so. Most of my job in the Great War was . . ." He faltered, looking away from her. "Was graves' registration — finding and identifying the dead, and that included bodies that did not obviously belong to any specific army, mostly parts of bodies." His eyes turned ancient again, fixed on memories rather than this afternoon.

Poppy took this in, and had to resist the urge to ask him if he knew anything about the death of her father. America had not entered the Great War yet when B. O. Thornton had been killed, so Loring would not know anything about it. "That's pretty demanding work."

"Yes, it is," he said bluntly. "But, as Chief Smiley said during our meeting with the Pearses, I have contacts no one else does, and I know how to keep my mouth shut." He offered a tentative smile. "And so do you."

"That won't be easy if things get out of hand," said Poppy, frowning. "Because Isadora Pearse is overwrought about GAD, he drives all other considerations from her mind. If she decides she should make a public announcement, she will, and no one, including her husband, can stop her." She reached for her coffee and tasted it; she found it cooler than she liked, but knew that was her own fault; she could have sipped it while they talked.

"I understand that." He unrolled his napkin and dropped it in his lap. "Can you tell me anything about GAD? Mister Pearse said a lot about him, but I think it would be useful to get your take on the boy."

"I don't know how useful it might be, but our families used to be on good terms, and if you think that would help . . ."

"It would give me some notion about GAD from someone other than his parents; you may know things about him that neither his father or mother do." Loring studied her. "That is, if you think it's a good idea."

"I understand what you're after," she responded. "The thing is, I don't know him very well. I haven't seen him for almost three years, and that last time was a month or so after HOB died, which hit him hard; he may have changed since then, but if you like, I'll find out what his friends are saying about him now. At that last meeting, he was just getting used to his brother's death."

"I'll bear in mind that it's possible that did change him to a degree, but you're observant, and at least you're not one of his immediate family; you have a clearer view of him," Loring said, a wry quirk to his mouth. "I would like your opinion of him. Tell me anything you think might help me be able to get a real start on him."

"I don't see him the way his family does, it's true," she said, and ruminated briefly. "All right. This is what I noticed about him." She stared into the distance of memories, trying to recall the boy she had known. "He was adventurous, always getting into things: climbing trees, running into streams, going up in tall buildings, that kind of thing. He did most of those things alone. He has a sympathetic streak, too, and that meant that every abandoned kitten, every injured rabbit, every fallen baby bird, every hapless puppy that came his way ended up in his room, much to the consternation of the rest of his family. When he thought something was unfair, he would rail at it, and upbraid his brothers and sisters for not being as upset as he." She paused, trying to summon up her memories of him as she had seen him the summer before she went to college — he was a little older, some of his character emerging more clearly than before he went to preparatory school. "He's athletic, but doesn't go in for team sports: he is an outdoors sort of man; he camps, and hikes, and canoes, and sails; every now and then he fishes. He told me once that nature restored his soul. He doesn't hunt, but I'm told he's a crack shot. He was talking about becoming a naturalist when he was younger — back then, he admired the work of John Muir, and President Roosevelt, and said that he wanted to follow in their footsteps — and he still might do something of the sort now."

"Then you would believe that he might take on the misfortunes of displaced Armenians," said Loring.

"I'll put it this way: it wouldn't surprise me if he has; he has always sympathized with those who are less fortunate than he is. His father was not pleased," said Poppy. "You should talk to his sister Genevieve, she's the most like him of them all, and if you can speak with her privately, she may tell you things she would never tell her parents. In fact, I think you should speak to all the children alone, if that's possible."

"I'll have to talk to everyone in the family eventually," he said, not pleased at the prospect. "I'll ask Mister Pearse if I can do this in private, and soon."

"Tatiana won't want to help you; if she tells you anything, it isn't likely to be the whole truth. She's secretive and she likes to mislead; if she smirks, it means she thinks she's getting away with something. A few years ago, she got in trouble for borrowing Auralia's pearl necklace. She and Auralia don't get along very well — never have. The twins, Felix and Berengaria — they call her Gari — are about twelve, as I recall, and they stick together; other than that, I haven't much to say about them. I don't know how reliable they are in regard to GAD."

"Twins often do stick together," said Loring. "Either that, or each resents the other."

"You might want to see them together when you go to interview the children," Poppy said, recalling the twins' shyness when alone. "They're fairly cooperative, or they were a couple years ago. They may not be now."

"What about Auralia?" Loring asked after looking through his notes.

"She's married, and lives in Connecticut with her husband, William Mikkelsohn. She's just twenty-two, if I remember correctly, and he's about twenty-eight; they married last year, at the end of January. I think she's pretty ambitious, and Mikkelsohn is from a political family; one of his forbearers signed the Declaration of Independence, and Auralia never lets anyone forget it. When I saw her at school, she was hard-working and eager for success, which for her meant a good marriage to a man interested in politics, so she's succeeded so far. At school, she was in charge of the Committee for Public Health. They raised money for families unable to afford medical care during the 'Flu. She managed to convince the dean to establish a clinic for mothers with young children in one of the old buildings on campus."

"That sounds commendable," said Loring.

"Oh, it was. Auralia garnered all manner of praise for what she did, and she deserved it, in a way. But I think Auralia would like to be in charge of almost anything if it had political worth." Poppy blinked at her own audacity. "I'm sorry. I shouldn't have said it that way."

"You said it just fine." Loring gave an amused single laugh. "Then, do you think it might be worthwhile for me to talk to her?"

Poppy was about to answer when the waiter appeared with a plate of rolls and butter. He did a quick survey of their cups. "I'll bring you more coffee. Your meals should be ready in about ten minutes. Sorry for the delay." Then he withdrew, taking care to make sure the curtain was completely closed.

Loring waited several seconds, then said, "Let's wait until he brings the coffee. We can have a little more privacy after he's gone."

Poppy nodded. "It's never easy when there's an interruption." She drank what was left in her cup and then made a few hasty notes. "Would you like to talk to Aunt Esther? About the Armenians? You could do it Friday night."

Loring stared around the booth. "Why don't you ask her if she would like to talk with me? A party might not be a good setting."

Poppy saw his point. "If that's what you'd prefer, I'll do it, of course." She sketched a star next to where she had written Esther — Armenians — GAD, so that it could be a more emphatic reminder to bring it up with her aunt that evening. "Is there anything more you'd like me to arrange for you with her?"

"Not that occurs to me," he said, closing the file in front of him and cocking his head in the direction of the curtain as the waiter came back, a large silver-plated coffee-pot in one hand, and small paper napkins in the other. As he refilled their cups, he set down the napkins. "Will you want anything else to drink? We have an array of sodas, and milk. Or, if you prefer, we have tomato juice, orange juice, and apple juice."

"I don't think so," said Loring, and nodded to Poppy. "Would you like anything? More coffee? A glass of water?"

"A glass of water when you bring the food." Had she been at home, she would have told Missus Sassoro for a glass of Sauvignon Blanc, but knew better than to do it here, in the presence of a police officer, even so accommodating a one as Inspector J.B. Loring.

"Very good," said the waiter. "And you, sir?"

"Water when the food comes would be fine," Loring said.

"Very good," the waiter repeated, and slipped back through the curtain.

"Now, where were we?" Loring asked rhetorically, taking a roll from the basket and setting it on his butter plate. "Weren't you about to tell me more about whom else you know who might be able to tell you something about GAD?"

"Was I?" Poppy asked, then tried to resume her train of thought. "Humphrey Fairchild knows the Pearses quite well, and he and Mildred will be at the party on Friday."

"You mentioned them." He thought. "If it looks promising, I'll make an appointment to meet with him privately. We're agreed, aren't we? That clandestine discussions don't usually go well at parties."

Poppy was convinced he was right, so she only said, "I'll introduce you. Mildred will probably pester you for information about Louise Moncrief."

"She's the one who called the police when you went missing, isn't she?" Loring asked.

"Yes, bless her. She's expecting, so they probably won't stay late — she needs her rest." Poppy heard steps approaching. "I think lunch is here," she said just as the waiter drew the curtain back; their conversation was once again abandoned.

Chesterton Holte was a filmy blur in the late afternoon sunlight that flooded Poppy's room, more like a flaw in the three tall windows than an actual presence. He watched as Poppy sat down on the edge of her bed to take off her shoes. On the end of the bed, Maestro raised his head to give a half-hearted hiss before curling himself into a tighter knot and going back to sleep. "Your Inspector Loring is in a difficult spot," he said as he drifted toward the chaise lounge next to the new chest-of-drawers standing against the north wall.

"He is," said Poppy, sounding a bit distracted.

"Would you like me to make some inquiries?" Holte offered.

"In the dimension of ghosts, or nearer to home?" Poppy countered, and immediately added,

"I apologize. I meant in the dimension of ghosts. Don't take offence at what I'm saying. My feet are killing me."

"I thought they might be, since you're rubbing them before you remove your hose."

"I'm not going to remove them. I want to get out my new low-heeled pumps, after I dress for dinner. There's no reason for anything fancier than they are." She smoothed the bedspread in a slightly distracted way, her thoughts in a jumble; Maestro raised his head to stare at her, then dropped it back on his pile of paws.

"That isn't for almost three hours," Holte observed.

"I know. But we'll have a drink together before we sit down to eat," Poppy said, stretching, "and that will be in about an hour and a half. Aunt Esther has been busy today, and she'll want to talk about it. She has an appointment with Lowenthal tomorrow, to discuss some articles on her travels. No doubt she'll want some pointers on how to approach him." She gave a little sigh and took a handkerchief from the nearer night-stand drawer, using it to wipe her face carefully, so as not to smear her mascara.

"When do you expect your Aunt Esther to arrive this evening?" Holte asked. "And does Miss Roth know when that will be?"

"I suppose she does." Poppy stared down at her feet. "I wish you were corporeal enough to manage a foot rub."

"My apologies," said Holte, thinking that even something so minor as that would be a most welcome reminder of the advantages of having bodies. "About the housekeeper?"

"Miss Roth has worked for Aunt Esther for nearly ten years. She started out as a maid and eventually became housekeeper. That was at the end of the 'Flu, I believe, when trained help was as hard to find as trained anyone." She started to stand, but changed her mind. "If you don't mind, I'm going to lie here for a bit."

"You were up late last night," said Holte.

"Ye gods!" Poppy exclaimed, straightening up in an effort to seem more indignant. "Don't tell me you were watching me?"

"No more than usual," was his oblique answer.

Poppy lay back, her left arm behind her head to serve as a pillow. "How comforting," she muttered.

Holte sank an inch or two into the chair. "Your lunch with Inspector Loring appears to have been a success. Did you know about graves' registration?"

Poppy shook her head slowly. "No. I thought he was probably in intelligence — he hasn't volunteered much about his activities until today. But a lot of soldiers don't say much about what happened to them."

"The same thing is true among the ghosts. If it takes them longer to remember, that means they need more time to go on to the next stage. Most of what they don't remember is what they are trying to forget. Unpleasant things."

Poppy gave a crack of laughter. "Does that include you?"

"It looks that way to me," he said, more solemnly than he had intended.

She heard the somberness in his answer, and nodded slowly, taking the time to consider what it might mean. Staring up at the ceiling, she thought about what might have happened to her father, and she found her recollections of him so overwhelming that she very nearly wept. After a few minutes, she said, "I'd better get changed."

"Don't worry, Poppy; it isn't as hard to do as you might imagine. There isn't much else to do in the dimension of ghosts but remember." He had deliberately lightened his tone, and he was rewarded with her rueful smile.

"What about you? You are spending a lot of time here. Is that slowing you down in going on?" Poppy asked as she got up and went to her closet to bring out her dinner ensemble: a drop-waisted dress with an ankle-length skirt in dusty-rose silk twill, neat but not girlish. She carried this back to the bed and dropped it onto the narrow bench at the foot.

"One of the main reasons we ghosts remember is to allow us to balance the books. We can't, or don't, go on until we do." He rose out of the chair to half-way to the ceiling.

She looked around for his ephemeral presence, and finally saw his shimmer on the level with the tops of the windows. "Do you know how much longer your . . . book-balancing is likely to take?"

Holte did something not quite visible that was probably a dismissive wave with his non-existent hand. "Not yet. I'm still dredging up memories, trying to find the balance-point. I don't have any notion of how long it will take me to go on. But I'm trying to talk about the things I can remember a little more: the Bastins warned me that refusing to speak could make it more difficult for me. Their son won't say anything about the Great War, and he's in a madhouse."

"Can ghosts go mad?" Poppy asked him, at once curious and abhorred by the idea.

"Not the way the living can, or none that I have seen or know of ever heard of that happening. Maybe if they were mad to begin with, in life, they might hold onto the madness for a time. Ghosts can become . . . less connected to their lives, and then it can take them decades to move on. I've seen the ghost of a young lieutenant in the Confederate Army who still cannot bear to consider what happened to him and his men at Gettysburg.

I've been told by others that he was one of the junior officers with Pickett, but he can neither confirm nor deny that."

"He's been in the dimension of ghosts for fifty years?" Poppy exclaimed. "Ye gods!"

"He's not the only one, but taking so long is rare." He paused, then said in a more subdued manner, "I think Poindexter may have gone on."

Poppy was startled by this news. "But from what I understood, he had not remembered who killed him, or even why."

Holte moved up from the chaise horizontally. "I'm not aware that he did, but he may have put it behind him, let it go, thought about other things. Maybe he was not as disappointed at having his life end as it did as Moncrief, or Knott are. Maybe he simply decided to let it go. Many of us do that when it is too painful to grasp the truth."

"Ghosts can do that?"

"A few can. Sibyl seems to have done it. I haven't been able to find her in the dimensions of ghosts for a while. I can understand why she might want to put her life behind her." The mention of his dead wife made Holte uncomfortable, making him fade in and out like a weak projector light at the flickers.

"I'm sorry?" Poppy said in a rush of sympathy. "Is that the appropriate comment?"

Holte swung around and slid toward her, now seven feet off the floor and almost horizontal to the ceiling. "I wish I knew." He dropped down from the height as if sliding down a waterfall feet first. "Is there anything that I can do to help you? About the Pearse boy?"

"I don't know. Since it's not a family matter . . ." She motioned him to turn around, then unbuttoned her suit-jacket. As she removed it, a possibility occurred to her. "Maybe you could find out if GAD is still alive? If he'd dead, someone in the dimension of ghosts should be able to help you find him. And if he has died, where we might look for his remains. Would you do that?"

"If you like." He floated down two more feet. "Would you like me to find out if there is any news about Stacy?"

She was surprised to discover that part of her had no wish to know, but that impulse was quickly overshadowed by her desire to make him answer for what he had done to her. "If you can do it without too much trouble." While she continued changing clothes, she said, "I'd so like to put that all behind me, but until Stacy is located, I can't. And neither can the law."

"True enough, about the law." Holte hung an arm's length away from Maestro, and was rewarded with a warning hiss. "He doesn't try to attack me anymore," he remarked, a bit wistfully.

Poppy shrugged. "He knows it won't do any good."

"Clever cat," said Holte, and swooped away from the disgruntled animal.

Poppy watched this as she removed her skirt. "I'm beginning to think you like aggravating Maestro," she said to Holte.

"Well, I prefer it to being ignored." He slipped into a small alcove with a bay window at the end of the room. "You have a very nice view of the garden."

Poppy slid her dinner dress over her head and shimmied it down her body until it hung properly. "That's better," she announced. "But I'll have to comb my hair again."

"Then you're dressed?" Holte inquired.

"I am: you may turn around." She curtsied a little. "You see? Not too formal, but not office-appropriate, either."

"Don't tell me that Aunt Esther bothers about that," Holte said, a bit stunned by this news.

"Oh, no, not as a matter of propriety. But after knocking about the world as she does, she likes to indulge in the niceties of society, and this is one way she can do it." Poppy went to her vanity table and inspected her reflection; she picked up her boar's bristle brush and went to work on the froth of short curls, going on while she brought her hair into order. "I need to go to Hannah's Beauty Box in a week or so. This is getting a bit too fly-away."